IN THE LIGHT OF DARKNESS

REVISED VERSION

BY

MISS CHEYENNE MITCHELL

Gotham Books

30 N Gould St.
Ste. 20820, Sheridan, WY 82801
https://gothambooksinc.com/

Phone: 1 (307) 464-7800

© 2025 *Miss Cheyenne Mitchell*. All rights reserved.

No part of this book may be reproduced, stored in a retrieval system, or transmitted by any means without the written permission of the author.

Published by Gotham Books (January 30, 2025)

ISBN: 979-8-3484-9430-8 (P)
ISBN: 979-8-3484-9431-5 (E)

Because of the dynamic nature of the Internet, any web addresses or links contained in this book may have changed since publication and may no longer be valid.

The views expressed in this work are solely those of the author and do not necessarily reflect the views of the publisher, and the publisher hereby disclaims any responsibility for them.

This book is dedicated to the Lord, my God,
The Giver of Creativity and Imagination
Whom I adore

Tyla Davidson Shelley is returning home from the funeral of a loved one she had not seen in many long years. Suddenly horrible, tragic and somewhat frightening memories of her past begin to flood her mind. Memories of terrifying and unbelievable family secrets and a childhood that was filled with fear.

CHAPTER ONE

The taxicab pulled up in front of my house. A warm feeling of arriving home swept over me. I was glad to be home after being away for a whole week. And, I had missed my son and my grandson.

After tipping the cab driver I grabbed my luggage and started up the walkway to my front door. I turned the key in the lock and opened the door. As I entered the house the familiar smells and sights inside greeted me. Without stopping I climbed the stairs to my bedroom. All I wanted to do was get out of the two-piece, black suit and high heeled shoes that I had been wearing. My feet were hurting me like crazy.

After tossing my suitcase onto the bed I stood there and stared at it for a moment. I didn't want to unpack it just yet and thought it could wait until later on. Quickly my clothes followed the suitcase onto the bed. I took off my shoes and put them inside the closet.

Then grabbed my most comfortable lounge dress from the closet, put on some slippers and went downstairs to the kitchen. I just wanted to make myself a hot cup of tea and relax. After fixing the tea I pulled out a chair and sat down at the table. As I began sipping the warm beverage my mind travelled to my past. I let out a long sigh.

The funeral was beautiful. I hadn't seen my brother, Nicholas, for many years. He had aged just like I had. But laying lifeless in his casket he looked as handsome as he ever had. Our family often wondered why we never heard from him again after he left home the second time years ago. Then, nearly thirty years later the letter came informing me that he was dead.

I looked out of my kitchen window. It was Autumn now. I marveled at the beautiful colors that the leaves on the trees had turned to, and they were still falling to the ground. This was the season and the time of the year that I loved the most. Not only because the weather was almost perfect in my mind, but I also had a birthday coming up.

I learned to appreciate birthdays a long time ago from my Grandmother. For more years than I cared to count my siblings and I never celebrated ours' or any- one else's birthday for that matter. In fact, we never celebrated any holidays or occasions.

As I sat at the table looking out of the kitchen window my mind drifted backward in time. I was six years old. And growing up in a small town called, Maron, with my brothers and my sister, Emmaline, who was four years older than me.

Autumn was the most beautiful time of the year in our small, southern town. A time when the lush, green leaves of the tree-lined streets turned to radiant colors of red, gold and yellow. It created an awesome picture of post-card beauty rarely seen anywhere.

The picturesque setting was enhanced even more by the neatly-kept, twin houses on every street. There were only a few houses that stood alone. Anyone who saw this wonderful sight would never guess that one of those larger homes in the quaint, little town harbored a dark and unbelievable mystery. A mystery that had plagued the family who lived there for a long time. It was my house and my family.

Maron was a typical small town of twenty eight hundred people. Everybody knew everybody else's business as is the case in small towns. But if someone needed help the people rarely, if ever, got involved in the matter. Gossip, rumors, and slander were commonplace. However, as small as it was Maron managed to publish a weekly newspaper.

It was more like a community paper than anything else. And its' focus was on what was going on in the local area and a few surrounding counties. There were teenagers who delivered the newspaper. Later on they would send some-one around, usually near the end of the month, asking for donations to it. Any amount of money that you wanted to give was fine. But if you didn't make a donation deliveries abruptly stopped.

The highlight of everyone's week in Maron was the town meetings that were held by the Sheriff and other town leaders. It was a chance for everybody to get together and catch up on the latest gossip if nothing else. Since nothing more spectacular than the town meeting ever occurred, most of the children who grew up there left as soon as they became of age.

A few citizens in Maron stood apart from everyone else. And, the things that they were doing or had done were regurgitated for months until some new gossip surfaced. Yet, for the most part everybody kept to themselves.

The heart of our town was Windre Street. On that street was the towns' only General Store that was owned and operated by Annie and Tom Greenley. A nice, elderly couple who had lived in Maron for decades. They were nice to everyone in town and everybody liked them.

For some reason they always quarreled with one another over the most idiotic things that anyone could imagine, and right in front of their customers. The fact that someone else overheard their quarreling and bickering didn't seem to bother them one bit. They had five children. But they had all grown up and left Maron. No doubt to get away from their ever feuding parents, most people surmised.

Next door to the General Store was Artie Jacobsen's Hardware Store. Artie was an elderly gentleman who lost his wife, Amanda, that same year when I was six years old. She was killed in a tragic car accident. The rumor around town was that Artie had been driving as drunk as a skunk that night, and crashed their car into a telephone pole on the way home from a party.

Amanda died instantly. It was right after that when Artie quit drinking. A little too late in my opinion. But at any rate it was an accomplishment for him the people in Maron thought. It was apparent that he had been a closet alcoholic for several years.

Further down on Windre Street was the only gas station in Maron. It was owned and operated by Sara Cosby and her town sons, Jimmy, and Danny. Both men were married and had families of their own. But Sara still treated them like they were ten year olds and couldn't think for themselves.

Ever since her husband, Terrance, walked out on her for another woman she had a hard time letting her sons go. Some people in town believed that she was afraid of being left alone. And was trying to her best to hang onto Jimmy, and Danny. It was known all over town that Jimmy and Danny's wives couldn't stand Sara. They were sick and tired of her interfering in their lives.

There were two churches in Maron. One was a Baptist church and the other one was a Methodist church. Also, there was St. Agnews Hospital and the Town Hall which was badly in need of repairs.

On the other side of Windre Street was the Court House, Sheriff Bicket's office, the Butcher shop owned by Mr. Thomas, a small bakery, a shoe repair shop, the only movie theatre, a Beauty Salon and a couple of department stores.

The only Barber in town was Ted Hurly who was considered by many young women and girls to be nothing but a dirty, old man. He was always lecherously putting his unwanted hands here or there on their bodies. Many husbands and boyfriends wanted to kick Ted's ass on numerous occasions.

Usually Sheriff Bicket or one of his Deputies would stop the upset man from committing any assault on the old pervert. To make matters worse, Ted had been accused by one woman of rape. But there was never any proof that he had committed such a heinous crime. Ironically, the same men who wanted to pulverize old Ted would still congregate in his Barber shop on a daily basis to gossip and visit.

Gladys Budsman had the only Beauty Salon in town. She was a nice lady and very pretty. The people in Maron thought of her as being wild and trampish. But I never got that impression about her. She was always nice to my sister, brothers and I.

Whenever somebody's boyfriend or husband suddenly started stepping out on them she would become the subject of most of the gossip in Maron. I don't think Gladys ever cared what people said about her.

The movie theatre was owned by Betty Abrams. A middle aged, black woman who had married her fifth husband the year before. Rumors were all over town that she murdered her previous four husbands. Yet, nobody could prove it.

All four men had died mysteriously. They were the picture of health one day then dead soon afterward. It was weird.

Betty was a pretty woman, too. And, everybody knew that she liked her men at least twenty years older than she was. However, that didn't keep the younger guys from trying to hit on her. Even though they knew they didn't stand a chance with her. Over the years and through her different marriages Betty became a rich woman. She showed all of the latest movies, too, for the small admission price of $2.00 per person.

Although most of the homes in Maron were beautiful, twin homes there were a few that sat by themselves and were just as beautiful. Those three houses were much larger and one, in particular, stood out from all of the rest. It wasn't because of its size. But because the people in town heard many ugly stories associated with the family who lived there. The Davidsons. Before I was married my name was, Tyla Davidson.

The townspeople considered my family and I to be strange people who never mingled with the other people in Maron. It wasn't that we wanted it that way but because we weren't allowed to associate with them.

My sister, brothers and I would have to sneak into town behind Mama's back just to look in the windows of the stores on Windre Street. There were nice things that were on display. If she knew about it Mama would have killed us, or at least tried to. We were terrified of her.

The people in Maron, in spite of Mama, got to know us pretty well. I think they felt sorry for us. We looked like little rag-a-muffins to say the least. Our clothes were clean only because our grandmother kept them that way. She made sure that Mama had money to buy us nice shoes and clothing. But Mama spent that money on herself not us.

Mama forced us to lie to our grandmother, too. When Grandmom Faya would see us after school she would look at the clothes that we had on. They were always the same ones that we had worn to school. But when she asked us if they were the same ones we told her 'no'. And, that we had changed our clothes as soon as we came home.

We knew if we hadn't lied like Mama told us to, she would beat the hell out of us. She feared our grandmother though. And we, in turn, feared her. The situation for us in our home was extremely abusive. I realize now that if it hadn't been for my grandmother living in the house with us we would have been living under even more dangerous, and perilous circumstances.

Mama hated all of us, even my grandmother. She waited like a lion waits on its' prey for one of us to do the slightest thing that she didn't like, just so she could beat us. We were beaten severely and often for no reason at all.

The five of us were certainly abused children and there was no one to help us. Not even my grandmother, who in the beginning, was completely unaware of the abuse that we suffered at Mama's hands.

Although Grandmom Faya lived in the house with us she did not stay on top of the things that were going on in the house like she should have. The house belonged to her. The day that she did find out about what had been going on for years right under her nose, the lives of my siblings and I changed forever.

Even at the age of six I knew there were rumors circulating around town regarding my family. Many of them involved murder, witchcraft, adultery and even incest. Other children talked as well. But I was too young to really understand.

I was a very pretty, little girl. I had gorgeous, dark-red hair almost brown which hung down to my waist, big, dark blue eyes and olive colored skin. Even then I knew that the people in Maron silently wondered about me. I didn't look like any member of the Davidson family that they had ever seen in person or in photographs.

I was a curious child, very bright and I had a vivid imagination. Also, I was prone to day-dreaming. People would often have to say something to me twice before I heard them and responded. In my mind I would be a million miles away, deep in thought, escaping the painful reality that I lived in. It was the daydreaming that helped me cope with the horrid home situation we had to endure.

Our mother's name was, Charon. She was dark skinned with long, dark, brown hair and light brown eyes. She ignored the people in town. And always seemed to be angry about something. She was distant, unfriendly and would be cold towards us. Her own children.

Our father's name was, Andrew, and he was dead. I saw photographs of him. He had olive colored skin like me, light brown hair and eyes. There was very little that my siblings and I knew about him, except that he killed himself when I was a baby. They had five children and I was the youngest.

Not one of my siblings looked like me in any way whatsoever and sometimes it bothered me. For a while I even thought that I may have been adopted but Grandmom Faya assured me otherwise.

My oldest brother, Andrew, Jr., was fourteen years old and very handsome. He had dark brown hair and light brown eyes. One day I overheard my grandmother say that he had to be at least six feet tall. He was a good boy. And he had thought about running away from home once.

But believed he had a responsibility to stay for the benefit of the rest of us. He thought that we would be safe from Mama as long as he remained there. Yet, he could not have been more wrong.

The next oldest was my brother, Nicholas. He was twelve years old with light brown hair and dark brown eyes. He had a rebellious spirit in him that none of the rest of us had. His biggest problem was not going to school and hanging out with boys who were much older than he was.

Then, there was my one and only sister, Emmaline. She was ten years old and had dark auburn hair and big, gray eyes. She was much more outgoing and friendly than I was. Also, she was willful, stubborn and headstrong.

Lastly, there was, Malin, who was two years older than me. He had red hair, hazel eyes and freckles. Malin was sensitive, kind-hearted and he loved to draw. Everybody loved him because he was such a sweet, little boy.

Nobody in our family resembled me. Even Grandom Faya looked nothing like me. I thought it was strange. Of course I never said anything to any of them about it. I was at an age when I really needed assurance from someone that I hadn't been found on the doorstep, and my dear grandmother gave it to me.

Grandmom Faya was my father's mother. She was still a very beautiful woman for her age. Her hair was completely white and it was beautiful. It was so long that she could sit on it when she sat down.

She had very dark blue eyes like me and dark skin. Sometimes she used a cane because she had a little difficulty walking. She told my siblings and I that something happened to her when she was a young girl. There was a bad accident and she was badly hurt.

The only love, kindness and affection we received growing up as children came from my grandmother. Never Mama. Grandmom Faya was a loving and caring woman. Unfortunately, she was also oblivious to the problems that Mama was causing us. Especially, Andrew, Jr.

The house we lived in with my grandmother was her house, like I said. After my father died we moved in with Grandmom Faya. It was very big house. And even had secret rooms in it that no one ever used. It was the only home I had ever known. Mama never talked about where we lived before that. She never talked about my father either.

My sister, brothers and I were all very close and loved each other dearly but Malin was my favorite. He was my constant companion. We went everywhere together. Also we got into a lot of trouble together.

Malin and I thought it was hilarious sometimes to leave Emmaline behind on the mornings that we caught the bus to school. We would tell the bus driver, Mrs. Fitz, that Emmaline wasn't going to school that day, so Mrs. Fitz would drive off without her. All day long we would laugh about it, imagining how Mama would have to drive her to school, or just make her stay home.

Our school was a half a mile away from where we lived. So we definitely had to ride the school bus. It was never funny to Mama though. And we decided, for Emmaline's sake as well as ours, not to do that anymore. Making Mama angry wasn't a wise thing for us to do. She could be very cruel to us when she got angry.

Malin and I had our own secret, hiding place that no one else knew about. It was a little spot under a big, old, oak tree down by the lake not far from our house. We would sit by the edge of the water and talk for hours. In warm weather we would take our shoes off and splash our feet in the water.

The two of us talked about anything and everything. We found peace there. "This will always be our secret place, Ty," Malin said to me one day while we were there. "You can't ever tell anybody about it no matter what. Okay?" I nodded my head in agreement.

Near this lake was a big, spooky-looking house that had been abandoned. We could tell that it had been a nice house at one time. On one particular occasion we decided to go inside the house and look around. The front door was unlocked when we turned the knob to go in.

Slowly entering the house, we stepped into the foyer. Immediately, it gave us the creeps. A sinister feeling seemed to permeate the air and chills ran down our spines. Terrified, Malin and I turned around quickly and ran out of the front door, never stopping until we reached home. Needless to say, we were so frightened that we never went inside that house again. And, it was a long time before we got up enough nerve to visit our secret place again.

The first time that we did go back to it we sat down, as usual, under the oak tree near the water. Suddenly, Malin turned to me and said, "Ty, if you or I ever get into trouble we can always come here and somebody will help us." Surprised by his remark I said, "Who?"

"I don't know who," he replied solemnly. "You just have to believe me. *Someone* will always help us if we come here. Not just you and me but Nicholas, Emmaline and Andrew, Jr., too. I promise you that. So don't forget it. Alright?" "Alright, Malin," I assured him. "I won't".

When he told me that I noticed that he had a strange look on his face. I thought it was odd for him to say what he did. I had the distinct feeling that it wasn't really him saying those words. Someone else was there with us. Someone who was telling him things and *someone* we couldn't see.

"What kind of trouble is he talking about?" I wondered. I was confused but I went along with him and said nothing else. The rest of that day we sat in silence. Neither one of us talking as we usually did. Malin was there with me that day but only in body. It was as if he was in a trance or something.

When it was beginning to get dark outside we started for home. We knew Mama would be angry at us for being out that late. When she got angry she did terrible things to us, except for me.

For some odd reason she never touched me. Malin, Emmaline and I were together one time and came home late like it was now. She said nothing to me but she surely went after Emmaline and Malin. That day, realizing we were in trouble, I recalled a time before that when we were out too late.

Emmaline and I had gone to visit Miss Miriam who lived about four blocks from where we did. She loved to see us children especially, Emmaline, and I. She would let us dress up in her old clothes and play in her huge attic. We were allowed to play with anything that she had up there, except an old trunk. She told us to never touch it but we could play with anything else that we wanted to.

Miss Miriam used to be very good friends with Grandmom Faya before any of us were born, she told us. When we asked her why their friendship had ended I thought I saw tears in her eyes. She turned away from us too quickly for me to be sure that's what they were.

As young as I was I could see that there had been much more than friendship between her and Grandmom Faya. "Girls," she said one day when we were there and questioned her again about her friendship with our grandmother, "it was a long time ago. I don't remember why or what happened." Then she started to talk to us about something else.

Emmaline and I had so much fun that day that the time slipped away from us. When we did get near our house Mama was standing on the front porch with her hands on her hips, pacing the floor. As soon as we got next to where she was standing she grabbed my sister's head, getting a hand full of her hair, so tight and hard that Emmaline screamed in pain.

Mama picked her up by her hair. Emmaline's feet dangling in mid-air and

threw my sister, bodily, against the front wall of our house. "You little bitch!"

Mama screamed at my sister. "I should kill you!" Then she looked at me. "Tyla," she said, "you get your little ass up those stairs and go to bed right now."

Running past her, I raced up the stairs as fast as I could. I was terrified! While running I began to think about how hungry I was. But I knew that we could for- get about any dinner that night. That's how Mama was when she got angry. She didn't give a damn if we ate or not. In fact, she barely fed us even if she wasn't angry.

When I got upstairs I walked past Grandmom Faya's bedroom. Her door was ajar. She was sitting up in her bed, probably awakened by all of the noise and commotion downstairs. She looked at me and I at her but neither one of us said a word. She only smiled at me. I went into my bedroom, took off my clothes, put on my pajamas and got into bed. I know it was a long time before I fell asleep.

The following morning I looked for my sister. I wanted to see if she was alright but I couldn't find her anywhere. I wouldn't see her for the next three days. Then it dawned on me suddenly that I hadn't seen Malin recently. I remembered that a few days before that he had gotten into trouble with Mama.

Worried, I tried asking Andrew, Jr. and Nicholas where Malin and Emmaline were. They just shrugged their shoulders and said that they didn't know. All of us knew that Mama had done something to Malin and Emmaline. It was nothing new or surprising to us. One of them often disappeared for a while after one of Mama's beatings.

I just couldn't understand *why* she refused to hit me. Or maybe it was because she was afraid to. Still, Mama's cruelty and abuse affected all of us in some way.

Andrew, Jr. always had a far-off, trance-like look in his eyes. I knew he was very sad and it was Mama who was making him that way. All of us knew, except Grandmom Faya, that Mama sometimes made Andrew, Jr. sleep in her bedroom with her at night. We knew there was something wrong with that. When our grandmother finally did find out about it she had a big fight with Mama.

My grandmother threatened to have Mama arrested and Andrew, Jr. taken away but it didn't stop Mama. My grandmother never did call Sheriff Bicket about it. *"Maybe, if she had,"* I thought, *"things would have turned out differently."* I felt tears welling in my eyes as I recalled that memory. *"Oh, Andrew, Jr."*

Nicholas, on the other hand, had no respect at all for Mama anymore. He cursed at her to her face whenever she made him angry. He even told her that he hated her. If she hit him he would immediately hit her right back. It had reached a point where she rarely said anything to him anymore.

Nicholas hardly ever went to school. He was always trying to be a tough guy. He smoked marijuana, cigarettes and also liked to drink beer. He even came home drunk a few times. He came and went as he pleased as if he dared Mama to say something to him.

Grandmom Faya was the only person that Nicholas would listen to. He respected and loved her. He was alright until Mama did something else to make him angry. Then he would start rebelling again.

If Sheriff Bicket or one of his Deputies caught Nicholas out on the street after curfew they would bring him home. But he would just wait until they were gone then he'd go back out again. If my grandmother intervened he would straighten up for a while. Yet, it was only a matter of time before Mama provided the push that he needed to get back into his old ways.

Inside, Nicholas was really a good boy but he was also a troubled boy, my grandmother told the rest of us. No one could have ever guessed that, eventually, the day was coming when my brother wouldn't come home at all anymore.

When I couldn't find Malin or Emmaline I didn't know what to do. I certainly didn't want to ask Mama where they were. Although I knew that if anybody knew their whereabouts it was her. Instead, I decided to talk to Grandmom Faya about it.

I knew she probably didn't know any more than I did. But I wanted to talk to her anyway. I went into her bedroom. She spent a lot of time in her bedroom back then. She informed us children that it was to keep from fighting with Mama.

"The less contact we have with each other," she said, "the better it is for both of us. Entering her bedroom I saw that she was asleep. I walked quietly over to the bed and gently touched her on her forearm. She opened her eyes and smiled when she saw me.

"Tyla, honey, how are you?" She asked me in that sweet voice she had. I said nothing and I don't know why. "Is there anything wrong, honey?" she asked me sitting up in her bed and resting against her pillows. "Come here and talk to me," she said patting the side of the bed.

"It's been a long time since you came in here to talk to me," she said. I stepped towards her. She put her arms around me and kissed me on my cheek softly. I smiled. "What's wrong, sweetheart?' she asked again. I thought about how much I loved her and I knew she loved me.

"Grandmom, do you know where Malin and Emmaline are?" I asked her. "I haven't seen Malin for a few days. And Mama beat Emmaline last night. It was terrible. Why is she such a bad person?" My grandmother shook her head sadly. I saw the sorrow in her eyes.

Hugging me tightly she said, "Honey, you have no idea what's going on in this family. It's a shame that you never knew your father. He loved you, your sister and your brothers very much and only wanted love and happiness for you. As for Charon, that's a different story and a long one that I'll tell you about when you're older. I promise you though, you will be alright. I'll make sure of that. She hesitated.

"I have to stay on top of what's going on in my own house," she continued. "I'm sure that Malin and your sister are alright wherever they are, sweetie. Charon's not that crazy. So don't you worry. Okay?"

At the time I didn't understand some of what she said, especially about Mama. But I nodded my head anyway. "You are a special, little girl, Tyla," my grandmother told me. "Don't ever be afraid of Charon. She cannot hurt you. Do you understand?" "Yes, Grandmom," I replied. "I understand."

My sister, brothers and I always felt safe with Grandmom Faya. Somehow, we knew that she would protect us from getting killed by Mama. I believed my grandmother knew that wherever my brother and sister were they were alright like she said. We laid back on the pillows. As I laid in her arms that day I thought about Miss Miriam and decided to ask her about their broken friendship.

"Grandmom?" I said. "Yes, honey," she answered. "Why aren't you and Miss Miriam friends anymore?" I asked. For a minute she was quiet. I could sense the sadness that was evident in her voice.

She told me, "Tyla, Miss Miriam loves you children very much. In fact, just as much as I do. And one day you'll know why. She and I were very close. But a terrible person deliberately destroyed our relationship with each other out of jealousy and hatred. It was our own fault in a way because we allowed this person to do it. We didn't realize just how wicked and treacherous she truly was."

For a moment I pondered what she said. Then I asked her, curiously. "What did she do, Grandmom?" "Well," said Grandmom Faya, "it wasn't only one thing that she did but many things over a period of time, sweetheart." "Why can't you and Miss Miriam be friends again," I asked her, "and forget about that bad lady?"

"It's not that easy, Tyla, honey," she said. "A lot of things were said and done that can never be taken back or undone. But let's not worry about all of that right now. Okay? You children go to visit Miss Miriam any time that you want to. I'm glad that you like to visit her. She is a very good person. One day we'll work out our problems for ourselves." She smiled at me.

Returning her smile I nodded. I was satisfied with her answer. Secretly, I hoped that she and Miss Miriam would truly become friends again. While laying there in my grandmother's arms I fell asleep and began to dream.

CHAPTER TWO

In my dream my grandmother and I were walking toward a big house that was surrounded by a heavily wooded area. There were beautiful pink, white and yellow carnations all around the house. Also, it was surrounded by a huge lawn. Grandmom Faya was no longer a middle-age woman but a beautiful, young girl. Her long, white hair was a deep, gorgeous dark-red like mine. And her dark skin was as soft as a baby's. She was slender in the dream and no longer stout like she was in reality.

Together we approached the house. My grandmother held my hand. At the front door she turned the knob, pushed it open and we went inside. The inside of the house was very nice. We went into the kitchen which was huge.

Grandmom Faya began to get various items out of the cupboards to make us something to eat. I sat down at the kitchen table. I was amazed at how much she looked like me in my dream. The only difference was that her skin was darker. But we could have been sisters or even mother and daughter.

While I was sitting at the kitchen table my grandmother began to talk to me. "I'm going to show you how to make my special salmon cakes, Miriam," she told me. I was confused. *"Why is Grandmom calling me, Miriam?"* I wondered.

I wanted to tell her, *"Grandmom, I'm Tyla! Who is Miriam?"* But I couldn't speak. No matter how hard I tried I couldn't make a sound. To my dismay, I realized that I couldn't move either. Suddenly, I was a fixture in that kitchen. Like one of the many pots and pans that hung from the kitchen ceiling. Yet, I was able to watch as well as hear everything around me.

I watched the beautiful, young woman in my dream move around the big kitchen getting things that she needed. It was more than obvious that it was her house. She knew, instinctively, where everything was and where it belonged.

She began to talk to me again. "Miriam," she said, "this is a special recipe that Mama gave me. Now I'm giving it to you. It will be a secret recipe that we will pass on to our daughters one day. Okay, Miriam?" She was smiling at me so sweetly.

"She really thinks that I'm this Miriam person," I thought. *"Why else would she keep calling me that name."* Without any warning I heard someone open the front door and enter the house. The sound of their footsteps approached the kitchen where we were. Grandmom Faya heard them, too.

She stopped preparing the salmon cakes as she looked toward the kitchen entrance. The sound of the footsteps were coming closer and closer to us.

Suddenly they stopped at the doorway of the kitchen which was behind me.

The whole room became as cold as ice and I felt chills run down my spine. Every hair on the back of my neck and forearms stood on end. I saw anger and rage come over my grandmother's face as she looked at someone over my shoulder.

I desperately tried to turn around so I could see who was standing there in the doorway. And who made Grandmom Faya so angry and enraged. But I still couldn't move a muscle or say a word as fear and terror washed over me. Suddenly, Grandmom Faya yelled at the person who was standing there.

"Get out! You get out of here and don't you ever come back!" She yelled at the person. "You don't belong here anymore! If you ever try to hurt my sister and her child again I'll kill you! Do you understand?! *I'll kill you!"* She paused, looking as if she was getting more and more enraged at the person that I couldn't see. "Get out!" She screamed. I couldn't believe this was Grandmom Faya.

I was stunned as I stared at my Grandmother. I had never heard her speak to anybody that way or in that horrible tone of voice she used. It was frightening. Her hatred for that mysterious person was more than evident. Again I tried to turn around so I could see who it was, yet still couldn't move or speak.

I never heard the unknown visitor leave from the doorway but I knew they were gone. My grandmother looked away from the kitchen entrance and back at me. Her face became soft and sweet again as she smiled at me and went back to preparing our meal. Then she said, "It's okay now, Miriam. She's gone and I'll never let her hurt you again."

As soon as she spoke those words to me the room became soft and warm again. Just as it was *before* the mysterious stranger entered the house so I relaxed. *"She!"* I thought. I realized that the *stranger* was a woman who came into the house and stood at the kitchen entrance.

After that, the back door, which was directly in front of me, opened. A handsome, young man with smooth olive skin and light brown eyes and hair came into the kitchen. He sat down at the table directly across from me. My grandmother looked at him smiling tenderly. He returned her smile but didn't say anything. He was still smiling as he turned to look at me. *"I hope he doesn't start calling me 'Miriam', too."* I thought. He just kept smiling at me as he sat there. Grandmom Faya walked over to him and kissed him gently on his cheek.

"That wicked bitch was here again," she told the young man. "She will never rest in peace because of all of the evil she has done in her life." She continued to speak. "I told Miriam not to worry, Andrew," she told the young man, "and now I'm telling you, too." With her hand she turned his face to hers and continued speaking. "I will always protect you and Miriam," she told him. "You'll see. And she will never hurt you again".

The young man faced me again. His eyes, filled with love, looked deeply into mine. And a tender smile was on his lips. Grandmom Faya turned to look at me, too. Just when I thought my dream would never end I awakened.

My mind was spinning, trying to remember everything that I had dreamed about. The first thought that hit me was, "Grandmom Faya was really pretty when she *was younger."* Suddenly I realized who I looked like in our family. It was my dear grandmother when she was a young girl and I was very happy about that. I wasn't the misfit in the family that I believed I was. Then I thought about the handsome, young man who was in the dream. *"Andrew*?" I said softly. *"I'll bet* that man was my Daddy that I dreamed about. Why didn't he say something to me?"

Slowly, I rose up from Grandmom Faya's bed trying not to awaken her. I was still recalling the strange dream as I walked down the hallway to my own bedroom. The dream had my full attention. As I laid down on my bed I wondered why my grandmother persisted in calling me 'Miriam' in my dream. My siblings and I never knew that Grandom Faya had a sister. *"Why didn't she* ever tell us about Miriam?"

I was anxious for Grandmom Faya to awaken and I could hardly contain myself. I wanted to tell her all about the mysterious dream that I had. I had a lot of questions that I wanted to ask her and my mind was racing. There was no way that I could have known it. But I would find out later that she had a dream, too.

It was an hour later when I walked past my grandmother's bedroom and saw her standing by her bedroom window. She was lost in her thoughts. I called to her four times before she heard me and answered. When she saw me she motioned for me to enter the room. We sat down on her bed. At that time I began to tell her about my dream as I was still excited about it.

"You kept calling me, 'Miriam', Grandmom" I told her. Somebody came into the kitchen that I couldn't see. The room turned really cold and I was scared. She listened as I told her everything about the dream. "You told the person who was there to get out, Grandmom." I continued while she listened. "Then this man, named 'Andrew', came into the kitchen and you kissed him on his cheek. You told him that the person wouldn't hurt him or your sister, 'Miriam', anymore. The man never said anything, Grandmom," I said. "He just kept smiling at me. You were showing me a secret recipe for salmon cakes. And you were young and really pretty, too. You looked just like me in the dream." By the time I was finished telling her about the dream I was breathless.

"Well, Tyla, honey," began my grandmother, "that certainly was some dream that you had. Let me show you something. Okay?" "Okay, Grandmom," I replied. Then I asked her. "Grandmom, why do you think that you kept calling me, Miriam', in the dream?" I was still excited. "Do you think that the man in my dream was my Daddy?"

"Tyla," said Grandmom Faya, "I have no doubt that it was your Daddy that you dreamed about. Would you like to see some old photographs that I have?" "Oh, yes, Grandmom," I replied happily.

Grandmom Faya got up from the bed and walked over to her closet. She reached up to the top of it and retrieved a big, metal box. She brought it over to the bed and opened it. Out of it came what seemed to me like a thousand old photographs.

"Wow!" I cried. "That's a lot of pictures!" "It sure is, sweetheart," said Grandmom Faya, "and we're going to look at all of them. You don't know a lot of these people in the pictures but they're all family." We began looking at the pictures. I noticed that most of them were photographs of me, my sister and my brothers.

My grandmother took out a photograph of a beautiful, dark, young woman with long, dark-red hair. I gasped as I opened my mouth wide in surprise. It was Grandmom Faya as a young girl and she looked exactly as she did in the dream. She even had on the same dress that she wore in the dream. I made my revelation known to her. As if she already knew she nodded her head and showed me a photograph of the same young man who was in my dream.

"That's your Daddy, Tyla," she told me. I felt happy after she said that. A feeling that was very rare in our household because of Mama. For the rest of that day Grandmom Faya and I looked through the many photographs that she had. The only photograph I saw of Mama was one of her as a young girl, maybe twelve or thirteen years old.

"Do you have any pictures of Mama when she was older than this, Grandmom?" I asked. "No, honey," she answered. "Charon doesn't believe in taking photographs and she has been that way since......" Suddenly, she broke off her sentence. I looked at her in confusion. "Since what, Grandmom?" I asked anxiously. After a moment's pause she spoke again.

"Oh," she replied, "some silly superstitious nonsense that she believes about them, honey. The only other photograph I have of her is when she was a little girl just a bit older than you are now."

After that she pulled out a faded, old photograph of Mama. She looked to be around ten years old and she was holding the hand of a woman who looked just like Grandmom Faya. "Who is that lady in the picture with Mama, Grandmom?" I asked. "She looks a lot like you."

"She is someone who died a long time ago, honey," said my grandmother. "She wasn't a nice person. We were all kind of glad when she was dead." "How did she die, Grandmom?" I wanted to know. "It's a long story, sweetheart," she replied. But said nothing else about the woman at that time.

I looked at the picture intently. I noticed that the woman in the picture with Mama had the same color hair, eyes and complexion as Grandmom Faya had when she was younger. They looked so much alike that they could have been twins. The woman wasn't as pretty as my grandmother. Her eyes were the same color as mine and my grandmother's but they were cold and eery-looking.

The woman looked menacing to me. Just looking at her in the photograph frightened me a little. I would learn that she was my grandmother's older sister, Marie. I wanted to know more about her but I could sense that Grandmom Faya didn't want to talk about this woman.

We looked through a lot of the photographs that day. I saw other pictures of the same mysterious woman, my grandmother, Mama and another pretty, young girl who seemed to be familiar to me. I had seen her somewhere before but I couldn't remember where. She looked a little bit younger than Grandmom Faya. Since I couldn't shake the feeling that I knew her I had to speak.

"I know this girl, Grandmom," I told my grandmother but she did not reply. I didn't want to upset her so I didn't persist at that time. As I continued to study the photograph I noticed how much this girl looked like Grandmom Faya, Mama and the woman that she told me was dead. Suddenly, it hit me. "*All four of them must be sisters.*" I hoped that my grandmother was willing to continue telling me about the people in the photograph that I didn't know.

Finally, I asked, "Who is the other girl in the picture, Grandmom? I know I've seen her before but I don't remember where. Who is she?" She stroked my small hand gently and said, "That's my sister, Miriam, Tyla?" "*So*," I thought, "*they* ARE *sisters.*" I held the photograph in my hand almost mesmerized by it. "Miriam," I thought, "I know that I know you from somewhere but why can't I remember where?"

After we finished looking at the photographs Grandmom Faya collected all of them and put them back into the big, metal box. Then she returned them to the top of her closet. I mustered enough courage to ask her, "Who do you think it was that you were telling to 'get out' in the dream, Grandmom, and who you were so mad at?" Ignoring my question completely she replied, "Tyla, you dreamed of your Daddy alright. And as for Miriam she is my younger sister. We were very close once.

I know that my grandmother must have breathed a sigh of relief when I didn't continue to press her with more questions about Miriam or ask where she was. "Do you know where that house is," I asked, "the one in my dream, Grandmom? Why do you think I dreamed about it? Did I ever live there?"

Grandmom Faya walked back over to the bed and sat down next to me. She answered none of the questions that I asked about the strange house in my dream. She told me in her soft, tender voice, "Tyla. I had a dream, too." "You did, Grandmom?" I asked curiously. "What did you dream about?" "I dreamed about my three sisters," she replied. "And, I dreamed about your Daddy." She spoke as if she was far away from me.

"Grandmom, you had three sisters?" I asked knowing the answer already.

"Where are they now? Why don't we ever see them? Why didn't you ever tell us about them?" "Well," she replied, "I was only close to my sister, Miriam." "Do I look like she did?" I asked her. "Believe it or not, sweetie," she said smiling, "you look exactly like she did when she was your age and you are just as sweet as she was, too."

Tell me more, Grandmom," I said anxiously feeling that she was finally ready to talk about her sisters. "Did you have any brothers?" "No, Tyla," she said. "I only had three sisters. We lost our mother when we were very young. She was taken away from us when she got sick and my grandmother finished raising us."

"Was your Grandmom, nice?" I asked looking into her eyes. "I wish she had been, honey," she replied. "She was not nice at all. In fact, I believe she hated us." "That's terrible, Grandmom!" I exclaimed knowing how much she, as my grandmother, loved my siblings and I. "Why was she like that?" I asked her.

"She was a wicked woman, Tyla," said Grandmom Faya, "and she was cruel to my mother, her own daughter. My grandmother began to look very sorrowful when she said that. "Nobody liked her," she continued. "She was especially cruel to Miriam and I. She did all that she could to make our lives as miser- able as possible."

"How did she treat your other two sisters, Grandmom?" I asked while my mind was contemplating why anybody's Grandmom would be mean to them. "Oh," replied Grandmom Faya, "she didn't care that much for them either. But she could use and control them. Whereas, she couldn't use or control Miriam and I." "How did she do that?" I asked her. I was captivated by then with the sad story of family members I had never known. And how my grandmother and her sisters were treated cruelly. My grandmother continued.

"Well," she began, "there were rumors that she practiced witchcraft. Miriam and I believed it, too. We would hear her and our other two sisters late at night upstairs in the attic. They would be chanting and making all kinds of weird noises. One day our mother investigated what they were doing up there. She found a 'witches' circle drawn in the middle of the attic floor. They were using it in their rituals." She paused for a moment. Then began to speak again.

"Our mother was so afraid of our grandmother that she never confronted her about it," continued Grandmom Faya. "She told Miriam and I that Ole Lucy was teaching that stuff to my sisters. She paused looking out of the bedroom window. She had that far-away look in her eyes again. As if she was straining to see something on the horizon. Then she continued.

"Miriam and I were always protected from Ole Lucy though," she said. "That's why she never bothered with us too much." "Who protected you, Grandmom?" I wanted to know. "We were never really sure, honey," she replied. "But someone always helped us in that horrid house. We believed back then that it was our grandfather because he often came to Miriam and I in our dreams. He would warn us about things that Ole Lucy and my sister, Marie, were trying to do to us through witchcraft to harm us. He would always be right, too." She hesitated again.

"You know, honey," said Grandmom Faya, "I think that old house was as wicked as Ole Lucy and my older sister, Marie, were." She spoke those words as if she was just realizing that fact for herself. "As beautiful as the house was inside and out," she continued, "there was never any love there, Tyla. None of us girls had any friends. Except for Marie, that is. She had one girlfriend who was just as bad as she was I think." Grandmom Faya paused again and seemed to be concen- trating on something. Then she spoke.

"Sheila Watson!" she cried. "That was her name. Nobody ever came to that house unless they had to. We were never allowed off the grounds or allowed to associate with the people in town. Our education consisted of tutors hired by

Ole Lucy to come to the house." "That sounds awful!" I cried trying to imagine never being able to leave the house or have any friends.

"Do you have any pictures of your mother and father or your grandmother?" I asked her. "No, honey," she said with a shake of her head. "You see, it was Ole Lucy who didn't believe in taking photographs. Which is where Charon got that nonsense from. I was shocked. "Mama knew your grandmother?" I asked in surprise. Grandmom Faya became very quiet.

"Grandmom?" I asked quietly waiting for her to answer. "O-oh, o-oh, yes," she said shakily. "Y-yes, she did, honey." She got quiet again. "Why was your grand- mother scared to take a picture?" I asked her.

"She thought people could harm you through your photograph," said Grandmom Faya. "Like hoodoo or something I guess. Which is witchcraft, too."

I was only six years old and very confused. I think she sensed my confusion, too.

"She thought everybody was like she was, Tyla," replied my grandmother. "She never allowed my mother to take a photograph. And the ones my mother already had of herself and my father were burned to ashes by Ole Lucy when she found them. Years later, after my mother had gone away, a friend of hers brought me the old photographs that I've shown you. This friend of my mother's saved them by keeping them for her. She instructed this friend of hers to give them to me after I left that horrible house and she did. All but the photographs of you children. I had them taken myself."

I could tell that she was thinking about her past and what she should tell me next. After several minutes Grandmom Faya asked me, "Do you know what we heard about Ole Lucy? I don't know how true it was or is," she admonished. "But there was a terrible rumor in our family that she murdered my father."

"What!" I cried horrified. "Yes," she said. "It was said, by many people in Maron, that Ole Lacy murdered my grandfather, too, her own husband." "I'm sure glad that I never knew your grandmother," I told her. "She sounds terrible." Grandmom Faya smiled softly and continued.

"I believe it's true," she said. "My mother told Miriam and I that our grandfather, her father, had come from a family that was heavily into witchcraft. His mother taught Ole Lucy a lot of things. She also told us that our grandfather was a Warlock." "What's that, Grandmom?" I asked. "It's a man who practices witchcraft,

Tyla, honey," she answered. "Anyway, they said that he caused a lot of problems for many of the people in Maron. He had a lot of enemies by the time he passed away. Yet, he adored my mother and she loved him. From what I can remember about him he used to play with Marie and I when we were small children." "He doesn't sound so bad to me, Grandmom," I said. "No, honey," she replied. "He doesn't, does he?" "Do you know how your grandmother murdered people?" I asked.

"Well," said Grandmom Faya, "they never found my grandfather's body you know. My grandmother told everyone in town that he just walked out on her. It never made any sense to us though. Everything he owned was still there in that house." "Maybe, he isn't dead," I suggested. "If he wasn't back then, honey," she said with a chuckle, "I'm certain that he is by now, after all of these years.

"Tell me what happened to your mother, Grandmom," I said. "My mother was very unhappy in that house, Tyla," she replied. "Ole Lucy, her mother and my grandmother made her that way. Ole Lucy drove my father away from us and a short time after that he was found dead in the wooded area in back of that house. The Coroner told my mother that he had a heart attack. But my mother demanded an investigation into his death. Naturally, Ole Lucy tried to prevent that. She blackmailed many people in high places who were afraid of her. She fought my mother every step of the way. As a result there never was any investigation into my father's death. However, my mother knew without a doubt that Ole Lucy had something to do with his demise. She knew it because she knew what Ole Lacy was capable of."

By that time I was completely enthralled with my grandmother's terrible memories as a young girl. I anxiously waited for her to continue.

"Lucilla Camay', was my grandmother's name," said Grandmom Faya. "She had no sisters or brothers that we ever knew about. And, she had the most evil and hateful looking eyes that you ever saw. Sometimes she didn't even look human to Miriam and I. Rather like a demon from the pit of hell. She acted like one, too. It seemed, for reasons that only she knew about, that she hated everyone and everything. My sisters and I had never done anything to her but she hated us anyway. Grandmom Faya's voice turned to an angry tone as she said in a low voice, "I'll never forgive her or Marie for what they did to our baby sister."

"What did they do to her, Grandmom?" I asked curiously. I thought I saw tears in her eyes then. She looked away from me and out the window. Like she was suddenly interested in what was going on outside. We could hear some of the children in Maron playing ball in the park not far from our house. From their laughter we knew they were having fun. Something that my siblings and I knew nothing about.

We didn't bring any of the children that we knew from school to our house. We never knew what kind of mood Mama would be in. We didn't want to be embarrassed by a sudden beating brought on by some small infraction committed that she didn't like. My grandmother started talking again.

"My baby sister was the sweetest, kindest human being that I had ever known," she said, her voice cracking as she spoke after a time. "She loved everybody. She could never understand why Marie was the only one who could have friends over to our house from town. My mother tried to explain things to her but she never understood. She looked up to Marie and trusted her. It was through that trust and love that Ole Lucy as well as Marie destroyed all that was ever good inside our baby sister. She became like them over time. Cruel and mean."

Something warned me that if I asked any more questions right then about her baby sister Grandmom would start to cry. Although I had a lot of curiosity and many more questions about her I kept them to myself. After she regained her composure Grandmom Faya began the conversation again but on a different subject.

"My father's name was, Armand Davidson," she said to me proudly. "He was young and handsome. When he died he was only thirty six years old and had been in excellent health. It was like he just dropped down dead, they said. My mother accused Ole Lucy of his death of course. She knew that she'd done some- thing to harm him. I believe she did, too. My poor mother was never the same after that."

Grandmom Faya stared out the bedroom window again. I could feel the sadness in her. She started talking again. "My mother always regretted having to go back to Ole Lucy's house," she said. "But my father lost his job and they had no money and four children. Therefore, they had no choice. There was nowhere else for them to go. My father had no family. Before they found him dead my mother never stopped hoping and praying that he would return to us. But when they found him dead she just went to pieces.

"That's so sad, Grandmom," I said with tears in my own eyes by then. "I remember the day that some people came to the house to take my mother away," my grandmother said sorrowfully. "They put her on a stretcher because she could barely walk by then. She lost so much weight because she refused to eat and was extremely weak. All she did was drink every single day from sun up to sun down. She would start in the mornings with a bottle of gin and go all day long until she passed out on the living room couch, or in her bed."

Grandmom Faya looked down at me and stroked my hair lovingly. "She was very sick Tyla, honey," she said of her mother. "We never saw her anymore after that day. Ole Lucy never told us where she was taken. She just woke us up one morning two weeks later and told us that our mother had died." My grandmother had an angry look on her face. Other than in my dream I had never seen that look on her face before. Little did I know that I would surely see it on her face again and for a totally different reason.

"I swear," she continued, "it looked to me as if she had a smile on her face when she told us that. But I never believed her and neither did Miriam. We didn't know why but we just didn't believe her. We knew in the back of our minds that she had done something terrible to make our mother lose interest in us and in life."

As I looked at my grandmother I saw tears form in her eyes. Tears that she couldn't hide. "Miriam and I cried our eyes out," she said to me in a choking voice. "But my other two sisters had become so much like Ole Lucy by that time I don't think they even cared about our mother. At least they never showed it if they did." Without thinking I asked, "I wonder where your sisters are now, Grandmom. Do you ever see them?" She fell silent and said nothing more on the subject. Then she looked at me and smiled.

"Honey, I'm going to lay here for a while and rest," she told me. "So you go on downstairs. Okay? We'll talk some more another time." "Alright, Grandmom," I said. As I slid off the bed I saw the heavy sadness in her eyes. I knew that she wanted to be alone with her memories. Leaving her bedroom quietly I went downstairs to see if I could find out where my sister and brother, Malin, were. A year had passed since that day.

CHAPTER THREE

I was so absorbed in my memories of that day one year ago I didn't hear Malin talking to me. He had been talking but I hadn't heard a word that he said. I hadn't realized that we were running either. It was already dark outside and Malin was holding onto my hand tightly.

"Did you hear what I said, Tyla?" asked Malin. "No," I replied. "What did you say?" "I said," answered Malin, "maybe Mama is busy doing something and won't notice how dark it is out here." "I sure hope so," I panted as we ran toward home. "You know how mean she can get if we make her mad." "I know," replied my brother. We were running to get home as fast as our little legs would carry us. It just wasn't fast enough.

As Malin and I were running I thought, "*She never puts her hands on me no matter what I do.*" Not that any of us ever did anything to cause her to be so mean to us. Little did I know that all of that was about to change and much sooner than I knew.

As my brother and I got closer to our house we saw Mama pacing back and forth on the front porch. Suddenly, she looked up and saw us running. I will never forget the evil smirk that she had on her lips. She stopped pacing the floor and reached down to pick up the electric cord that she used to beat my siblings with.

Practically running down the front steps she grabbed Malin around his neck with one hand. Then she hit him as hard as she could with the cord that she held in her other hand. My brother screamed in pain but she kept on hitting him. My dear brother could not stop screaming and I was horrified.

I began to hope that Grandmom Faya would hear his screams and come to our rescue. Malin's little body was trembling and jerking from the pain that Mama was inflicting on him. It looked the same way that Emmaline and I had seen Miss Miriam's body do when she got sick. She called them 'epileptic seizures' that started when she was a young woman. She told us what to do in case it ever happened while we were visiting her. Miss Miriam told Emmaline and I that it was a blow to her head that knocked her unconscious. Two months after that she started having the seizures. She told us that she rarely had them as she got older. Yet, they still occurred without warning once in a while. Those seizures that she had were terrible to see. My sister and I felt sorry for Miss Miriam. She was such a nice lady.

As I watched my dear brother going through something like that, and my grandmother nowhere in sight to help us, I got angry at Mama. I began to sob hysterically. Before I knew it I ran over to her and bit her as hard as I could on her right side.

Still holding onto my brother with one hand she dropped the electric cord from her other hand and grabbed her side screaming in pain. "Ow!" she yelled. "You stinking, rotten, little bitch! I'm going to kill you for that shit!" With that she grabbed me by my hair and threw me against the wall of the house. Just as she had done to my sister that day. In all of this she was still holding onto Malin who was crying uncontrollably. Mama came at me.

"I'll kill you!" she yelled. "So help me will!" Her teeth were clenched together in rage and anger. I was dazed from her attack on me. Sprawled on the floor of the porch I was too scared to move. I saw something in her face that day that I had never seen before. It was pure hatred. "*She is really going to kill me!*" I thought terrified. I began to cringe before her.

As Mama reached for me the screen door swung open violently and there stood Grandmom Faya. Her eyes blazed with anger like fire. Both of her fists were clenched into tight, little balls. Immediately, she stepped between Mama and I.

"Touch any of these children again, you bitch," she told Mama. "And I'll make you wish that you hadn't!" I saw Mama become visibly shaken and scared. Another smirk came upon her lips. She reached down to pick up the electric cord that had fallen to the porch floor. But Grandmom Faya put her foot on it. "Not today, bitch!" she told Mama, her eyes blazing with rage.

"If you think I'm playing," continued Grandmom Faya talking to Mama "you can try me right now. Let that child go." She was staring directly into Mama's eyes. But she still wouldn't let my brother go. Grandmom Faya got right into Mama's face and I heard her whisper, "I'm ready to do this. Are you?" It was an outright threat and Mama knew it.

The two women glared at one another for what seemed to me like a long time, but was only seconds. They could feel each other's breath on their faces as they stared one another down. One daring the other to make a move to harm

Malin or me. "Well," my grandmother said to Mama, "what's it going to be?" Mama grinned wickedly at her then she let Malin go.

As Mama went back inside the house my grandmother watched her with rage and anger still in her eyes. After that she wrapped both Malin and I in her arms and hugged us tightly. My brother whimpered in pain. "Oh, honey, I'm so sorry," said Grandmom Faya. She kissed each one of us on our foreheads.

"This shit is going to stop right now, children," said my grandmother. "I promise you that. It's time that someone dealt with that witch once and for all. And that someone is going to be me. From the look on her face I knew things were going to be very different for my siblings and I after that day. "Grandmom," I said, "you should have seen her face when she was coming after me." I was still shaken from the ordeal. "It was terrible. She hates me. I saw it in her face." Malin had stopped crying but his little body was still trembling from the horrible beating. He was very angry. He wiped his tear-streaked face.

"I'm going to kill her one of these days." he said seriously to my grandmother and I. "I am," he said. "You just wait and see. If I don't kill her she's going to kill me." My grandmother and I both realized how much he hated Mama and wanted her dead. He continued speaking. "I know she will, Grandmom. She's going to end up killing all of us or at least one of us. She really wants to you know."

I had never seen Malin so angry. I knew he meant what he was saying, My grandmother knew it, too. "Now, now, child," she said to Malin soothingly trying to calm him down. "She's not worth it. She'll get what's coming to her. Believe me. You won't have to do anything to her. I have a feeling that what is coming for Charon Davidson is already in the works."

Malin and I looked at one another in confusion at what she said. "What do you mean by that, Grandmom?" Malin asked her. "Don't you worry your little heads about it," she said evasively. "It's not your problem. Not anymore."

"Let me see your back, Malin," said my grandmother changing the subject. She raised his shirt and saw many ugly, red welts on his back. There were bruise all over his torso, too. Also, there were old bruises and scars on his arms and legs. "Come into the house," said Grandmom Faya. "Let's go into the kitchen so I can put something on these bruises for you."

The three of us went into the kitchen. My grandmother got some ointment and dressing to care for my brother's bruises. After she took care of Malin she made us some hot cocoa and sandwiches. No dinner had been prepared for us by Mama and of course it was intentional. Grandmom Faya thought no more about the words of anger that Malin spoke regarding Mama. But those words were soon to come true.

My grandmother sent me upstairs to get my other siblings so they could eat, too. Mama disappeared into her bedroom and closed the door. The only time that her bedroom door was ever closed was if she was in there. I hoped she would stay in her bedroom and never come out. It was only wishful thinking.

I found Emmaline in her bedroom and told her to come downstairs to eat. Nicholas was in his bedroom but I couldn't find Andrew, Jr. anywhere. Startled, I recalled the night before that. I saw him going into Mama's bedroom with her. He looked so unhappy and sad but when he saw me he smiled.

I recalled the week before that when I overheard Mama trying to make him come into her bedroom but he refused. Mama cursed him out badly, yet he still refused to go. The day after that no one saw Andrew Jr. and every- one wondered where he was.

It was the same night that Nicholas told Emmaline, who wanted to be called Emma by that time, and I that Mama locked Andrew Jr. in the basement. She was angry with him for not doing as she told him. We had wanted to tell Grandmom Faya but we were too scared to say anything. Now I wished we had told her about it.

Nicholas told the rest of us how Mama always did those kinds of things to Andrew Jr. and him. She would be nice and sweet to them. Then do something to hurt them when they least expected it. She was very sneaky and dirty. However, she didn't bother with Nicholas anymore. She knew he was not afraid of her.

Nicholas informed us that on the day of the bedroom incident and Andrew, Jr.'s refusal Mama started treating him really nice. She asked him to go down into the basement and get something for her. When Andrew Jr. went down to the basement she shut the door on him and locked it. Nicholas said that he would have let Andrew Jr. out of the basement but Mama took the key and hid it.

As usual, because he knew there would have been a big fight between my grandmother and Mama, he didn't tell. Also, he knew that somehow if he had told on her she would have made Nicholas pay for it. Mama would see to that no doubt.

According to Nicholas, hours later when she knew Andrew Jr. was asleep she went downstairs to the basement and tied him up. She beat him with the same electric cord that she used on Malin. She kept Andrew Jr. down in that cellar for days Nicholas told us. It was then that he made up his mind to leave home for a few days. Before she gathered enough courage to start in on him. Thinking back now I wondered why I hadn't seen Nicholas for a few days.

Grandmom Faya called Sheriff Bicket but they didn't do much. Because Nicholas had a history of running away from home.

Andrew Jr. and Nicholas were both big enough and strong enough to fight Mama off. That was the reason why she would wait until she knew they were asleep. Then tie them up and beat them until they were bloody

When we saw Andrew Jr. again it was the previous night when I saw him with Mama going into her bedroom. He looked so thin, bruised and sickly to me. I couldn't fathom why Andrew Jr. never ran away like Nicholas did. But they were opposites of one another.

He had the mistaken idea that since he was the oldest it was his responsibility to look out for the rest of us. Nicholas tried his best to tell him otherwise but he wouldn't listen. He just kept on taking Mama's cruelty and abuse, physically, mentally and emotionally.

I went back downstairs to the kitchen and told Grandmom Faya that I couldn't find Andrew Jr. anywhere. Also, I told her about the last time that I saw him and all that Nicholas told us.

"Oh, no!" cried my grandmother. "Oh, my God!" She hadn't realized that Mama had taken things so far in her abuse toward us. She began to look worried and frightened. We got scared, too. "I didn't know she was such a sick woman," said my grandmother. "You children should never be afraid to tell me anything any- more," she told us. "Do you understand me? Never." We looked at her and nodded our heads. I thought happily, "Things are going to change around here now just like she promised."

"After you all are finishing eating," said Grandmom Faya, "we're going to tear this place apart until we find Andrew, Jr. Okay?" "Okay, Grandmom," we replied. "I don't have good feelings about this," said my grandmother. "Especially after what Tyla just told me."

My grandmother recalled the time when Emma and Malin had been missing for a few days. "Emma, when you and Malin were gone that time after Charon beat you," asked Grandmom Faya, "where were you?" Malin answered her question. "Mama locked us up in the shed out back, Grandmom," he told her. "Every day she came out there and gave us each a slice of bread to eat and some water to drink. Then she would beat on us some more with that electric cord that she uses." "Yeah," said Emma angrily, "she made us stay out there all tied up with no clothes on. It was cold and we were freezing, Grandmom. But she didn't care one bit. All she did was laugh like it was funny to her." Emma paused for a moment then said, "Do you know what she said to us?" "No, tell me," said Grandmom Faya. I could tell that she was dreading what she was about to hear from the look on her face. Malin answered. "She told us that we were nothing but pieces of shit," he said. "And if she ever got a chance she would kill all of us, Grandmom."

My grandmother put her head down on the kitchen table. She didn't want us to see the tears that were in her eyes. "How could I have ever let these things happen in my own house, right under my nose?" she asked herself truly bewildered. "Are you going to beat her up for hurting us, Grandmom?" asked Malin hardly able to contain himself. All of us would have loved to see that.

My grandmother answered, "Not unless I have absolutely no other choice, sweetheart." She raised her head up from the table and continued to talk. "There are other ways to deal with people like Charon Davidson believe me. Let's just find Andrew Jr. first." She shook her head in disbelief at the things that she was learning.

We were eating but my grandmother lost her appetite. I knew she wanted to kill Mama. And, it was all she could do to keep the rage that she was feeling inside her from spilling out. For our sakes she tried her best to remain as cool and calm as she could. "As God is my witness," she solemnly said "She will never hurt you children again. I just hope a and pray it's not too late for Andrew Jr."

After we finished eating my grandmother cleaned up the kitchen. Then we began to search for Andrew Jr. We searched every room in that house and even out back in the shed. Also, we looked in the basement. We couldn't find him anywhere. "I know that child is in this house," my grandmother said worriedly.

"What do we do now, Grandmom?" asked Emma. "Well," she said, "you children go to bed. It's getting late and you have school in the morning." Together we headed upstairs to bed. My grandmother told us that maybe Andrew Jr. was visiting with someone he was friendly with. But we knew she didn't really believe that. She decided after we were all asleep that if he hadn't come home she was going to confront Mama with her suspicions.

After tucking us into our beds that night Grandmom Faya kissed all of us goodnight.. Then she went to her own bedroom. She changed into her nightgown. Then laid across her bed to rest for a little while. She wanted to be sure that we were all asleep before she confronted Mama.

I remembered everything that my grandmother told me about that night. As she laid in her bed she got angry. Not just with Mama but with herself for letting things get so out of control. She drifted off to sleep as she laid there.

It wasn't until many years later that she told me about the eery visitations that she received. The truth about our family history and the secrets that she and her sisters tried to keep buried would soon be revealed.

She told me that she was suddenly awakened that night by something unknown at first. A gust of wind blew into her bedroom window that had only been cracked a little. A very cold chill came over her that made her shudder violently. Sitting up in the bed another cold chill came over her. And the beside lamp started to grow dimmer and dimmer until the room was almost completely dark.

Then at the foot of her bed she saw Andrew standing there. My father and her son she told me. He looked very handsome but his face was drawn and haggard as if he was worried about something. The sorrowfulness of his spirit was more than obvious to her as she looked at him. "Andrew, honey," she asked, "what do you want?"

"Mama," he said to her, "don't be afraid for Andrew, Jr. Be afraid for my other children because Marie is in this house with you. She controls Charon just like she always has. I've tried to help them but there isn't too much that I can do. She is very powerful Mama just as she was in life. The children need you. You are the only one who can save them. Marie fears you Mama just as she always has."

The spirit hesitated for a moment. Then he said to her, "One more thing. Mama." "Yes, Andrew," she said. "Please forgive me for all of the pain that I caused you and Aunt Miriam." Then his spirit vanished and her bedroom became bright again. The chill she felt had vanished as well,.

"My, God!" she exclaimed. "Marie is in this house?" She sat on the side of her bed. Her worst fears were about to come true. Andrew Jr.had been murdered and his body was somewhere inside the house. My grandmother told me that she began to cry. The horrid memories of her past came flooding back to her mind. Terrible memories that she had managed to suppress for a long time.

"Dear, Andrew," she said softly, "how could I have ever called Miriam a bad mother?" It was never her fault that you got caught up in a bad situation. Your father was an evil man. Marie was determined that he would marry her instead of Miriam. .Although it was Miriam who was carrying his child. She caused so much pain and heartache with her hatred, wickedness and jealousy. She hated her own sister because of a man." My grandmother calmed herself for a moment.

"Now she is back," my grandmother said softly. "Even in death she cannot rest until she destroys your children just like she destroyed you. It was then that

Grandmom Faya knew what she had to do. First, she had to find Andrew Jr. wherever he had been hidden. Then she would confront Mama.

There was something else that my grandmother knew she had to do. "It's time for me to make peace with my sister," she said to herself. "*I will need her* help to keep these children safe. We have to stand together now it's the only way."

After Andrew's appearance Grandmom Faya looked at the clock. It had only been a half an hour since she put us to bed. She knew how we liked to talk among ourselves before falling asleep. Laying back on her pillows she wanted to wait a little while longer before she began her search for Andrew Jr. She drifted off to sleep and began to dream.

In the dream Grandmom Faya saw Andrew Jr. He was standing down by the lake near the spot under the big oak tree that Malin and I called our 'secret place'. We didn't know that my grandmother knew about it but she did. I learned about that years later.

My oldest brother began to speak to her. "Grandmom," he said, "your house has a couple of hidden rooms behind the walls in the basement. If you go down there and search them you will find me." She awoke with a start. A horrible feeling clutched at her heart.

"Oh, no!" she cried. She looked over at the clock and saw that an hour had passed since she fell asleep. We were definitely asleep by that time. She got up to search the basement as my brother told her to do.

She put on her housecoat and slippers. She knew about the rooms that my brother mentioned in her dream. However, she was surprised that Mama knew about them. My grandmother often suspected that my siblings and I may have discovered them. Yet, she never questioned us.

Once she got downstairs Grandmom Faya got a flashlight from a drawer in the kitchen and turned it on. She headed for the basement. Before going down the stairs she already knew from her two ghostly visitors what she would find.

"My, God," she murmured to herself, "how could I have let this happen? How? After what happened to their father I should have known better. I should have been on top of things in this house." She chastised herself for being so unaware of Mama's cruelty that was most likely connected to some mental issues,

In the basement she pushed open a panel in one of the walls that revealed a hidden room. It was small and dark inside. A feeling of dread washed over my grandmother and the hairs on the back of her neck stood on end. As she entered the hidden room the dim light of the flashlight shone on the figure of a young boy. He was hanging from one of the beams in the ceiling.

She put her hand over her mouth as if to stifle a scream at the sight. She stood frozen in terror as she stared at the limp body whose face and head were almost unrecognizable. The boy had been beaten as well as tortured to death. The scratches and cuts on his now thin arms and hands revealed that he tried to defend himself from his attacker. He looked so small and fragile to her.

Grandmom Faya's eyes filled with tears that spilled over onto her cheeks. She took his body down from the thick rope that it was hanging from and held Andrew Jr. in her arms. She sobbed heartbreakingly as she gently rocked his body back and forth. "Oh, Andrew Jr." she sobbed. "This is all my fault. Oh, God, forgive me please. I'm so sorry that I let this child down."

My grandmother held my brother's body in her arms for a long time. Then, laying him on the basement floor, she telephoned Sheriff Bicket. She never at any time had to wonder or guess what had happened to my dear brother, Andrew Jr.

CHAPTER FOUR

My grandmother was shocked and horrified when she saw Andrew, Jr.'s Death Certificate. It read that he had died as a result of "*suicide*". She was outraged and argued, vehemently, with Sheriff Bicket and the Coroner. She condemned publicly and privately the so-called 'investigation' they had conducted but it didn't do any good. They refused to change my brother's cause of death. The Coroner, James Witley, was an old boyfriend of Mama's. My grandmother knew that she must have promised him something in order for him to outright lie about my brother's death. On the other hand, Sheriff Bickett knew better but wanted to keep his job. He didn't have any political 'clout'. Therefore, Grandmom Faya had no way of dis-proving Coroner Witley's lie.

Something was terribly wrong in more ways than ever when an obvious beating caused my brother's death but a Coroner said it was a suicide. After Sheriff Bicket went along with it his and Grandmom Faya's long friendship was irreparably compromised. Needless to say, my grandmother wanted to hurt Mama as badly as she knew Mama had hurt Andrew Jr.

However, years would pass before my grandmother revealed to my siblings and I how Andrew Jr. really died. The burial was private and only attended by Grandmom Faya, Emma, Nicholas, Malin, me and to our surprise, Miss Miriam. The few friends that Andrew Jr. had were also invited by my grandmother. Grandmom Faya requested an open casket but that didn't happen.

The Undertaker, Wilson Evans, did a good job on the body but he wasn't a miracle worker. He also wasn't fooled by the cause of my brother's death. Not surprisingly Mama was not there. A few days before that my grandmother confronted Mama about Andrew Jr.'s death. She let her know, without a doubt, she knew that Mama murdered my brother. Then she told Mama to pack her bags and leave immediately. Never to come back. My Grandmother never wanted to see Mama again. My siblings and I would not be leaving with her. I cannot tell anybody how grateful we were for that.

The confrontation occurred on the same night that Grandmom Faya found Andrew Jr.'s body in the basement. My sister, brothers and I were awakened by the heated argument between the two women. We heard the accusations that Grandmom Faya hurled at Mama. "I know you murdered Andrew Jr., Charon." We heard her say to Mama.

"You don't know what the hell you're talking about, Faya." Mama shot back at her. "Why don't you just mind your own damn business anyway?" "I am minding my own damn business," shouted my grandmother. "This is my house not yours. And I don't want a lying, murdering bitch like you inside it any longer. So pack your things and get the hell out of my house. You have twenty four hours to do it."

"Oh, really?" retorted Mama sarcastically. "What about my children? If I go they go with me. You know that don't you, Faya? I will make sure that you never see any of them again. You'd better believe it, too."

Suddenly, it got quiet. I knew my grandmother was probably staring. angrily at Mama. "Whatever happened to you, Charon?" she asked Mama. "You've always had your faults like everybody else. But in the past eight years you've become a monster." We could tell from the tone of her voice that Grandmom Faya was doing all that she could do to control her anger and rage. "You *will* leave those children right here when you go, Charon," she told Mama. "Do you really think that I would let you kill them off as you've murdered Andrew Jr.?"

"I didn't murder anybody you stupid, crazy bitch," Mama shot back at Grandmom Faya. "You're a sick woman, Charon," my grandmother said to her. "You need help. Like I said, you have twenty four hours to get your ass out of my house and don't even think about coming back here or ever coming near those children again."

"I don't ever want to see you again, Charon" said my grandmother, "as long as I live." She was speaking to Mama in a low threatening voice. "Don't make the mistake of thinking that anyone will help you fight against me on this either, Charon." My grandmother spoke as if Mama would understand exactly what she was saying.

"I-I d-don't know what the hell you're talking about, Faya," said Mama shakily. Yet, it was plain from her tone of voice that she knew *exactly* what my grand- mother was referring to. "Oh, yes, you do," said Grandmom Faya. "You know damn well *what* and *who* I'm talking about. Don't play dumb with me. I disown you as my sister, Charon. I hope to God that you burn in hell for what you have done to these children and to *my* son."

Mama chuckled that time. It was evil and wicked. "*Your son,*" she mocked. "I guess you've really believed that nonsense all of these years huh, Faya." She hesitated. "You poor stupid fool. Andrew was not your son, dear heart." Mama chuckled again.

"Get the hell out of here you wicked witch," Grandmom Faya hissed at her.

"When you go the evil that is here in my house now will go with you."
"What evil?" asked Mama sounding surprised.

"You really don't know do you, Charon?" asked my grandmother. "Well, that's too bad for you but I think you do know. You know *exactly* who it is that has controlled you all of these years. Even if you won't admit it. She has you in the palm of her hand like a puppet on a string. Just like she always has even from the grave." She hesitated.

"How could you ever forget all of the hell and despair that she brought upon this family?" continued Grandmom Faya. "Or all of the lives that she destroyed with her wickedness?" As we listened to them arguing we were hearing about things in our family that we never knew about. Suddenly, Mama became silent. To our shock and surprise we heard her crying.

All four of us had been listening to everything they said to one another. We were shocked to say the least. We never heard or saw Mama cry. We didn't even think that she could cry or would cry.

"Sister?" whispered Emma in shock. "Mama and Grandmom are sisters?"

"Shhh", I said. We listened as my grandmother began to speak to Mama again. "When you leave here Charon," said Grandmom Faya, "we'll all be better off. I should have gotten rid of you a long time ago, before Andrew died. Maybe Andrew Jr. would still be alive. You killed my grandson. I know you did that for sure. Although I can't put all of the blame on you for his father's death without proof." "Andrew wasn't your son, Faya," Mama said through tears. "You know that and so does Miriam. He blew his own brains out because he found out about you two. You both did that to him, Faya. I didn't. How can you blame me in any way for Andrew's death? What do you think the good people of Maron would think of you if they knew the truth about you and the Davidson fam- ily huh?"

"You knew *everything* that was going on with Andrew and Teresa back then, Charon," said Grandmom Faya refusing to back down from Mama. "Yet, you stood by and did nothing. Nor did you say anything to anybody about it. It could have been prevented, Charon. Therefore, that makes you just as bad as the true killer and we *all* know who that was."

Again things got quiet. We knew Grandmom Faya was probably glaring at Mama. It was as if she knew what Mama was saying was true but it was something that they could never do anything about. We heard my grandmother say, "Twenty four hours, Charon, not a minute more. You'd better be gone by this time tomorrow. Don't even think about coming to the funeral." We heard Grandmom Faya leave Mama's bedroom.

My siblings and I looked at one another that night in disbelief. We couldn't believe all of the things that we heard. After all of that time we discovered that Mama and our grandmother were sisters. And, that our father wasn't the child of our grandmother. "*Who is Teresa?*" we were all asking ourselves. "*Where does she fit into all of this?*"

There was something else that didn't fit into the puzzle. It was something truly strange. If my grandmother wasn't our father's mother who was she?

Where did our father fit in all of this? After all, he certainly wouldn't be married to his own aunt would he?

There were pieces of this drama that were missing. It didn't make any sense to us. There was definitely something wrong. For most of that night we whispered among ourselves. We even heard Mama packing her things to leave. As hard as we tried to come up with answers we couldn't figure out what was going on between Mama, Grandmom Faya and our father.

The biggest question was, "Are they who they say that they were in connection to us? Was Mama really our mother? Was Grandmom Faya really our grandmother?" We even began to ask the question, "Was Andrew really our father?"

We were so confused. Not to mention the fact that my grandmother had accused Mama of murdering our dear brother. "Andrew Jr. is dead?" Emma asked her face breaking up to cry. Silently, we all sobbed. "It can't be true," said Malin who wasn't supposed to be in Emma's and my bedroom. Both he and Nicholas snuck into our bedroom when the argument between Mama and our grandmother awakened them, too.

Each one of us hoped that we had heard wrong. None of us wanted to believe that part of the conversation about Andrew, Jr. Our dear brother couldn't be dead. Grandmom Faya said that she would always protect us. Eventually, all of us drifted off to sleep.

It was the following morning when Grandmom Faya woke all of us up and told us about Andrew Jr. What we had overheard was true. He was dead. All of us cried for what seemed like a long time. We loved our brother so much and we couldn't imagine living without him in our lives anymore.

When our crying quieted into gentle sobbing Malin asked Grandmom Faya what happened to Andrew Jr. All she said was that he had been involved in a tragic accident. Then she told us that Mama was gone and wouldn't be com- ing back. We were very happy about that. It was a very bright spot in an otherwise dark day of heartache.

We already agreed not to let Grandmom Faya know that we had over- heard the argument between her and Mama. So we asked no questions about the things that we heard them say to one another. Looking back now I don't know how my grandmother kept so many things about our family to herself for so many years.

Later that morning I stared out of the window and watched as two men from town dug Andrew Jr.'s grave. All of our family members were to be buried in the plot which was on the rear grounds of the house when we died. It was the way that our family did things Grandmom Faya told us. No one ever went into a pub- lic cemetery. I thought, *"There must be a family plot near the house where Grandmom used to live, too."*

Saying goodbye to Andrew, Jr. was so hard for us. We all had tears running down our faces. He looked so handsome in the dark blue suit that Grandmom Faya bought him. It was difficult to accept the fact that he was dead and was never coming back. He looked so peaceful. Like he had just fallen asleep.

Andrew, Jr. was laid out in the big living room of our house. A lot of people from Maron came to pay their respects. We didn't know that he had so many friends and they in turn brought their families. He was well liked in spite of how hard Mama tried to keep any of us from having friends. "They probably just came to be nosey," Miss Miriam said in disgust. He laid there in the living room all that day and all that night until the next morning when we buried him.

At the gravesite that day a strange thing happened that would stay with me for the rest of my life. The large floral arrangement from Miss Miriam was placed atop Andrew Jr.'s casket. As Grandmom Faya, Miss Miriam, the Priest, the two grave diggers, my sister, brothers and I stood around the grave the floral arrangement was lifted off the casket by unseen hands into mid-air. It stood above the casket for at least ten seconds as we watched in horror. Someone unseen was there with us and we were terrified.

It was as though some invisible person was holding the arrangement in the air while we watched. The Priest began to tremble as he stopped reading from the Bible. He just stood there like the rest of us in shock. A look of fear on his face. Suddenly, as if deliberately dropped by someone, the floral arrangement fell neatly back atop the casket. I, nor any of the others would ever forget what happened that day.

However, over the years and as we grew older the incident seemed to stay with me longer than with anybody else. Miss Miriam told us, "It's a sign that his spirit is not going to rest in peace." That incident caused me to have a great fear of graves, cemeteries and anything else to do with dead people for years to come.

Once my oldest brother was laid to rest our family settled in and began to live a life of peace and happiness with Grandmom Faya. Two things we had never had in our home when Mama was there. Then Miss Miriam and Grandmom Faya became friends again. Miss Miriam would come over and visit with us almost on a daily basis. She and my grandmother sat and talked for hours as if they were making up for lost time.

Their friendship was rekindled when Andrew Jr. died. Grandmom Faya tele- phoned Miss Miriam to tell her about my brother's death and how she suspected Mama. One word lead to another and soon they had been on the telephone for two whole hours. Finally, I heard my grandmother ask her to come over so they could talk face to face. Within the hour Miss Miriam was there.

When she walked up to the front door my grandmother threw the door open and hugged and kissed Miss Miriam as if they hadn't seen one another in years. Each one of them had tears in their eyes and were crying all over one another. Emma and I were overjoyed. Our secret wish had come true. Miss Miriam didn't go back home. She stayed with us until well after Andrew Jr. had been buried.

During the months that followed my brother's death our home was filled with something else that had never been there before. Laughter. It seemed strange at first. We were so unhappy for so long because of Mama but my grandmother made a vow that things in our home would change and they certainly did.

Everything we had been denied that other normal children took advantage of was now ours. We had birthday parties, went to the amusement parks, carnivals and to the zoo. Things we had never dreamed of doing with Mama we were now doing on a regular basis with Grandmom Faya and Miss Miriam. All of us were completely happy with our new lives.

Miss Miriam became like a second grandmother to us. We were happy to see her whenever she came to visit. I even heard Grandmom Faya trying to talk her into moving in with us. However, she told my grandmother that she didn't want to leave her home. For our part Emma and I certainly wished she would move in with us. Little did we know our wish would come true in the near future.

Miss Miriam was so sweet and kind to all of us. She was a beautiful woman, too, just like my grandmother. She and Grandmom Faya always laughed about something during their many conversations. They looked much happier, too, now that they were friends again. It was easy to see that they truly loved each other. It was rather strange that they looked so much alike Emma and I thought. "They could easily pass for sisters, couldn't they, Ty?" Emma asked me one day. "They sure could," I replied secretly wondering if she was one of my grandmother's sisters.

CHAPTER FIVE

As the years passed by Emma and I grew into beautiful young women, and Nicholas and Malin became very handsome young men. It was then that Nicholas started staying away from home more and more. He changed a lot after Andrew Jr. died. We knew he missed our oldest brother more than the rest of us did because they were so close.

The day finally came when he left home altogether. Nobody in our family was surprised. He left home one day to go to the store down the street and he never came back. Even my grandmother wasn't surprised.

Of course, she initiated an all-out search for my brother after he'd been gone for a week. Sheriff Bicket, his Deputies and many people from town joined in the search, and that surprised us. Since the people in Maron rarely got involved in one another's problems.

My grandmother even put up posters bearing Nicholas's picture all over Maron and in surrounding counties but it didn't do any good. He was gone. Although everybody else gave up hope of ever finding my brother, Grandmom Faya never gave up hope.

Years later, out of the blue we received a letter from him. He told us in the letter that he had enlisted in the Air Force and he was stationed in Paris, France.

My grandmother was overjoyed to hear from him as were the rest of us. When she opened the letter that day she shrieked with joy. For nine long years she worried about him. Not knowing whether he was dead or alive. She had imagined all kinds of terrible things that could have happened to him but that day, at last she knew that he was alright and her mind could rest.

Also, in his letter Nicholas told us that he was going to marry a girl that he met in Paris, but he didn't say anything in the letter about coming home. And, he didn't mention where he had been for all of those years before he enlisted in the Air Force. Yet, it was still good to know he was alive.

Malin was going to be a senior in high school that year. Furthermore, he earned a basketball scholarship for college. He chose a school that was almost five hundred miles away. It didn't seem that far away to him but it did to me. He was seventeen years old and I would soon be fifteen. Emma had just turned nineteen years old.

As young as Emma was she was considering marrying some guy who lived in town named, Artie Weston. She didn't know it at the time but I had heard rumors that he was already married. Besides, I thought he was too old for my sister. Artie Weston was thirty four years old and very nice looking but he was much too jealous.

I found out that most older guys who had young girlfriends were overly jealous. To me, that made them dangerous. Also, I thought, *"He's got a lot of nerve and he's married."* Artie wasn't any different from any other man in my opinion, who always wanted their 'cake' and eat it, too.

He would freak out if he telephoned our house and Emma wasn't there. He wanted to know where she was every single minute of the day. I couldn't understand why she put up with him. She thought it was funny how he would act like a complete idiot over her. I saw *nothing* humorous about it. I didn't trust him at all.

Grandmom Faya didn't know how old Artie Weston was. Or, that he acted like an imbecile when he couldn't put his hands on Emma's whereabouts at all times. For her he put on a good disguise and acted like a perfectly mannerable gentleman. However, my grandmother wasn't fooled by him and she didn't like him. She said, "There's just something about that guy that I don't like."

She was right. I could sense it, too. There was just something about him that didn't sit well with us. Grandmom Faya knew his family and she thought of them as uncouth characters. Right up to and including his grandmother, Sheila Weston, she told me. "Where have I heard that name, before?" I thought.

It was then that I recalled Grandmom Faya telling me long years before that, when I was a little girl, that Sheila Weston was the only outsider ever allowed in their home when they were young. She was friendly with Marie, my grandmother's evil older sister.

Anyway, it didn't matter what anybody said to Emma about Artie, she wouldn't listen. Emma was head strong and believed that she *everything*. My grandmother got tired of trying to warn Emma about Artie.

After that she told me that it was sometimes best to let hard-headed people like Emma find out things the hard way. I agreed. "For some people, Tyla," she told me, "the hard way is the best way."

In the year that I was going to turn fifteen my grandmother was sixty two years old but she looked like a woman of fifty years old. She seemed to get renewed strength and vitality after Mama left. She and Miss Miriam would sit outside on the front porch when the weather was nice and gossip for hours. When the weather wasn't so nice they would sit in the kitchen and gossip.

I will never forget the day that I overheard Grandmom Faya talking about us moving back into her old family home. The house where she lived many years ago with her evil grandmother, Ole Lucy.

Miss Miriam objected bitterly and didn't want to go with us when my grandmother asked her to. I could tell from the way she reacted that Miss Miriam knew about that house, too. And I thought I detected a touch of fear in her voice as she told Grandmom Faya that she wouldn't go.

As close as the two women were Miss Miriam was adamant about not going to live in that old house. I understood perfectly. After all of the bad things that my grandmother told me about that place. I didn't think moving back there was a good idea either.

Since Grandmom Faya hadn't said anything to any of the rest of us about moving yet I said nothing to my sister and brother about it. Besides, I didn't want Grandmom Faya and Miss Miriam to know that I had been eavesdropping on their conversation. That wasn't the only thing that I overheard them talking about that day.

I heard my grandmother telling Miss Miriam about how she believed that someone named 'Marie' had probably left the old house by then and that we could live there in peace and safety. After I heard that, as if they knew I was listening, they began to whisper. I hated that. I couldn't hear anything else that they were saying. I started thinking.

"I wonder if this 'Marie' person is Grandmom Faya's evil sister? No! She couldn't be! She told me that 'Marie' was dead." I began to recall the many bad stories that my grandmother told me about her older sister and I shivered in horror unconsciously. *"No," I thought. "It must be some other woman named "Marie'."* I would find out later on that it was the same person that I overheard them talking about that day. I didn't know it then but after all that my grandmother told me about her sister, Marie, she softened the part about how truly evil her sister was.

One day after school I was walking home from the bus stop. As usual my mind was occupied with all kinds of thoughts. Grandmom Faya and Emma called me "the thinker" like the statue. I was always day-dreaming about one thing or another. Often a million miles way in thought.

That particular day was no different and my thoughts were sifting through the reasons why I didn't have a boyfriend yet. I thought there might have been some- thing wrong with me. A lot of boys at school liked me but none of them interested me, and I made that known to them. I just wasn't interested in any of them. Besides, Grandmom Faya told me just as she told Emma that I wouldn't be able to date until I turned sixteen years old.

Even Emma said to me, "Something must be wrong with you, Ty," she told me one night while we were in her bedroom talking. "Why don't you like the boys?" she asked me. "You never go out anywhere or have any friends. It's weird." "I do so have friends," I replied stubbornly.

"Oh, yeah?" she retorted. "Who? Crazy Karen?" she chuckled. "She's the only friend that I've ever seen you with. Silly Karen Bullock and that's because she's as strange as you are." I didn't say anything because I knew Emma was right. Karen was my only friend outside the family.

"You need to branch out more," continued Emma. "As pretty as you are the guys should be knocking our door down to get to you, girl. Be like your big sis- ter." She said that with a smirk on her face that made me angry. "What?" I snapped at her. "Mess around with married men?" She stared at me in shock. As soon as I said it I was sorry. The last thing that I wanted to do was hurt Emma.

"Oh, I'm sorry, Emma" I said sheepishly. "But I heard that Artie is married." Her countenance changed quickly. "That lousy son of a bitch," she snarled angrily. "Thanks for telling me, sis," she said glaring at me. "How long have you known about this, Ty?"

"It's only a rumor, Emma," I said. "You should talk to him about it before you go off the deep end." She was quiet as she pondered over what I told her. "Okay," she said finally. "You're right, Ty. I'll ask him about it before I dump his ass like a hot potato."

She reached for the telephone and dialed the number to Artie's mother, Beverly. She asked to speak to Artie. Beverly told her that Artie wasn't there but that she would have him return her phone call as soon as possible. Emma hung up the telephone.

"Now that I think about it," she told me, "every time I call there he's not there. But he always calls me back five or ten minutes later." "That ought to tell you something right there, Emma," I told her. "She probably calls him wherever he really lives and tells him that you called for him."

"You can't be too careful about some of these men, Ty," she warned me. I could tell that she was really angry with Artie. "Don't ever trust them," she continued to tell me. "If you're not with them you can't trust them." Then she laid across her bed and became silent.

It was obvious that she was thinking about all of the other little hints that Artie gave her that she missed. Hints that she never paid any attention to. Hints that had "*MARRIED!*" written all over them. She was wondering how she could have been so stupid.

I knew that it was because she was willful and stubborn. She was a 'know-it-all' and the rest of us were the dummies. Grandmom Faya always told her that she would get hurt one day. If she didn't stop '*knowing*' everything and refused to listen to somebody else for a change.

I decided to leave her alone with her thoughts. I told her that I would talk to her later on and went to my own bedroom. I sat down on my bed and stared out of the window. I thought about Karen. Maybe I did like her because we were a lot alike.

Karen was a year older than I was and she was very pretty. She kept her hair dyed dark auburn. I knew it was out of jealousy since my hair was naturally dark red. She had light brown eyes and smooth brown skin. Karen was tall and slender like a model. She dressed real sharp, too. Although she was old enough to date I never saw her with a guy ever since we had been friends.

Karen came from a strange secretive family like me. They were fairly wealthy, she told me. The Bullocks were very well liked by the people in Maron. Mrs. Bullocks' family had lived in Maron for four generations. But Mr. Bullock,

Karen's father, came from a big city in the East. He was in town on business when he met Karen's mother.

They fell in love and got married after only one month. Karen and I both thought that was kind of quick to jump up and marry somebody. But she told me that her mother thought she was pregnant at the time. So they just got married to save themselves a lot of slander and gossip. Karen was an only child.

Good looks were not the only thing that Karen had going for her. She was extremely smart. Almost a genius. She always did well in school and was at the top of her class. Yet, when it came to boys she shunned them. "They only want one thing," she told me. "After that they'll leave you alone." With no social activity all she did was go to school or to my house and help her Mom around their house.

Jacqueline Bullock, Karen's mother, was very nice. She reminded me of one of those Southern belles that you see in old movies like 'Gone With the Wind'. She was very lady-like and almost dainty and delicate in her mannerisms. I never heard her raise her voice or say a cuss word as long as I knew her.

Otto Bullock, Karen's father, was a nice man. He wasn't at home very often though. Karen and her mother spent a lot of time alone or rather with one another. There were rumors around Maron that Otto Bullock was having an affair with a lady named, Olivia Laws, who lived in Tolstoy. The rumor was that Olivia was married, too.

"He must have heard the rumors, too." Karen told me one day speaking about her father. "How could he not have heard them?" Yet, he still stayed away from home a lot. As if he didn't care about the rumors or how much he was hurting his family. He was an Executive Vice-President of the company that he worked for in Tolstoy.

Tolstoy was where many people who lived in Maron went to look for work. It was very industrial and five times the size of Maron. Also, Karen told me that her mother caught her father and Olivia together on more than one occasion.

But she didn't want a divorce because she still loved him. And thought they would be able to work things out. She told Karen that her father was just going through a phase that would pass. Well, after eight years it hadn't passed yet.

Karen's family lived in a big house similar to the one that my family and I would be moving into. According to what I heard my grandmother telling Miss Miriam. I hadn't seen the house yet but I knew we would be moving into it soon. I finally got up enough nerve to ask Grandmom Faya where the house was. As she had described its' location, to my horror, I realized it was the same old house down by the lake that had scared Malin and I when we were little children.

"That old place?" I asked her, the surprise and fear echoing in my voice. "Yes, honey" she said, "that's the one. Why? Is something wrong?" "No," I lied to her. I was terrified of that old house. The chill and terror that swept over me that day long ago when my brother and I opened the front door would never be forgotten. Now, to find out that it was the same spooky house that my grandmother told me all of those scary stories about I was shocked as well as scared.

In spite of my fear I wanted to go back and see that old house again. So I left the house one day and headed down to the lake to look at it. I promised myself that I would only view it from a distance. I wasn't about to go near that place.

When I arrived at the lake area to see the old house I was amazed at what I saw. There were contractors and workmen all over the place and they were making it into a beautiful home. The grounds were mown and manicured. New shrubs and flowers had been planted. The flowers were all carnations, my grandmother's favorite flower. They were pink, white and yellow and they looked beautiful.

The long, marble walkway leading up to the front door of the house was sparkling. Since the old house sat so far back from the lake it had to be at least fifty yards long. The workmen and contractors were busy on both the inside as well as the outside of the house. To look at it, it was hard to believe all of the horrifying stories that Grandmom Faya told me. When the workmen were all done it would truly be a beautiful house. At least on the outside.

"Grandom Faya certainly is full of surprises," I thought as I turned around and began to walk back home. She had many more surprises for my sister, brothers and I. We had no idea they were coming either. When they did, needless to say, we were not prepared for them. I thought to myself that there was no one on the face of the earth who could keep secrets like Faya Davidson could.

CHAPTER SIX

Right after he got his driver's license Malin tried to talk Grandmom Faya into buying him a used car. She refused. My grandmother tried to teach him about responsibility by letting him drive her car to and from school every day. But when he wrecked it, trying to show off for his friends, that was the end of that.

My grandmother went out of her way to spoil my siblings and I. And so did Miss Miriam. I believed they were trying to make up for all of the misery and terror that Mama put us through. Since Nicholas left home they didn't want any of the rest of us to do that, too.

With Mama gone life became very different for us. We were happy. My grandmother made sure that we knew how much we were loved. She and Miss Miriam showered all of us with nothing but love and kindness. But at the same time they were also strict with us. There were rules to follow in our home. And if those rules were broken we paid for it. However, the 'punishments' were nothing anywhere near what we had experienced with Mama. After she left we never heard from Mama again. I often wondered where she could be or if she was still alive. It had been nine years since she left. Emma and Malin could have cared less about her. They refused to even mention her name. When Nicholas wrote letters to us he never asked about Mama.

Sometimes I would hear my grandmother and Miss Miriam talking about Mama. It was always at the same time they were talking about "Marie' and my father, Andrew. Lately, a new name began to surface in their whispered conversations. A man by the name of 'Roy'. Apparently, this man was connected to 'Marie' in some way. Also, another woman's name was mentioned.

One that I hadn't heard before. "*I could find out so much more if they wouldn't start whispering,*" I thought. I was wrong. There were actually two people, not one, as I previously thought who had as many secrets as Grandmom

Faya did. Miss Miriam kept secrets pretty good, too. I couldn't have known then how right I was.

Before I knew it I was home and opening the front door. As I went inside the house I could hear Grandmom Faya and Miss Miriam laughing about something in the kitchen. They heard me when I came in the house and turned to see who it was.

"Hi, honey!" my grandmother said with a smile. "Hi, sweetheart!" Miss Miriam said. "How are you? How was school today?" "Okay" I answered. "Would you like a sandwich or something, honey?" Grandmom Faya asked me. "No, Grandmom" I replied. The two women resumed the conversation they had been having when I came in. I put my school books on the coffee table in the living room. Suddenly, I began to feel tired. So I headed upstairs to take a nap.

It was a lovely, warm, summer day when the letter came in the mail. There was no school that day because of a teacher's conference. The school usually had those conferences at the end of the school year. I was home that day and got the mail when it came.

Bernie Brown had been our mailman ever since I could remember. Back then you could see that he was getting on in age but he still waited in the General Store very morning until the mail truck arrived. He took on the job of hand delivering everybody's mail many years before that. It was a nice gesture as people didn't have to pick up their mail themselves. They just let Bernie do it.

My grandmother told us that he just needed something to do to occupy his days after his elderly mother passed on. He was an only child and he had never been married or had any children. He lived with his mother all of his life. In all truth, he and his mother acted like an old married couple instead of mother and son. I don't think Bernie ever had a girlfriend in his whole life. His mother's death had been very hard on him.

Whenever he brought people's mail he would always sit down for a spell and chat with people. He loved to talk with Grandmom Faya and Miss Miriam. Or, any of us who happened to be at home when he arrived with the mail. Then he would start talking about how he missed his mother. He loved to talk about her, too. "He must live a very empty life now," I thought. Bernie was a good man.

Mr. Greenley and his wife arranged with the local Post Office in Tolstoy for Bernie to be paid a small salary like a regular mailman. Also, the Post Office gave him one of their little mail trucks to drive around in while he made his deliveries. Bernie never missed a day. Except, Sunday when there was no mail delivery in Maron. If he did miss a day, Billy Greenley, Mr. Greenley's grandson who lived with them would make the deliveries.

After Bernie arrived that day he and I talked for a few minutes. Then he went on his way. I was the only one in the house that morning. As I looked down at the mail I saw a letter addressed to "The Davidson Family" and postmarked "Paris, France". Right away I knew it was from Nicholas but the handwriting on the front of the envelope wasn't his. Before I opened the letter and read it I knew my brother was finally coming home. At that time I often 'knew' things before they occurred and so did my sister.

Gradually, I became aware of this ability in the past three years. Both Emma and I seemed to 'know' many things were going to happen long before they actually did. Either she or I would have a dream about something. Then whatever happened in our dreams would happen in real life a few days later. Sometimes things would just pop into our heads. As if someone we couldn't see was telling us about something or someone. Whatever we 'heard' would happen shortly afterward.

Also, this ability we had worked in other ways. We 'knew' when somebody was coming to our house to visit long before they got there. Or if someone was coming with any kind of news. We 'knew' what the news was going to be. We would be right every time, too. It scared us a little bit.

We didn't know what was happening to us. And neither one of us told the other one that we were going through the exact same thing. Until later on. It wasn't just a little scary but it was also strange.

Grandmom Faya and Miss Miriam told us not to worry about it or be afraid of it. They told us that a lot of people could 'see' or 'hear' things that others couldn't before they occurred. It was called ESP and it was a gift. Well, if you asked either Emma or I we certainly didn't consider it a 'gift'. Of course, at first we didn't understand the power that we had. For Emma, and I we couldn't understand why anybody would consider what we had a 'gift'. As I said, at first I didn't know that Emma was experiencing the same 'gift' that I was. I found out when I finally broke down and told her what was happening to me. I was totally surprised when she exclaimed excitedly, "The same things are happening to me too, Ty!"

Emma gave a huge sigh of relief after I told her. "You don't know what a relief it is," she told me, "to know that I'm not going crazy or something" "Well," I said, "if you are I am, too. So don't feel bad."

It was after that when we decided to tell my grandmother and Miss Miriam about what was happening to us. After the two women assured us that there was nothing abnormal about us we didn't feel so spooked about it anymore. They told us that many other people had 'the gift just like we did.

To our surprise, we heard Grandmom Faya say to Miss Miriam when she thought we were out of hearing range, "I was wondering when it would finally come to the surface," she said. "Me, too," said Miss Miriam.

My grandmother never told us that her mother and grandmother both had psychic abilities. Yet, 'the gift' was not inherited by her or any of her sisters. Standing there with the letter in my hand I just stared at it. My mind began to wan der again. Back to the night that Emma and I were watching a movie on television. As we watched the movie suddenly Emma screamed.

"What's wrong?" I cried scared out of my wits. "Why did you scream like that, Emma?" A terrified look was on her face. And she whispered, hoarsely, "It's it's Miss Miriam." "What about her?" I asked.

By then, Emma's eyes were wide-open with alarm. She looked at me and said, slowly, "Miss Miriam is going to be sick again, Ty. And, this time if we don't get her to a hospital fast she's going to die." "What?" I cried. "Yes," replied my sister more calmly. "I just saw it all. Right before my eyes, Ty. You believe me don't you?"

"Sure, I do," I told her becoming more frightened by the minute. We had never been wrong about those things and I believed Miss Miriam was in danger. "We'd better get over to her house right away," I said jumping up from the chair, quickly.

Ever since we were little children we always called Miss Miriam's seizures 'being sick' instead of having a seizure. Suddenly, it dawned on us that she hadn't been over to our house that day. That was unusual. Grandmom Faya was outside working in her garden and hadn't heard my sister scream. Finding her, we told her where we were going and why.

Standing up, she announced that she would go along with us. When we got to Miss Miriam's house we rang the doorbell and waited, impatiently. But when she answered the front door she looked like the picture of health. Emma and I began to feel very foolish. But my grandmother told us in a soft voice, "Don't be so quick to write things off, girls."

"Hi, Miriam," said Grandmom Faya. "We were a little concerned about you over here. So we decided to pay you a visit." "Well," said Miss Miriam with a smile, "come on in. But as you can see I'm doing just fine. In fact, I was just get- ting ready to fix myself a big bowl of chocolate ice cream. Then sit down to watch the rest of the movie on television. Since you're all here you might as well join me."

She knew that Emma and I were fools for chocolate ice cream. She always kept some in her freezer in case we came over to visit her. The thing was we hardly ever had to visit her anymore because she was always at our house.

My sister and I looked at one another. Then we looked at our grandmother who nodded. We followed Miss Miriam into the house. "Remember what I just told you, girls," Grandmom Faya said quietly. "We'll stay for a while just to make sure she's okay. Alright?" We nodded.

Miss Miriam happened to be watching the same movie that Emma and I had been watching at home. "At least we can see the rest of the movie," she said to me. My grandmother and Miss Miriam went into the kitchen while Emma and I sat down in the living room and watched the rest of the movie.

"Are you sure you saw what you say you did, Emma?" I whispered to my sister. "Yes," she replied. "I saw it all just as clearly as I see that movie on that television set, Ty. It was as plain as it could be. I saw her have one of her seizures and she was all alone. There was blood on her head but I don't know how it got there. As she was laying on the floor I saw a clock over her head. The time was 12:15. There was an ambulance and paramedics there but they said that it was too late, because she had been lying there too long before someone found her. I saw it all, Ty. All of it. I swear." Emma was visibly shaken. This was the first time that she saw something in such vivid detail.

"I've seen crazy weird things before, Ty," she told me. "But never anything like that." I knew Emma was telling the truth. Also, I knew for a fact that since Miss Miriam hadn't been over to our house at all that day we certainly would have checked in on her tomorrow. "*It would have been too late,*" I thought. "*If all that Emma saw came true.*" It made perfect sense. Then we noticed Grandmom Faya watching us from the kitchen smiling. She winked at us. The four of us got our ice cream and sat down in the living room to watch the movie that was playing. When it was over we sat around and talked. Then my grandmother and Miss Miriam started talking about all of the old boyfriends that they used to sneak around with when they were young girls.

"We would have to wait until late at night when everybody was asleep," my grandmother said. "We had to be careful that no one in town ever saw us, too, because of Ole Lucy." "Yeah," added Miss Miriam, "she was a mean one alright. We would have to go twenty miles away from that house just to have some fun." She chuckled. Unwittingly, I asked Miss Miriam, "You knew Ole Lucy, too?"

For a minute she looked surprised then said, "O-oh, o-oh, yes, I did, Tyla, honey. I sure did." Suddenly, she was very nervous and so was my grandmother. It was like she had been caught off-guard by my question and said something that she shouldn't have. Both women got very quiet afterwards. Emma and I thought it was very odd that both of them stopped talking about 'the good old days' so suddenly. I think it was then that I got suspicious of their true relationship to each other.

The conversation started up again but on a different subject. They were laughing up a storm until the name, 'Roy', was mentioned. My sister and I noticed again how quiet the two of them suddenly got. That was a strange night. After a long silence Grandmom Faya said, "Well, girls, we had best be getting back home now." Emma had calmed down by that time so we got up to leave.

"Oh, wait a minute, Faya," said Miss Miriam. "Let me get that old locket for you that I told you about. If I don't get it now I'll forget it again. Wait right here for a minute while I go upstairs to get it for you."

My grandmother, Emma and I sat back down on the sofa to wait. Idly, I thought about Miss Miriam. Her black hair was almost as long as Grandmom Faya's and had one thick, white streak down the middle of her head. It looked odd but it made her more attractive than she already was.

Amazingly, she had the same skin color as my grandmother. And light brown eyes like Mama had. Their features were very similar to one another's. *"Surely these two women could pass for sisters with no trouble," I thought.*

Suddenly, we heard a loud thud followed by an even louder crash upstairs. We raced up the stairs to see what happened. Miss Miriam was laying on the floor of her bedroom near a big bureau dresser faced down. There was blood coming from one side of her head and she was unconscious but convulsing. On the corner of the bureau was some blood. It was apparent that she had fallen and hit her head.

Grandmom Faya quickly grabbed the first thing she got her hands on. Which was Miss Miriam's hairbrush. She placed the handle between her teeth so she wouldn't swallow her tongue and choke to death. It seemed like she knew exactly what to do for Miss Miriam. As if she had seen her that way before. At first I didn't hear my grandmother yelling at Emma and I to go call an ambulance. I don't think my sister ever did hear her. We were both standing there stunned.

"Move it!" I heard Grandmom Faya say. That time I heard her and ran to telephone for an ambulance. Emma remained frozen to the floor. When I returned I told her that the ambulance was on its' way. Then I looked at Emma and followed her disbelieving gaze to see what she was staring at. There was a clock atop the bureau dresser just above Miss Miriam's head. It had stopped at 12:15 exactly as my sister had 'seen' in her vision.

The ambulance arrived quickly and the paramedics took over Miss Miriam's care. All of us rode in the ambulance with her to the hospital. "She's a real lucky lady," said one of the paramedics. "If no one had been there with her there's no telling how long she would've been laying there. She might have died."

My sister and I will never forget the way that my grandmother smiled at us after he told us that. Emma started to sob softly. Grandmom Faya put her arms around her. "You saved her life, Emma", I heard her whisper into my sister's ear. "You sure did, Emma," I added. "Everything is going to be alright now girls," said my grandmother comfortingly.

Miss Miriam stayed in the hospital for a whole week because she hit her head so hard on the bureau dresser. They ran a lot of tests on her to be sure that she was okay before they let her go home. Also, they told Grandmom Faya that she really shouldn't be living by herself anymore in light of what happened to her. The next time she might not be so lucky.

Coming back to reality, from my memory of that night I looked at the envelope in my hand. I knew it was great news and I eagerly tore it open. As I read the letter I was overcome with joy. Excitedly, I ran to the backyard where my grand- mother was tending to her flower garden.

"Grandmom, guess what?" I cried when I saw her. "My goodness, girl," she said stopping her work to look up at me. "What is it that's go you so worked up?" "Look," I said holding up the letter for her to see. "Nicholas and his wife are coming home to stay with us. He's coming home, Grandmom. He's out of the Service now. Isn't that great?" I was so excited as I spoke to her.

As she read the letter I noticed that she wasn't sharing my joy and excitement. "What's the matter, Grandmom?" I asked worriedly. "Aren't you glad that Nicholas is finally coming back home?" She smiled at me and folded the letter. Then she put it back inside the envelope. "Yes, I am, Tyla, honey," she said. "I truly am after all of these years. I don't know how he will like staying in my old family house." I listened to her intently.

"I know none of you are crazy about the idea of moving in that house," she continued. "In fact, by the time he and his new wife arrive we may already be living there. I'm not sure yet. Even Miriam doesn't want to go. But she has no choice anymore as sick as she is." I understood what she meant. We didn't want to move into that old house.

"I don't think he'll mind too much, Grandmom," I told her. "You're probably right, honey", she agreed. "Anyway, at my age it doesn't make sense to live here when I have much more room and space over there." She paused again then sighed. "I've had contractors over there fixing up the place. It'll be ready soon."

"But, Grandmom," I said, "I didn't think you would want to live in that old house anymore. After all of the bad things that you told me that happened there." "It wasn't a nice place to live in back then, honey," she replied. "But the same love that we have in this house we'll be taking into that one with us. That love is like a bright shining light in the midst of all of the darkness that may still try to linger there. It will overcome any darkness don't you think?" I wondered. "Besides," she said with a secretive, little grin, "you, and Malin can be closer to your 'secret place', too."

I was shocked. "How did you know about our 'secret place', Grandmom?" I asked her. "We never told anybody about it." "I know a lot of things, Tyla sweetie," she said still smiling slyly. "Did you know that your brother talks in his sleep?" "Malin?" I asked surprised. She kept smiling at me. Then a more serious look came across her face and she asked me, "You're not afraid of that old house. Are you, honey?"

I was deathly afraid of that old house. Even though I didn't know why. Maybe it was because of all of her stories about it. Whatever the reason was I didn't want to live in there that was for sure. I would never forget how badly that place had scared Malin and I that day.

"No, Grandmom," I lied. "I'm not afraid." "As for Miriam," she said accepting my outright lie, "she can't be alone, anymore. It's either that old house or a nursing home for her. I already told her that and she knows I'm serious. Which one would you choose if you were her?" "I guess it's okay if you say so Grandmom," I replied meekly. Silently, I couldn't have agreed more with the way Miss Miriam felt.

Grandmom Faya put her arm around my shoulders. "If it will make you feel any better, honey," she said, "I've already had a Priest from each of the churches in town go inside the house and bless it for us. They will do it again, too, before we move in."

"Why did you do that, Grandmom?" I asked surprised that she would have something so solemn done if our love could out-shine any darkness there. "Oh," she replied, "because of all of the trouble and evil that went on inside there so long ago. But I don't think we will have anything to worry about."

No one could have known at the time, but Grandmom Faya had her own reasons for moving our family into that old house. Together, she and I went inside the house. I went upstairs to my bedroom and closed the door. I sat down on my window seat and stared out of the window. I was a little worried in spite of what Grandmom Faya told me.

I smiled to myself as I continued thinking about what she said. *"Just imagine, all of us being the light in that darkness. I sure hope you know what you are doing, Grandmom! I don't have good feelings about this move at all. There's still some thing not quite right about that place. I don't think any of us will do any good in there. No good at all."* I continued to stare out of my window and think about the move we would be making.

"Then again," I thought, *"maybe all of our love for each other will be able to destroy all of that darkness of the past like she says."* Over the following years and even now as old as I am, many times I still recall my grandmother's words.

CHAPTER SEVEN

On the same day that we received Nicholas's letter I decided later that evening to visit Karen. After all, Emma wouldn't be home until late that night and Malin would be out with his friends. I needed to talk to somebody about the up-coming move that my family and I were making. Someone other than my grandmother and Miss Miriam. First, I wanted to take a nap so I laid on top of my bed.

As I laid there, still thinking about our moving into that old, spooky house I dozed of to sleep. I slipped into a strange dream. In my dream I saw Andrew Jr. We were at the 'secret place' where Malin and I used to go to when we were children. It was weird to Malin and I how, even after Mama was gone, we didn't want to go there anymore.

Andrew Jr. started talking to me in the dream. Although I was terrified of dead people and anything remotely connected to them I was not afraid of my brother's spirit. A relaxing peace washed over me. I thought about how strange it was to see my oldest brother as the young boy he was when he died. He would have been twenty three years old at that time if he had lived.

"That's silly," I thought. "Dead people don't age. Why shouldn't he look the same as he did when he died?" I was so preoccupied with my thoughts I hadn't heard anything that his spirit was saying. I pushed those thoughts aside and listened to him carefully.

"Ty," he said to me, "there is nothing you can do to stop Grandmom Faya from moving back into that old house. She thinks it's safe to go back there now but it isn't. The woman named, Marie, is still in that house, Ty. She is very evil. Her spirit cannot leave that house for some reason." He stopped talking for a bit then continued. "Also, she comes to the house where you are now," he said. "But she has no power there. Listen to me, closely." My ears were glued to my brother's words.

"She is following you, Ty," my brother's spirit told me. I was shocked. "What?" I cried. "Listen!" he admonished me. "You're the one that she is angry about for some reason. Her anger and rage have made her spirit more evil and more dangerous after all of these years. She is more vile now than she ever was in her lifetime." "Why is she following me?" I asked the spirit still stunned. "Why me?" He kept on talking as if he hadn't heard my question.

"Marie is determined to do a lot of harm to somebody, Ty", he continued. "But whoever it is, it's someone that she feared when she was alive and still fears them in death. I just don't know who it is. She has help with her evil in that old house, too. There are others there. Others who are just as evil as she is. I hear them talking, Ty!" He hesitated.

"There's the spirit of a man whose name in life was, Roy, and another woman but she won't tell me her name. She died a long time ago like the others. It was at the hand of Marie, she told me. She said that she is there to protect her children. None of those spirits can leave that house, Ty." Suddenly, he stopped talking. His spirit looked sad and forlorn.

"Why does this Marie person follow me around, Andrew Jr.?" I asked calmly. "What does she want with me? I don't even know her. Tell me please if you know." Andrew Jr.'s spirit turned and looked toward the old abandoned house that sat back in the woods near the lake. I followed his gaze. But the house wasn't spooky looking anymore. It had been fixed up beautifully.

I would never forget how badly it scared Malin and I that day we went inside it. Since we were small children at the time we never realized that it was the pure evil inside there that frightened us. It was filled with evil, anger, rage and hatred that had been festering there for many long years.

"I've got to leave you now, Ty," said Andrew Jr., suddenly. "They are coming so you'd better go, too." "Wait!" cried. "You've got to tell me more Andrew Jr." "All I can tell you, Ty," he said, "is that a lot of terrible things that went on in this family had to do with Marie and that house. There is something else you should know too." "What is it?" I asked curiously.

"It has something to do with you turning twenty one years old, Tyla," he said. "I'm only fourteen now, Andrew Jr." I said. "That's a long way off."

"Yes," he answered, "but you'll be fifteen soon, Ty. It's not as far away as you think it is. Grandmom Faya knows a lot more than what she has ever told you or anybody else. She knows exactly what she's doing. I believe, for some strange reason, you have to be living in that old house when you turn twenty one." It all sounded incredulous.

"I'm telling you this," he continued speaking, "because of what I hear the others saying. They never say much around me or the lady whose spirit is good. They know that we're not like they are. Our father isn't like them either. He is there sometimes, too, but not all of the time."

Andrew Jr.'s spirit hesitated again. Then he said, "Did you know that whenever you and Malin came down here to your 'secret place' that our father was here with you, Ty? He and the woman whose spirit is good." He was now smiling at me. Then he was gone.

Immediately I awakened from my dream and bolted upright in my bed. I was surprised and stunned by what my dear brother's spirit told me in the dream. I got scared! "Why would someone as evil as Marie had been in her life *be following me around?"* I wondered, getting more and more afraid at the thought.

I recalled the day when Malin and I were at our 'secret place', and he told me that someone would always help us if we came there when we were in trouble. "Poor Malin," I said to myself smiling. *"He didn't know it was our father's* presence that he was feeling that day. Also, that it was he who was speaking those words that he said to me that day. But who is this woman who was there with him? Who are her children that she is protecting and from whom?" My mind was going over everything that the spirit said.

I got off the bed and went downstairs to see if dinner was ready. It was six o'clock. Grandmom Faya was a stickler for having everybody present and on time for dinner at six thirty every evening. But as hard as she tried it never happened. It was usually my grandmother, Malin and myself. Or, just Emma, Grandmom Faya and myself. Sometimes Miss Miriam was there, too. However, it had been a long time since everybody in the house was there at dinner time. Someone was always missing in spite of all that my grandmother did to have us all together at the dinner table.

As I made my way down the stairs I decided not to tell anybody about my dream. *"Well," I thought, "maybe Emma."* As I approached the kitchen I could hear my grandmother talking and moving around in the kitchen as she got dinner ready. There was another woman sitting at the kitchen table that she was talking to.

"Hi, honey," she said when she saw me. "Did you have a nice nap?" "Yes, Grandmom," I replied while looking at the other woman sitting there. She noticed me looking oddly at the stranger and said, "Good!"

The woman nodded at me in greeting but said nothing to me. "Tyla," said Grandmom Faya, "I want you to meet Mrs. Josette Marshall. She's going to be helping me out around the house where we are moving to. It's much too big for just Miriam and I alone to try to keep up. And you girls have school work as well as work to do. Don't you think that's nice?"

Before I had a chance to answer her she continued speaking. "Josie, this is my granddaughter, Tyla." Josie extended her hand to me. "I'm very please to meet you, Tyla," she said shaking my hand. "I've heard a lot about you, your sister and your brothers. Your grandmother is very proud of all of you."

I smiled as did my grandmother. "I'm very glad to meet you, too, Miss Josie," I replied. "No, sweetheart," said Josie. "Please call me, Josie. Okay? I don't need you to put a handle on my name. Although, I know that's how your grandmother raised you all."

"Okay, Josie," I said. She flashed a big, friendly smile at me. Then the two women resumed the conversation they had been having before I came into the kitchen. While they talked I studied Josie.

Josette Marshall was short, stout and had short white hair, dark skin and dark eyes. She was Native American, very gentle and soft spoken. Also, she smiled a lot. I liked her immediately.

As I listened to them talking I learned that Josie lived in Maron, and had recently lost her husband of twenty seven years to a long illness. They had never had any children. His illness was some kind of genetic disorder. She wanted to have children but she and her husband loved each other so much, they were content just to have each other. They never even considered adoption she told my grandmother.

Josie, as Grandmom Faya had said, was going to be a live-in housekeeper for our family at that old house that we were moving into. I was a little taken aback by that. Since my grandmother hardly ever bothered with any of the people in town. Not until lately that is.

We had started bringing friends home from school and Emma from work. This provided a push for my grandmother to start attending town meetings. Or, other events in town to improve the quality of life there. She became one of the most important and influential community leaders, too.

Contrary to how Grandmom Faya felt Emma and I could have helped her and Miss Miriam with the housework. Why we needed a housekeeper suddenly I didn't know. But I was totally unaware of just how big that old house really was. I found out for myself that she did the right thing. We could have used another one like Josie because the house was so big.

At the dinner table that evening there was only my grandmother, Josie, Miss Miriam and I. Josie helped with the clean up afterward then went home. I went into the living room to watch television before going over to Karen's house.

I recall that it was a warm, lovely evening and Karen was sitting outside on her front stoop when I got to her house. "Hey, kiddo!" she said with a smile when she saw me. "I was hoping you would come over tonight. Do you feel like taking a walk into town with me? I thought I'd check out some of the Halloween costumes. How about it?" "Yeah, why not?" I told her. "Let's go before the stores close up." We started on our way.

"Are you planning on going out trick-or-treating?" I asked jokingly. "As a matter of fact," said Karen, "I am. Don't you think it would be fun to dress up as something or somebody and walk around town all night like the other kids our age do?" "I guess so," I said nonchalantly. Halloween was only five days away. I hadn't thought much about it even though it was my birthday.

Emma, Nicholas, Malin and I had never gone out trick-or-treating until after Mama left. Grandmom Faya bought all of us costumes the following Halloween and she took us out for an hour. We had a lot of fun, too. And got lots of goodIes. When we came home that night she made a cake for my birthday. We had a party with ice cream and balloons. Also, she had all kinds of party favors. It was really nice and something that I never had before. After that my grandmother did the same thing for us every year on Halloween.

As Karen and I were walking home from window shopping that evening, an eery feeling suddenly came over me. I didn't know what it was and I had never felt anything like it. It was a feeling of deep dread. No matter what I did I couldn't shake it. It made me feel sick to my stomach, because it began to weigh down on me heavily. It felt like some great sorrow was coming my way. I had experienced strange feelings connected to *'the gift'* that my sister and I had but nothing like I was feeling then.

The bad feeling came over me first while Karen and I were looking around inside the stores. I fought it off. Now the intensity of it was greater. I wanted to leave Karen right there and run home. But I knew she would think that I was losing my mind. Yet, she noticed that I didn't look so good. "Are you alright, Ty?" she asked me concerned. I didn't say anything because I didn't know what to say or how to explain what was happening to me. "Is something wrong?" she asked me. "I don't know," I said finally. "All of a sudden I just feel down and depressed."

She put her arm around my shoulder and said, "Maybe we'd better hurry up and get you home, Ty." I felt faint. She tried to steady me by putting her arm around my waist as we walked. I noticed her hand touched one of my breasts and lingered there longer than it should have. I pushed the thought out of my head when she let go of me. We reached a park bench and sat down.

"What is this?" I wondered. *"Why is this terrible feeling on me? It came out of nowhere."* Karen and I were silent as we sat on the bench. Suddenly, I felt her arm around my waist again. What I had thought was my imagination before was happening again. Her hand was full on my breast gently massaging it. I went into shock. Then she turned my face to hers and kissed me full on the lips.

"What the hell are you doing, Karen?' I shouted in anger, surprise and disbelief. I pushed her away from me so hard she fell to the ground. She got up and brushed herself off. "Oh, come on, Ty," she said. "You can't be that naive. Why do you think I don't date guys?" "I don't know," I told her a little pissed, and I don't care. I thought you just weren't ready to date yet that all."

"Well, girlfriend," she told me, "that's not it. It sure as hell isn't because I can't get a guy either. I like you, Tyla, and you know it."

"Now just a minute, Karen," I said my mind whirling at the strange twist in our relationship that I wasn't expecting. "I don't know any such thing. All I know is that we are friends. *That's all I know."* She could see my anger at her. "I don't appreciate you doing that to me, Karen." I said. "Please for the sake of our friendship don't do it again. We are friends. And no matter what or who you like respect my feelings. Okay?"

She stood there in silence for a minute. "Okay, Ty," she said, "you're right. I had no right to do that to you. I promise it will never happen again." "I would like that," I told her sighing with relief. I didn't want to have to fight off my friend's unwanted advances. Karen sighed.

Then she said to me, "All of those times, up in my bedroom or if we were in your bedroom trying to see who had the biggest tits, remember? Me pretending to be the man and you the woman sometimes in our games? What did you think all of that was about, Tyla?" "To me," I replied, "it was just that. A game that we played." Karen chuckled a little. "Ty," she said, "I could see it if we were little girls but we're not. I thought you knew how I felt that's all." I started to recall those games that we used to play and it became obvious to me that to her it had never been just a 'game". *"Maybe that's why I have this bad feeling. It's a warning that this shocking revelation about her was coming to light,"* I thought. However, that deep, horrible feeling stayed with me.

Karen's voice interrupted my thoughts. "Can you imagine what the good people around here would say," she asked, "if they knew about me, Ty?" "Yeah," I replied, "I can but don't worry. We are friends, Karen, and your secret is safe with me for as long as you want it to be. You'd better keep it to yourself though. At least until you're out of high school and moved away from this place."

"That's a good idea," she said. We got up from the bench and started walking toward her house again. We were almost to Karen's house when she asked me, "Are you still feeling badly?" I noted how genuinely concerned she sounded for me. "I can't understand it," I told her. "It came over me so fast. It seems to be get- ting worse and worse. It's so sorrowful, Karen. I feel like breaking into tears.

"Well," she said, "it seems like after we started talking about Halloween, and it being your birthday, is when it happened. Maybe that has something to do with it?" "I don't know," I replied weakly. "I just want to go home and talk to my grandmother for some reason."

"Yeah," Karen agreed with me. "She could probably help you. They say that your great-great grandmother knew a lot about spooky feelings and stuff." "What?" I asked puzzled. "What do you mean by that, Karen?" "Oh, well, Ty," she said, "I'm sorry to bring this up now. But I have heard people say things about your family." She shrugged her shoulders.

"What kind of things?" I asked her. I had never heard anything except the things that Grandmom Faya told me when I was a little girl. Karen hesitated. "Tell me, Karen," I insisted. "I wouldn't say anything if I wasn't your friend," she said. "Out with it!" I snapped at her.

"Well," she began, "first of all, they say that the lady named, Charon, wasn't really your mother, Ty. It was another one of those sisters who was your mother. People in Maron said that your real mother dabbled in witchcraft and was very powerful. They say she even caused the deaths of a few people in this town."

"Who?" I asked. "What people? And how do you know all of this stuff? I guess my father wasn't really my father either huh?" I was being sarcastic by then.

"Please, Tyla," said Karen, "don't be angry with me. I'm just telling your what's been said around here about your family that's all. But, yes, Andrew Davidson was your real father I heard. Only the lady named, Charon, was your aunt not your mother. She was one of the four sisters who lived in that big, old house down by the lake. People around here say that your real mother and her sisters were all powerful witches like their grandmother was. Their mother's mother. Which would make her your great-great grandmother. They say that two of the sisters were really nice people. You know, kind-hearted and all? As powerful as those two were, people say that they always helped others and never hurt anybody."

"I can't believe this," I said to Karen shaking my head in disbelief. "Yes, Ty," Karen replied. "Rumors have it that your grandmother was a very good witch. But she was overpowered by the others and almost destroyed." "My grandmother is just fine," I said defensively. "No, Ty," continued Karen. "People in town also say that Miss Faya is not really your grandmother but another one of those sisters is." "What?" I cried stunned. Everything was getting very confusing around me.

"People around here say that your real grandmother was messed up for life," said Karen, "at the hands of her own sister through witchcraft." "How so?" I asked getting more and more interested in what she was telling me. She continued telling me shocking things about my family that I had never known.

"It was over a man that she wanted," said Karen. "But the man didn't want her. This sister was angry about that and caused a bad accident to happen to your real grandmother, Ty. The accident involved two guys that were friends with her. Suddenly, they turned on the one who is your real grandmother for no reason that anyone knew. I don't know what occurred. All I ever heard was that it was an accident."

"I don't understand, Karen," I told her. "Neither do I," she replied. "Because these two friends of your grandmother's jumped on her out of the blue for nothing. They were all out at some club or party or something they say. They beat her up pretty badly and they raped her." My mouth fell open in horror. "The beating she suffered caused her to have seizures for the rest of her life after that. She was pregnant at the time that it happened, too, and almost lost her baby," said Karen.

"My, God!" I cried. "That's terrible!" "They say she did have a baby though," continued Karen. "He was your father, Andrew, Ty." Karen paused and looked at me. But I was staring at the ground beneath my feet trying to make some sense out of what I was hearing about my family.

Karen started talking again. "This wicked sister she had is supposed to have murdered your great-grandfather, too," said Karen, "with the help of your great great grandmother. He was your grandmother's father."

"She murdered her own father?" I asked even more stunned. "That's what they say," answered Karen. "They ran him away and later on he was found dead in the woods behind their house." "Oh, my God!" I cried. "Please finish telling me the rest of what you've heard, Karen."

She took a deep breath and let it out. "From all that I've heard," continued Karen, "there was a lot of jealousy and hatred among those sisters and their grandmother. I hear her name was, Lucy. The evil sister was just like your great-

great grandmother. Just pure evil. Anyway, Lucy taught her all of this supernatural stuff. She was going to murder her own sister, Ty, because of a man." I couldn't wrap my mind around all that Karen was telling me. It was unbelievable.

"This man, they say," said Karen, "loved your real grandmother and the baby that she had was his. He loved herb but the evil sister began to hate them both because he didn't want her. His name was, Roy Oberon. I hear that he was young and handsome. He, too, was into black magic just like the evil sister and her grandmother were."

By that time my eyes were wide-open in shock. I couldn't believe what Karen told me. All of the conversations that I'd overheard between my grandmother and Miss Miriam began to make sense to me. I could fill in all of the blank spaces then. All of the things that Grandmom Faya already told me when I was a little girl were true. I sat down on another bench that was nearby. Karen fol. lowed me and sat down next to me.

"There's more, Ty," she said. "If you want to hear it." Numbly I nodded my head. Of course I wanted to hear everything that she had heard about my family. I wanted to know everything that she knew. She began to tell the rest of what she had heard around town about the Davidson family.

"Your great grandmother," began Karen," the four sister's mother met and married the love of her life." Her voice turned low. "They had four daughters and no sons. There was some kind of financial trouble that forced them to move into your great-great grandmother's house. That's when everything fell apart for them and their daughters." Karen looked at me sympathetically. "Your great great grandmother set out from day one to destroy her own daughter's marriage, Ty," she told me. "Her own daughter, Ty," she was in disbelief herself by that time, "your great grandmother. And from what I've heard, Ty, she almost succeeded, too!" "What do you mean 'almost succeeded'?" I asked Karen turning to look at her. Karen sighed. "Well," she said, "like I already told you, two of the sisters Lucy couldn't control or destroy. It seems that they had the same supernatural powers that she did. I don't think she bothered with those two that much. Also, they prevented a lot of bad things from turning out much worse than they did in that old house."

"What happened to those two men you told me about earlier, Karen?" I asked. "They were both found murdered, Ty." She told me with a shudder. "Somebody had slashed their throats." "This is getting worse by the minute," I said sadly. "I don't know all of the names that the townsfolk have called, Ty," she said. "But I do remember that the wicked sister was named, Marie." My heart felt like it had stopped beating for a moment. "Marie?" I said in a low voice that Karen couldn't hear. "Grandmom Faya's evil sister."

Karen had heard a great deal about my family that she never mentioned to me. I wondered why but I didn't dwell on it. I thought she was probably trying not to hurt me. I listened as she continued to tell me things.

"Your great great grandmother was named, Lucilla," said Karen "But they called her Lucy." My spirit was sinking lower and lower as I recalled all that Grandmom Faya told me about her grandmother. "She tried to force this guy, Roy, to marry Marie. Even though she loved him, too." Karen said. "But he was in love with the one who is your real grandmother, Ty. But she wouldn't have him."

I couldn't recall where I had heard the name, Lucilla, before. Then I remembered the night that Emma had the vision about Miss Miriam getting sick. It was Grandmom Faya who had called that name. She called her Ole Lucy. Also, she mentioned her older sister, Marie, in all of her many gossip sessions with Miss Miriam. I began to wonder about Miss Miriam again. As I had been doing for quite some time but no one knew.

"Anyway," continued Karen unaware that my mind had wandered away from her. "This guy, Roy, decided that it was time for him to pack up and leave that house. He supposedly threw himself out of a window of that house and killed himself. Nobody ever believed it though. Too many strange things went on inside that old house back then." Karen looked at me as if to silently ask if I want- ed her to go on. I looked at her and nodded my head. I had to hear the whole story. I just had to.

"Well," she began again, "the battles between those sisters and the grandmother grew worse and worse when your father, Andrew, was born, Ty. As he got older the worse things got inside that house. The rumor is that Marie seduced him. Her own nephew. He was a grown-up man, married and had a family of his own. She ended up getting pregnant by him, too, they say. She was just so wicked and vengeful."

By that time I was so overwhelmed by the tales of horror that I was hearing my mind refused to believe them. Although, I knew that Karen wouldn't lie about something like that. "I just can't believe those terrible things happened in my own family," I said sadly. Even as I said those words deep inside me I knew all that Karen said was the truth.

"Well, they did," she continued, "and you know I would never lie to you, Ty. I'm your friend." "You're right, Karen," I said. "Is there anything else that I don't know?"

"I'll have to think on it," she said. "But you know that great great grandmother of yours was the root of all of the evil that went on inside that house, Ty. She plotted to take the baby that Marie had by the nephew, your father, Andrew. It was a little girl. She gave the baby to the nephew and his wife to raise. After all, he was the baby's father. When evil Marie protested there was a real battle between her and the grandmother. Marie lost the battle. Not long after that they found Marie on the floor of her bedroom one morning. She had been poisoned by somebody. The people in Maron always said that it was one of the other sisters that killed her." "Oh, God!" I said.

Karen continued talking. "The nephew's wife's name was, Teresa, Ty," she informed me. "She came from Tolstoy. They had four children, her and Andrew. No one ever knew where that fifth child came from later on. However, they did find out that the little girl was the baby that Marie had. The youngest sister that Lucy tried to force the baby girl onto to raise refused to do it at first. She didn't want any trouble from Marie. And Marie wanted revenge for her grandmother taking her child away from her. She couldn't hurt Lucy. So she set out to destroy the nephew and his family." Karen paused again. I struggled to keep following the story that she was telling me.

"Again," she said, "one of the kinder sisters intervened. She was alone by that time because the other nice one was put into an asylum by Lucy. She was the same one that this guy, Roy, had been in love with and is your real grandmother. Your father, Andrew's mother, Ty. Anyway, this one good sister saved all of those children. But the nephew ended up blowing his brains out with a sawed off shotgun. It happened after his wife, Teresa, was also found dead in that old house one morning and guess what?" I looked at her as if I couldn't wait to hear what she was about to say. "She was poisoned."

"All of this is so terrifying and incredible!" I gasped. I felt nauseated. Karen nodded then said, "There's a little more, Ty. Marie thought she would get her daughter back after Teresa and Andrew died, but she didn't. Lucy made sure of that. That's when she forced the youngest sister to take all of those kids and raise them as hers."

Karen and I were silent for several moments. My mind was still racing trying to tie everything she told me into the things that Grandmom Faya told me long years before. Finally, I just shook my head, still trying not to believe all that I heard. "It's all just so terrible, Karen." I said.

"I know, Ty," she said. "Maybe you should talk to your Grandmom Faya about these rumors. She would know all about it. And if they're really all true or not." "Yeah," I mumbled, "maybe I'll do that." I already knew that Karen was telling me the truth. My grandmother told me a lot of the things that she had said anyway. "Oh, there's something else, too," said Karen.

"Do you think I really need to hear anymore, Karen?" I asked her sarcastically. "I know," she said as she put her hand on my shoulder. "But there is something about that old house being cleansed forever by someone on their twenty first birthday. It's a different witch whose name has never been mentioned before."

My mouth fell wide open again in shock. It felt like my bottom lip had reached my knees. I recalled the dream that I had about Andrew Jr. that afternoon. Karen immediately noticed my reaction. "What's wrong, Ty?." she asked. I couldn't answer her. I remembered what Andrew Jr. said to me about my twenty first birth- day and my having to be living inside that old house at that time. "Oh, it's nothing," I lied.

"Nobody knows about this person, Ty," said Karen almost in a whisper. "Marie was very fearful of one of the two nice sisters. Truly scared they say. She was no match for that one whichever one it was."

I couldn't say anything else to Karen except, "I'm going home now, Karen. I'll see you later." Dazed, I started for my home while Karen walked in the other direction toward her home. The heavy sorrowful feeling was still upon me.

When I got home that evening I went straight up the stairs to my bedroom. I never heard Grandmom Faya calling to me, or noticed Emma standing in the kitchen doorway waving to me. I never answered Malin when he spoke to me as he passed me on the stairs. I didn't want to be bothered with anybody. Yet, I knew Grandmom Faya would follow me upstairs to see what was going on with me. So I locked my bedroom door behind me.

Sure enough I heard her outside my bedroom door a few minutes later. She called to me but I pretended not to hear her. I said nothing to her. I knew she started to knock on the door. But changed her mind when I didn't answer her calling to me.

I heard her talking to herself softly. She didn't know that I could hear her. She said, "It's finally happened, huh, Tyla, honey?" She knew that sooner or later somebody was going to tell my sister, brothers and I about our ugly family past. That's how the people in Maron were. They loved that kind of gossip best.

"Don't be sad, Tyla, honey," I heard my grandmother say softly through the door. "There's more to this story than they know. It will all be taken care of. I promise you that." Then I heard her go back downstairs.

I laid on my bed and thought, "One thing is for certain. There must be some thing to the rumors that she had supernatural powers. How else would she have guessed what was wrong with me?."

A little while later I heard our doorbell ring. "*It's probably Miss Miriam,*" I told myself as I heard Grandmom Faya going to answer the door. "What's wrong with Ty?" Malin asked her.

"She's just fine," my grandmother lied. She thought it was Miss Miriam at the door, too. Because I heard her say that to Emma and Malin. "We'll be moving soon," she said to them. "I don't understand why she can't stick it out in that house of hers until then."

CHAPTER EIGHT

Recently, Miss Miriam began to have ghostly visitors during the night. *Visitors* that she didn't want. She was hardly able to sleep at night in her own home anymore because of *them*. When she did fall asleep spirits would shake her awake by moving her bed or call to her from the foot of her bed. The toilet would flush all by itself whenever it got ready to. To top that off, Marcus, her cat of fifteen years suddenly left home and didn't come back. It was no wonder that she didn't want to stay in her home alone.

But it was not Miss Miriam who was at our front door that evening. Before Grandmom Faya could open the front door it was pushed wide open and a voice yelled, "Hey! Where is everybody?! Come here and greet your long lost brother!" It was Nicholas. My grandmother shrieked with happiness and delight. And I heard Malin and Emma running from the kitchen. From my bedroom I could hear all of them hugging and kissing one another.

"Nicholas!" cried Grandmom Faya. "We're so glad you're finally back home!" I could hear her kissing him. "We weren't expecting you this soon," she told him. "Why didn't you call for one of us to pick you up from the airport?" "I'm sorry about that Grandmom," Nicholas told her. "But I just couldn't wait to get home and see my family again. I missed you all so much."

I stopped going over in my mind all of the things that Karen told me. I jumped up from my bed and hurried downstairs to see my brother. With a squeal of delight I jumped right into his arms when I saw him. In fact, I nearly knocked him off his feet. I kissed and hugged him as the others did then I said, "I'm so happy you're home, Nicholas." I held onto him tightly. As if I thought he would get away from us again.

"I am, too, Ty," he whispered in my ear. "My, you and Emma sure turned into a couple of beauties," he observed. "I'll bet the guys are tearing the door down to get to you two." Then he laughed and said, "Please just tell me the truth.

Is there anybody around here that I have to go to war with over you two?" We knew he was joking with us. All of us laughed.

Nicholas looked very handsome and I could tell that he worked out a lot, too. He held me with just one of his muscular arms. I didn't know for sure but I had to weigh at least one hundred and twenty five pounds.

He reached for the hand of a lovely, young woman who was standing behind him the entire time. He pulled her in front of him and told us, "This is my wife, Linda, everybody." Anxiously, each one of us introduced ourselves to our new family member. I could tell right away that Linda was very shy. Nevertheless, she politely reached for each of our extended hands and greeted us one by one. "I'm very pleased to meet all of you," she told us in a kind, sweet, gentle voice.

Later, Grandmom Faya told us, "She is just the type that Nicholas would go for. Someone who is just the opposite of himself." We could tell that Linda was a quiet person. Whereas, Nicholas had never been quiet and far from shy.

My new sister-in-law was tall and slender with short, dark brown hair and big, dark eyes. Her skin was a beautiful coffee and cream color. When my grandmother took her hand to greet her their eyes met. And it was as if they already knew one another. It wasn't in the physical sense but in the spiritual sense. Both of them would become very good friends in the coming years.

"At last you've come," Grandmom Faya whispered in Linda's ear. It was only for the two of them to hear but I heard what she said. At first Linda looked a bit confused. And so did I but then she smiled at my grandmother as if she knew what she meant by what she said to her. *I didn't.*

When Linda reached for my hand that night she said to me, "So you're, Tyla. I'm glad to finally meet you." Apparently, Nicholas told her a lot about me. As our hands touched I felt the same thing that my grandmother must have felt about Linda. I knew without a doubt that she and I would become very close.

Over the years Linda was much more than a sister-in law to me. She became another sister just like Emma. I would never realize just how close we really were, or how much I truly loved her until another tragedy touched our family years later.

Nicholas and Malin brought their suitcases inside the house. Then they took them upstairs. After that all of us went into the kitchen. We sat down at the table and started to talk. The first thing my grandmother wanted to know from Nicholas was where he had gone when he ran away from home so many years ago.

"I couldn't stay in this house anymore, Grandmom," he said softly. "Especially after Andrew Jr. died. I knew Mama murdered him. And that she would probably get away with it." He was right about that. All of us felt that way. "I knew if I stayed here," continued Nicholas, "sooner or later she would have gathered enough courage to come after me. And I would have had to kill *her*. She just wasn't worth it so I left."

Grandmom informed him then that she had thrown Mama out of house. He was surprised to learn that none of us ever heard from her again. Also, he was surprised how our lives had changed so dramatically after that. "Wow!" he said. "Maybe I should have stuck around."

The entire time we were all talking with each other Linda remained quiet. Nicholas told us how he traveled around the country for many years before he joined the Air Force. Then we asked and learned about Linda.

Linda Arniste Davidson was born in Cuba to a highly honored and well-known voodoo Priestess. Her mother was a 'healer' for many years before she died two years before we met Linda. Linda herself was a fourth generation 'healer' from a long family history of voodoo Priestesses like her mother before her. The people of Cuba, bound and tormented by all kinds of evils, were set *free* by the 'healing' powers of Linda's famous mother. And she passed all of her know- ledge to her only child who was Linda.

My sister-in-law was educated in Paris, France where she met and married my brother while on her way to school one day. It was love at first sight they told us. Of course we wanted to know all of the details about how they fell in love and got married. They provided them for us, too.

"I'm so glad it's all over now," said Nicholas. "Now I can settle down with my baby here." He smiled at Linda and put his arm around her shoulders. But Linda didn't look very happy to me. I could see as all of us could that she loved my brother. It was all over her and in her eyes when she looked at him. She was so sweet, kind-hearted and the most unselfish person that I would ever meet in my life.

But I didn't think as Grandmom Faya did that they were really suited for one another. Nicholas was the most out-going and out-spoken of all of us. I knew he was not the type to be tied down to any *one* woman. That just wasn't the kind of man he was.

Secretly I believed, that no matter what she told us, Grandmom Faya knew it, too. I think I was more surprised than anything else when he wrote to us saying that he was getting married. Somehow in my spirit I knew that Linda knew *exactly* what kind of man my brother was. I believe my beloved sister-in-law knew way back then that hers' was a marriage not meant to last. She loved my brother and he loved her I knew. But it wasn't going to be enough. Not for Nicholas.

There was one characteristic that my brother had possessed all of his life that I knew he would never be rid of. *He was easily bored.* If something didn't hold his interest he dropped it quickly. I had the heart-breaking feeling that Linda was somewhere on that list. And more than likely right at the top. I didn't like thinking that way about him. But *I knew my brother.*

He was older then. But he hadn't changed that much. Also, we would find out shortly that he was a ladies' man. He had been that way in Paris before he and Linda got married. She told me all about him. And how he acted before they got married. She thought by marrying him Nicholas would change and settle down.

She was wrong. I couldn't help asking myself the question that I wanted to ask Linda but didn't. "Why in hell would you marry a guy like that? They never change. If anything they get worse."

The sad thing about it is that Linda wouldn't learn how wrong about her husband she was. Until after a lot of sorrow, tears, heartache and two wonderful, little children later. As much as I loved Nicholas on the day that I lost my dear sister-in- law from my life I began to feel anger and resentment toward him.

We were still in the kitchen talking when my grandmother announced, "Well, Nicholas, you and Linda arrived just in time. We'll be moving in a few days into my old family house down by the lake."

"That old place was your family home, Grandmom?" Nicholas asked her in surprise. "You never told us that was where you grew up. It sure is a spooky-looking place." "Not anymore," I replied. "Oh, yeah?" he asked looking at me. "Why not?" Before I could answer him Grandmom Faya said, "Because I've had it all fixed up for us. It's really a beautiful place. You should see it."

"I'll bet it is," he said, "knowing you, Grandmom." Everybody talked well into the night but work for Emma and school for Malin and I were fast approaching. Emma, Malin and I said our 'good-nights' and went upstairs to go to bed. Besides, I recalled that Malin hadn't been feeling like himself all that day.

My grandmother telephoned Doc Walker and asked him to come over and have a look at Malin. He advised her to keep him in bed for a few days and to give him the medication that he prescribed for him. He couldn't find any physical problem that was wrong with my brother. "He may be coming down with some kind of virus," Doc Walker told my grandmother.

That night after we went upstairs to bed Grandmom Faya, Nicholas and Linda remained in the kitchen talking. It was only later that my grandmother told me what was said and what happened.

At last, after much conversation, Grandmom Faya decided it was time for her to retire to bed, too. "I have to start packing up some of these things around here, tomorrow," I heard her say to the others. "So I'd best get some rest. I have to make sure that Miriam is packed, too." "Miss Miriam is moving in with us?" asked Nicholas smiling. "Yes," Grandmom Faya answered, "she is. She's been sick lately so she doesn't need to be alone anymore. I told her that she had no choice in the matter."

"Ole Miss Miriam," Nicholas said in a low, loving voice as if to himself. He always loved Miss Miriam as all of did. She was as dear to us as Grandmom Faya was. "I can't wait to see her again," he continued. "You will," replied my grandmother with a smile. "You will." Neither she nor Nicholas had any idea that they would be seeing Miss Miriam sooner than they thought. "I'm glad you two made up after all of these years," said Nicholas. "Yes, honey," she said, "I am, too." "You go on up to bed, Grandmom," Nicholas told her. "Linda and I are going to sit up for a bit. Okay?" "Sure, sweetheart," she answered. "I'll see you two later." She went upstairs to bed after that.

It was some time later that she told me as she passed by my bedroom that night she overheard me praying. I remembered the prayer that I said that night as if it was yesterday. "*Lord*", I prayed, *"please come with us into that evil old house."* Then she whispered but I hadn't heard her, *"Tyla, honey, you have nothing to fear. If you will only believe that."*

Grandmom Faya knew that nobody else wanted to move into that old house. No matter how nice they fixed it up. We were all afraid. Including Miss Miriam. But it was something that she would tell all of us later on that had to be done if our family was ever going to be free. We never had a choice.

As she readied herself for bed that night she told me years later that she recalled three weeks before. A woman in town by the name of, Ethel Rosekiln, came to our house with Josie. She had a little boy around eight years old who loved playing in the wooded area behind our new house.

Ethel's little boy told her that he saw a woman go into that house but she never came out the whole time he was there. Grandmom Faya thought about what the child told her. "That's so strange," she said to herself. *"Since all of the workmen and contractors have finished their work and gone. There shouldn't be anybody around there."*

"We thought you and your family had already moved into the house, Faya,". Ethel told my grandmother. "So Josie and I decided to come over here to see if you had moved without telling us." "That's right," said Josie. "I knew I was supposed to move into the house with you all. I was wondering why you hadn't contacted me."

She didn't now why at the time but Grandmom Faya had the strangest feeling that the woman the little boy saw at the house was Mama. "*She could have* been living there all of these years and nobody knew it," she told herself. She was disturbed about it but got into bed. She was very tired but so happy to have Nicholas home again and with a nice wife who would make him happy she hoped.

It seemed like she had barely fallen off to sleep when a noise awakened her. Looking at her beside clock she saw that it was four o'clock in the morning. She put her robe and slippers on. Then went downstairs where the noise came from to investigate.

The noise came from the kitchen. When she entered the room she was surprised to see Linda bending over to pick up pieces of a cup that she had accidentally dropped to the floor and broken. She looked up as Grandmom Faya came into the kitchen.

"Please don't tell me that I woke you up, Miss Faya," said Linda sheepishly. "I'm so sorry. But the cup slipped from my fingers. I was trying to make myself a cup of hot chocolate."

"Don't worry about it, Linda," Grandmom Faya told her sweetly. "I often get up in the middle of the night to make myself a cup of tea or something." "I could use some company if you don't mind," said Linda. "I'm not very sleepy at all. Nicholas is fast asleep. I didn't want to keep him up by tossing and turning all night because I can't sleep." She was a very considerate person. As long as I knew my dear sister-in-law she was always concerned with how others were doing. She always asked how 'so-and-so' was doing.

"Oh, honey," my grandmother said to her, "if only you knew how many sleep less nights I've had. Just lying awake and thinking mostly. Your problem is that you're in a strange place that's all. That and probably some jet-lag." She went out of her way to make Linda feel comfortable with us and part of our family.

"You're probably right, Miss Faya," Linda agreed with her nodding her head. The two women sat down at the kitchen table and began to talk to one another. Just as my grandmother thought they were becoming fast and life-long friends.

They exchanged stories about past events and relatives that each one of them had. Also, they talked about Nicholas. Linda's ears were glued to Grandmom Faya's every word that she told her about my brother. She was fascinated by our family history, too. And she was shocked at some of the things that my grand- mother told her.

"So the house that we're moving into is haunted huh?" asked Linda with a little skepticism. "That's right," replied Grandmom Faya. "It has been for a very long time." "So," asked Linda, "do you know who *they* are?" My grandmother understood what Linda meant by *they*. She began to tell Linda things about our family. I believe Grandmom Faya was relieved to reveal a lot of things that she kept hidden for many years.

"Well," she said to Linda, "I believe that my older sister, Marie, his never left that house. She was so wicked in her lifetime. I'm sure her spirit is forever earth- bound. Then there's, Roy, the man that she loved but he never loved her. He was wicked, too, just like she was. They would have made a perfect couple. Then, there's my grandmother. Her name was Lucilla Camay and she was one of the most evil and dangerous people who ever lived on the face of this earth I believe."

Grandmom Faya paused and Linda was listening to her story with deep intensity. "She was the root of all of the evil in our house when I was growing up," continued my grandmother. "There was absolutely *nothing* beneath her. I know that wicked spirit is not resting believe me. Even the devil doesn't want her." Grandmom spat in disgust remembering how malicious her grandmother was. She slipped into the past and began to think about Roy Oberon.

She relayed to me when I was a little older all that she told Linda. Roy had a gift of gab for all of the ladies. His family lived in Brewer. In fact, they owned most of the town. They were filthy rich.

He met Marie at a poker game in Brewer one night. She gambled a lot but not as much as he did. He definitely had a gambling problem. And it had gotten him disinherited by his grandfather. Apparently, it was a sickness with him but not with Marie. They ran into each other many times after their first meeting. And always in gambling houses or speak-easies where gambling games were going on. They started dating about one month after they met.

Marie fell in love with Roy. She fell very hard for him knowing as did everybody else that he had at least four or five other women that he was seeing at the same time but she didn't care. She was in love with him. She mistakenly believed that she could change Roy and make him into a one-woman man. She couldn't have been more wrong. Roy's mother's name was, Berta. She tried to warn Marie not to waste her time with him because other women had tried and failed. Marie still wouldn't listen. She was bound and determined to have that man no matter what anybody said about him. That was Marie. Headstrong and willful.

When she brought Roy home to meet Ole Lucy it turned out to be the greatest mistake that she could have ever made. Ole Lucy like him right off and started to monopolize him from the beginning. After a while Marie realized that she shouldn't have brought Roy to that house.

As evil as Ole Lucy was she found her match in Roy Oberon. He was into witchcraft as heavily as she was and Ole Lucy learned a lot from him. She was especially interested in how to harm people. Little did she know that that was Roy's specialty. A talent that he learned from his mother, Berta. Marie and Ole Lucy swallowed him up like two man-eating sharks. He never stood a chance.

When Roy finally realized how truly evil Ole Lucy and Marie were and that they had no intention of ever letting him leave that house he became afraid of them. Then he fell in love with Miriam who couldn't stand him by the way. Marie's love for him turned to hatred and worse so did Ole Lucy's. That's right, she was in love with that man, too.

It never occurred to Ole Lucy that Roy was far too young for her. She wanted him and she was willing to fight her own granddaughter for him. Miriam could've cared less but they got rid of her anyway by having her committed to an asylum. Roy went off after he found out about that but there was nothing that he could do. He tried to leave that house but it was only a matter of time before they killed him.

Then there was old man, Lucas, Roy's grandfather. He controlled all of the family fortune. He invested in some stock that after a considerable loss paid off very well. In one week he made millions of dollars from that stock. Then he sold it off at three times what he paid for it. He and his family were set for life.

Lucas's only child, Berta, was Roy's mother. She was an alcoholic in the worse sense. And eventually, still a young woman, drank herself to death. She said that she never knew who Roy's father was. Therefore, neither did Roy. It was some- thing that bothered Roy all of his life. According to rumors Berta had been a victim of incest inflicted on her by, Lucas, her own father for almost thirty years. No one ever knew much about her mother. Only that she had gone insane before she died.

While growing up Roy desperately needed a man in his life, a father figure at least, but Lucas never had time for him. He seemed to have disliked Roy for some reason. There were rumors that he was Roy's father. Also, he was always busy preserving the family fortune.

There were rumors that Berta, Roy's mother, had the 'gift'. It was said that all she had to do was touch a person and she could 'see' things that were going to happen in their lives. But she was never able to handle the 'gift'. It drove her to alcoholism that took a terrible toll on her life. Also, Berta dabbled in witchcraft. She learned many things from an old girlfriend of Lucas's named, Cairo. Cairo was a middle aged, black woman who came from Cuba before Berta was born.

It was after Cairo arrived that Berta's mother's health began to mysteriously deteriorate rapidly. No doctor was ever able to help her and it was a matter of months before she died of unknown causes. Therefore, heart attack was listed on the death certificate as the cause of her death.

Berta learned all that she could from Cairo. In turn she taught what she learned to her son, Roy. Together they became very powerful in the black arts and they targeted many people that they didn't like. These people, usually from Maron, never did anything to hurt them. They didn't care and Cairo had no idea that she was one of their prime targets until it was too late.

Apparently, Berta always knew that it was Cairo's witchcraft that killed her mother. She caught Lucas and Cairo together late at night too many times not to know that there was something going on between them. Berta tried to tell her mother. But by that time she was too sick to care.

All Berta and Roy did was give Cairo a dose of her own evil. They used a doll which had been made up to look exactly like Cairo. They used hairs taken from her comb and saliva from her mouth as she slept at night. Berta knew how to use those things to make the doll *become* Cairo herself.

Roy and Berta targeted the head of the doll using it to drive Cairo insane as she had done to Berta's mother. It took them three weeks to do it but it worked. Cairo was out of their lives for good. They believed Lucas knew what they were doing but he didn't say anything. By that time he had become frightened of Cairo, too. Actually, Berta and Roy believed he was glad to be rid of her.

Berta Oberon had never been married but she gave birth to three more sons after Roy. Not one of them knew who their fathers were. Berta would go into Brewer's night life section of town and get stinking drunk. The next morning she would wake up in a motel room somewhere. Or, in a place that she had never heard of before. Men saw her as an easy mark. The reputation that Berta Oberon had was a terrible one to say the least.

In her father's opinion she was nothing but a tramp who didn't have the sense to protect herself from getting knocked up. She was fast and loose. No man would have married Berta anyway. Men knew about the bad reputation that she had around town and in surrounding areas. Lucas was disappointed with her to put it mildly and he never failed to let her know it. Yet, a lot of her problems more than likely came from his abuse to her.

Well, one morning the inevitable happened. Berta was found hanging from a rope in the ceiling of a motel room in Brewer. After she committed suicide Roy moved out of their house. Lucas was left alone after that. However, he lived long enough to see Roy buried.

But Roy's three brothers were still alive somewhere. Although nobody knew where they were. They left Brewer a long time ago. Not being able to overcome the vicious rumors about their mother. Grandmom Faya was brought out of her reverie by Linda's soft disbelieving voice.

"My, Lord!" said Linda. "How did all of those people get so wicked, Miss Faya?" My grandmother smiled at Linda and said, "Linda, honey, some people are just born wicked I believe." She shook her head sadly. "Then there's poor Teresa," she continued. "She was just a victim of circumstances. A very nice girl who got caught up in the horror of that old house. And the dark forces in this family."

"That's such a shame," said Linda. "I have so many questions that I want to ask you, Miss Faya." "Well," said my grandmother, "ask away." "I want to know more about your grandmother, Miss Faya," said Linda. "Linda, honey," replied Grandmom Faya, "to tell you the truth the only thing I know about that woman is how wicked she was. And how badly she treated us. My mother told me a lot of things about her and I have no doubt that all of those stories are true." "Like what, Miss Faya?" asked Linda curiously.

"My grandmother was in a situation similar to the one that my sister, Marie, was in," said Grandmom Faya. "She loved a man who never loved her but he was in love with another woman. My grandfather never wanted to marry my grandmother. He only wanted to fool around with her. In fact, he was all set to marry the woman that he truly loved when Ole Lucy turned up pregnant with my mother." She paused for a moment.

"My mother told me that my grandfather was furious," said Grandmom Faya. "But his parents made him do the right thing by her. Yet, he never stopped seeing the woman that he was in love with. That made Ole Lucy mad as hell and very bitter. That's when she started dabbling into the supernatural." "Maybe," said Linda, "she wasn't so bad, Miss Faya, until after he started to have an affair with the other woman."

"Linda, honey," replied Grandmom Faya, "if she went that far knowing that the man didn't love her or want her do you really believe she hadn't always been treacherous and conniving?" "Hmm," said Linda nodding her head. "I guess you're right. Please, Miss Faya, go on with your story."

"The rumor is that she learned all that she knew about witchcraft and the supernatural from her mother-in-law," said Grandmom Faya. "She liked my grandmother and never liked the woman that my grandfather was in love with. Well, she threatened the woman and forced him to leave her and stay with my grandmother. Nobody knows what she said to her but my own mother told me that at first the woman paid no attention to the threats." My grandmother hesitated.

"Then," said Grandmom Faya, "a sudden and mysterious fire engulfed this woman's parent's home. Her parents as well as her two sisters perished in that fire. An investigation into the fire was spooky to everybody because no rea- son could be found in that house why it occurred."

"Witchcraft?" exclaimed Linda stunned. "What else?" said my grandmother. "How horrible that must have been for that poor woman," Linda said softly. "Yes, I know," answered Grandmom Faya. "My mother told me that the other woman left town after that. My grandfather never knew where she had gone and he never saw her again. He resented his mother for what she did and refused to speak to her for the rest of his life. We never knew her because of that. Also, he started to hate my grandmother after that but he loved my mother dearly," Grandmom Faya spoke fondly as she recalled her memories of her mother.

"What was your grandfather's name, Miss Faya?" asked Linda. "His name was, Richard," replied my grandmother. "Richard Oliver Camay. I remember how he used to play with Marie and I when we were children. He was a very handsome man and always very good to us. He was a ladies' man, too. My mother loved her father very much. He was good to her, too, and he made life in that old house with Lucilla bearable."

"I can certainly understand that," replied Linda. "Ole Lucy was extremely jealous of the relationship that my mother had with my grandfather," said Grandmom Faya. "So she made life as miserable as she could for my mother when my grand- father wasn't around." My grandmother paused as though she had come across a bad memory that she wanted to forget.

"You know, Linda," she said, "when my mother was fifteen years old my grandmother, Ole Lucy, set her up to be raped by some man who was a friend of hers. Where he came from I'll never know. Because as I said nobody liked Ole Lucy. Unless they were as devious and treacherous as she was." "Birds of a feather," said Linda smiling slyly. "I can't see how anybody would have wanted to be around that woman."

"Well," said Grandmom Faya, "I use the term friend loosely. There were those people that Ole Lucy did have under her control. They would have done anything that she told them to do out of fear of her. But somebody warned my mother about her evil plot against her. I believe my mother told me that she had even paid this man to rape her. My mother. Her own daughter."

"I can see what you mean now," said Linda, "about how evil that woman was. Any woman who would do that to her own child deserves every terrible thing in existence to happen to her. She was truly a wicked witch."

"My mother ran away from home when she found out about it," said Grandmom Faya. "She didn't want to tell my grandfather because she knew he would have killed that guy and Ole Lucy ending up in jail. So my mother just took off." Grandmom Faya pondered over that memory with tears in her eyes. Then she continued.

"After my mother ran away," she told Linda, "my grandfather never did any good after that. He looked forward to the times when we would visit him. But we didn't do that very often because my mother couldn't deal with Ole Lucy. We hadn't been to see him in about three for four weeks I recall. Then my mother got the news that he had suddenly died. She was twenty-one years old by then."

"I remember that it took everything that my father had in him," continued Grandmom Faya, "to persuade her to attend my grandfather's funeral service. She didn't want to be within one hundred miles of Ole Lucy and always suspected that she murdered my grandfather. Her own husband. Even though she would never be able to prove it."

"Oh, boy," said Linda, "this is getting worse and worse." "I know it is, Linda, honey," replied Grandmom Faya, "but it all happened because I know my mother would never have lied about any of these things." "She hated her mother." said Linda. My grandmother nodded. "You see," said Grandmom Faya, "my mother could never stand to be around Ole Lucy for too long. If she went to my grandfather's funeral as any daughter who loved her father would do she would've had to be near Ole Lucy. Even when we would visit my grandfather we never stayed near that house. We would always go to the park or something. Anywhere that was away from that house and Ole Lucy."

"How about your father?" asked Linda. "Oh," said Grandmom Faya, "he never went there at all." "I see," said Linda. "Besides Ole Lucy, my mother and only three other people from in town came to my grandfather's funeral," Grandmom Faya told Linda. "He lost a lot of his friends because he became hard-hearted before he died. He made life a living hell for quite a lot of people in Maron I heard." She paused then began to speak again.

"He just wanted everybody around him to be as unhappy as he was I guess," continued Grandmom Faya. "My mother told me that he was a Warlock, Linda, but he never used any of his knowledge or power against anyone until he lost his only child. My mother."

"You do have a terrible family history, Miss Faya," said Linda. "Did you know the name of the other woman that your grandfather was in love with?" she asked. "I think her name was, 'Sophia' something," answered my grandmother. "Do you truly believe we will have peace in a place like that?" asked Linda after pausing for several seconds absorbing what she learned from my grandmother about our family.

"Well," said Grandmom Faya, "I'm having another Priest go inside the house and bless it for us from top to bottom, Linda. Maybe there will be some disturbance for a while but I don't think we have anything to worry about. Okay?" She patted Linda's hand gently in reassurance.

"Oh," replied Linda bravely, "I'm not worried." My grandmother wasn't convinced by her pretense. She knew that Linda was getting just as concerned as the rest of us already were.

My grandmother and Linda had been so engrossed in their conversation they hadn't noticed that the sun was beginning to shine through the kitchen window. Then they heard commotion upstairs. It was 7:30. Emma and I were talking as we got out of bed and they could hear us.

"My, goodness," said Linda. "Where in the world did the time go? I haven't even been to bed yet." My grandmother smiled. Then she began to get breakfast ready. Linda excused herself and went upstairs to lay down. Even though she still wasn't sleepy. Then the doorbell rang.

"Who is that so early in the morning?" said Grandmom Faya softly. When she opened the front door there stood Miss Miriam. She was still in her pajamas, slippers and bathrobe visibly upset about something. "Miriam!" exclaimed Grandmom Faya. "What in the world is wrong?" She became agitated at the sight of Miss Miriam.

"Did you walk all the way over here in nothing but your night clothes?" Grandmom Faya asked her. Without answering her Miss Miriam brushed past my grandmother and hurried into the house. It was as if someone or something was chasing her. My grandmother closed the door. Then turn around with a confused look on her face. "What's wrong?" she asked Miss Miriam again.

As Miss Miriam tried to compose herself my grandmother sat down on the sofa beside her. Finally, the words just spilled out of her. "I-I c-can't spend another night in that house, F-Faya," said Miss Miriam shakily. "I haven't been to sleep all night. I spent the whole night sitting in one corner of my bedroom with an opened Bible in my lap." Grandmom Faya listened as she kept on talking.

"*People*' were downstairs in my living room talking, pots and pans were being thrown around the kitchen." said Miss Miriam. "There were shadows of people on the walls of my hallway. *People* kept calling to me and there was no one in that house but me. If it wasn't for a shame I would have been over here hours ago." She paused and sighed.

"Things finally quieted down around daybreak," said Miss Miriam. "I didn't bother to get dressed. I just got out of there. I thought about running over here instead of walking, Faya. That's how scared I was. I'm not going back there. No, sir," she said. "Not me. I've had enough of this bullshit."

"Soothingly, Grandmom Faya agreed with her. She knew as we would all find out in the years to come that Miss Miriam was not a very courageous person. Although it was certainly understandable why she was so frightened. Anybody would have been frightened if what happened to her had happened to them.

I never liked to call people cowards but if I had to use a word to describe dear Miss Miriam it would be 'coward'. She just wasn't what you would call a fighter. According to my grandmother, Miss Miriam had never been a fighter. No matter what the situation was. When they were younger it was always Grandmom Faya who had to take up for Miss Miriam and encourage her to fight back to keep people from walking all over her.

Oftentimes, that is what happened with Miss Miriam. Someone could always take advantage of her and it was my grandmother who would confront these people on Miss Miriam's behalf. She was a person who just didn't like to fight or quarrel with anybody. She yearned for peacefulness. Which was fine but not a total reality.

"*Who doesn't want to live in peace?*" I thought. As young as I was then I knew that the real world didn't work that way. When all of the truth was known to us it was evident that *peacefulness* in their house when they were young was next to impossible.

Also, Grandmom Faya felt that if they could have made more friends instead of having to stay away from people Miss Miriam might have been more outgoing than she was. She would have learned how to stand up for herself by being exposed to other children and teenagers.

Miss Miriam was gentle and kind just as my dear grandmother had been. But they were as different as night and day when it came down to a good fight for what was right. Grandmom Faya had been a fighter all of her life she told me. While Miss Miriam, on the other hand, was just the opposite. She hadn't changed after all of these years. I doubted back then that she ever would.

My grandmother patiently listened to Miss Miriam talking about the horrifying night that she had spent in her house. And so did Emma and I from the top of the stairs. Their conversation would become very interesting.

CHAPTER NINE

After my grandmother calmed Miss Miriam down, she said, "Okay, Miriam. I'll Malin, Nicholas and the girls to go over to your house later and pack up your things. We're moving into that old house, soon. So, you'll stay here with us." "I don't know if I want to move back into that place, Faya," said Miss Miriam. "Not after all that's been happening to me, lately." She spoke, in a small, soft voice, that bordered on whimpering. Something, or *someone* had really scared her.

When Emma and I heard that we looked at one another. "Move *back* there?!" My sister whispered in surprise. It sounded, to us, like Miss Miriam had lived in that house before, too. "Maybe, it's not such a good idea." We heard Miss Miriam say. Her voice was still trembling. She was truly fearful of that house.

Grandmom Faya sighed and sternly said, "Now, listen, Miriam. We've been " over all of this, before. You know that it's the right thing for us to do. Don't you see what's going on here? They don't want us to move in there. If we do, they know what will eventually happen to them." She sounded more and more mysterious as she spoke to Miss Miriam.

"Can't you see that *they're* trying to scare us off?" She asked Miss Miriam. "We have to stick together," she continued. "We have to! If we don't, *they* will win and I will never let that happen Miriam! No way!" Grandmom Faya was vehement and adamant about our moving into that old house. She was not going to be swayed by anybody. Her dogged determination had my sister and I wondering more and more about what was really going on that we didn't know about.

Emma and I looked at one another again. "Tyla?" asked my sister, "are we talking 'ghosts' here?" She sounded quite alarmed and I began to feel the way she sounded. I just shrugged my shoulders. I didn't tell Emma, but *they were talking about ghosts!"*

Miss Miriam thought about what my grandmother told her. Finally, she said. "You're right, Faya! I just don't know about this! Are you sure we're doing the right thing?" "Quite sure," replied Grandmom Faya, confidently. "After all of the long talks that we've had about this, Miriam! About what we need to do, how can you ask me that? We only have each other, right now. But, remember, I promised you that another person is going to help us?" Miss Miriam was silent.

"There is also, Tyla and Emma," continued Grandmom Faya. "They don't even know that they are the main reason that we have to do this. We have to help them understand the 'powers' that they possess. You do realize that don't you, Miriam?" From the top of the stairs, we could sense our grandmother staring into her friend's eyes.

With a loud sigh of despair, Miss Miriam agreed with my grandmother. As if she knew that she had no other choice and no way of escaping the inevitability of our move. "I do know we have to help them," Miss Miriam said, softly. "After all, they didn't ask for this."

"Neither did we," Grandmom Faya pointed out with a slight chuckle. "But, what does that matter? It's settled, then! When the time comes all of us together will deal with the problem that we're facing. Then, we'll be rid of it forever and free." "I'm still wondering who this person is, who will help us," said Miss Miriam, after a moment.

"I don't know yet, Miriam," my grandmother told her. "At first, I thought it might be Linda, Nicholas's wife but more and more I'm feeling that it's not her."

Through the entire conversation, Emma and I were listening intently from the top of the stairs. "What's going on around here, Ty?" Emma whispered to me. "What kind of 'powers' are you and I supposed to possess? What is it that we have to do?" "I don't know, Emma," I replied.

Suddenly, it dawned on Miss Miriam what my grandmother had just told her about Nicholas. Emma and I went downstairs. Her eyes widened with joy and surprise. "Did you just tell me that Nicholas is here, Faya?" cried Miss Miriam. "And with a new bride?" "I certainly did" said Grandmom Faya.

"Oh my" said Miss Miriam, excitedly. "Where are they? I can't wait to see him, and meet his new wife." By then, she had calmed down considerably.

"You'll see them, shortly," my grandmother told her. "I think everybody is get- ting up now. All but, Linda! She just went to bed before you rang the doorbell!" "After all of these years," said Miss Miriam. "He has finally come back home!" There was much joy in her voice, as she spoke. She had missed Nicholas as much as the rest of us had.

"Come on into the kitchen, Miriam," my grandmother told her. "I'll fix all of us some breakfast and some coffee!" She followed Grandmom Faya into the kitchen and sat down at the table while my grandmother made her a cup of coffee. Miss Miriam started talking, again.

"You know, Faya," she said, "I'm really tired of all of these secrets that we've been carrying around. Also, I'm tired of Ole Lucy and Marie, too!" She hesitated before speaking again. "And, please, let me not forget to include that rotten bastard!" My grandmother said nothing, as she set the table, for breakfast.

Miss Miriam laughed softly and said, "Those dear children! How shocked they will be on the day that they find out that I am their grandmother and not you!" "Yes," said Grandmom Faya. "But, how will we ever tell poor Tyla the truth? All of the children have the same father but her mother was a different woman than the mother of the other children!" Miss Miriam agreed with her.

"I know exactly what you mean," she said. "It wasn't fair that Ole Lucy forced Charon to raise those children as hers, you know. She was their aunt and much too young for the heavy burden of raising five of someone else's children. That's why she began to resent them so much." "That resentment turned to hatred, I think," said Grandmom Faya. "And that hatred turned deadly for those children." "A direct result," added Miss Miriam, "to Ole Lucy's wickedness!"

"I know, without a doubt," replied Grandmom Faya, "if Charon had the chance, she would've murdered all of them, like she did Andrew, Jr." Miss Miriam agreed. "And, why not?" said my grandmother. "She murdered their mother, didn't she?"

"We don't know that, for sure, Faya," continued Miss Miriam, but she didn't sound sure of herself. "If Charon did kill Teresa, you can bet that Marie was behind it. She hated Teresa, more than she hated us, her own sisters."

"You're right about that," said Grandmom Faya. "She had a hard time working her evil, while Terry was around." "she was so full of fire, and life," Miss Miriam said. "Marie always could use poor Charon to do her dirty work for her." "Well," said my grandmother, "Charon was so naive! She was kind, and gentle, until Marie, and Ole Lucy destroyed those qualities she had in her. She's trying to destroy you, again, too, Miriam! Right from the grave!"

"How can any human being be so filled with pure evil?!" asked Miss Miriam. "The answer to that, my dear sister, is, *'Lucille Camay'*!" Grandmom Faya replied, with a soft chuckle.

Needless to say, as their conversation unfolded Emma and I had come downstairs but they didn't know it. We were still listening to them, talking. We were absolutely stunned! Our minds started spinning around in circles as we looked at each other with our mouths open in shock.

"They ARE sisters! Just like we thought a long time ago, Ty! Remember?" Emma was whispering recalling many years before when we had noticed how much the two women looked alike. "Yes, I do remember, Emma," I whispered back, still in shock. I was stunned more than she was.

"I can't believe that Mama wasn't really our mother, Ty," said my sister. "If she wasn't, who was? Who is this person named Teresa?" "I don't know, Emma," I said, unconsciously, still hearing the conversation between the two women. "I am as in the dark as you are!"

I was lying to Emma. I had already put some of the pieces of the puzzle in this saga, together. By using much of the information that Karen gave me. "What is this truth that they have to tell you, Ty, I wonder?" Emma looked thoroughly confused. "I don't know what to tell you, Emma," I said. "But I think they are about to tell us before too long." "Maybe, Ty," she said. "My, God! How can two women keep so many secrets between them?" Often, I wondered about the same thing, myself, over the years.

Suddenly, part of their conversation struck Emma. "Did you hear what else they said, Ty?" she asked me. However, I was lost in my own thoughts. Only vaguely did I hear her questions. "No," I said, "what?" "Miss Miriam said that she is our true grandmother! Not Grandmom Faya!" I had heard that part of the conversation but I wasn't as surprised as Emma was. Then, the two women began to talk, again. And, we strained our ears to hear every word they spoke. I was hoping I had heard them wrong when they said I had a different mother than my siblings.

"Well," began Miss Miriam, "I'm not getting any younger, Faya. I just want all of this to be over, forever. So, we can live, in peace, like a normal family. I'm so tired of it all!" She sounded disgusted with her past, in particular.

"It will be over soon, Miriam," my grandmother assured her. "You'll see! But first, let's get moved into that house. Then, we'll take it from there. One day at a time, alright?"

I know Miss Miriam smiled at Grandmom Faya, then. Because she didn't respond to her question. Emma and I decided to go into the kitchen, then. Because we could hear the rest of the family awakening. We didn't want anybody to know that we had been eavesdropping. In fact, we were both almost late, because of our being nosey. As we walked into the kitchen, we were greeted by both women.

"Good morning, girls!" Miss Miriam said, cheerfully. "Hi, darlings!" added my grandmother. My sister, and I dutifully kissed each of them on the cheek and said, 'goodmorning'. At that moment, Nicholas came into the kitchen, too. "Hey, Miss Miriam" he cried, when he saw her, joyfully. "Give me one of those big, sweet kisses that you're famous for" Eagerly, she arose from the kitchen table. They hugged, and kissed each other fondly.

"My, Lord!" she cried. "How handsome you've become, Nicholas, darling!" She smiled at him. "You finally remembered that you had a family back here, huh? Where is your new bride? I'm anxious to meet her." At that moment, Linda, who still couldn't sleep, entered the kitchen.

"Well," Miss Miriam said to her, opening her arms, "you must be the bride and a very pretty one, too!" Linda shyly went into her arms. "How do you do?" asked Linda. "I'm Miss Miriam," she told Linda. "And you're Linda. I'm very happy to meet you, Linda!" "Same here, Miss Miriam," replied Linda, smiling.

I wondered how long it would take for her to get used to our family and become comfortable with us. I could tell that she was very comfortable with Grandmom Faya but she was still a little uneasy with the rest of us. We were all talking and laughing as we sat down at the table to eat breakfast. "Miss Miriam is like a second grandmother to us, baby," Nicholas told Linda, jovially.

My grandmother and Miss Miriam glanced at one another when he said that. But, we're unaware that Linda, Emma, and I, had also caught the look that passed between them. "Nicholas has already told me a lot about you, Miss Miriam," said Linda. "Don't believe everything that you hear, Linda, darling," said Miss Miriam, jokingly. "I'm really not that bad!" Everybody at the table laughed at her comment.

It was a wonderful loving time for all of us and none of us wanted to go anywhere. Not to work, or to school, nowhere! I'm sure we could have sat there, all day long and just talked and laughed with one another but it was time for me to leave for school. As it was, I had already missed my first class and Emma had to go to work. Her boss was on vacation that week. So, she was responsible for opening and closing the office where she worked.

We said our good-byes for the day. Then, hurried out the front door, Nicholas was going to see if he could find a job that day. So, soon after we left home, he did, too.

After the three of us had left that morning, there was only Linda, my grandmother and Miss Miriam in the kitchen. Since Miss Miriam hadn't slept all night, either, my grandmother suggested that she go upstairs to the other guest bedroom, and lie down. Gladly, she did.

But, Linda decided to clean up the kitchen before trying to get some sleep. herself. So, Grandmom Faya took the chance to go upstairs and check on Malin. She had been worried about him. Although Doc Walker gave him medication. And, recommended bed-rest the day before, he still had a slight fever, and seemed to be getting weaker, and weaker. Nicholas' home-coming had perked him up a little. But, when Malin tried to eat something, it wouldn't stay in his stomach. Nothing would.

When Grandmom Faya reached his bedroom, she knocked on the door. But, got no answer. It was not locked, so she went inside. He was asleep. Touching his forehead, to see if the fever had broken, he felt hotter than he had before. Worried, she shook him awake. "Oh, hi, Grandmom," he said, groggily. His eyes had a dazed look in them, that she didn't like. He seemed to be getting worse, instead of better.

She went back downstairs, and telephoned Doc Walker. She requested that he come back to the house, to take another look at Malin. He arrived in less than half an hour. As soon as he saw my brother, he knew something was terribly wrong. It was something he couldn't put his finger on and was bewildered.

Doc Walker had been practicing medicine in Maron, since I was a little girl. Even longer than that, I think.

Everybody knew that he came from a big city up north, where he was the Chief Surgeon, in some big hospital.

He lost his wife, and three sons, to a drunk driver about twenty years before. After the tragedy, he began drinking heavily, he wouldn't go to work, eat, or do anything. Except get drunk. It was understandable, I guess. The hospital didn't look for him to return to work, any time soon, after that happened. They offered him a one year leave of absence but he decided to return to work after only three months.

Doc Walker scheduled a liver transplant, on an eighteen year old girl. Although, he was a fine Surgeon, and highly regarded in the medical field, and by his colleagues at the hospital where he worked, everybody insisted that it was much too soon for him to return to surgery.

He didn't agree! Instead of the transplant patient receiving a new liver, all she got was a new kidney. There was nothing wrong with her kidneys, at all. Only, her liver. Unfortunately, the girl died, on the operating table and the Medical Board of the hospital decided that it was time for Doc Walker to resign, for good. A law- suit, by the girl's family nearly bankrupted the hospital. The girl's family won, because of 'negligence'.

After that, he vowed never to perform surgery on another human being, again. He moved to our small town, and after all of those years, kept his word. He referred any surgical matter on patients to St. Agnews. He wouldn't even do stitches on anybody.

Doc Walker arrived that morning and examined Malin, thoroughly. He decided to keep him on the medication that he had prescribed. Also, he advised Grandmom Faya to give him lots of fluids. And, to keep him in bed. However, he did admit to my grandmother that he was puzzled. He couldn't find anything wrong with Malin. After practicing medicine for forty years, he told my grandmother that he was completely stumped by my brother's illness. He had never seen a case like Malin's.

When he left our house that morning, Malin said, "Grandmom, if I tell you something, do you think you can believe me?" "Of course, child," replied my grandmother, reassuringly. "What is it?" "Well," he began, "I had a dream a few days, ago, Grandmom." "You did?" she asked. "Yes," he replied. "In the dream, I saw Andrew, Jr. He kept telling me to 'run', Grandmom! He said, "Run, Malin! Run to the 'secret place! If you don't you're going to die! Hurry! Run! Run!' I was so scared, Grandmom! Someone was chasing me but I couldn't see who it was. Then, Andrew, Jr. disappeared, and I could sense this horrible, evil presence, chasing me, as I was running! I knew, in the dream, if they caught me, they were going to hurt me! Maybe, even murder me! It was so real! I woke up, soaked in sweat! I was still scared after I woke up!" He began to shudder and my grandmother knew it wasn't from the fever he had. He paused for a minute, as she continued to listen.

"The next day," he continued, "when I was coming home from school, I sensed that same inhuman presence, again, Grandmom! It was all around me! Like a covering, or something! I wanted to run but I couldn't! I tried to tell myself that it was stupid because there was nobody there! Then, I heard him!"

"Who?" asked Grandmom Faya, quickly. "Andrew, Jr.," said Malin. "I heard him, as clearly as I can hear you, right now, Grandmom! He was telling me, again, to 'run'! He said to me, 'Run, Malin! Run to the 'secret place'! Hurry!! You don't have much time! And, you'll be safe there! You know that!" But, instead, I came home. As soon as I got inside the house, I started to feel sick and I've been sick ever since, Grandmom! I'm getting worse, too! I can tell." Then, Malin looked up at my grandmother, expecting her to do something to help him.

Stroking his cheek, gently, my grandmother was really worried. "I don't know what to make of that dream, honey," she told Malin. "Why don't you tell me what you thing about it?"

"Grandmom," he said, "you may think I'm crazy. But, I believe, if I don't do what Andrew, Jr. said, I am going to die, just like he told me. Nobody will ever know why. I know that I won't get better." "Oh, sweetheart," replied Grandmom Faya, "don't say things like that, please!" "It's true, Grandmom," insisted Malin. "I just had that same dream, again. Before you woke me up!"

At that, his eyes widened, in fear. "Of course," she mumbled. "First, Miriam, now, one of the children" Then, looking at Malin, she said, sharply, "Get up, right now, Malin" Asking no questions, he trusted my grandmother implicitly, as did the rest of us. We did whatever she told us to do. Whether it sounded strange, or not.

Malin knew, if she told him to 'get up', even as sick as he was, she had her rea- sons. As she helped him out of bed, my grandmother got some clothes for him, and helped him to them on. Then, she got his slippers onto his feet. My brother was so weak, she had to help him to his feet. She called for Linda to help her. Because, Miss Miriam was fast asleep.

Linda heard my grandmother calling for her. She went running up the stairs, to Malin's room. "What's wrong, Miss Faya?" she asked. But, when she saw my brother, she knew.

Together, Grandmom Faya and Linda put each of Malin's arms over their shoulders. Even with their help, he could barely walk. "Where are we taking him?" Linda asked my grandmother. "There's place where he and Tyla used to go when they were little children. Remember, I told you about it?" asked Grandmom Faya. "Oh, yes," said Linda. "I remember but why are we taking him there?" "Because, of a dream he had about Andrew, Jr. He told Malin, in the dream, to go there or he would die. We have to hurry, Linda!" "Okay," replied Linda.

My sister-in-law had seen many people, in the same shape that Malin was in. They were being overcome by demons or evil spirits her mother told her. "That place is near a lake?" asked Linda. "Yes, it is," replied Grandmom Faya.

Linda's mother always took her along with her. Whenever someone needed her 'healing', or 'cleansing' powers and she recalled how her mother never failed to use water, in all of her rituals. They even lived near a like in Cuba. "Demons have no use for God's water, sugar plum," her mother always told her. They let Malin lean on them, as they helped him down the stairs, and into the car. They headed for the spot that Malin had been instructed to get to.

As they drove there, a strong, powerful gust of wind suddenly came out of nowhere and struck the car nearly causing my grandmother to lose control. Desperately, she yanked the steering wheel, and just missed crashing into a tree.

But, it was several minutes, before she regained control of the car. The strong was spinning the car around, in every other direction but the one that they wanted to go in and my grandmother actually felt as though she were wrestling with *someone, or something unseen*, for control of the automobile. wind

Suddenly, Linda yelled out, "Stop! We're continuing on! So, get back! Now!" As soon as she said that, just as suddenly as the mysterious, and powerful force had come upon them, it vanished! By that time, Malin was unconscious, in the back seat. My grandmother drove as fast as she could, knowing that time was of the utmost importance!

As they neared the spot, where Malin needed to get help, a huge tree, split right down the middle, and fell in front of the car, blocking the road. There was no rea- son, whatsoever, for it to happen. But, both Grandmom Faya, and Linda knew that *something, or someone evil*, was trying its' best to stop them. And, it, or they, were very strong.

Linda knew it would take more than both, she, and Grandmom Faya, to deal with the situation. My grandmother threw the car into reverse, backed up, then, drove around the fallen tree limb. Finally, they reached the old 'secret place'. My grandmother, and Linda almost had to carry Malin to the tree. The same one that he, and I had sat under, for hours talking.

Leaning him up against the tree they stood back and watched him. Neither one of them knowing just what they were watching for! Or, what was going to happen! From where they stood, they could clearly see the old house that we'd be moving into, soon. It was beautiful! "Is that going to be our new home?" Linda asked my grandmother. "Yes," answered Grandmom Faya. "It is!" "Why, it's beautiful," exclaimed Linda. "I can't believe there was so much evil there!"

"It was just as beautiful back then, too, Linda," my grandmother told her with a touch of sadness in her voice. Suddenly, they both shuddered, violently, as a cold chill ran down their spines. "She's here," Grandmom Faya said, softly. "Who?" asked Linda. "It's not Marie!" my grandmother told her. "I believe, it's the child's mother, Teresa!" Linda was confused. "Teresa?" she asked. "I thought their mother's name was Charon?"

My grandmother looked at Linda. "Don't worry," she told my sister-in-law, "She's not here to hurt anybody! She's here to help her child, that's all! Marie cannot come near this spot. I don't know why, for sure. But, if I was a betting person, I'd say that it's because of the running water!" "And, you'd be correct," Linda said, nodding her head. "My mother always told me that evil spirits despise water. Especially, *running* water."

Just then, a great feeling of peacefulness washed over Linda, and my grandmother. "Look!" cried Linda, pointing to Malin, who was beginning to stir. As they watched, he was transformed right before their eyes. Instead of looking sick, pale, and weak, he began to look like his normal, robust, and healthy self. He looked like he had never been sick, at all.

Opening his eyes, Malin looked around, as if he was wondering where he was. The cold chill swept over my grandmother, and Linda, again. But, this time, it was different. It felt rotten, clammy, and evil, as if there was a danger present with them: Malin's eyes got a dazed look in them. "Malin, are you alright?" asked Linda.

But, he just looked at her, and my grandmother, as if he had never seen either one of them before, in his life. Suddenly, a strange, eery smile formed on his lips. And, the most sinister demonic voice spoke to the two women, through him. It was the voice of a man: A voice that m grandmother hadn't heard, for many long years. But, one she would never forget.

"You still look good, Faya!" said the strange man's voice. My grandmother was terrified! "Who are you?" yelled Linda. The voice wouldn't answer her. "Be gone, now!" she commanded the spirit. "Leave here, In the Name of the Lord! You have no power, here! Be gone! Now!" Amazingly, the spirit promptly left my brother's body. Linda looked at my grandmother, who was still staring, with a stunned look on her face, towards my brother.

"Who was that, Miss Faya?" asked Linda, again. After a moment of hesitation, my grandmother looked at her. "It was 'Roy Oberon' " she said, slowly. She had already told my sister-in-law all about this guy, 'Roy'. "Oh, my God!" cried Linda. "Are you alright, Miss Faya?"

"Yes, honey," said my grandmother. "I'm okay. He's gone, now!" The cold chill was replaced by a warm, peaceful feeling. It was a feeling of love, and tenderness. Malin became himself, again. And, said, "Linda! Grandmom! I'm okay, now! I feel great! Someone touched me, and it was like all of the sickness, or whatever it was, just drained from my body! It was weird!"

Yet, he had no memory of what happened to him, there before he came back to himself. My grandmother and Linda would wait to tell him what happened. They began to help Mallin get up but he stopped them. "No!" he said. "I'm alright, now!" "Okay," my grandmother said. "Let's go home, then."

On their way back home, they passed by the fallen tree limb. Then, saw all of the skid marks left by the car, where my grandmother had struggled against whatever it was, to maintain control.

"Grandmom?" said Malin, "it's just like I told Ty, years ago!" "How's that, sweetheart?" she asked him. "I told her, that if we were ever in trouble and needed help, we could come here to our 'secret place' and somebody would help us he said. "How do you figure I could've known that, back then?" "I don't know, Malin," she answered, shaking her head. "But strange things do happen! All that matters, is that you're okay, now." "That's right," replied Linda, with a smile. "I just met my new brother-in-law: So, you can't leave me, yet!"

Two hours after leaving home, my grandmother Linda and my then-cured brother returned home. As they approached the house, they saw Miss Miriam on the front porch pacing the floor, nervously. When she looked up and saw them coming, she hurried down the steps, to meet them.

"Faya!" she shouted, noticeably upset, before the car even came to a stop. "I woke up, from my nap, and went downstairs to the kitchen, to make myself a cup of tea. I was sitting at the kitchen table when I heard the front door open. Then, close! I didn't hear anybody come in! I sat there, waiting for whoever it was and guess who I saw from the kitchen entrance, standing in the livingroom and smiling at me?"

"Who was it?" asked my grandmother. "It was 'Marie', Faya!" she said. "She had an evil grin on her face, too!" "What?" cried my grandmother, surprisingly. "Are you sure, Miriam?" "She was just standing there. looking at me, with an evil smirk on her face, Faya," said Miss Miriam, in a trembling voice. She was obviously upset at what had happened to her. "I think she's trying to scare me, Faya!" My grandmother thought, for a second.

"She's definitely getting bolder, now," my grandmother said to the others. "But, I doubt if she will come back, Miriam. We can't do anything, anyway, until we get settled into that house. Just in case though, you know what to do. She always hated the 23rd Psalm" "Don't I know it" replied Miss Miriam.

Linda listened, but, said nothing. Then, the three women and Malin went inside the house. "I'll make us some tea," Linda volunteered. "Sounds good to me!" Malin said, with a grin.

As they sat around the kitchen table, they began talking. They told Miss Miriam where they had gone and why. Also, they told her what happened while they were there. "Oh, Malin, honey," said Miss Miriam, "I'm so sorry that happened to you!" "It's okay, Miss Miriam," he assured her. "I don't remember any of what Grandmom Faya and Linda said happened but I'm glad it's over! I feel great, now! Like I was never sick!"

"That's very good," my grandmother said, "because, when the girls, and Nicholas get home, I would like for you to go over to Miss Miriam's house, and, pack her things up. Then, bring them over here, okay? She's going to be staying here, with us?" "Great!" cried Malin. "I'll get the girls, as soon as they get in!"

At first, Miss Miriam was a little apprehensive about us going into her house. Especially, after what happened to her, in there. But, then she thought, "*It's okay!* The light in those children, can overcome any darkness, or evil! They'll be fine!" WE would have to tell her, later, how wrong she was!

"By the way," Malin said, casually, "who is this 'Marie', that I heard you talking about, Grandmom?" "We'll tell you about it later," she told him, with a smile. "Okay," he said. "Whatever!" However, Miss Miriam and, Grandmom Faya would both end up wishing they had told my brother about 'Marie', right then, and, there. At least, he would have been warned. *All of us would have been warned!*

CHAPTER TEN

For the rest of that day, things were quiet. Emma came home from work early. And, I arrived home from school around my usual time. Miss Miriam and Grandmom Faya were both napping. Linda, Nicholas and Malin had all gone out. Emma and I fixed ourselves something to eat. Then, we sat down in the living room to watch television. We had no idea of what had taken place, earlier that day.

Soon afterwards, Malin came home and we were surprised and happy to see him looking like his old self. Then, he asked us if we would help him pack Miss Miriam's things and bring them back to our house. We agreed to help him. "I need to get out, and do something, anyway," said Emma. "I haven't been feeling like myself, all day."

Malin had already gotten Miss Miriam's door key from her and Grandmom Faya's car keys. Together, the three of us went over to Miss Miriam's house. When we walked inside the house, we were appalled at the mess the place was in. Things had been thrown everywhere. Dishes had been broken in pieces. The floor was covered with glass. All of the contents of the drawers had been dumped onto the floor and lamps were turned over. It looked like a hurricane had come through there. The upstairs was in a shambles, too.

"Damn!" said Emma. "What the hell happened in here?" "I don't know," told her. "But, let's get whatever we can pack up, and get out of here, fast!" "Yeah," said Malin. "I've got a funny feeling about this place, that I never had before, when I came over here." Quickly, we began putting Miss Miriam's clothes, and other belongings into suitcases, and trash bags. Suddenly, I noticed that Emma had a strange look on her face.

"What's wrong, Emma?" I asked her. "Are you alright?" Malin stopped packing, and began to walk over to where she was standing. Suddenly, she broke out into a bone-chilling unnatural laughter. And, looked at Malin and I as if we were Strangers. Her face was no longer soft and pretty. But, contorted, hateful and filled with rage.

Malin reached for my hand. Then, said, to Emma, in a soft voice, "Are you okay, sis?" But, the voice that answered him, was not Emma's! instead, it was cold, sinister and evil and it wasn't human. "What do you know?" The voice, coming from my sister asked us. "All of you are dead! Do you hear me! Dead! Tell your grandmother that, too! Or, do you know who your grandmother really is, yet?! In fact, tell Miriam to come back here, and get her own damn things, the bitch! She's scared of us! And she'd better be! Faya can't protect her, or you, forever! I'll get her! I'll get them both, and you brats, too! The same way that I got your lousy, sorry mother! But, I have other plans for you, Tyla, girl!" The voice said, then, laughed, evilly.

"Who are you?!" shouted Malin. Both he and I shuddered from the sudden coldness that engulfed the room. "My, God," said Malin, "you're the one that Andrew, Jr. warned me about it in my dream! It's you, and some man that with you, who were trying to kill me!" I stood, frozen. But, Malin became angry. He forgot that it was Emma's body, that this things was speaking from, and lunged for her! He put his hands around her throat, and began strangling her!

Emma began gasping for air! The eery laughter started again. But, it wasn't coming from my sister. Instead, it seemed to be coming from the walls, themselves. Frantically, Emma tried to pry Malin's hands from her neck. In a barely audible voice, she said, "Malin, Malin, p-please! Don't! It's me, Emma!" "Stop it, Malin!" I screamed. "Stop it! It's Emma!"

I jumped onto his back, and helped my sister pry his hands away from her throat. When I saw that she was beginning to change colors, I reached for a lamp that was lying, there, on the floor. Before I knew it, I swung it and hit my brother upside his head. I just hoped that I hadn't hurt him, too badly.

Fortunately, I hadn't! He was still conscious, when he let Emma go. She dropped to her knees, gulping down air. Malin realized that he had almost killed Emma. And, he shook his head, as if he was trying to shake himself awake, from a bad dream. "I-I don't know what came over me, just then," he said. Then, he wrapped his arms around my sister's shoulders. "Oh, sis," he said, "I'm so sorry! Please, forgive me! I would never knowingly hurt you! You know that!"

All of us knew that! But, we didn't know what was going on in that house. All we did know was that we were going to get out of there, as fast as we could. "What happened?" asked Emma. "Suddenly, I went into some kind of trance. I didn't know you two, or where I was!" Quickly, we told her what happened to her.

"Look," said Malin, "let's get this stuff, packed, and get the hell out of here!" "I don't think we should even be in here without Grandmom Faya." I added. "Well," said Malin, "it's too late for that now, Ty! We're already here! So, let's just hurry up and get done!" "What about the furniture?" I asked. "Who cares?" Emma snapped, now frightened, too. "This furniture can stay here for the movers, whenever the come!" "All we're taking, is what we've alright packed up," snapped Malin. Grabbing the suitcases and trash bags which we had already packed, we ran toward the front door to leave. Suddenly, the whole house trembled right down to its' foundation. The walls shook, and the floors reeled! It felt as if it was getting ready to collapse on us.

Running quickly out of the house to the car, it was not a moment too soon. The entire house caved in. In fascinated horror, we watched as first the roof, then the walls then the rest of the house collapsed to the ground. I utter disbelief and terror, the three of us stood there on the sidewalk and watched the dust settle over the mangled wood and brick that used to be Miss Miriam's house.

Also, passersby were staring in disbelief at what they saw. "How could a house just cave in like that?!" We heard someone ask. Somebody called the Sheriff and the Volunteer Fire Department but there was nothing that anyone could do. No one had gotten hurt, luckily.

When we got home, Miss Miriam and Grandmom Faya were still napping. Quietly, we set the suitcases and bags down on the living room floor. Then, we went into the kitchen. As we sat down at the table, we were still in shock at what had taken place. "I've never seen anything like that in all of my life!" said Emma. "Me, neither," I replied. "I don't know how we are going to tell Miss Miriam, when she wakes up," said Malin. "I wonder how she'll take the news?"

"I don't know," said Emma. "But how do you tell somebody that their house just suddenly collapsed, for no reason?" As it turned out, we need not have worried about it. When we did tell her, she was not the least bit surprised. In fact, she seemed to have expected something like that to happen.

"If you children had experienced the things that I had in that house, lately," said Miss Miriam, "you'd know why I'm not a bit surprised, or upset! I'm just glad that none of you got hurt!" We were going to tell her what occurred while we were getting her things. But, we decided not to and kept it to ourselves.

However, both Miss Miriam and Grandmom Faya insisted on going over to the house. So, they drove over there to see, for themselves. A crowd of spectators surrounded the property, where the house once stood. Most of them were still shaking their heads, in disbelief. The two women saw the rubble, and decided to remain inside the car. "Well," my grandmother said, "I can't say that I'm surprised, Miriam. After all that you've told me. I'm just glad that you weren't inside that house, when it happened!" "You're glad?" echoed Miss Miriam. "So am Then, they returned home.

I hadn't known it, at the time, but Miss Miriam and Grandmom Faya, were only concerned about a single item, that was inside that house. The trunk that Miss Miriam kept locked inside the attic. The same one that she always told Emma and I, to never touch when we were little girls.

One week after the house collapsed, two men from in town brought that old trunk over to our house for her. And, put it into our basement. They managed to find it, after searching through all of that rubble. Everybody was dying to know what was in it. But, Miss Miriam refused to tell us. When we did find out, it was a day we would never forget.

As it turned out, we weren't able to move into that old house that year, after all. The place needed a lot more work done on it, then originally thought. Every time my grandmother had one thing fixed, something else was found to be in need of repair. I heard her remark to Miss Miriam one day, that it seemed like someone or *something* was trying to stop us from moving into that house.

Immediately, Miss Miriam got frightened, all over again. She had been pretty cool, lately. And, hadn't seen, or heard anything unusual, in quite some time. But, I couldn't blame her. I wasn't anxious to move in there, either. However, in Autumn of the following year, everything was all set for us to move. Fortunately, during the course of that year, there were no more weird or strange incidents, to disturb our family. Everything was peaceful for us. But Grandmom Faya felt that things were a little too peaceful. And, always remained on her guard, for any unexpected *visitors*, or events, in our house.

A couple of weeks after the collapse of Miss Miriam's house, Emma did tell my grandmother, and Miss Miriam, what happened to us, while we were in the house, packing her things, that day. They were both very troubled about it. And, it frightened them. They felt that Emma and Malin were in some kind of danger. Since, they had been so easily over-taken by the evil, that was plaguing our family. At my grandmother's urging, the whole family made a commitment to pray and to read the Bible, daily.

Grandmom Faya and Miss Miriam felt it was the only thing we could do, to protect ourselves, from whatever was trying to harm us. As the time came closer, and closer for us to move into the old house, we began to fervently read the Bible, and pray. In particular, we read the 23rd Psalm, on a daily basis, if nothing else. Yet, I still had a bad feeling about the new house.

CHAPTER ELEVEN

Malin and I attended high school in Tolstoy. Amaretto Mardez Sr. High, was a fairly large school, accommodating over twelve hundred students from surrounding counties as well as Maron. I was attending it as a sophomore, while Malin was a senior. Karen was a year ahead of me. She had already made up her mind that she would leave Maron for good after she graduated.

Also, she promised me that she would keep in touch with me, after she left. But, I knew how that was. She would get involved with new friends and a new lifestyle, then, forget all about me. Although I would miss her, I was discovering something new that I liked, at that time. Boys!

There were plenty of guys at school, who liked me. And, one, in particular, who went out of his way to try to talk to me, whenever he saw me. His name was Gary Shelley! He made no attempt, at all, to hide how he felt about me. And, I was flattered by the attention. He was tall, slender, brown-skinned and handsome. There wasn't a girl, in the whole school, who didn't want him for a boyfriend. He wore a small earring in his left earlobe. And, kept his hair cut short, with waves in the top of it. He had a light, thin mustache and dressed sharply. Every girl's dream.

But, Gary was not only something to look at. Also, he was very smart. Among the students had a good reputation, as well as, with the teachers. He was very well liked, and anyone could tell that he had been raised very well. Also, he was from a well-to-do family. As a senior, he had just earned a full scholarship to one of the best technical institutes, out West.

Through hearing the other girls talk, I learned that Gary didn't live too far from where I did. He was always asking me to study with him. But, I knew it was just a ploy, on his part, to see me. He was a senior, and I was a sophomore. So, what did we possibly have in common, to study? However, he never stopped trying. And, I never said 'yes'.

To tell the truth, I was a little scared of Gary. But, I didn't know why. Often, I would find little notes from him, taped onto my locker. Other times, he would give them to Karen, to give to me. I did not know how he knew that Karen, and I were friends. Because, she, and I, hardly ever talked, at school. Only later, when school was out! It wasn't until later, that I realized he had been watching me, for a long time.

The last note that Karen gave me from Gary read, "Tyla, why are you so afraid of me? I won't bite you, you know! Please! Give me a chance to show you what you're missing! Be my girl, please! Love, Gary!" "So, what are you going to do, now?" asked Karen, after she read the note, along with me. "I don't know," I told her.

She looked at me, strangely, then, said, "Ty, what is your problem? Either you like this guy, or you don't! Do you know how many girls in this school are falling all over themselves, to get to this guy?! It's your move!" "I'll see," I said, rather lamely. But, Karen persisted. "Do you really think that you'll see, Ty? I wonder! A girl that's as pretty as you are. But, is never seen with a guy?! People will begin to wonder! If you know what I mean?" Inside, I knew she was right!

"Just give him a chance," urged Karen. "What can you lose? You may find out that he's the best thing that ever happened to you!" Hedging, I told her that I would think about letting Gary visit me. If my grandmother allowed it!

When I did decide to say a few words to Gary, I immediately found out that he was truly a nice guy. Although, he was also a bit on the wild side. And, hung around with a wild bunch of guys, and girls. I heard that a couple of his friends had babies by girls, in Maron. I personally knew that Gary, himself, had a child by a girl named, Tisha Poree, who went to school with us.

Tish, as everyone called her, was a nice looking and, shapely blonde, from Brewer. She thought she was the best looking thing in school. Until, *I* got there, that is, I don't mean to sound arrogant, or vain. But, it was the truth. I was far prettier than she was. Though, not stuck on myself. My grandmother taught me better than that. I didn't need to show off, for anyone, like she did. I knew I looked good, and could get any guy that I wanted, any time.

After having Gary's baby, Tish had come back to school. She ended up in one of my classes. She was still in love with Gary, and everybody knew it. She was crazy about him. However, Gary ignored her. Although, I heard that he did give her money, for the baby. He could afford to. He had a part time job, after school, and worked, five days a week, and on weekends, sometimes. I thought that was admirable. It showed me that he was responsible. I liked that about him.

Tish, however, made it no secret to anybody, at school, that she absolutely despised me. I didn't have any reason to care what she thought about me. I ignored the snide, rude remarks, and slurs that she hurled my way, whenever she saw me. Or, when I passed by her, and her girlfriends, in the hallways, at school. Personally, I felt she was nothing but a damn fool.

Finally, I realized the reason that I was so wary of Gary. It was because of his reputation with the girls. *"I ought to start letting him come to see me. Then, make a fool out of him,"* I told myself. *"It would serve him right!"* After all, he had done the same thing to more girls than anybody cared to count. Tish was the only jerk, who ended up getting pregnant by him.

One day, I heard Tish tell one of her friends, in the girl's bathroom, that I was the one who was chasing after her boyfriend. Meaning, Gary! The girl was nuts. Gary ignored her, and wouldn't even speak to her anymore, in school. *And she thought I was chasing him?* She was such an idiot.

My mind was finally made up. It would be easy to trick Gary up. Since, he liked me so much and I really didn't like him. I would make him fall madly in love with me. Then, dump him. The problem was, *Gary was already madly in love with me!* I just didn't know it.

The next day at school, I started to put my plan into action. Since it was still pretty warm outside, for Autumn, I dressed my short, black, lycra chemise, which fit me, perfectly. The stretchy material hugged every curve of my body. Of which I had many! To top that off, I wore black nylon stockings, and black, four inch, high heeled pumps, that belonged to Emma. Dressed to kill, I knew I looked good.

On my way to school, that day, there were more men's eyes on me, and more wolf-whistles, than I cared to have. But, I had to admit to myself, that it was fun, as well as flattering. My hair hung, loosely, around my face, and down my back. It wasn't as good a grade as my grandmother's, and Miss Miriam's, but, it wasn't what you'd call *nappy* either!

Purposely, I made it a point to go where I knew Gary, and his friends would be. I saw them, and they saw me! One of them must have told him that I was coming down the hall. Because, he turned around, immediately, and saw me. A huge smile came across his lips.

As I saw Gary, I was struck by how handsome he was. Also, I noticed all of the other guys watching me, too. But, strangely, all I could see was Gary, who had become my 'target' by then. I was surprised at myself, for my heart seemed to go down to my stomach, when I saw him, too. God! He was good looking! Hurrying up, I tried to push that thought out of my head. If I kept thinking like that, I would surely blow it. And, end up like Tish, and the others he'd had.

Walking toward Gary, I saw his eyes, watching my every movement. And, I could feel them, as they slowly ran over my body, from my head right down to my feet. Then, back upward. *"He sure is bold!"* I thought. He didn't even try to be discreet, as he looked me over. I saw hunger in his eyes. Like a wolf would look at a roasted leg of lamb, that it was ready to dive into, and devour! And I liked it.

When, I reached him, I said, casually, "Hi, Gary! Can I please talk to you for a minute?" My looks, and the casual way that I asked to talk to him, caught him completely off guard. I could tell. Especially, since I hadn't shown any interest in him, inspite of his persistence. I could tell that he was shocked! It was all over his face! Later he would inform me that, at that instance, he said to himself, *"Wow! At last! The girl of my dreams wants to talk to me! Finally!"*

If I had bothered to pay attention, I would have seen all over his face, that he was completely infatuated with me. His eyes were sparkling! And, there was nothing that he wouldn't have done for me. I was the beautiful creature who occupied his every thought, day, and night. That was something else that he would inform me of, later, in our relationship with each other.

For once, the confident, and suave Gary Shelley, was at a loss for words, with a girl. Finally, he stammered, "S-sure, Tyla!" Then, he turned to his friends, and said, with a sly grin, "Excuse me, fellas," and started walking with me. Once we were out of earshot of his friends, he stopped, and looked at me. "What did you want to talk to me about, Tyla?" Gary asked me, softly. Too softly, if you asked me.

I won't say what I was thinking about, right then. But, it wasn't lady-like! My grandmother sure would've been shocked but it couldn't be helped. Because, when describing Gary, 'sexy', is one of the first words used, along with 'handsome'. For a moment, I forgot all about my devious plan but I caught myself and tried to concentrate on it.

"I was wondering, if you still wanted to come over to my house, some night, Gary," I said, looking him right in the eyes. Immediately, I could tell that he couldn't believe his ears. I knew he was probably thinking, *"My, God! Is this really happening? My dream is finally coming true!"*

"Well?" I asked, waiting for his answer. "Sure, I do," he replied, quickly. "When can I come over, Ty? I can come tonight, if that's okay? Please!" Inwardly, I smiled at myself. He sounded just like an anxious, little boy! *"My plan is working out well!"* I thought.

"I don't know about tonight, Gary," I told him, acting a little disinterested. "Please, Ty!" he pleaded, touching my hand, gently. When he touched me, I felt a jolt like an electric shock. For a minute, we stared into each other's eyes. Then, turned away. Although, I tried my best to shrug the feeling off, I knew inside that I was already in trouble. My plan just might backfire in my face! Already, I felt something for Gary. I didn't know it then, but those feelings for him would grow deeper than I could have ever imagined.

"Alright," I said, before I realized it. "What time do you want to come over?" "Is eight o'clock, okay, Ty?" he asked me. "I get home, from work, around seven thirty." "Sure," I told him. I wrote my address, and telephone number on a piece of paper, for him. He was still looking, deeply, into my eyes. "I don't need the address, Ty," he confessed to me. "I already know where you live but I will take your telephone number! I don't have that!"

Needless to say, I wasn't surprised. Eagerly, I gave him my telephone number. "Okay, Ty," he said, with a boyish grin. "I'll see you, later on, then." He touched my head, gently, a second time. *"I must be going crazy! What have I gotten myself into here?"* I asked, myself.

Suddenly, I began to get scared, thinking about Gary coming over to my house, that night. But it was too late, now! I had never had male company, before. Other than my brothers. Nervously, I realized I would have to ask Emma what to do! School was no longer important to me and I couldn't wait to get home. I had to talk to Emma or even Grandmom Faya about this.

As I walked away from Gary, that day, I could feel his eyes all over me, again. Inside, I was thrilled. Instead of going to my next class, that day, which was on three doors away from where we had been standing and talking. I made up my mind and went straight out the front door of the building and headed for home. All the way there, I couldn't stop thinking that I had made a mistake, by inviting Gary over to my house. "Grandmom Faya will wonder why I'm home from school, so early. What am I going to tell her?" I thought.

My mind raced the rest of the way home, that day but when I arrived home, all of my anxiety disappeared. My grandmother had already moved almost every thing we had into our new house. And, only a few boxes were left sitting in the middle of the living room floor. Surprised, I stood there in the middle of the floor, looking at all of the boxes. I hadn't had the slightest clue that we were moving that day. Because, she hadn't told me anything about it.

"Tyla, honey," Grandmom Faya said, from the kitchen doorway, "why are you home from school, so early? Are you sick?" "No, Grandmom," I replied. "I'm fine! I just wanted to talk to you about something! You didn't tell me that we were moving, today!"

"I wanted to surprise you, sweetheart," she replied. "I know that you're feeling spooked about moving into that house. So, I thought, if I didn't tell you, you wouldn't have time to psyche yourself up, about it!" "Does everybody else know?" I asked her.

"Yes, honey," she said, "they do! What's wrong?" She put her arm around my shoulders. "Oh, nothing," I said, with a shrug. "It's just that I invited somebody over tonight from school. Now, what will I do when they come here and find that there's no one living here, anymore?"

"Oh, sweetheart," she said, "we can leave a note on the front door, for them. Telling them where we've gone, okay?" It's not that far from here, you know." My mind whirled. "That's it! unwittingly, Grandmom may have solved my problem!" At least, I had a way out. If Gary came over and we were all gone, that'll be the end of it! I would just take the note off the door, when she wasn't paying attention. "Tyla, what did you want to talk to me about?" She asked, remembering what I had said to her.

"Oh, that's okay, Grandmom," I said. "It's no one special, anyway. I just didn't know that we were moving, today. I don't need to leave a note on the front door. He probably won't come over, anyway!"

"He!" She cried, pleasingly surprised. "Why, Miss Tyla Davidson, you mean to tell me, that you have a gentleman caller? Well, I'm very glad to hear that and I can't wait to meet him. If you don't leave a note on the door, I will! What time is he coming over?" I told her what time Gary was supposed to come by.

She was surprised and happy, that her *strange granddaughter*, who would soon be sixteen years old, had developed an interest in the opposite sex. Together, we loaded the last of the boxes into the car. Then, she and I headed for the new Gary, telling him our new address. Then, she locked all of the doors. But, when she wasn't looking, I took the note off the door.

Before we left, my grandmother said that she had to go back into the house to get something that she forgot. She knew me well enough to know that I would probably take the note off the door, out of fear and nervousness regarding my new date. Without me ever knowing, she replaced the old note with another one.

She told me later, as she was putting the new note on the door, she thought to herself, *"Poor Tyla, so afraid of boys! It's time she knew what it's like to be a woman! I sure hope this one is better than what Emma brings home!"*

My grandmother never liked any of the guys that Emma dated. she had bad taste in me, to say the least. She seemed to attract guys who were married or had 'hand-trouble' (liking to hit women). Or, they drank too much, Grandmom Faya complained. I agreed with her.

Grandmom Faya returned to the car, started the engine and drove off toward the new house. One the way there, she talked to me about men, saying that no matter what, I should always be myself, and things would work out fine. Inside, I was thinking, *"I'll be sixteen years old, tomorrow! What a birthday present this is!"* I was still very apprehensive about moving into that house.

Then, I thought about how eery it was, to be moving into that spooky old house, on devil's night. The day before Halloween. Fear shot through me but I decided to make the best of it because there was nothing that I could do about it, anyway. I pushed my worries out of my mind.

Nicholas, Miss Miriam, Josie and Linda were already there at the house when we arrived. Malin was still in school. Looking around, I saw that the extra months that the workmen needed to fix the house up properly, had been well worth it. The house was more beautiful inside and out than it was the last time that I had seen it. It was a completely different place than it had been, when it scared me, as a child. All of the furniture was in place, as well as a few new pieces that my grand-mother bought. I felt as if I were coming home from a long trip, or something. For some strange reason, there was no fear in me, at all.

Standing in the house, looking around, I suddenly recalled the dream that I'd had, so long ago. In it, Grandmom Faya, and I had walked into the house. And, this was the very house, that I saw in that dream. It was exactly the same! I went into the kitchen, where, in my dream, I had been unable to move, and see who was behind me.

Walking into the kitchen, I saw that it was the same one, I had seen in that dream. *"Maybe, it's meant for me to live here! Why else would I have dreamed about this house, so long ago?"* The thought popped into my mind. At the time, I had no way of knowing how close to the truth I was.

Josie was busy in the kitchen stocking the cupboards and the big refrigerator, with various foods and staples. While Nicholas and Linda were chatting happily about how much they loved the third floor of the house. There was an entire three bedroom apartment up there, now. And it was theirs! It had formerly been the attic, that Grandmom Faya told me about when I was a little girl. The very place where her evil grandmother and her sisters had practiced witchcraft during the night.

All of the bedrooms, in the house, were very roomy. Emma's bedroom, was right next to mine. And, we had an adjoining bathroom. Grandmom Faya gave Malin the guest house, in the back of the property. He was thrilled to have a place of his own. Then, something strange occurred.

Miss Miriam immediately claimed the downstairs bedroom. "It looks just the same as it did a long time ago," she said, with a smile. "I always loved this room!" My sister and I looked at one another curiously. We were puzzled by her statement. We made no comment. But, it was more than obvious to us, that Miss Miriam had lived in that house before. "*When?*" I thought.

We didn't know it at the time but that bedroom had been hers and Grandmom Faya's, when they were young girls. My grandmother made an all out effort to have the room re-done, just the way it had looked, when they were girls.

When Malin came home from school, he asked why I left early. Then, he told me that, after school was out, Gary Shelley was looking for me. He told Malin that he wanted to remind me, that he was coming over that night. I thought Gary was crazy. How could I forget that? I didn't need to be reminded.

"So," said Malin, with a big grin, "you're going to start seeing Gary Shelley, huh, Ty?" "I don't know," I replied, casually, as if I didn't care. But, Malin was still grinning, like a Cheshire cat. "Well," he said, "he deserves a nice girl, like you, for a change. I like Gary!"

Around six thirty that evening, Josie had dinner on the table for all of us. For once, the whole family sat down together at the kitchen table to eat. My grand- mother was tickled pink. Because, she had tried, for so long, to get all of us there, at the same time, for dinner.

The food was good. And, we were busy passing plates of food to one another, and talking. Suddenly, Grandmom Faya got an icy chill, which shook her whole body.

She stopped talking and looked down the hallway toward the living room. Instantly, the rest of us stopped talking too and stared at her. She appeared to be in a trance like state. "Grandmom, are you okay?" asked Emma, nervously.

But, Grandmom Faya didn't say anything. All she did was keep her eyes on the living room. Just then, a great gust of wind, violently, blew open the big, front door, startling everybody. We turned to see what was there. The whole room became as cold as ice. And, Josie and Emma began to get up from the table. "No!" snapped Grandmom Faya. Immediately, they sat back down.

"I'll go shut the door," said Nicholas. "Stop!" shouted Grandmom Faya and everyone froze. "Don't go near the door! Stay right where you are!" Her tone of voice filled us with fear. And, we realized something awful was occurring or getting ready to occur. Then, she closed her eyes and concentrated. She was the only one who could see who or what had entered that house.

"What do you want?" she asked the *unseen* visitor. Several moments passed. Then, my grandmother spoke, again. "We're all here, now. And, we are going to stay!" She said, firmly. "You are welcome here, too! You don't have to leave! We welcome you!"

As everybody watched my grandmother, we became more and more scared. We could neither see nor hear anybody but instinctively, we knew there was something, or someone in the room with us.

"Yes, we know that!" Grandmom Faya said, nodding her head to some information only she could hear. A few minutes passed by. Then, we distinctly heard the front door close. Whoever, or whatever had been there had gone! The room became warm again and Grandmom Faya opened her eyes. She looked, slowly at everybody sitting around the kitchen table. All eyes were on her, too.

"Teresa is here with us," she told us. "But, don't worry! She is a good spirit! And would never harm any one of us! She is here, only to protect her children, that's all! We need not fear her!"

Inspite of her words, we were all very frightened. She smiled at us and said, again, "Have no fear!" "My goodness," exclaimed Miss Miriam. "Teresa is here? In this house?" "Who in the world is, Teresa? "Josie asked, before anybody could answer Miss Miriam. Grandmom Faya, and Miss Miriam turned, and stared at Josie, intently, for a minute.

Josie's mouth fell open, in shock! "You can't mean.." she began. But, my grandmother cut her off. "Yes!" she answered Josie. "But, where are her children, Faya?" asked Josie. My grandmother hesitated, for a moment. Then, turned to Miss Miriam. Then, she turned, and looked at Nicholas, Malin and Emma. "*You three are her children,*" she said, in a low voice.

"What?!" they cried, in unison, surprised. "We don't even know anybody named, Teresa," Nicholas pointed out, and Linda reached for his hand. "I know you don't," said Grandmom Faya. "You were too young to remember her. But, evidently, she has watched over all of you, over these past years." "You said, "we three', Grandmom," Emma finally spoke up. "What about Tyla?" "What about her?" asked my grandmother.

"You didn't include Tyla, Grandmom," said Malin. "Why not?" A few minutes passed, in silence. Then, my grandmother said, sweetly, "Because, Tyla, is not her child, Malin." All of our mouths opened, in surprise, just as Josie's had. "I don't understand," Emma said, with confusion all over her face. Up to that point, I hadn't said anything, sensing that something extraordinary was about to be revealed. Suddenly, I began to recall all of the things that Karen told me about my family. Then, I remembered my dream about Andrew, Jr. At that moment, I knew what Grandmom Faya, and Miss Miriam were about to tell us.

"Tyla has a different mother than the three of you, and, Andrew, Jr. had," began my grandmother. "But, you all have the same father! Tyla's mother is dead, also. I have wanted to tell you children a lot of things about this family, for a very long time. You are adults, now. So, it's as good a time as any, to tell you the truth. Right, Miriam?" Grandmom Faya asked, as she turned to Miss Miriam, who nodded her head, in agreement with her.

"There are many things that Faya, and I need to tell you children," began Miss Miriam. "Linda is family, now, and Josie is, too, in a way. She'll be living here with us." "I remember it all, now," replied Josie, numbly, still in shock. "There was a lot of trouble here, in this house, years ago. Your grandmother found out that Andrew was married and had a family! He had been secretly married for years to Teresa Boleyn, am I right?" Grandmom Faya and Miss Miriam nodded their heads.

"She couldn't stand the thought of anyone being happy because she was so miserable, and unhappy," said Miss Miriam. "What about Tyla's mother, Grandmom?" asked Malin. "Who was she?" My grandmother looked at me, and smiled. "She was my sister, Marie," she said.

For the first time, I joined the conversation. "Marie?" I cried in horror. "That's the name that Andrew, Jr. called in my dream that day. He said she was very wicked and that she was following me. Also, he told me that she was angry with somebody. Somebody that she was afraid of, when she was alive!"

"Why didn't you ever tell me about that dream, Tyla?" asked Grandmom Faya. "I don't know, Grandmom," I said. "I guess I just forgot about it, until now, I was going to tell Emma but I never did."

"Well," my grandmother said, looking at me. "Marie was my older sister! She was angry at a man, by the name of Roy Oberon. He was a very handsome but evil, young man. He had supernatural powers and he was to marry Marie but while he was staying here in this house, as a guest, he fell in love with Miriam!" She sighed. Then, gazed off, as if collecting her thoughts.

"You all may as well know this, also," she continued. "Miriam is my sister, too." Everybody was stunned. Except Emma and I because we already knew that. We heard it on the day we eavesdropped on her and Miss Miriam's conversation but Grandmom Faya didn't notice that we were the only ones at the table, who didn't look surprised. As if on cue, Emma, Nicholas, Malin, and

I looked at one another and recalled the argument between our grandmother and Charon many years before.

"Was Charon your sister, too?" asked Nicholas. "Yes, honey," said Miss Miriam, "she was!" "So, everything Karen told me about our family is true, then," I said out loud to myself. Grandmom Faya heard me. "That may well be, Tyla," she said. "But I would rather you heard it from us, okay?" "Okay," I replied.

"Charon was our youngest sister," said Miss Miriam. "She was forced, by our grandmother, to raise your children as if you were hers after your mother was found dead." "What happened to her and our father?" Nicholas blurted out with out waiting to see what she was going to say next.

"After your mother was found dead," continued Miss Miriam, as if she hadn't been interrupted, "and, believed to have been murdered, your father committed suicide. He couldn't take anymore. A lot of things had happened in this house, because of my grandmother, Ole Lucy, and Marie. Well, he took a gun and shot himself to death!" "My, God!" cried Linda, who had been silent, up to that point, "someone murdered Teresa?"

"Of course, they did!" my grandmother said, emphatically. As if there was no doubt about it. "We just never found out who did it but we always suspected Marie because she hated Teresa so much." "Yet," said Miss Miriam, "as in the case of Andrew, Jr., a clear case of murder was ruled as a suicide. Ole Lucy had friends in high places, you know. Just like Charon did!"

"But, you told us that Andrew, Jr. had an accident, remember Grandmom?" asked Malin. "Yes," she replied, nodding her head. "I did! I remember!" "So, now you're telling us that he was murdered, too?" asked Nicholas. "Yes," she said. "He was murdered. And, by Charon!" "I knew it! I knew it!" cried Nicholas in anger. Then he put his head down onto the kitchen table. His body began to heave and we knew that he was crying. Sympathetically, Linda rubbed his back trying to soothe him.

My oldest brother's death had really hit Nicholas the hardest and for the first time, we saw just how badly it had. Everyone sat there, silently, absorbing all that was being told to us. Finally, Miss Miriam continued the story.

"Anyway, Marie seduced her own nephew and got pregnant with Tyla," she said. "All because she hated Teresa so much." "Why?" asked Emma. "Because, Teresa had something that she didn't have," my grandmother joined in.

"Teresa was happy! She had a man who adored her. Also, Marie and ole Lucy couldn't control Teresa but the main reason for her hatred was because Ole

Lucy took Tyla away from her and gave her to Teresa to raise. See, Ole Lucy had total control over Marie and Charon. She told them that they were never to marry any man. Or, have any children, as long as she was alive."

"What?" cried Linda. "Yes!" Miss Miriam added. "Ole Lucy was just that hateful!" "Then, Marie got pregnant by Andrew. Ole Lucy wanted to kill her. Instead, she took Tyla away from her, as soon as she was born. Marie already hated Teresa and Andrew out of jealousy. But, by giving them Tyla, she really had a reason to hate them, both," Miss Miriam explained.

"Ole Lucy destroyed everyone and everything she came into contact with." added Grandmom Faya, angrily. "Andrew waited for years before he came back to this house with his family. All he wanted was to be close to his mother whom he loved, dearly. He didn't have to come back but he chose to!" Miss Miriam had tears in her eyes and my grandmother gently squeezed her hand. "It's okay, now, Miriam," she said comfortingly. "Our mother was Ole Lucy's own daughter," my grandmother said. "But, she hated our mother, too. Because, she was jealous of the relationship our mother had with her father. Our grandfather, and Ole Lucy's husband. Ole Lucy was so wicked, she managed to destroy our parents, too."

Miss Miriam agreed. "She drove my father out of the house and a little while after that, he was found dead in the wooded area behind the house, here. After that our mother was never the same, again." "What kind of monster was that woman?" asked Linda, horrified. Grandmom Faya chuckled, softly. "You have no idea, Linda," she said. Then, she turned and said, "Why don't you continue from here, Miriam? I think it's time that they heard it all. And, from us, don't you?"

Miss Miriam blew her nose and wiped her eyes. Emma, Malin, Nicholas and I had figured out by this time, that it was Miss Miriam, who was our true grand mother. And, not Grandmom Faya! Of course, as I said, before, Emma, and I already knew that.

"Another thing that helped to destroy your father," added Miss Miriam, "was the truth about Faya, and I." "What was that?" asked Emma, anxiously. Miss Miriam hesitated. "Marie told him that I was his true mother and not Faya, who had raised him, as her own," she said. "I couldn't accept him as my child for a very long time. Because of *who* his father was, Roy Oberon! He raped me and I ended up getting pregnant. I let my hatred come between my son and I I felt so ashamed after a while. Andrew, your father, was grown and married when he found out the truth!" She paused.

"We found out after he died," she continued, "that he'd been told the truth by Marie. She was only too happy to tell him, you know. She did, just before she died. She had been poisoned, too. Like Teresa was!" Miss Miriam began to sob. All of us had tears in our eyes. "This is like a terrible nightmare," Emma commented, looking as distraught as I felt. "It's terrible!"

No one said anything. Each lost in our own thoughts. However, the whole story was far from over. There was a lot more for the two women to tell us. It was a horror story from start to finish but from what we had been told up to that point at least, I understood why Grandmom Faya had been so dead-set on moving back into that house. It held something for her and for us as well. Our future if things worked out, as Grandmom Faya wanted them, too. Or, our demise, if they didn't Either way, she felt that we had nothing to lose, and *everything* to gain.

I still didn't know if I agreed with her on that, or not. But, as I look back, now, I can see her wonderful insight, and wisdom, and appreciate it. She truly *had known* what she was doing. Just like Andrew, Jr. told me, in the dream, that day.

CHAPTER TWELVE

"Charon was so young," said Miss Miriam. "She wasn't much older than Andrew, my son and your father." She was looking at Malin, Emma, Nicholas, and I. "So, you are our real grandmother, then?" asked Emma. "Yes, baby," Miss Miriam said, with a proud smile. "I am!" "But, why didn't you ever tell us all of this before?" asked Nicholas. "Listen to all that we have to tell you," said Grandmom Faya, "then, maybe, you'll understand, okay?" We nodded, hanging onto Miss Miriam's every word, after that.

"Charon deeply resented what Ole Lucy did to her and took it out on you children," she continued. "For us, we had no one to stand up to Ole Lucy, except Faya. She challenged both Ole Lucy and Marie who were both very powerful in the black arts but there wasn't much that they could do, with Faya. So, they took it out on me because they felt they could intimidate me," she said. "Faya was just as powerful as they were. And, they knew it! Our mother tried to send Marie away, years before all of this happened but Ole Lucy intervened."

"Then," she continued, "two years after our father died and our mother was taken away, Roy Oberon raped me. And, I ended up getting pregnant. I gave birth to you children's father and my son, Andrew! Shortly, after that, I was locked away in an asylum for the mentally unbalanced for no reason. Except, that Marie wanted me out of her way. She *still* wanted Roy!" Miss Miriam stopped and dabbed at her eyes with the back of her hands. Then, she continued.

"Roy raped me and got me pregnant!" She said. "But, when I tried to tell someone about it, Ole Lucy would convince them that I was crazy! She lied and told the authorities that I never had a baby. She said that it was Faya who had the baby. She made them think that I was totally insane. They thought it was so funny, her and Marie but they actually did me a favor. I was glad to get away from them. Even though I knew Faya would be left alone, to fight them!"

"You were sent away?" Malin asked, incredulously. "Yes!" she said. "I pretended for three years to be insane! Just so I wouldn't have to go back into that horrid situation that we lived in. I knew what was happening to my sisters. But, I did nothing to help them! I was a coward!" She said, looking down. "No, no, darling," Grandmom Faya said, as she squeezed Miss Miriam's hand, gently. "You did what you thought you had to do, to protect yourself, Miriam. That's all!"

Maybe, Grandmom Faya really felt that way but I felt that Miss Miriam was right on the money. She was a coward, for running away from her own child like she did. Miss Miriam continued.

"After Marie set me up, many months before Andrew was born," she said, "and, I almost died. I couldn't face her and Ole Lucy, anymore! I was tired of constantly fighting them! I couldn't protect my baby son or help my sisters! I didn't have the courage that Faya did."

Grandmom Faya was still holding her hand and gave it another gentle squeeze as if to encourage her to keep talking. "You would have thought that I'd stick around and do something, said Miss Miriam. "Especially, after they ran Faya over, with the car and nearly killed her. I found out about that while I was in the hospital!" "What?" asked Emma, in disbelief.

"Oh, yes," said Grandmom Faya. "Marie tried to kill me by running over me with her car one night! She was the only one who had one, you know. We weren't worthy in Ole Lucy's eyes of owning a car, or anything else, for that matter! I didn't even see or hear the car coming up on me. I was sweeping the driveway, when she purposely pulled into it, doing at least fifty miles an hour. The car hit me and ran over me. For two hours, I was pinned beneath it, before the ambulance came. I knew she went inside the house and told no one that I was out there lying on the ground, injured! It's a good thing that some man, who had been down to the lake, fishing, was coming home and saw me lying there. I probably would have laid there and died!"

"My, God!" exclaimed Linda, in horror. I wondered if she now had doubts about marrying into our family. If she did, I certainly couldn't blame her. "What did you do to her, Grandmom?" asked Emma. "Well, nothing at the time, Emma," she said, with a little laugh. "I had two broken legs and couldn't walk for three months. But, believe me, I had no intention of letting her get away with it!" She didn't elaborate. Instead, she said, "Go on, Miriam, finish the story, please!"

"Okay, Faya," Miss Miriam said, again dabbing at the tears, that were, again, forming in her eyes. She was such a sensitive, loving person. I felt sorry for her, in a way. Also, I was happy to know who she really was, in relation to us. It was good to finally know the truth. It always is.

"After I had been in the hospital, for two years," continued Miss Miriam, "I met a woman who looked very familiar to me. She looked very old, though and she was always lethargic because of the medicine that they gave her. I tried to talk to her every day inspite of that. The fact that she looked like someone I knew, worried me but I could never get her to tell me her name. One day, I asked one of the nurses on duty, what the woman's name was. She told me that her name was, 'Selena Davidson'." She hesitated, for a moment, then said, "That was our mother's name!"

We were all stunned! I recalled Grandmom Faya telling me that she never did believe Ole Lucy when she told them that their mother was dead. Miss Miriam smiled at Grandmom Faya who had tears in her eyes by that time, too. "She was our mother!" Grandmom Faya said, sobbing softly.

"I thought that your mother died, Grandmom," Emma said, confused. "That's what we'd been told, sweetheart," she said, composing herself, again. "But, we never did believe it! Miriam and I that is!"

"Your grandmother must be burning in the fires of hell," Josie said, angrily. She wasn't a member of our family but she felt anger and rage for all of the wrong that had been done, just as the rest of us did.

"Probably," Grandmom Faya, agreed. "Anyway," said Miss Miriam, "I kept this woman company, constantly, after I learned who she was but she never did recognize me. She was always in a dazed state!" Then, Miss Miriam began to sob, softly, as she remembered the pain she felt back then and the fact that her own mother didn't know her. After a few minutes of silence, she continued her story with tears in her eyes.

"To top that off, she was buried in a pauper's grave when she died in that hospital," said Miss Miriam. "Because neither Ole Lucy or Marie ever claimed her body. Faya never even knew about her. Until, I came home from the hospital, a year after that."

"That must have been horrible, for you girls!" said Josie, a look of horror and disbelief on her face. "It was!" said Grandmom Faya. "Believe me, it was!" Her voice was breaking up, as if she wanted to cry, again!

"Our mother was a beautiful, vivacious woman, full of life and love for everyone who crossed her path," said Miss Miriam. "But, she died a broken woman, aged far beyond her years, all alone except for me. Although she never recognized me." Tears were rolling down her cheeks, now.

"I *am* very grateful to the hospital personnel for letting me attend the small funeral service they gave her. I never did admit to them that she was my mother." She stopped talking and wiped the tears from her face.

"Go on, Miriam," prompted Grandmom Faya, as she held her hand to give her support. Miss Miriam smiled at my *grandmothe*r, lovingly. Then, continued to tell the story of horror.

"Faya is the person that both Marie and Ole Lucy feared when they were alive," she told us. "She had supernatural powers that we equal to theirs. The only think we didn't inherit from Ole Lucy was the 'gift'. The same thing that people refer to as ESP." She looked at Emma and I.

"Your powers were equal to theirs', too, Miriam," said Grandmom Faya, "but, they had you too afraid to use them, that's all!" Miss Miriam nodded, in agreement with her.

"We always used our powers for good, never evil, like Marie, and Ole Lucy did," said Miss Miriam. "That's what our mother taught us! I will always believe we could have saved Andrew, Teresa, and our baby sister, from those two wicked monsters of the pit of hell! If only I had not run out on Faya, like a coward! I *knew* Faya couldn't do it, all alone!" Miss Miriam stopped and began to sob again, silently. Her frail shoulders, shaking. It was easy to see that she was filled with regret, and sorrow.

My grandmother smiled at her and held onto her hand. She knew this was something that had haunted Miss Miriam all of her life but now it was time to let it all go. Regaining her composure, Miss Miriam continued her story.

"When we were young girls, in this house," she said, "my grandfather's spirit would come to Faya and I in dreams and visions whenever Ole Lucy or Marie were up to their evil tricks trying to hurt Faya and I. Because of that, we knew that as long as we were living in this house, his spirit would remain here, too. It was our grandfather who always protected us from them, we believed. Also, I don't think he was at peace because his disappearance was never solved! They never did recover his body!"

"Yeah," added Grandmom Faya. "But, guess what?" "What?!" we all asked in unison. "We were awakened one night, Miriam, and I," she said. "By the sound of someone dragging something heavy across the attic floor but we didn't pay too much attention to it at first. There was always some kind of noise or disturbance going on up there at night. We went back to sleep."

"The next morning, the house was unusually quiet," she continued. "I swear, we didn't think Ole Lucy ever slept! You would be awakened by the sound of her voice from somewhere in the house, every morning and hers was the last voice we heard, every night. But, that morning, we didn't hear her. I woke Miriam up. Together, we looked all over the house, to see where she was but we couldn't find her. Then, we remembered the noise we heard the night before, in the attic. Opening the door, that lead to the attic, we still heard nothing. So, we decided to investigate!" She paused.

"The first thing we saw was Ole Lucy, stretched out on the attic floor, flat on her back. Her mouth was open, as well as her eyes and she looked like she had been scared out of her wits. Unfortunately, she wasn't dead. Beside her, was a big, old trunk. It was obvious that it was what she had been dragging across the attic floor, in the night. Before we called for help, we wanted to have a look inside the trunk." Then, my grandmother paused.

"What was in there?" Malin asked, breathlessly caught up in the suspense and mystery. Miss Miriam and Grandmom Faya looked at one another and smiled. "Our grandfather!" they said.

All of us just stared at the two women numb with shock. What a horror story. After that revelation, I didn't think anything could shock us anymore. "Well," said Grandmom Faya, "what was left of him, anyway! He was almost a skeleton, by then." "Oh, my God!" cried Emma, shuddering. "Oh, yes," replied Miss Mariam "She had his body so well preserved, we never smelled any terrible odor in the house, or anything!"

"That's unbelievable!" cried Josie, shaking her head. "Well," said Miss Miriam, "believe it!" "That's macabre!" added Nicholas. "Well," continued Miss Miriam, "we never told the Sheriff about the trunk. Or, about our grandfather's body being found but Faya and I moved it over to a corner of the attic. Then, we called the doctor for Ole Lucy! She had only been in shock, he told us." She paused, again.

"The day after that, I packed my things, and told Faya that I was leaving, and not coming back!" said Miss Miriam. "I left my son with her! She vowed, that if I left she would never speak to me, again, in life! But, I didn't care! I had to go! That is why we never spoke to each other for so many years!" We could tell that she truly regretted her actions. After another short pause, she continued talking

"Although I wasn't coming back, here, anymore to live," she said, "I still came to visit Andrew, at least, three times a month, until, he became a teenager, and was old enough to come to me. He knew me as 'Aunt Miriam', and I was overjoyed on the day, that he told me he had fallen in love, and was getting married! By then, he was a grown man! When I met Teresa, I liked her, immediately!" She paused, again.

"After they got married, they would both visit me regularly and kept me informed about the things that were going on in this house after they moved in here. I should have warned them but I didn't! I will never understand why I didn't!"

I looked around the table and saw that everyone was as caught up in the sorrowful story, as I was. All eyes were on Miss Miriam and I wondered what other surprises we might find out.

"By that time," she said, "I had bought the house that collapsed! Then, many years later, I had some movers come over here, for the trunk! It was when Faya moved out of this house, and after Marie, and Ole Lucy died. I knew Faya didn't want it, because she'd left it behind. According to Charon who was still here, with you children! I still have that old trunk!"

My sister and I looked at her strangely. "Is that the same old trunk that you told us never to touch, when we were little girls?!" I asked her. "It certainly is, honey!" she answered.

"Only now there is nothing left but his bones," she continued. "I took part of the remains to Tolstoy some years ago, to have them analyzed. Also, to make sure of who it was. They asked me a lot of questions but I told them that I didn't know the person. That I was just curious. They told me that it was a man and that he had died from arsenic poisoning. They told me that it had been given to him, over a long period of time! I guess now, we'll get around to burying him."

"We don't have to guess who poisoned him, do we?" Nicholas commented, dryly. Grandmom Faya, and Miss Miriam gave him a look, as if to say, "are you kidding?!" "Right!" said Nicholas.

"Ole Lucy and Marie ruined Teresa and her family, you know," said Miss Miriam. "After that, they turned their hatred and jealousy on your father, Andrew. It was Faya who finally destroyed Marie, after your father killed himself." "How did you destroy her, Miss Faya?" asked Linda, eagerly.

"Well," said Grandmom Faya, "she came at me, out of the clear blue, one evening, with a hunter's knife. We started fighting and while we were wrestling with the knife, she was stabbed in the side." "Oh, my Lord!" cried Josie. "But she didn't die from that!" said Miss Miriam. "No," said Grandmom Faya. "But she was severely injured! After that, Ole Lucy, to be smart, wanted only me to wait on Marie, hand and foot while she was recuperating. I fixed her meals every day and every day she would taunt me. Because of what happened to her. So, I started mixing arsenic in her food!"

My *grandmother* paused and looked at each person sitting around the table waiting for our reactions. Disbelief and horror were all over our faces but no one said a word. I think, secretly, we were all glad at what she had done to such a wicked person as Marie. Not one of us blamed her for what she did.

"It took about a week, I guess," she added, nonchalantly. "Ole Lucy found her, one morning and I knew she knew what had happened to Marie but she never once confronted me about it. Not one word!" "You're right!" exclaimed Josie. "Nobody in Maron, ever knew how Marie died!"

"That's nothing new, Josie," observed Miss Miriam. "This family has many hidden secrets!" "I don't understand why our father didn't just take us and leave," Malin said, softly. "Sweetheart," Grandmom Faya said to him, "before Marie died, he and Teresa were raising Tyla right along with the rest of you. Ole Lucy took Tyla away from Marie, as soon as she delivered her. When Ole Lucy found out who Marie was pregnant by, she was thoroughly pissed to put it, mildly but that's how jealous Marie was of Teresa's happiness." She paused.

"She couldn't have Andrew's father," she continued, "who was the man she had become obsessed with, so she went after his son. Her own sister's child. She was too afraid of Ole Lucy to challenge her. Before she ever seduced Andrew and got pregnant by him, Marie had him under some kind of '*spell*', that I couldn't seem to break. No matter how hard I tried, or what I did!"

"She went after Teresa, with a vengeance," added Miss Miriam. "The thought of Teresa raising *he*r child, enrage Marie. She poisoned Teresa a little bit every day. Just as Ole Lucy had done to our grandfather. Teresa was loving, and trusting. Really believing that Marie was her friend! In reality, Marie hated her!" She paused, again.

"After it was revealed that Teresa had been poisoned," she continued," Andrew went to pieces. Marie taunted him after that, and kept telling him that *'he was next'*. Then, you children. All, but Tyla! She tried to drive him insane. The last straw was when she finally told him that Miriam was his *true* mother and not me. I think he just couldn't take anymore!" Grandmom Faya had tears in her eyes, then. She stopped talking, and stared off into the distance, lost in her thoughts. Miss Miriam continued the story from there.

"After Teresa's death," she said, "And, the knowledge that I and not Faya, was his real mother, Andrew changed! He just wasn't himself, anymore. I never knew Marie told him about me being his real mother. Until, Faya told me years later. I can't tell you how painful that was for me."

"Andrew walked around in a trance-like state, all of the time, after that, Grandmom Faya took over the story, again. "I *knew* something was wrong. But, no matter what I did, to break Marie's hold over him, nothing worked. I found out, after he was dead that she'd told him about Miriam, and I, *and* about his father!" Miss Miriam began to speak again.

"Ole Lucy forced you children onto Charon!" She said. "At first, she refused, and when Marie died, she thought she was free but she wasn't. Before her death, Marie insisted that Charon raise you children by putting it in her will. She even left Charon two hundred thousand dollars on the condition that she raise you children. Otherwise, she would never see a dime of that money. Charon *never* had any money, before. Ole Lucy saw to that!"

"Well, backtracking a little," she continued, "Marie thought that with Andrew, and Teresa out of the way and with Charon raising you, she would be able to have close contact with her child, Tyla. But, she forgot about Faya, who wisely did- n't want Tyla anywhere near Marie." She took a sip of her water, then continued. "She never got a chance to put her wicked plan to work because she died, soon after Terry did."

"There were many battles between Marie and Faya even before that stabbing incident." she continued. "Charon was completely and totally under Marie's control. Almost as if she was possessed by Marie, or something. Well, the battles ended on the morning Ole Lucy found Marie, dead! Her plan had failed! And, she carried her anger and rage to the grave with her!"

"My friend, Karen, told me about a lot of this stuff," I finally spoke up. "But, she also left out a lot of details." "People who gossip tend to do that, honey," said Grandmom Faya. "Now, you're getting the story straight from the horse's mouth. The best place, don't you think?" I nodded. Miss Miriam smiled at me. Then, *she* began talking.

"Roy Oberon was your grandfather, children," she said. "He raped me, when I was fifteen years old! I was only a child and I hated him, for what he did to me! It was another reason that I let Ole Lucy put me away. I *wanted* too get away from all of them! Even, Faya! Marie tried over and over again, to make us turn on each other. But, she failed! No matter what, I *knew* Faya was on my side!" She paused.

"Even Roy told lies to Marie about he and I," she said. "Nothing he ever said about me, was true but naturally she believed every word he told her. Then, I came back to this house after three years and Faya told me that Ole Lucy and Marie, through witchcraft, had *forced* him out of a window to his death. They did it because he tried to leave this place! I was just glad that he was dead!"

"I came back to this house for reasons that I'll never understand myself," continued Miss Miriam. "But, it wasn't for long! I hated this house and I hated *all* of them! I even blamed Faya, for my son's death!" "Why didn't all of you just leave this house?" asked Linda. "You have to understand the forces of darkness, Linda, honey," said Grandmom Faya, sweetly. "I know you do, because your mother did. Ole Lucy had tremendous power over *all* of us. Even though

Miriam, and I fought her and Marie every step of the way. This house had a *'hold'* on us, too! We couldn't shake it, no matter what we did or where we went! It was only *after* Ole Lucy and Marie's deaths. Especially, after Ole Lucy's, that we were free from it! Miriam had been strong enough to leave but she still couldn't stay away," she explained.

"It wasn't easy, either," added Miss Miriam. "This house kept pulling me back to it. But somehow, I had the strength that I needed, by then. Andrew was the only reason I kept coming back!" "When she did that, just as she's told you," leaving also gave *me* the strength to leave here, years later. After I had already dealt Grandmom Faya admitted, "I vowed never to speak to her again in life but her with Marie and Ole Lucy. I left Charon here, with you children, which was a mistake!"

All eyes were on her, waiting for the rest of what she had to say. "Bernie Brown, our old mail man," said Grandmom Faya, "kept me informed on how you children were doing over here. When he told me that he'd seen bruises on Andrew, Jr., and Nicholas was always in some kind of trouble with the Sheriff, I came over here to see what was going on. Sure enough, I saw the bruises, too. I had a huge quarrel with Charon. Also, I informed Sheriff Bicket and old Judge Marsdensen, who was still living at that time of my suspicions of child abuse."

"I was so angry," she continued, "I took Charon to court, to get custody of you children. But, when it was all over and done with she was given two options. To move in with me in the house where we used to live and where I could keep y eyes on her. Or, she could go to jail for child abuse. You know the rest." "And, now, you've come back here?" cried Emma, with fear in her voice. "Believe me, child," said Grandmom Faya, "we do *know* exactly what we're doing. You have to be free of this evil, too. And you aren't!" "Oh, no!" I cried. I didn't want to deal with it anymore.

"That's right," Miss Miriam affirmed, "you four are the light that is going to destroy this darkness, that's hovering over this place and over our family! We have to be rid of this wickedness and this evil forever! It's still around us. And, it refuses to let go! That's what caused my house to collapse, like it did! The people in town are still wondering how that happened! Also, it's why Emma, and Tyla, have the dreams they have!" Then, she turned toward Malin.

"Even you, Malin," she continued. "When you got sick! It's why Teresa is *still* around you, too!" "Those evil spirits are *still* occupying this house," added Grandmom Faya. "They would like to occupy your souls, in all truth! Your grand- father, Roy, our sister, Marie, and our grandmother, Ole Lucy! All had power, in their lifetimes that has been passed onto you! In particular, you girls!

Even our grandfather, Richard, came from a family that delved into the supernatural! His family dated back as far as the fifteenth century!"

"Ole Lucy, had the gift of second sight, just as you girls do, Emma, and Tyla," she continued. "But, she learned other things about the black arts from her mother-in-law, and some things from Roy Oberon, too. Some of her in-laws were evil. But some were good! Unfortunately, her mother-in-law wasn't one of the good ones," Miss Miriam told us.

"Your grandfather, Roy Oberon," added Grandmom Faya, "had learned all that he knew from his mother and your great grandmother, Berta. They say that she could touch a person and see their whole future. She naturally possessed the '*gift*' of second sight. But it drove her to alcoholism and eventually, to her death."

"Wow!" said Nicholas, "Ty is really our cousin and our sister, then!" "That's absolutely true," replied my *grandmother*, "And, I'm your aunt, *not your grandmother!* Charon was also your aunt. She wasn't always mean and evil either children. She was made to be that way, by two wicked people that she believed cared about her! But, they didn't! I became angry at Miriam, here, for a very long time. Because, I thought she had run out on me Andrew and Charon when we needed her the most! I thought she didn't care about us! But I was wrong!" She paused.

"She was just very scared," she continued, "and I should have understood that! I let Marie come between us, when I shouldn't have. She made sure that your father knew Miriam was his true mother. And, not me! It hurt him very, very badly! That shock, the witchcraft Márie used on him, and the death of Teresa! All of this pushed him to the point of no return!"

At that point, Grandmom Faya, who had been as steady as a rock, broke down, and cried. She was remembering her dear nephew, and my father, Andrew. It was Miss Miriam's turn to console her sister and she patted Grandmom Faya's hand, gently. "It was my fault, too, Faya," she said, quietly. Then, she turned to us.

"Marie wanted us to hate each other," she said. "But our love was too strong for one another! She lost! Poor Charon was like a puppet on a string. She never could stand up to Marie! She loved her from the time that she was a little girl. She wouldn't listen to anything that Faya or I had to say against her!"

"After your father killed himself," said Grandmom Faya, after drying her eyes, "the battles really did begin in this house and I won!" "How did you win, Grandmom or should we start calling you, Aunt Faya?" asked Emma. "Yeah, what should we call you two, now, anyway?" asked Malin

"You can call us the same things that you've always called each of us, or whatever makes you comfortable," replied Miss Miriam. "We're telling you all of this, because we want you to know the truth! You deserve to know the truth!"

"Anyway, to answer your question," continued Grandmom Faya, "after what Ole Lucy and Marie did to your father, Teresa, Miriam and Charon, I made up my mind to make them pay for it. I gave Marie a dose of her own medicine. A little bit at a time. Just as I have already to you. If you had known Marie Davidson, none of you would be surprised that I did it!" She hesitated, before speaking again.

"As for Ole Lucilla," she continued, "I knew, after what happened to Marie, she would try something. She planned to have me murdered as I slept, one night. By a man she knew who lived in Maron. A man that she had completely under her power and control. I saw this man do many wicked deeds for her when I was growing up. Let's see! I can't remember his name, can you, Miriam?" She asked, looking at her sister.

"No," answered Miss Miriam. "I can't think of it, either. I think it was 'Jack' something, or other. I just can't remember, for sure!" "My, God! My, God!" said Linda, shaking her head. "Your own grandmother?!" "Don't tell me that you're surprised after all that we've already told you about her, Linda!" Grandmom Faya said with a little laugh. "I just can't believe it all!" replied Linda.

"Anyway," continued Grandmom Faya, "Ole Lucy never knew that I overheard her plot against me. She thought I was outside on the front porch, the day that this man came over to see her but I came back inside the house without her knowing it. I heard the whole plot! Every detail! I realized that I could never go to this man, and, try to talk him out of it! Because, he certainly would have told her, if I had!"

"So, what did you do, Grandmom?" asked Emma, anxiously. "Well," she said, "I had a habit of sleeping on the sofa, in our den, at night. And, that was where he was supposed to murder me! On the particular night it was to happen, I fixed Ole Lucy her usual cup of tea, with a shot of Rye in it. Only that time, I added a half- dozen sleeping pills." She paused.

"Ole Lucy always watched me, as I made her tea, at night," she continued. "But, I guess she never saw me put the pills in it. That was her way of taunting me, by having me make her a cup of tea, every night. It was as if to say to me, "*If you're* going to do anything to me, you'd better do it now! Or, forget about it!" She wanted to believe, that I was afraid of her. When she really knew that I wasn't! She fell asleep, right there, at the kitchen table, that night!"

Everybody was staring at Grandmom Faya, waiting to hear what happened to Ole Lucy! Even though it was a horrible story about our family, each one of us was on the edge of our seats, in surprise!

"As soon as Ole Lucy fell asleep," she said, "I struggled to drag her to the sofa where I usually slept. I laid her there with her face toward the back of the sofa and covered her up. Then, I went to the top of the stairs and waited." She paused, again.

"At the scheduled time for the murder," she continued, "I heard the man come in the front door using a key that she gave him. I was listening at the top of the stairs." Grandmom Faya paused, again, as if reliving the incident. She didn't say anything for a moment. "Grandmom, what happened?" Malin asked, when he couldn't take the suspense anymore.

Malin's voice caught Grandmom Faya's attention! "Well," she said, slowly," I need not tell you the rest of the story but I do know that her spirit will never be at peace because I turned her own plot against her."

Grandmom Faya wasn't going to say anymore about it but all of us just had to know what happened to Ole Lucy. "Come on, Grandmom!" cried Emma, voicing everyone else's thought. "Finish the story, please!" After a moment, she complied.

"Ole Lucy was bludgeoned to death, with a baseball bat," continued Grandmom Faya. "Right there, on that sofa!" I thought I caught a smug tone, in her voice. She was glad that she killed her grandmother.

"Then, as planned," she continued, "I heard the man tearing up the place, to make it look like a robbery! He broke out a window pane as if somebody had bro- ken into the house. Instead of using a door key! The Sheriff never knew what really happened because I didn't tell anyone!"

"That's certainly horrifying!" said Josie. "Everyone in Maron always wondered who murdered Lucy Camay! But, nobody ever knew!" "I know," Grandmom Faya said, nodding her head, vigorously. "When the man found out that he'd murdered the wrong person, he was frantic! He went around town, ranting, and raving, like a madman!" She paused, again.

"He would even get out into the middle of the streets," she continued, "get down on all fours and bark pretending to be a dog sometimes or even a cat. Apparently, he completely lost his mind, after that. Later, they found him lying faced down in an alley with not a mark or scratch on him anywhere. The Coroner said that he had a heart attack but I will always believe he was frightened to death!"

"You believe that Ole Lucy reached out from the grave out of anger and killed that man, Miss Faya?!" asked Linda. "Sure, I do," replied my grandmother, matter of factly. "There is no doubt, in my mind, whatsoever and there never will be!" At that time, Miss Miriam joined in. "So, you see, children, there are evil, wicked forces here but there are also good ones, here, too!" She told us.

"I wonder whatever happened to Mama, or Charon?" asked Nicholas. "We don't know," answered Miss Miriam. "But I do have a feeling that we'll find out, sooner or later!" These were more words that would prove to be true, and even prophetic.

"I know you're all curious as to why I wanted to move back here," said Grandmom Faya. "And, I think you have the right to know. Don't you, Miriam?" She asked her sister. Miss Miriam agreed with her, whole-heartedly.

CHAPTER THIRTEEN

Taking a deep breath, Miss Miriam began talking. "Before Marie died," she said, "she cursed me, Faya, and you children! She vowed never to rest, until she had destroyed all of us, on her daughter's *twenty first* birthday! Right here! In this house, where she had so much wicked power!" "So, why didn't we just stay where we were, then?" I asked. "No, Ty," my sister-in-law said, "don't you understand what she was *really* saying?!"

"Tyla doesn't," said Grandmom Faya, "but, I do! She was talking about demonic possession! She will possess her daughter's soul, on her twenty first birthday, to accomplish the fulfillment of her curse on all of us!" "That's right!" Linda agreed. "I saw many cases of such possession when I traveled with my mother. It was always on the victim's *twenty first* birthday! And, *it was always someone very close to the evil spirit!"*

A cold chill caused me to shiver, involuntarily. I became very frightened. "Can she really do that to me?"

I asked, in a fearful voice. "Yes, she can," answered Linda, gravely. "But," Miss Miriam added, quickly. "We are going to stop her! This way we can destroy her and *'the others'*, at the same time! Once, and for all! The thing is, it has to be done on the demon's *own ground!"*

"So," exclaimed Emma, "that's why we're here!" "Right," said Grandmom Faya. "This is *her power base'*, so to speak! If we wipe her out in this house, she'll be destroyed, out of our lives, forever!" "But, how?" asked Emma. This time, Grandmom Faya refused to tell us. "We'll get into the details of that, later," she said. Then, she changed the subject. Things were getting more and more mysterious.

"After Marie died," Grandmom Faya started, again, "I saw the drastic change in Charon. She went from being passive, gentle and naive! To evil, selfish and hateful. I knew, immediately, that Marie's wicked spirit was beginning to take hold of her. Especially, when she started abusing you children.

She became angry about having to take the responsibility of raising you! At first, though, she loved every one of you and wouldn't have hurt you! You have to believe that, children, okay?"

"Yes, it was only Marie's evil that caused Charon to act the way that she did" emphasized Miss Miriam. "She hadn't always been that way!"

"Charon was a beautiful young woman" said Grandmom Faya with a faraway look in her eyes. It was as if she was *seeing* her sister in her mind. "She loved to be around people when we were growing up! She had that long dark hair that was down her back and those big pretty light brown eyes. She was well built too!" Then she laughed softly. "I will never forget the day that she snuck out of the house and went into town! Remember, Miriam?"

"Yeah" said Miss Miriam, rolling her eyes. "Boy, do I remember! Lucilla had a fit!" "She sure did" Grandmom Faya laughed some more. "Charon went into town and took her sweet time browsing in the stores and talking to various people in town. The young guys who saw her went absolutely *crazy*. She was a knockout children and to add to that, she was very sweet too! She loved people and if she could help anybody, she would."

"Gee" exclaimed Nicholas. "That sure doesn't sound like the woman that we knew!" "I know honey" said Grandmom Faya softly. "But it's true! Charon was a very good person until hatefulness and wickedness destroyed her life!"

"It's truly sad" added Miss Miriam. "If Faya hadn't forced her to come and stay with her, Charon would have killed all of you children a long time ago! Andrew Jr. is dead because Faya let her guard down! She'll never let that happen again, I'm sure!"

"You are right about that dear" Grandmom Faya agreed. "*Marie knows it too!* I'm right on top of everything that goes on with your children! And now I've purposely brought the battle to her!" "So" asked Nicholas. "Now you two can battle it out over us for real huh?" "Right again" Grandmom Faya said with a smile.

"But I don't want to be fought over! I just wanted to be left alone!" I wanted to shout at all of them, but I kept my thoughts to myself. "Is that the reason why Tyla and I have this *gift?*" asked Emma. "Yes sweetheart" replied Grandmom Faya. "My mother and my grandmother had it. Then it skipped over me and my sisters. Now you two have it."

"Why didn't you ever tell us all of this stuff before?" asked Emma, obviously wishing we had known the things they told us a long time ago. "We wanted whatever *powers* that you have to manifest themselves first so we could be sure that you had them" answered Miss Miriam.

"That's right" said Grandmom Faya. "When you had the *vision* of Miriam getting sick we knew! Also I knew that Tyla's was coming to the forefront when she was a little girl and told me that she dreamed about this house! Remember that honey?" she asked, looking at me. I nodded my head.

"There are powers that you have" said Miss Miriam. "But you have to be taught *how* to use them! There are various plain old household seasonings used for cooking food that can be used to cast different spells either for good or for evil! You don't know these things now. But you will!" "How about Nicholas and Malin?" asked Emma. "Do they have these powers too?"

"They probably do," answered Grandmom Faya. "But you know how men are! They have a tendency to shrug things like that off as *coincidences* or something! A lot of things have probably happened to them that they never told about! Right fellas?" Nicholas and Malin both remained quiet. Which was all the answer that any of us needed. "I'd like to be included in this," said Linda shyly. "If no one minds!"

"Dear Linda," said Grandmom Faya graciously, "I've had you in mind to help us from the day that you came here with Nicholas! And I think you know that already don't you?" Linda smiled but didn't say anything. "*So everything that Andrew Jr. said in my dream is true!*" I thought. Everyone at the table got quiet! The food had long ago become cold. But nobody was hungry anyway. Time passed rather quickly!

Just then the front doorbell rang. We wondered who it could be. Since very few people knew that we had moved! For a minute I wondered if the evil spirits had the decency to ring the doorbell before they came calling. It was just a small joke that I kept to myself. Malin jumped up to answer the door. And I glanced at the clock! It was eight thirty already!

"Oh Ty!" Malin called to me from the living room. "You have a visitor!" "*Who is it?*" I asked myself. I had completely forgotten about Gary Shelley! Then as I started into the living room I saw him standing there. Instantly I knew that Grandmom Faya had put the note back on the front door.

As he stood there in the doorway Gary looked so handsome! I don't know how I could have ever forgotten that he was coming over. But somehow I had. Malin stood beside Gary grinning from ear to ear!

"Hi!" Gary said when he saw me. "I saw the note on the front door of your other place. And came right over! You must've forgotten to tell me that you were moving huh?" "I didn't know it myself," I told him glad that he came. "I'm sorry about that! I only found out when I got home from school!"

"I'm Malin, Gary," my brother said extending his hand to Gary in greeting. "I know you from school!" They shook hands. "Yeah," said Gary. "I've seen you around too!" "Well," Malin said enjoying himself, "come on into the kitchen and meet the rest of the family!" It was like I wasn't even there anymore.

Gary followed Malin past me into the kitchen. My brother introduced him to everybody as *my friend from school*. As I watched from the living room Grandmom Faya and the others absorbed Gary like a sponge absorbs water! He didn't stand a chance! And I couldn't rescue him! From the look on their faces both Grandmom Faya and Miss Miriam approved of Gary a lot! And so did the others! He was very nice and extremely mannerable!

"Well well," said Grandmom Faya with a big grin. "You're the gentleman caller huh? My you are a handsome one! Do I know your family?! Are you from Maron?" "*Oh no*," I thought. "*Here comes the third degree!*" The entire time I stayed in the living room watching and listening! Miss Miriam pulled out a chair for Gary to sit down in which happened to be right next to hers.

"No Maam," said Gary politely as he sat down in the chair. "We moved here two years ago from Vaira County. Just south of Tolstoy! My father retired from the railroad there and decided to move here because he said it was nice and quiet!"

Everybody was familiar with Vaira County. It was at least thirty miles from Tolstoy. And a fairly big county too. In fact, it was larger than Tolstoy! All of the things that any big city had, Vaira County had twice over. Including crime! A lot of people there wanted to leave. But they couldn't afford to move anywhere else. I knew immediately that Grandmom Faya was thinking that Gary's family was fortunate. And I could tell that she was thrilled to meet this young man who came to visit me.

Even though he had come to see *me*, Gary handled the informal interview well. He charmed Grandmom Faya and Miss Miriam and got along well with Linda, Emma, and my brothers! He told me later that he liked them too. For at least a half an hour, he sat in the kitchen with them talking and laughing.

Then I heard him excuse himself! He came into the livingroom where I was watching television. "So hi again!" he said to me softly. Then he sat down next to me on the sofa. "Hi," I said shyly. I hoped my nervousness wasn't apparent to him. "Well," Gary started making conversation, "it's the weekend. And there's no school work to be done! I forgot that if you can believe it! Did you?"

"I sure did," I told him. "I'm usually not that absent-minded, are you?" he asked me. "No, not usually," I answered. "Maybe it's a sign or something," he joked with me. "You know, when we start forgetting things like that whenever we're around each other." I smiled. He had a wonderful sense of humor. And he could always make me smile. Somehow I knew Gary would never break my heart! Yet I was still wondering how to begin putting my *plan* to work!

"We can just sit here and watch television Gary," I told him. "Is there something that you usually watch on Friday night?" "It doesn't matter to me Ty," he said staring hard at me. "Anything that you want to watch is fine with me! I'm just glad to finally be here with you." His voice was soft and tender. As if he was making love to me with only his voice! It was nice too! He wasn't wasting time coming on to me!

Turning the channel to a comedy program I thought he might like, we watched it together. And laughed at some of the funny parts in it! Suddenly Gary held my hand and gently squeezed it. My first instinct was to pull my hand away. But I couldn't! I liked his touch! Also, I felt the same electric jolt again as I had in the hallway at school when he touched my hand.

For several minutes, we stared at the television set. But all of our concentration was on the contact of our hands! Then he put his arm around my shoulders. This time I didn't want to pull away! I liked his arm around me. And the wonderful scent of his cologne was intoxicating! To my surprise, I began to relax because it felt so natural to be in his arms! All of my anxiety and worry had been for nothing! I was comfortable with Gary! *Very comfortable*!

Linda and Josie started to clean up the kitchen while the rest of the family were still chattering away. After a while, Malin and Nicholas went out to the guest house to talk. "Would you like a soda or something Gary?" I asked him politely. "No Ty," he said. "I just want to sit here with you in my arms like this!"

My *plan* wasn't working out like I thought it would. I found myself thinking thoughts that I had never thought before. When I had been silent for a while, he asked me, "What are you thinking about Ty?" "Oh nothing," I lied. "I'm just watching the show that's all." "Do you think we can talk then?" he asked me. "About what?" I asked him. "About us!" he said. I started to get nervous again.

"There is no us, Gary," I said with a little chuckle. "We just met!" But even as I spoke those words, I found myself truly *falling* for Gary Shelley! He was kind, considerate, gentle, soft-spoken, intelligent, and unselfish. And he treated me like I was his queen! I enjoyed that!

As we sat on the sofa, I could feel Gary's urgency in wanting to talk to me. Finally, he blurted out, "Ty, I sure do like you! I have for a long, long time too! Since the first day that I saw you in school two years ago!" My head whipped around in surprise! I stared at him stunned. "You've been watching me for two years?" I asked incredulously. "Are you that surprised?" he asked me with a chuckle. "Yes," I said, "I'm stunned!"

"Well you stay in my thoughts Ty," he said softly. "Like no other girl ever has or ever will! It's *you* that I really want to be with! When I had other girlfriends, it was always you that I wanted! Only you Ty!" I couldn't seem to get your attention though. Then I got tired of watching you from a distance and waiting for you to come to me. So I started leaving you messages on your locker! Or I would give them to your friend Karen to give to you!"

"Oh yeah," I said. "How did you know that Karen Bullock and I are friends anyway Gary?" I asked him. "Because different people that I asked about you told me who your friends were, what you liked to do, and where you hung out. The thing is you didn't hang out anywhere Ty! You'll never know how many Friday, Saturday, and even Sunday nights I've gone out into the streets to various parties and hangouts hoping and praying that I would run into you!"

I couldn't find any words to respond to what he said to me. So I just kept my mouth shut. It was a shocking revelation that he was so serious about me!

Then he tried to kiss my hand. But I pulled away from him. I was scared for sure by then. And I think he knew it! I had never been kissed by a boy before. Except by my brothers on my cheek. "*What am I going to do now?"* I wondered, my heart beating fast! "Don't be afraid of me Ty," Gary said to me softly. "I would never hurt you! All I want to do is love you! If you'll give me a chance! Please?!" He was pleading with me by then. But I couldn't say anything because I was so scared.

"Can I have a kiss from you?" he asked me tenderly. I *knew* he could sense my fear by then. "I'll bet you've never been kissed have you Ty?" he asked in a low sweet voice. His face was close to mine! "By a lover I mean," he added hastily. "No," I said. It was all I trusted myself to say. By then, my heart was racing, and my palms were sweating!

"It's nice," he told me. "And I'll bet you will like it very much. In fact, I promise you that you will! Just let me show you how nice it is!" Then he gently turned my face to his. This time I didn't move away from him.

Gary stood up and pulled me gently up from the sofa. Putting his arms around my waist and never taking his eyes away from mine, he pulled me close to him. Lifting my lips to meet his, he kissed me deeply. And tenderly, parting my lips with his tongue. It was a long deep kiss, and he held me tightly to him. As our lips touched, there was fire between us that we both felt! At that moment in time, no one else existed in the whole world but the two of us. And we were not even aware that the remaining members of my family were watching us from the kitchen and smiling.

"You'll never forget that one, Miss Tyla," Linda said to the others softly. When it was over, Gary tenderly kissed my eyelids one at a time. Then the tip of my nose and my forehead. Then our lips met again in another long sensual kiss. This time when the kiss ended, I had to sit back down. Because my heart was pounding like crazy! And my knees were knocking! Strange feelings coursed through my body that I had never experienced before.

Gary sat down next to me, putting his arm around my shoulders again. And pulled me closer to him. "I don't think I'm ready for this, Gary!" I told him nervously. "We just met each other!" He grinned at me.

"I know Ty," he said. "But I'm in no hurry! I'll wait for you forever! If I have to! After all, I've already waited for two years, haven't I? I plan on being around for a long time, Tyla Davidson! Now that I finally have you. I'll never let you go! I don't have to *dream* about you anymore! Because I have you in my arms now! All I want to do is love you Ty! And I want you to love me too. In time, okay?"

At that moment, I knew it wouldn't be hard for me to do. Gary, without a doubt, was the one for me! He was my first love! And although I didn't know it then, the only lover that I would ever need or want in my life! As we talked, we discovered that we had a lot of things in common too.

Later on that evening, Grandmom Faya, Miss Miriam, and the others came out of the kitchen. And said their 'good-nights' to Gary and I. Then went upstairs to bed. All except Miss Miriam, who had the downstairs bedroom. Suddenly the house became very quiet!

Sooner than I realized, it was midnight. I knew it was time for Gary to be on his way home. Before Grandmom Faya came downstairs and told him so. Also, I knew that she and Miss Miriam were not asleep yet. They were waiting to see if Gary was responsible enough to leave on his own at a respectable time.

Of course, Gary didn't want to leave me. But at the front door, he pulled me into his arms again and kissed me. "Can I come over to see you tomorrow Ty?" He asked me gently. "Sure," I said without hesitation. "Tomorrow is my birthday," I added. "Well," said Gary with a smile, "I'll have to buy you a birthday present then, won't I?"

"You don't have to do that Gary," I protested. But he ignored what I said. "Oh yes, I do," he said. "I *want* to do it! I want to give you everything that you..." could ever want Ty! I want to spoil you to the point where no other guy will ever be any good for you! Except me!"

Gary was truly sincere about that. And I knew for certain he had fallen in love with me as I did with him! But I tried not to let him know it. Needless to say, my *plan* to teach Gary Shelley a lesson about girls went out the front door with him that night. I wanted him in my life. And since I would be sixteen years old the next day, we could go out on dates together! "*At least we can go somewhere and have some privacy!*" I said to myself.

Before he left me, I told Gary that we could go out on a date sometime. "Whatever you want to do Ty," he said, "just tell me." I nodded, smiling at him. I mean *really* smiling! *I was in love!* I knew exactly what I wanted to do with Gary Shelley. But I quickly pushed the thought out of my head. He had awakened desires in me that I had only read about women having in the books that Karen and Emma showed me. But I didn't want to scare him off by acting like Tish Poree. Or some of the other girls he'd had at school.

I could certainly understand why they were ready and willing to drop their panties for him though. They were absolute tramps for him! But he didn't want any of them! He wanted me! And I knew he was truly in love with me!

After Gary left, I went upstairs to my bedroom. And laid down on the bed. My mind was in a whirlpool! I decided to do as Grandmom Faya suggested and take things slowly! I would always be a lady, as she taught me to be. "*Gary does deserve that,*" I told myself, remembering what Malin said about him. I had no choice but to admit to myself that I had fallen in love with Gary Shelley! Then I finally drifted off to sleep. I slept better than I had in a long time too!

CHAPTER FOURTEEN

The next morning, Emma came into my bedroom, wanting to know everything about Gary. She liked him! "He seems like a real nice guy Ty," she said. "I wish you a lot of luck with him!" Immediately, I detected a note of sadness in her voice. But I didn't question her. The same sadness was in her eyes too. Nobody knew it! But bad problems had begun to develop between Emma and Artic.

It was Halloween, and Grandmom Faya, Linda, and Miss Miriam put up decorations inside and outside of the house. "I hope the children in town aren't afraid to come here for trick-or-treat because of all of the rumors about this house," Miss Miriam said as she taped up a cardboard ghost.

"They won't be afraid to come," Grandmom Faya assured her. "We'll make sure that it's brightly lit up." As it turned out, she was right! Every child in Maron came to our house for goodies that evening.

For my birthday, Gary took me out to dinner. Then, we went to the movies. He bought me a beautiful golden anklet with the words *Love Forever* engraved on it. He was so thoughtful! Around midnight, we came home from our date. Everybody in the family was waiting up for us. So we could have a late birthday celebration! Even Karen came over.

The birthday celebration went on until two o'clock in the morning. And everyone was having a lot of fun! Suddenly, the bathroom toilet on the first floor began to flush by itself. Looking around, everyone was in the kitchen. Nobody was in the bathroom! Before anybody could say anything, the television set came on by itself! Every time one of us turned it off, we would hear a click and the set would come on again. At Grandmom Faya's urging, we decided to ignore it.

Gary and Karen thought it was spooky. But the rest of us knew that our ghostly *visitors* were right there with us! Then, as we sat at the kitchen table talking, every light in the house except the one in the kitchen where were went out! It was pitch black in the rest of the house.

Suddenly, a woman dressed in black from head to toe with eyes blazing red like fire appeared standing in the middle of the dining room floor. Her hair was a deep dark red like mine! She wore the most evil-looking grin on her face that I had ever seen! Our family knew exactly who she was! *'Marie'*!

Marie glared at all of us angrily. Then she turned around and walked toward the front door as if to open it and leave. A powerful gust of wind blew the front door open violently! Then all of the lights suddenly came back on! Marie had vanished!

"Whoa!" cried Gary excitedly. "Who was that?!" Nobody answered me. "That was cool!" he continued ignoring our concerned looks. "How did you all do that?!" he asked.

We still didn't answer him! Evidently, he thought it had been some kind of Halloween prank that we arranged for the purpose of entertaining him and Karen. He wasn't afraid like I thought he would be. But Karen was! She wanted to leave immediately. Nervously, she asked Gary if he would give her a ride home in his car. "Sure," he told her, "It's time for me to go too."

Gary asked me to walk him to the front door. However, he noticed that I seemed to be a little fearful of going near the door. Placing his hands on my shoulders, he turned me to face him. The others watched us as he said to me gently, "You don't have to be afraid of anything or anyone Ty! I'll never let anything happen to you, okay?" I smiled. Then, he took me by the hand as we walked to the front door. Just before leaving, he kissed me good-night. I was smiling at him.

"I love you Ty," he said in what was almost a whisper. "I really do love you!" "I know," I said, still grinning. "I'll see you tomorrow, okay?" he asked. "Yes," I replied. "Tomorrow!" Over the months after that, our relationship blossomed into something truly beautiful! I was envied by every girl at school. A few of them tried to break us up. Especially Tish's girlfriends! They told lies about Gary! But we never let anything or anyone come between us!

Then, Gary graduated from high school. Although he didn't want to go, I convinced him to utilize the scholarship that he earned. It would have been foolish to throw it away! So, he went off to college. And, we were nearly two thousand miles apart. I missed him terribly. But we talked on the telephone every other night. And we wrote letters to each other every week! For holidays and semester breaks, he would come home.

The summer that I graduated from high school, Gary came home for the summer break. We decided to sleep together. It was better than anything I had ever read about in the books that Emma and Karen had. Our relationship became even stronger after that! We decided to get married as soon as he graduated from college!

Grandmom Faya and Miss Miriam wanted me to go to college too. Or at least to a business school in Tolstoy. But I wouldn't hear of it! Instead, I got a job as a Clerk in the Sheriff's office. It didn't pay a whole lot. But I didn't care! It was a job. And that's all I wanted for the time being!

In the meantime, Linda and Nicholas made me an aunt with the birth of my nephew Nicola. He had grown quickly and was two and a half years old when I graduated. Malin was off at college on the East coast. And Emma was finally seeing another man. His name was Ray Jamison!

Ray was Emma's age, very nice, and most of all, *unmarried*! In fact, he wanted to marry my sister and take her away from Maron. He came from a hardworking family of mechanics. And was a mechanic himself. He and his father owned their own garage. And they made pretty good money! He even told Emma that she never had to work another day in her life if she married him! All he wanted her to do was be his wife and the mother of his children!

Ray loved Emma very much. And he was extremely good to her! Our family adored him. Especially Grandmom Faya and Miss Miriam. Everybody believed he was good for my sister! So we couldn't understand why she hesitated to marry him. At first, we thought it was because she didn't want to leave home. But when Ray told us that they didn't have to leave if Emma didn't want to, we couldn't understand what her problem was! All she would tell us was, "It's not the right time yet!" No one questioned her as to what she meant by that.

Then Tom Garrison, a new butcher in town, started coming around to see Grandmom Faya. He lost his wife four years earlier to cancer. He was a nice man.

A few weeks before he met Grandmom Faya, he moved to Maron. Then she came into his store to buy some meat, and they hit it off right away. She told us how he immediately came on to her. Right there in the store, in front of fifteen other people!

Tom and his wife never had any children. So he adopted us as his 'grandchildren'. Grandmom Faya explained to him that she was really our 'aunt'. But it didn't matter to him. He cared about all of us!

As a butcher, Tom was very hard and muscular. Especially for a man his age! And he was big! The hair at his temples was graying. But the rest of his hair was the natural dark brown color. He was a handsome man. And I patted Grandmom Faya on her back for obtaining such a 'good catch'! I really hadn't thought that she was interested in men anymore. But what did I know?!

My siblings and I, as well as my sister-in-law, all referred to Faya as 'Grandmom', and we called Miss Miriam "Grandmom Miriam" to keep down confusion for little Nicola's sake!

The eerie, spooky events which had been going on in our house were still happening. But not as much or as severe. Malin, in fact, was the only one who had seen anybody! It was before he left for college! Other than that, nobody had been bothered by anything or anyone since that Halloween night when the woman we believed to be 'Marie' had stood in the middle of our dining room floor glaring at us!

However, her spirit did make its presence known occasionally. Not only *her* spirit but *others* as well. Rooms in the house would suddenly become so cold and frigid we couldn't stay in them. Also, things would move by themselves, steps would creak loudly as if somebody was walking up and down them. The toilets were always flushing by themselves when nobody was in the bathroom. And many other spooky things would occur!

Before Malin left for college, he had seen "Teresa" so often that when he wrote home from school, he asked about her like she was a living person. The first time he'd actually seen her though was when he had just stepped out of the bathroom one night. There she was right in front of him when he opened the bathroom door! She startled him! However, he later told us that he thought she was just a friend of mine or Emma's who was visiting and had needed to use the bathroom upstairs.

"Excuse me," was all he said to her as he walked past her to go downstairs. Once he got downstairs, he told Grandmom Faya about 'the girl' who scared him half to death as he stepped out of the bathroom. He asked them who she was. "What girl?!" asked Grandmom Faya. "The girl who just came upstairs to use the bathroom," he told her.

Grandmom Faya and Grandmom Miriam looked at one another strangely. Shrugging, Malin said, "I guess she'll be back downstairs in a minute." "I don't think so, Malin," said Grandmom Miriam. Then, she asked him, "What did she look like?" "She was real cute!" Malin answered with a grin. "Describe her!" insisted Grandmom Faya.

My brother gave them a brief description of 'the girl'. As they listened to him, they realized he was describing "Teresa" right down to every detail of her appearance as she looked in life.

"Just a minute," said Grandmom Faya. She got up and went to her bedroom where she got a photograph of Teresa from the metal box at the top of her closet. Then, she hurried back downstairs to show my brother the picture. "That's her!" cried Malin, surprised. "Oh my God!" cried Grandmom Miriam. "What?" asked Malin. "What is it?" "Malin," said Grandmom Miriam slowly, "you just saw your mother, Teresa!"

Malin was so afraid after that, he wouldn't go back up those stairs that night for anything. He couldn't sleep at all either that night. Both of our 'grandmothers' sat up with him until he finally dozed off to sleep. Sitting in a living room chair! It was the wee hours of the morning by then.

They were always on guard because the 'others' as they called them had been quiet for too long. And they figured 'Teresa' was hanging around for a reason. They knew that something was going to happen sooner or later. And whatever it was certainly wouldn't be good.

Linda kept a watchful eye on Nicola too. On two different occasions, he was asked about his invisible 'friend'. When asked, he described his invisible 'friend' to his mother as a lady with dark-red hair and dressed all in black! Right away, Linda knew it was the spirit of Marie.

But except for that, our family gave a lot of credit for the peace that we enjoyed in our house to a renewed effort on the part of all of us to pray day and night. Especially to reciting the twenty-third Psalm that Marie loathed so much.

Another strange thing we began to experience was the fact that somebody else was living in the house with us. It wasn't one of our '*ghostly'* inhabitants either. We noticed portions of food missing that none of us had eaten. Appliances were being used and sometimes left running. Also, personal items would be missing then found in places where they should not have been.

One night, little Nicola awakened by a bad dream got up from his bed to go to the bathroom. When he opened the bathroom door, he told us that a dark-colored woman with dark brown hair and light brown eyes was standing there looking down at him.

"Nicola," she whispered to him. "Don't tell anybody that you saw me okay? It will be our little secret." Indeed, he never told anybody until much later on after a long series of other events occurred in our house. Curiously, he asked the 'lady' who she was.

"I'm Charon," she told him. "And I'm your great-aunt. I've been living here for a long long time. But nobody knows it. So you can't tell anybody! Okay sweetheart? It's our secret!" "Okay Aunt Charon," he told her. He kept their secret! He used the bathroom then went back to his bed and went to sleep.

After that, he and 'Aunt Charon' had many secret nightly rendezvous while everyone else in the house would be asleep. They would always play games together. She would even come to his bedroom and awaken him. Then they would go down to the kitchen and make hot cocoa with marshmallows in it. Just the way that he liked it! Nicola liked his 'Aunt Charon'.

"Aunt Charon, why don't you let the others know that you're here?" Nicola asked her one night during one of their secret meetings. "Baby boy," she said using her *pet name* for him, "I've done some very bad things in the past. Because I was so angry with my family. But now I'm sorry. And too ashamed to face them again. And ask for their forgiveness."

"I forgive you Aunt Charon," Nicola told her solemnly. "So I know they will forgive you too if you ask them." Hearing those words, Charon wrapped him in her arms. She had truly grown to love that dear little boy who was her only company. He eased the loneliness that she felt tremendously. She looked forward to their secret nightly meetings.

Charon thought of all of the times that she stood over Grandmom Faya and Grandmom Miriam while they were sleeping in their beds at night. She wanted to talk to them but just didn't have the courage to do it. "Not yet!" She told herself.

"We are buddies, you and I, Baby Boy," Charon told Nicola. "And when the time is right, I'll go to them. I promise you okay?" "Okay," he said to her happily. His trusting loving eyes looking into hers. Then she looked out of the window and saw it was almost daybreak. "It's going to be light outside soon sweetheart," she whispered to Nicola. "We'd better get you back to bed now."

"Okay Aunt Charon," he whispered back to her. She carried him back to his bed tucked him in and kissed him on the forehead. "I'll see you tomorrow Baby Boy," she said to him softly. Then kissed him again on his cheek.

"See you tomorrow Aunt Charon," he whispered to her.

Linda often wondered why Nicola slept so late in the mornings. But she didn't worry about it too much. He was healthy and nothing seemed to be bothering him. There was no need for her to worry.

Charon made her way back to her hiding place, which was a room in the basement of the house that everybody had completely forgotten about. It hadn't been used for many years. Also, the room could be accessed by a hidden door in the living room floor. The panels of the door perfectly matched the floor panels so no one ever guessed that it was a door leading into the basement.

Only the coffee table covered the spot and both our 'grandmothers' often wondered why the table had always been moved slightly each morning. It was so well hidden that there was no way to know that the door was there in the floor if you didn't know about it already.

Although we didn't know it at the time, Charon also helped us to keep peace in that house. She read the Bible every day and prayed just like we did. Also, she burned white candles to ward off evil spirits! By helping us, she felt that she could make up for some of the hurt that she caused so many years before. Fortunately, she was no longer under Marie's control. She hadn't been for a long time.

Smiling, Charon thought about the little boy asleep upstairs. She would do anything to protect him! After all, he was the only bright spot in her lonely life! She told herself that she needed to reveal herself to the family soon. She promised Nicola that she would. And lately, she hadn't been feeling very well.

Her left arm was almost numb sometimes! And she was having severe pains in the middle of her chest. Fearfully, she knew the warning signs of heart failure. And she had run out of her medication three days before.

Doc Walker was Charon's long-time friend and confidante. Also, he was one of the only two people who knew she had been living in that house for all of those years. He always made sure that she got her heart medicine. But she hadn't heard from him lately. "*Something is wrong*," she thought.

As she laid down on her small bed, she decided that in the morning she would try to get word to Doc through Patrick, our mailman. When Doc Walker had examined Charon, he found that her blood pressure was so high, she was on the verge of having a stroke! He gave her medication to control it.

But the side effects were that it would affect her heart. He told her not to worry because they would be minimal. He was wrong! By the time he gave her a better medication, it was too late! The damage had already been done to her heart.

Charon was afraid to let him touch her sometimes because he smelled like a bottle of gin. But she had no other choice! Besides, she knew she could trust him.

Patrick Davies was the postman in Maron after Bernie passed away a year before. He and Doc Walker worked hand-in-hand to make sure that Charon got her medication. They kept her 'secret' too. She would wait until everyone in the house was asleep at night. Then, she would go to the front porch. There, on the side of the stoop, under a hedge, would be a carefully wrapped package for her from Doc Walker. However, lately, there had been no package for her.

The next night when Nicola went to bed Linda read him a bedtime story. He fell off to sleep with a happy little smile on his angelic face. He awakened at five thirty that morning and looked out of the window. It was beginning to get light outside. Everyone was still asleep. But someone had awakened him. It was Aunt Charon! He rubbed his eyes.

"Aunt Charon," he said with disappointment. "You're late! It's almost time for everybody to get up! We won't have time to play!" Then he noticed that she looked different that morning. She was beautiful. And there was a glow around her. She was smiling at him.

"Baby Boy," she said sadly, "we won't be able to play at night anymore okay?" "Why not, Aunt Charon?" he asked her. They were both whispering. He had no way of knowing that only *he* could see and hear her then.

"I'm going home now, sweetheart," Charon said to him happily. "But you're already home, Aunt Charon," Nicola said, confusion on his delicate little face. He didn't understand what she was saying to him.

"One day you will understand, honey," said Charon sweetly. "But I'm not talking about this house here. I won't see you anymore." "No!" cried Nicola, his face breaking up to sob. "Shhh!" Charon put her finger to her lips, telling him to be quiet. "You don't want to wake anyone up, do you?" she asked him.

"No," he replied, his lower lip quivering. "Don't be sad, Baby Boy," she said. "I'm happy now! Be glad for me, okay? I'm free!" "But," said Nicola, "I don't want you to go! Don't leave me behind, Aunt Charon. Take me with you!" "Oh, sugar," she said. "I can't take you with me now. But I promise you, when it's your time, I'll come back for you. No one else but me, okay?" "Okay, Aunt Charon," said Nicola.

"Listen," she said, "I'll miss you! But you'll be alright now!" Aunt Charon looked so beautiful to him. And her smiling face was filled with peace and happiness. He didn't cry. "So, I *will* see you again?!" he asked her. "You sure will, honey," she answered him with a big smile. "One day, you'll certainly see me again. I promise you that! You're going to have a happy and full life, Nicola. Now, I have to go! So you go on back to sleep, okay?"

He reached for her so that he could give her a hug and a kiss, like he always did. But she stopped him. "No, sweetheart," she said, "you can't touch me. But remember, 'Aunt Charon' loves you very much. And I always will, alright?" "Alright, Aunt Charon," he replied sleepily. Then he turned over in his bed and closed his eyes to go back to sleep.

Being a small child at the time, Nicola didn't know that it was the spirit of his beloved Aunt Charon that came to his bedside that morning to say goodbye to him. She suffered a massive heart attack in her sleep only a half an hour earlier. It would be five days before her body would be discovered. There was an unbearable odor that permeated our house. Also, it was at this time that Nicola would reveal to Linda finally everything that happened to him with his dear Aunt Charon!

CHAPTER FIFTEEN

Two days after 'Aunt Charon' died, unbeknown to us, all of the peace our family had enjoyed in that house began to slowly deteriorate. The presence of evil was felt strongly by everybody in that house. Especially by myself and my sister. Grandmom Faya had the house blessed all over again. But we knew that something was terribly wrong. We didn't know that the presence of death was what we were also feeling. In the next few days, everything would fall into place for us.

Early the following Wednesday morning, Grandmom Faya got up to make breakfast. Everybody else was still asleep. As soon as she started down the stairs, she got a whiff of the most horrid odor that she ever smelled. All of us had been smelling the awful odor for days. But this particular day, it was stronger than ever.

At first, we dismissed it thinking there must have been a dead animal around somewhere. But as the odor grew stronger, we knew it had to be something else.

"My God! That's a terrible smell!" Grandmom Faya blurted out as she stepped into the living room that morning. "I can't stand it! We have to find out what that is!" She opened all of the windows and the front and back doors to let some fresh air into the house. Then she woke everybody up.

"Come on, get up!" she told us. "We've got to search this place and find whatever it is that's causing that horrible smell!" As each one of us awakened, we caught the putrid odor. It almost gagged us, it was so bad. "Ugh!" said Linda disgustedly. "Something is dead in this house!"

Spreading out, we began to search the house from top to bottom. "It seems to be stronger here in the living room," said Nicholas. He was standing right next to the coffee table. Suddenly, Grandmom Faya yelled and scared all of us. "Oh Lord!! I remember now!!" "What?!" asked Nicholas, looking confused. "There's a room right below the floor where you're standing, Nicholas!" she said.

Quickly, they moved the coffee table out of the way and found the trap door leading to Charon's hidden room. The odor grew even stronger. "Oh yeah," said Linda, gagging slightly. "Whatever it is, it's down there!"

As soon as Nicholas opened the trap door, the terrible smell of dead flesh was so powerful, we were barely able to breathe. Looking down into the room, it was dark. But, he could barely make out the form of a woman, lying on a small cot.

"It's a woman, Grandmom Faya!!" shouted Nicholas, stunned. He jumped back, so he could breathe some fresh air. "She's dead!!" he gasped. "Who in the world is she?!" Grandmom Miriam asked, worriedly. "I wonder how long she's been down there?!" "We'd better not touch anything else," said Grandmom Faya. "I'll call Sheriff Bicket!"

Sheriff Bicket arrived on the scene, with two of his Deputies, and the Coroner. Grandmom Faya, and the rest of us stayed outside. Because, we couldn't bear the terrible stench of dead flesh, any longer. The Sheriff called for assistance, to help him remove the body.

"We'd like to know who it is, when you bring her out," said Grandmom Faya. Sheriff Bicket put his hand on her shoulder, and said, gently, "Faya, it's your sister, Charon!" I think Grandmom Faya went into shock, at that time. She got so quiet. "Charon?!" cried Grandmom Miriam. "My, God!" The Coroner opened the plastic body bag, so we could see her face. "It's my Aunt Charon!" cried little Nicola, who had wanted to see who the person was, too.

"You know her?!" Linda asked him, surprised. "Yes," he said. "It's my Aunt Charon!" "*How* do you know her?" Nicholas asked him, sharply. "Aunt Charon said she was going home, and wouldn't see me, anymore!" Then, he proceeded to tell all of us about the '*secret*', nightly games, that he, and his Aunt Charon played, while everyone else in the house was asleep.

Our 'grandmothers' were not surprised that Charon had been living there, in that house, all of those years. Grandmom Faya remembered how Ethel's little boy had told his mother, about seeing a lady enter the house, long before we were to move in there.

"She must have truly changed," said Nicholas, "if she played with Nicola, every night. That's not the woman that I remember!" "You're right!" Emma agreed. "She must have changed a lot!" Grandmom Faya smiled, weakly, as the Coroner drove away with Charon's lifeless body. "Oh, Charon," she said, "why did it have to end like this?"

Grandmom Miriam put her arm around her shoulders. She, too, had tears in her eyes. Through all of the pain, and turmoil of the past, they had never stopped loving their baby sister. "She's at peace, now, Faya," said Grandmom Miriam. "If God can forgive her, so can we!" "Yes," said Grandmom Faya. "We can!"

Aunt Charon was buried in the family plot, behind our former house. Right next to Andrew, Jr. It was a solemn affair. And, all of us felt sorry that we didn't have the chance to forgive her. Even though she had been mean, and cruel to us, when we were children. It was obvious, from little Nicola, that she had, indeed, changed.

That same day, Doc Walker was buried, in the town cemetery. Patrick Davies told Grandmom Faya, and the rest of us, all about Aunt Charon's heart condition. And, how he, and Doc Walker had been looking out for her, for a long time. Also, he told us that Doc suffered a massive stroke, two weeks before that.

He had been in a coma, right up until the day that Aunt Charon's body was discovered, in our house. He never regained consciousness. And, he never revealed her 'secret' to anybody, other than Patrick. That was why Charon couldn't get anymore medication, which caused her death!

The Coroner told us that Charon died of a massive heart attack. Apparently, he said, he heart had been weakened. Without the medicine to control her blood pressure, her heart burst.

As Josie, and our 'grandmother's were cleaning out the little, hidden room, where Charon stayed, they realized that she *had* changed! Also, they realized the reason the house had been so peaceful, was because she became a hindrance to the evil one, who controlled her, for so long! Aunt Charon held Marie's spirit at bay, through her prayers. And, the daily reading of the Bible. They found it, lying next to the cot that she slept on. But, with Charon now gone, Grandmom Faya, and Grandmom Miriam, both, knew that Marie's evil spirit would become more aggressive, than ever.

They cried, when they saw the walls of that little room, covered with drawings that little Nicola made for his dear, Aunt Charon. Each one of them was signed with the words, "*I love you*", at the bottom, in a three year old's scrawl. Nobody at the funeral had taken Charon's death as hard as my little nephew did.

CHAPTER SIXTEEN

Time passed by. Autumn turned into winter. Winter turned into spring. Spring turned into summer. And summer turned into autumn again. Malin arrived home from school and announced that he was going to attend a school closer to home. He wanted to be near the family now after being away for so long.

However, he had declined to come home for Aunt Charon's funeral. He still couldn't find it in his heart to forgive her, no matter how much she had changed before she died. During that time, our family welcomed the new arrival of Angelina Mae Davidson, the second child of Linda and Nicholas.

While at the movies one night with Ray, Emma met another young man named Oliver Turner. She decided *he* was the man that she'd been waiting for all of her life. She wanted to marry him. Ray was devastated when she broke up with him. And our family also was stunned. Emma set her wedding date for the following summer.

Oliver was five years older than Emma was. He was tall, dark, and handsome. He claimed to never have been married before. Coming from a wealthy family, he was unspoiled, unselfish, kind, and considerate. Or so we thought. Emma was very happy with him at first. Yet both of the 'grandmothers' detested him. They said that they didn't know why. But there was just something about him. He came from Watsonville, a little borough of maybe four thousand people, which was about one hundred miles away from Maron.

Only rich people lived in Watsonville. They had yachts and sprawling estates. We passed through there a few times in the car. But we never knew anybody who lived there. It was fun sometimes, though, to go out for drives with the grandmothers and go through Watsonville pretending we owned one of those huge mansions there.

Oliver was the only child of elderly parents. Emma's wedding would be the *second* wedding in our family. Grandmom Faya finally decided to marry Mr.

Tom, whom she'd been seeing on a regular basis for quite some time by then. At least a year. Their wedding was set for New Year's Eve.

As for myself, I could hardly keep my mind on anything except counting the days until Gary came home for a late semester break in the fall. I truly missed him! Work was getting boring at the Sheriff's office by then. I began to think about other areas of work. I would be twenty-one years old that coming Halloween.

Emma and I became even more beautiful the older we got. Also, we discovered what the '*powers'* were that both 'grandmothers' told us about. The two older women taught us to always use them carefully for good and never for evil. Neither of us really wanted them. But we had no choice. We inherited them.

"If you love and you are loved," Grandmom Faya told us, "you won't be able to use your powers for anything but good!" And that we found out was absolutely true! It just wasn't in us to hurt people. We would talk to many different people that we would meet in various places. They always seemed to open up to us and tell us their problems. It was fascinating. Complete strangers that we had never seen before would just begin to talk to us about something that was bothering them.

When that would happen, Emma and I would go home, and with different mixtures of concoctions and '*spells,*' we would help those people to eradicate their problems and concerns. It worked every time! We knew it did. Because when we saw those same people again, they would tell us how their problems suddenly disappeared. We would smile at them and tell them how happy we were for them. "It's a shame we can't get rid of our own problems in this house," Emma said to me one day. She was right! No matter what we did, it always worked for other people. But never for us. "It's crazy, isn't it?" she asked. I agreed.

Despite not being able to help ourselves, we were very happy knowing we had helped others. It was a good feeling, too. I shared our experiences with Gary, too. He was very supportive. I told him about my '*gift*' when we first started going out and about my family.

One morning, I was staring out of my bedroom window, daydreaming. Gary called me on the telephone the night before to tell me that he would be driving home around noon that day. He couldn't wait to see me and told me how much he missed me. I couldn't wait to see him, either.

As I stood there by the window, lost in my thoughts, I heard a voice behind me. It was a woman's voice! Quickly, I turned around because it startled me. There stood the spirit of the woman that we saw that Halloween night many years before. She was dressed completely in black as she had been that night. And her eyes blazed with anger like fire.

"Did you hear me, girl?" The spirit hissed at me. *"What do you want?"* I retorted, a little frightened. *"You know what I want, girl!"* The spirit spat at me. *"Do you really think that boy cares about you? Well, he doesn't! You're MY daughter! No man can ever love you because you're just like me!"*

From somewhere inside me, I got courage. "I am NOTHING like you!" I said to the demon. "You're a liar! We are going to destroy you once and for all!" I was not afraid of her anymore. But the spirit laughed at me. It was an evil sinister laugh. *"And who pray tell is going to do that? You?"* the spirit sneered. Suddenly, the room felt like a freezer. It got so cold. It was filled with her demonic presence.

"You're not afraid of me anymore, are you, girl?" she asked. *"Faya and Miriam are teaching you well!"* Then she laughed again. Her ugly laughter was bone-chilling, and it seemed to echo throughout the whole room. But I was still not afraid of her. "Get out of here in the Name of The Lord!" I shouted at her spirit.

Immediately, I saw the demon become visibly shaken. But it quickly regained its composure. The room darkened. But I could still see her. The spirit of a man appeared next to her, a spirit just as evil and wicked as hers, if not more so.

"You can't fight us both!" he told me. *"You're coming with us soon. You AND your sister. There is nothing you or anyone else can do to stop us, either!"* I knew right away that the man had to be the spirit of Roy Oberon, my grandfather. Defiantly, I faced them both. "You will stay away from me, my sister, and the rest of our family," I told them. "I rebuke you BOTH in the Name of The Lord Jesus!" Both spirits vanished quickly, and my bedroom brightened up and was warm and cozy again.

"Tyla!" Grandmom Miriam yelled, knocking at my bedroom door frantically. "Honey, are you alright in there?" Without waiting for me to answer her, she flung open my bedroom door and stepped inside. She could feel the cold icy chill left behind by the two demonic spirits and shuddered.

"Are you okay, honey?" she asked again, looking at me closely. "Yes," I said with a sigh. The rest of the family at home then came running up the stairs and into my bedroom. "Tyla, who were you screaming at, honey?" asked Grandmom Faya breathlessly as she entered the room. I told them what had happened. Grandmom Miriam sat down on my bed, and Emma put her arms around my shoulders.

"It's getting near to their time," said Grandmom Faya, "and they know it. Charon certainly put a dent into their evil scheme against us by holding them back as long as she did!" Grandmom Miriam got up from the bed and walked over to me. She put her arms around both Emma and me. "Don't worry, darlings," she told us. "Tyla, you did the right thing. But the next time, SCREAM!"

"That's right," Grandmom Faya added seriously. "Let's see how well they can handle all of us together!" "They can't hurt anyone else, can they?" asked Linda. "What do you mean, honey?" Grandmom Miriam asked her as she turned to look at Linda. "You know," said Linda, her voice filled with concern. "Like a person very close to you, meaning the family?"

"Why do you ask that, Linda?" Grandmom Miriam wanted to know. "Well," replied Linda, "I had a dream last night." "Oh, really?" said Emma sarcastically. "Well, dear sister-in-law, you're definitely in the right house for that!" "Hush up, girl!" Grandmom Faya told her. Then she looked at Linda. "What did you dream about, sweetheart?"

Linda took a deep breath. Then, let it out, sharply. She sat down on my bed. "I dream of a terrible car accident," she told us. "I couldn't see who was driving the car. All I saw in the dream was a red car with black stripes on its sides!"

"Oh no!!" I cried, terror gripping my heart. "That's Gary's car! He just bought it! He sent me a photograph of it! He's driving home and told me he would be here by noon today!" Grandmom Faya hugged me tightly. I could see the worry on her pretty face.

"Oh, Grandmom Faya," I cried, "what are we going to do? He told me that when he gets to Brewer, he would call me again!" Brewer was sixty miles away from Maron. I was in a state of panic by then. Both my 'grandmothers' tried their best to calm me down. "Did he give you a time when he would call you from Brewer, Tyla?" asked Grandmom Faya.

"Yes," I told her, recalling our telephone conversation. "He said he would call me around ten thirty this morning!" I was in tears by then. "Well," she said matter-of-factly, "there's nothing that we can do until he telephones. So, let's all keep calm!"

"Neither Marie nor Roy can touch him outside of this county," added Grandmom Miriam. "Really, are you sure?" I asked, somewhat relieved. "How do you know?" "Because," she said smugly, "he's not connected to us yet, Tyla, honey. Not until he marries you!"

"Oh, thank God!" I said, the relief flooding my body. "We'll just wait for his phone call, Ty," said Grandmom Faya. "Then, I'll tell him what to do to make sure he arrives here safely. You have to trust me, Tyla, and he'll have to trust me too! Do you think he will?"

"Oh yes, Grandmom Faya," I replied with certainty. "I'll make him!" "Good!" she said with a smile. "We won't let anything happen to Gary, Tyla, sweetheart. Okay?" I nodded. I could feel the tears welling up in my eyes. I wiped them away. I knew what both Grandmom Faya and Grandmom Miriam were capable of. All of us trusted them implicitly.

There was nothing for us to do but wait for Gary's telephone call. So, we went downstairs to the kitchen. No one felt like talking. I was still somewhat worried. So, Grandmom Faya held my hand and continued to try to console me.

When the telephone finally rang, all of us nearly jumped out of our skins. I grabbed it and said into the receiver, "Hello?" "Hey, baby!" It was Gary on the other end of the line. "Gary, please, listen to me," I spoke rapidly into the telephone receiver. Immediately, he noticed the anguish in my voice and asked me, "What's wrong, sweetheart?"

"Grandmom Faya is going to tell you something, Gary," I explained to him. "You must listen to her carefully and do exactly as she tells you to do, okay?" "Sure, baby," he said. Then he asked me again, "So, what's wrong?" "You do trust me, don't you, Gary?" I asked him. "You know I do, baby," he replied sweetly. "So, what's the matter? You're scaring me!"

"We'll explain everything to you when you get here," I said. "But for now, it's very important that you do what my grandmother tells you to do! Please! Do it for me! No matter how crazy it may sound to you, Gary," I pleaded. "Okay, honey," he replied in a reassuring voice. "I will!" Then, I gave the telephone receiver to Grandmom Faya. "Hi, Gary," she said in a friendly voice so he wouldn't be afraid. "Hi, Miss Faya," he responded, anxiously waiting to hear what she had to say.

"This is what I want you to do, Gary," she told him. "It's important that you do just as I tell you, too. Do you understand me?" "Yes, Ma'am," he told her. "Okay," she said. "Is there a store near where you are now?" she asked him.

"Yes," he replied. "There's one right across the street from where I am." "Good," she said. "I want you to go in there and buy a bottle of olive oil, a whole clove of garlic, and a box of plain salt, right now! I'll hang onto the line until you come back to the phone. Go now!" "Okay," he said. He laid the telephone receiver down, told a person standing nearby that he was coming right back, then went to do as Grandmom Faya had instructed him to do.

About ten minutes later, he came back on the line. "Miss Faya?" he said. "I got everything that you told me to get." "You are sure you have everything?" asked Grandmom Faya. "Yes, Ma'am," he replied. "Now, what?"

"I want you to get a bucket," she told him. "I know you have something like that in the trunk of your car. If not, you'll have to go back to the store and buy one!" "I have one in the car," he assured her.

"Fill the bucket only halfway with water," she told Gary. "Do that now, while I wait!" "Okay," Gary said. He got the bucket from his car and ran up the street to a little coffee shop for the water. Then, he returned to the telephone. "Okay, Miss Faya," he said, panting. "I filled it halfway!"

"You're doing fine," she told him. "Now, pour the whole bottle of olive oil into the water, then the whole box of salt, okay?" "Okay," he replied, leaving the phone again to do as she told him. When he had done that, he grabbed the telephone receiver and said, "Okay, it's all in!"

"Alright," said Grandmom Faya. "Now, break the garlic apart into separate pieces and put them into the water also. Then, mix it all up with your right hand." Dropping the telephone receiver again, Gary broke the garlic up and dumped it into the bucket, stirring the concoction with his right hand. Then, he picked the receiver up and said, "Okay, what's next?"

"Now," she said patiently. "I want you to take a clean rag from the trunk of your car, Gary. I know you have rags in the trunk of your car." Gary later told me that he was confused and had asked himself, "How does she know that I have all that stuff in the trunk of my car?" As if she was reading his mind, Grandmom Faya said, "I've never known a man to buy a new car and NOT keep a bucket and clean rags in the trunk to wash it with!"

"What do I do now?" he asked her nervously, wondering if she was really reading his mind. "Now, I want you to wipe that car down, Gary," she told him. "Do it thoroughly, inside and out. Don't miss one spot, understand?" "What?!" he asked, surprised. "Gary," she said firmly. "I thought you were going to trust me and do what I tell you to do?"

"Yes, I will," he said meekly. "Well, then, you have to do this! DO NOT MOVE that car one inch until you have done it!" she spoke to him sternly, trying to empathize the importance of what she was having him do. "Is that clear?!" she asked.

"Yes, Ma'am," Gary said, a little bewildered. "We'll see you when you get here," said Grandmom Faya sweetly. "Miss Faya?" asked Gary quickly before they hung up. "Yes, Gary?" she said. "WHY am I doing all of this stuff?!" "Just believe me, Gary," she answered. "You won't be sorry that you did it! Even if it sounds crazy and weird to you! Just do it, okay?"

"Alright, Miss Faya," he told her. "Tell Ty that I love her!" "I will, Gary," she said and hung up the telephone. Grandmom Faya put her arms around me, and I started to sob softly. I didn't know what I would have done if something had happened to my beloved Gary that day.

"Everything is going to be alright, Tyla, honey," Grandmom Faya said softly. "You'll see!" It would take Gary at least an hour and a half to reach Maron, considering the time he would need to wipe the car down thoroughly. My family and I began to pray for his safety.

As I prayed, I began to reflect on our relationship and the future that he and I planned together. Soon, he would be home from school for good. But now, I understood fully, for the first time, just what our 'grandmothers' were really up against in our house. So did Emma and Linda.

Those evil demons from the pit of hell itself had to be destroyed. They had plagued our family in life as well as in death for far too many years. Now, it was time, as Grandmom Faya put it, "for them to go!"

Looking at the clock on the kitchen wall, I realized that I had been so preoccupied with my thoughts, time had passed quickly. A half hour more, and my beloved would be home. Wearily, I laid my head down on the kitchen table. As the other women talked among themselves softly, I drifted off to sleep and began to dream.

Suddenly, I was standing under the big oak tree down by the lake with another man. Instantly, I knew it was my father, Andrew. He was dressed in a beautifully tailored gray suit. Beside him were two beautiful little children. They stood silently, each of them holding one of his hands. They were dressed all in white, a little boy and a little girl. I guessed they were around two and three years old.

Hi, Tyla," the spirit spoke to me warmly. "Are you my father?" I asked the ghostly figure. "Yes, Tyla," he answered with a smile, "and these are your children!" He told me their names, but strangely, I couldn't hear them. I knew in the dream that I was not meant to KNOW their names. I smiled. "MY children?" I repeated, overjoyed with happiness. "That means that Gary will be alright! He'll be safe!"

"Oh, yes, Tyla," my father's spirit replied. "Gary will be just fine. Thanks to Faya and Linda, who received the warning through a dream. Also, you and your children will be safe! You'll see! On your twenty-first birthday, everything evil around you will come to an end, forever. You're going to be happy for the rest of your life, Tyla! Just be strong. And listen to Faya and Miriam. They know what they are doing. Trust them, always! Okay?"

"I will" I replied, still smiling as I looked at the two children. Then the spirit and the children turned and walked away from me. As I stood there watching them, they vanished right before my eyes. "Ty! Tyla, wake up!" Someone was excitedly shaking me awake. It was Emma. I opened my eyes. There stood Gary, safe and sound.

"Oh, Gary!" I cried, jumping up from the kitchen table and throwing myself into his arms. We kissed each other passionately, oblivious to everyone else in the kitchen or in the world for that matter.

"Wow!" said Gary. "That's well worth coming home to any time!" "You two need to be alone for a while" Grandmom Faya said with a smile. "But first, Tyla, Miriam, and I would like to have a talk with Gary. If you don't mind." "I don't mind, randmom Faya" I said. Then I went into the dining room to sit down.

My 'grandmothers' made it clear to everybody that they wanted to talk to Gary alone. Everybody left the kitchen. But from where I sat, I could still see them. They spoke with Gary for hours. I watched the expression on his face as the two women told him about the things that had gone on in our family. Grandmom Faya told him WHY he had to wipe his car down with the items that she asked him to buy. He listened to them intently, paying careful attention to all that they told him.

"I wonder if he'll still want to marry me after this?" I thought. But I need not have worried. When their conversation was over, the three of them began to laugh and joke among themselves. I felt relief.

Gary came into the dining room where I was sitting and pulled up a chair beside me. He was smiling at me tenderly. He reached for my hand and said with a grin, "Wow! You have quite a family history, Tyla Davidson Shelley! But there is nothing on this earth, living or dead, that will ever keep us apart" he said sincerely as he looked deeply into my eyes.

My eyes welled up with tears of joy. "I am so lucky to have this wonderful young man in my life!" I thought. Then I snuggled into his arms.

Gary gently kissed each of my eyelids, one at a time. Then we went into the living room and silently sat down on the sofa. We watched television for the rest of that afternoon. That evening, Gary stayed for dinner. Then he and I went out for a long walk. We called it an early night since he was tired from the long drive home that morning. Also, I was exhausted.

CHAPTER SEVENTEEN

Autumn went by quickly. And soon it was the end of December. It was the day before Grandmom Faya's wedding. The house was alive with hustle and bustle as everyone got the place ready for the ceremony. All of the decorations were put up the previous night. But there was still food to be prepared as well as a few last-minute details to be ironed out. To everybody's surprise, Grandmom Faya allowed Mr. Tom to invite a lot of people from in town to the wedding.

"Can you believe Grandmom Faya is getting married for the first time at her age?" Emma asked me. "It is something, isn't it?" I replied with a smile. Everybody in the house was laughing and having fun. It was a very joyous time for all of us.

My best friend, Karen, came back to Maron after she had been gone for nearly two years. To my surprise, she brought a man home with her. His name was Billy Cartier, and they met in college. I never asked her what happened to her professed life of lesbianism. And she never told me. But I was happy for her.

Karen's mother passed away that previous year. Neither she nor her father knew that Miss Jacqueline had liver cancer until one month before she died. Karen was devastated. Her mother kept up a good front for her and Mr. Otto, her father. She never wanted them to feel obligated to her in any way. Also, she didn't want them to feel sad and sorry for her. Yet her passing hit them both very hard.

Apparently, Mr. Otto never stopped seeing Olivia. They got married six months after Jacqueline Bullock's death. The disrespect to her mother's memory angered Karen deeply. It strained her relationship with her father for a long time. She vowed never to speak to Mr. Otto again as long as he stayed married to Olivia.

Billy and Karen lived together in a small house that they bought in Maron. They were happy together. I was envious of them. But I knew Gary and I would be married soon. And live as happily together as they did. I thought about Gary's family and slipped into one of my day-dreams.

Gary's two sisters, Amelia and Dana, were teenagers. They adored their brother and they loved me. Often, they would spend the night with my sister and me. I heard stories about "in-laws" before that, and they were not very good. But it certainly didn't apply to my future "in-laws".

MaryAnne Shelley, Gary's mother, was a sweet, soft-spoken, intelligent woman from a well-to-do family herself. She was only seventeen, she told me, when she gave birth to Gary, who was her second child.

Mark, her oldest son, had been murdered by a drunk driver just before they moved from Vaira County to Maron. He was two years older than Gary. And she almost suffered a nervous breakdown when he was killed.

I saw a lot of photographs of Mark Shelley. He had been just as handsome as Gary was. They looked a lot alike. Gary's family became a part of a counseling group. And it helped their family cope with the loss of Mark. Also, it helped Miss MaryAnne to hold onto her sanity.

Ernest Shelley, Gary's father, was very nice too. He was a kind-hearted man who loved people! He was extremely outgoing and loved to have fun. He was the life of the party wherever he went. People loved being around Mr. Ernest! He was loud at times. But Gary confided in us that his father had a hearing problem in his right ear, a problem he incurred while on a tenure in the Armed Forces.

Mr. Ernest refused to wear a hearing aid! He didn't want people to know that he had a hearing problem. I thought that was silly because most modern-day hearing aids couldn't be easily seen. But he came from a family who liked perfection and tolerated nothing that was flawed, especially people.

I met them all one time, and I never cared if I ever saw any of them again. They were people who looked down their noses at others! Very snooty and high and mighty! Snobs!! I didn't like that, and neither did Gary's mother, MaryAnne. She told me how they gave her a bad time when she and Mr. Ernest ran off and got married! They had to elope because his family didn't approve of their marriage.

In my opinion, Mr. Ernest's family was crazy to think that people didn't have faults or flaws! *"Where in the world did these people come from?"* I wondered to myself. Nobody was perfect! But God Almighty! Didn't they know that? *It was obvious that they didn't!* Truly silly people! Over all of the years that Gary and I were together, we never bothered much with Mr. Ernest's family unless it was a critical situation, such as a death in the family or something!

Gary's father, Mr. Ernest, was raised by parents who wanted perfect children. And they tried to hide their son's hearing problem from people by not acknowledging that he had one! It didn't matter that it wasn't Mr. Ernest's fault! It was an injury that he incurred during his time in the Service. Their wanting *perfection* made Mr. Ernest feel bad. They even had people thinking he might be a little 'slow,' when in reality, he was no such thing!

A caring friend helped Mr. Ernest to cope with his parents. He understood his dilemma, coming from a similar kind of family himself. Needless to say, Ernest Shelley's parents didn't make a very good impression on people who knew them and knew how they were! "That's the only way he copes with them," Gary told me and my family once. "How sad!" Grandmom Miriam commented.

Gary's parents and sisters loved me and my family though. They could hardly wait until that next Autumn when it would be time for our wedding. Emma still planned to marry Oliver Turner. Our weddings were barely one month apart. I couldn't wait either! I became giddy with excitement just thinking about it.

Soon, it was New Year's Eve! Everything was ready for the wedding. Around ten o'clock that night, we started to get dressed because the ceremony was to begin at midnight! Most of the guests began to arrive around eleven o'clock. And soon the whole house was filled with people, laughter, and joyous conversation.

Then BAM! Every light in the house suddenly went out for no reason! It was pitch black inside. We couldn't even see our hands before our faces! "Maybe it's the circuit breaker," said Nicholas. But when he and Mr. Tom checked, the circuit breaker box was fine. All of the switches were on! Looking out of the window toward the town, we could see that the lights were on in all of the other homes and buildings. Ours was the only house in the dark.

"Oh my," Gary's mother MaryAnne exclaimed. "It's as cold as ice in here!" She was right! Everybody in the house felt the sudden icy chill that came out of nowhere. "Look!" cried Amelia, pointing toward the stairs.

There was an eerie strange light at the top of the stairs. It had a dark depressing red glow, which began to spread out and cover every room in the house. The *presence of something unnatural and frightening* was felt by everybody in the house. And nobody spoke or moved!

It was as silent as a tomb inside the house that night. Then everybody heard the soft sinister laughter of a woman. It was so wicked it sent chills down our spines. The *laughter* came from the top of the staircase.

Just then, Grandmom Faya came out of her bedroom dressed in a beautiful white laced wedding gown. Grandmom Miriam was with her. "It's pitch black in here!" exclaimed Grandmom Miriam. "What happened to all of the lights?!" "Is everybody okay down there?!" yelled Grandmom Faya to all of us there. "Yes!" cried Emma. "We're all okay down here, Grandmom Faya!" Then we heard her speak to the weird mysterious ghostly red glowing light. "Who are you?!" she asked, although she knew what the sinister apparition was doing there and who it probably was.

All of a sudden, the front door blew open violently, slamming against the wall hard. A strong wind swept through the house. Decorations were sent whirling everywhere! The wedding cake on the dining room table was *lifted* up by unseen hands and thrown to the floor! Our family as well as our guests could only watch and stare in fear as the scene unfolded. The light from the street outside enabled us to see a little. No one could move because we were all frightened.

A car drove up to the front of the house. We heard its door open, then close. Someone was walking toward the open front door. Then they knocked.

"Hello!" cried Reverend McIntosh. "Is anybody here?" He entered the house and was puzzled to see everybody standing and sitting around too scared to move or say anything. "What's going on in here?" he asked. Not one person answered him. But *someone else did.*

"Get out!!" shouted an evil, mysterious voice that couldn't possibly have been human. It came from the top of the stairs. Reverend McIntosh didn't move! He looked at the house full of terrified people who were surrounded by that evil red glow that seemed to fill the house.

"Will somebody please tell me what's going on in here?!" the Reverend asked again. He was confused but not frightened like the rest of us were. "Get out!" the inhuman voice shouted at him a second time. Everybody heard it. "You cannot help them, Preacher! So get out of here! Now!" the voice told him.

"No, I will NOT get out of here!!" Reverend McIntosh shouted back. "YOU get out of here! Now!" He knew he was speaking to *someone* so wicked and despicable it was unbelievable. He walked to the front of the staircase and looked up at the red light.

"YOU are NOT welcome here!!" he said. "Nor are you wanted here!! So BE GONE! RIGHT NOW! BE GONE, IN THE NAME OF CHRIST!" As soon as he said those words, both the evil glow and the eerie darkness that filled the house vanished! All of the lights immediately came back on, and everybody began to stir. Then they started talking, all at once, wondering what happened in there.

"Reverend, I'm so glad you're here!" Grandmom Faya said, relief in her voice. She and Grandmom Miriam joined the rest of us downstairs without our knowing it. "Now, you see what I was telling you about, don't you?" she asked him. "Yes, I do," he said sympathetically. "You really do have some problems in here, Faya!"

"The funny thing is," said Grandmom Miriam, "their 'visits' are becoming fewer and further apart now. But more violent! We don't know why!" "Well," said the Reverend, "we will need to do something about them, won't we?" Grandmom Faya smiled, taking his arm. "It's all going to be taken care of, Reverend," she told him confidently. "Believe me! In the meantime, come on into the kitchen and have a bite to eat!"

When Grandmom Faya led him into the kitchen where the food was, she immediately saw her beautiful wedding cake on the dining room floor, smashed to pieces. A look of sadness came upon her face. "Don't worry," Linda told her. "We'll get it cleaned up!" "Alright, everyone!" cried Grandmom Miriam. "We're going to have a wedding tonight! And a good time too! So relax and enjoy yourselves!" A few moments later, everything was back to normal.

The guests were talking and laughing as they helped us collect and restore the scattered wedding decorations. And by the time the wedding was over, Linda had made another cake for my grandmother and Mr. Tom. It wasn't as nice as the original one. But at least they had a wedding cake. The ceremony was absolutely beautiful. Grandmom Faya and Mr. Tom were truly happy and in love.

MaryAnne Shelley, Gary's mother, cried throughout the whole ceremony. "I always cry at these things," she told us, dabbing at her eyes with a tissue. house was full of laughter, and gaiety, that lasted well into the wee hours of the morning.

Grandmom Faya, and Mr. Tom left to go on their honeymoon, as soon as the sun started to rise. It was a brand new year. And, a brand new life, for both of them. We were so happy for them. They went to Bermuda, for two weeks. I think it was one of the few times that Grandmom Faya had ever been away from Maron, for so long.

When they returned home, from their honeymoon, both of them looked radiant! Married life agreed with both of them. "They truly love each other," Grandmom Miriam told Emma and I.

CHAPTER EIGHTEEN

Tom Garrison settled in with our family as if he had always been a part of it. And a part of us! He was a good, kind man. We loved him very much. And over time, we grew to love him more and more, as if he had always been our grandfather. I thought, "*My grandmother deserves someone like Mr. Tom!*" I recalled her words to me so many years before that. Before we moved into that house.

She told me, 'we would be bringing a lot of love into that house with us!' Her prophetic words came true! That love was 'the light' in the midst of the darkness that tried and was still trying to destroy our family. We had to stay in that *'light'*. Because if we did, eventually, we would be free! I thought about how lucky my siblings, our family, and I had been to have the wisdom of not one, but two *'grandmothers'*.

To everybody's surprise, Emma changed her mind about marrying Oliver Turner. She wouldn't say why! All she said was that it *wouldn't work out!* Therefore, the next wedding in our family was my own.

Before I knew it, it was my wedding day! I stood in my wedding dress and veil, made by Grandmom Miriam and looked out of the window across the beautifully manicured lawn. It was a lovely, sunny day. Just what I had hoped for, since the wedding was to be held outside in our yard. As I stood there, staring out of the window, I began to daydream again.

I thought back to the turning point in my life! In all actuality, it was the day that I approached Gary in school. After that, we fell in love and realized that we wanted to be together forever! We promised the 'grandmothers' and the rest of the family that we would live there in that house with them for a while. It was made clear to me that I had to be living there when I turned twenty-one years old!

I didn't have much longer to go by that time. And I was glad. I didn't want to leave home, anyway. Gary wanted to move to Tolstoy. But he wanted me to be happy more than anything else that he wanted in the world. Then I thought about my dream.

I still hadn't told anyone about it. Even though it had occurred over a month before. It was a strange dream! But then, all of my dreams were strange ever since I could remember.

In that dream, 'Marie' approached me and said, *"You should go away from this house, with your new husband! Don't stay here! If you do, something might happen to you or him!"* It was more like a threat than a warning! "Something bad?" I asked her. "Like what?!"

The spirit laughed at me. It was the same sinister laughter that it always had been when she came around us. I got the feeling that she had something planned for Gary and I that wasn't good! But I wasn't afraid of her! I *knew* it was 'she' who feared me by that time. Also, she feared Emma, Grandmom Faya, and Grandmom Miriam.

Marie was tricky too! Of course, she wanted me to leave that house! Because if I did, all of our 'grandmothers' plans would be foiled. Everything that they planned for so long to get rid of her and the *other* ones!

"If Marie has been following me around all of these years, as Andrew Jr. told me," I thought. *"She should be able to use me ANYWHERE that I live!"* But then, I recalled what Grandmom Faya and Linda told me. "This house is *Marie's power base!"* The sound of someone knocking gently at my bedroom door interrupted my thoughts.

"Ty, are you dressed yet?" It was my sister. "Yes, Emma, come in," I told her. She entered the room. She looked lovely in her pale green chiffon and lace gown. She was my Maid of Honor. "You look absolutely breathtaking!" she told me. "Me?!" I replied playfully. "Have you looked in the mirror, sister?"

Emma and I were both very beautiful women. And we had a deep, loving relationship with each other. We were very close! She just couldn't seem to find the right man. "They're always trying to be slick," she told me once. "They're all a bunch of low-down, lying dogs, Ty!" She seemed to be very bitter at times. And I felt sorry for her. She was not only beautiful on the outside but even more on the inside! She deserved someone who would be good to her. Unfortunately, she always made bad choices when it came to men.

Ray, who was long gone by then, was the only good man that she ever had. Then, the last we heard about him, he had gotten married to someone else and had a family. I knew Emma had to be hurt by that news. But she never showed it.

"Here I am, getting ready to marry the only boyfriend that I've ever had," I thought. "And Emma has had dozens of boyfriends! None of them ever seemed to measure up to her standards, though!"

"I'm really happy for you and Gary, Ty," she said sweetly, breaking into my thoughts. "I wish you both all of the happiness in the world!" I smiled at her. Then we sat down on my bed. "Are you alright, Emma?" I asked her.

"Sure," she said. "I'm fine!" She had a smile on her face. But it looked like it was forced to me. "I just wanted to come in here and chat with you for a few minutes. I know you must be nervous, Ty. I am!" She pulled out a cigarette, lit it, and took a puff. Then she blew the smoke into the air.

Smoking was a habit that she had taken up since her breakup with Oliver. To me and the rest of the family, this last breakup seemed to push Emma right over the edge. She was so sure that he was the man for her. But she never told us what caused their breakup for good! We respected her privacy and didn't press her about it. We felt if she wanted us to know, she would tell us.

"God, if I was getting married," said Emma, "I know I'd be a basket case by now." "I AM a little nervous," I admitted to her. "But I'm far more happy!" Then, I noticed a strange eeriness about my sister. It was as if a dark cloud of doom was hanging over her and wouldn't go away! I never noticed it before that day.

"Emma," I said, "are you sure you're feeling okay?" "Sure, Ty," she replied. She smiled that 'forced' smile at me again. Her eyes were sad too that day. "There's something different about you today," I told her, hoping she would open up to me and tell me what was wrong.

"Well," she said, "I don't feel any different." She stared down at the floor for a minute. "I did have a dream last night, Ty," she said solemnly. My heart fell to my stomach. My family and I had come to dread Emma's dreams, which were more like visions of things to come. They were truly prophetic and scary.

In fact, we hated it whenever she told us that she had a dream about something or someone. Because we knew that whatever she 'dreamed' about would come true. And it was almost always something bad. No matter how long it took, whatever she dreamed or 'saw' would come to pass. Exactly the way that she 'dreamed' it.

"What did you dream about, Emma?" I asked her, although I didn't really want to know at that time. Not when I was so happy! Not on my wedding day.

"In my dream," she began, "I was trying to swim in this dark, murky water! It was hard to swim in it, Ty! I thought I was going to drown. But I did get out.

When I did, I was covered with blood! I had on this same dress. But it was cut shorter. It looked like I had been in a terrible accident or something!"

"That sounds spooky, Emma!" I said. "How did you get into the water in the first place?" She sighed. "You know how dreams are, Ty," she replied. "I have no idea! All I know is that I got really scared! Because when I saw that I was covered in blood, I looked up and saw Andrew Jr. He was standing in front of me, and he was crying, Ty!" I felt fear grip my heart. "Oh, Emma," I said worriedly. "I don't like the sound of that!"

"Well," she said, "that's not the best part, sister dear." "I don't know if I want to hear this," I told her, shaking my head. "I know," she said, patting my hand gently. "But he told me that he would be seeing me soon, Ty!" I jumped up from the bed and walked over to the window, not wanting to hear anymore. Nervously, I started chewing my bottom lip, which was what I usually did when I was upset about something. I dreaded my sister's 'dreams'! All of us did! Emma looked at me and smiled. "That's how I felt," she said. She knew that I was frightened for her.

I walked back over to my bed and sat down next to her. I took both of her hands in mine. "Oh, Emma, I know it will be alright," I told her. "Did you tell the 'grandmothers' about the dream?"

"No," she said, shaking her head. "I'm not going to let it worry me, Ty. This is *your* day, little sister. I'm going back downstairs to see how things are coming along, okay?" "Okay, Em," I said. She kissed me on the cheek, then got up and left my bedroom. Her 'dream' really did upset me. I decided to tell my 'grandmothers' if she didn't.

Worried about my sister, I finished dressing for my wedding. It was only thirty minutes away by then. It looked like Grandmom Faya and Grandmom Miriam had invited everybody in town to the wedding.

Finally, the Pianist began to play. I walked down the path, which was strewn with flowers, on Mr. Tom's arm. I smiled at Gary, who was waiting for me at the end of the pathway. He smiled back at me. I could hear my soon-to-be mother-in-law, MaryAnne, sobbing softly. It was another beautiful wedding.

This time, there were no *unwanted or uninvited visitors*. Everybody had a great time that day. Gary and I received a lot of beautiful gifts and lots of money. Also, there was a great band, and Linda and Nicholas had hired a Caterer. There must have been over two hundred people there. The wine, beer, liquor, and champagne flowed like water. Emma certainly took advantage of that. It was another habit that she had started—drinking heavily.

The whole family was concerned about Emma. She was hurt badly by the breakup with Oliver. But she still refused to talk about it. On the night that occurred, she came home and took an overdose of Grandmom Miriam's sleeping pills along with some whiskey. Luckily, Malin came home early from a party and found her because everyone else was out. She was on the bathroom floor, unconscious.

At first, we didn't think that Emma was going to make it. She was in a coma for eighteen hours. After that, she seemed to get herself together after spending ninety days in the Psychiatric Ward of the hospital. They released her only three weeks before my wedding.

Immediately, everybody noticed that she was drinking heavily and smoking lots of cigarettes—two things that she never did before in her life. Many nights, we would hear her in her bedroom, screaming. When we would run into the room to see what was wrong, she would be fast asleep. *I was worried out of my mind about my sister.*

"I don't like this," Grandmom Faya said, worriedly. On a few occasions, we heard Emma screaming for Andrew Jr. to leave her alone. "I don't want to go with you!" she would yell out in her sleep. Grandmom Faya and Grandmom Miriam were so worried about her, they hardly ever left her alone in the house anymore. They made sure that someone was always at home with her.

Grandmom Faya, while searching Emma's drawer for a pair of nylons to wear one day, found a loaded revolver hidden in the bottom of her drawer. When she confronted my sister about it, she told her casually that it was for protection.

"Protection from what?!" Grandmom Faya asked her. But my sister wouldn't give her a straight answer.

We got even more concerned when Linda told us that she'd come home from shopping and found Emma crouched in a corner of the dining room with the loaded revolver pointed at her head, ready to pull the trigger. "Emma!!" Linda shouted at her. "What the hell are you doing?" My sister smiled at Linda and put the gun down. She got up from her crouched position, looked at Linda strangely, then went upstairs to her bedroom.

"She looked terrified of something or *someone!*" Linda told us. "It was like she was *trying to hide from somebody!*" This occurred on the weekend before I got married.

Then Emma started sleepwalking. If Grandmom Faya hadn't stopped her one night, she would have gone right out of the front door to God knows where. I believed it was more than the breakup that was causing the drastic change in my beloved sister. We talked about *everything*. But she never told me *why* she and Oliver Turner had parted ways. Or had they? I began to wonder what was really going on with my sister by then.

Oliver Turner owned a white BMW. Different members of our family had begun seeing his car parked down the road from our house on many occasions. It was like he was *watching* our house or something. He would sit there in his car for a few hours, then leave. It was Nicholas who told us that Emma would be rushing to go out somewhere. But when she got to the front door, she would look down the road and change her mind about going out. She acted like she was afraid to go out. He told us, "She goes back upstairs to her room." She would stay in her room for hours.

Also, Nicholas told us that each time she did that, he would go to the door to see what was wrong. And each time, he'd look down the road, and there would be Oliver, *sitting in his car*. For some reason, only she knew, Oliver was stalking my sister.

Grandmom Faya and Grandmom Miriam started getting strange telephone calls at all hours of the day and night. None of the rest of us had telephones in our bedrooms. Therefore, if any phone calls came in late at night, they would be the ones to answer the telephone. The person on the other end of the line would not say a word.

Emma answered the telephone one afternoon. Whoever it was, and whatever they said, caused her to turn pale. I was watching her. She became nervous and scared. But a few minutes before the call came, she and I had been laughing and talking.

Emma would always retreat to her bedroom whenever she was depressed or

sad about something. When I asked her who was on the telephone and what they said, she answered, "Nobody important."

Before Oliver and Emma broke up, one night, the entire family was sitting around the table in the kitchen. Everybody was there except Emma, who wouldn't come out of her bedroom all day.

Linda mentioned the fact that she had walked in on Emma as she was dressing for work one morning by accident. She saw black and blue bruises all over my sister's body. The bruises were in places which could be easily hidden with makeup.

That comment made me recall how I thought I had seen Emma with a black eye. But I told myself it was just my imagination. It had been covered up really well with makeup. But I could still see the darkness and puffiness around her eye a little. I wouldn't have believed that was what I'd seen anyway. After all,

Emma told us that Oliver Turner was very good to her and how happy she was with him. Suddenly, it dawned on me. It had been a long time since she said those nice things about Oliver.

Then there was the time that Malin picked her up from the hospital. She had a broken arm. When he asked her what happened, she told him she had stumbled over a piece of tree stump that was sticking out of the ground, landing on her arm. Of course, it didn't sound right to him. But he took her word for it. It was shortly after that when she broke it off with Oliver.

After the breakup, Oliver would telephone Emma every day. But she wouldn't talk to him. That went on for quite a while. Then she started acting strangely.

"Something is happening here with Emma and Oliver," said Grandmom Faya as we were all sitting down at the kitchen table for dinner one evening. "I have a bad feeling about this!"

The funny thing was that the entire time Emma was in the hospital, the weird telephone calls stopped. And Oliver's car hadn't been parked down the road from our house. Only since she came home did both start up all over again. *We knew it was him.*

We began to notice that Emma rarely went out alone anymore. Whenever she got ready to go out somewhere, she would check to see if Oliver's car was around anywhere first. If it was, she would change her mind about going out. And if she and I were out shopping or something, I noticed how she kept looking over her shoulder.

"Who are you looking for, Emma?" I asked her once. "Oh, nobody," she answered too quickly. I recalled those things as I tried to put two and two together. "Penny for your thoughts," Gary said as he came up behind me and put his arms around my waist. "You're in deep thought again, Mrs. Shelley. Is anything wrong?"

"No, hon," I lied. "Everything is okay!" Truthfully, I became more and more worried about Emma. Suddenly, I became afraid for her. But I didn't know why. I tried to force myself not to let it interfere with my honeymoon. But it did.

During the wedding reception, Emma seemed like her old self again. The disc jockey played the oldies from the 50s and 60s, which I loved. I heard the song California Dreamin' by The Mamas and The Papas. It filled the air, and it sounded good. I loved that song, although it was much older than I was. Also, I heard my brothers and Gary trying to sing along with the record. It made me smile. Not one of them could sing. Everybody was having a good time.

Emma caught my bridal bouquet. "I should have let somebody else catch the damn thing," she said almost angrily. "I'll never get the chance to carry one anyway!"

She sounded so sad. It bothered me a lot to hear her talk like that. I knew that Oliver was still harassing her. Nicholas and Malin offered eagerly to kick his ass! But, my sister told them that things were alright. And, not to say anything to him.

For our honeymoon, back then, Gary, and I, went to Jamaica, for two weeks. We had a wonderful time, in the sun, and water. And, when we came home, everybody told us how in love with one another we looked. We were in love, and happy!

The only thing that dampened my joy, when my new husband, and, I returned home, was seeing my sister, after almost two weeks away. I almost broke down, and cried, when I saw her.

CHAPTER NINETEEN

When we got home from our honeymoon, I almost didn't recognize Emma. She looked like she lost at least twenty pounds in the two weeks that I was gone. She had dark circles under her eyes like she hadn't slept in weeks. Her hair, which was usually immaculately done, looked like it hadn't been combed in a long time. To me, she looked twenty years older than she was. She was chain smoking too and drinking all day long every day.

I found out that Emma hadn't been to work since Gary and I got married. She called in sick the Monday following my wedding and stayed home ever since. "I don't know what the hell is going on with her, Tyla," Grandmom Faya said to me in frustration and worry.

But no matter how hard we pushed her, trying to find out what her problem was, Emma wouldn't talk to us. She wouldn't even talk to me. All she would do was retreat to her bedroom.

Finally, I decided that enough was enough. I confronted her in the kitchen one day when she came downstairs to clean out her whiskey glass. Everybody else was out of the house that day. When she came downstairs, she was surprised to see that I was at home. "Alright, Emmaline Davidson," I said firmly. "Sit down! I want to talk to you!"

Already, she had a bottle of gin in one hand and a half-filled glass in the other. Without a word, she sat down at the table. "Let's hear it!" I said, staring hard into her bloodshot eyes.

For a minute, she looked back at me, then looked away. "Let's hear what, Ty?" she asked me, pretending she had no idea what I was talking about. "You know what, Emma!" I said angrily. "What is going on with you that you're not telling me? *Look at yourself!* You're a mess! I *know* something is going on. And it has to do with Oliver! *Doesn't it?"*

Again, she looked at me, but she didn't say anything. "Emma, talk to me, please!" I begged her. "We've always been able to talk to each other, haven't we?"

Suddenly, a tear rolled down her cheek. I put my arm around her shoulders. "Oh, Emma, please tell me what it is!" I said.

My sister put her head down. Then raised it back up and looked at me. "I'm still having that same dream that I told you about, Ty," she said in a weak, scared voice. "The dream that you told me about before, with Andrew Jr.?" I asked her. "Yes," she replied.

"Oh Lord, Emma!" I cried. Then I sat down next to her. "After all of this time?! You're still having that same dream?" "I sure am," she said, her voice getting stronger. "It's just a dream, though, right?" she said and tried to force a smile. "Emma," I said, "is that what is destroying you?"

"I know he's trying to tell me something, Ty," she replied. "Nobody has a dream like that over and over again for no reason. If anybody knows that, it's me! You know how my dreams are! Remember what the 'grandmothers' told us?" "Yes," I said, nodding my head. "I remember, Emma. So, what do you think he's trying to tell you?"

She looked into my eyes and smiled. This time, it wasn't a 'forced' smile but a genuine one. She knew I would never be able to accept the answer that she was about to give me. She reached for my hand and said calmly, "*I'm going to die soon, Ty!*"

"No!" I yelled, snatching my hand away from hers. "How can you say such a thing, Emma?! I don't believe that for one minute! Not even for a second! Have you told the 'grandmothers' about this?! They can help you, Emma!"

She took my hand in hers again. "*No one can help me, Ty,*" she told me, resolved in her belief. "*not even them!* What will be is going to be! I know that he's going to kill me! I've known it for some time now! He's just biding his time!"

"Who?!" I cried. In the back of my mind, I knew who she was referring to. "You know who, Ty," she said. "Oliver!" She was right! I did know it was him that she was talking about before she even said his name.

"We can call the Sheriff and have him arrested," I told her. "Have you told Nicholas and Malin? They can do something about that bastard! I know it. Even Gary will help!" In my mind, I was thinking of all kinds of things to help my dear sister.

"No, Ty," Emma said firmly. "It's too late for that now. He's not threatening me outright. He's too smart for that! But I know him." "But, Emma," I cried, "you told us that he was the one that you'd been waiting for all of your life. I don't understand what happened."

Then she told me a horror story that I would never forget as long as I lived. It was a story about the mental, physical, and emotional abuse that she had been suffering at the hands of a man she thought loved her. Finally, she got enough courage to leave him. The problem was, he wasn't the kind of man who would let go easily. Oliver actively stalked Emma. He was the one making the strange telephone calls and many subtle threats against her life since she broke up with him. "I found out that six months before I met him, he did the same thing to his former girlfriend," Emma admitted.

"What happened to her?" I asked, horrified. "Is she the one who told you about him, Em?" Emma hesitated for a moment. "No, Ty," she said numbly. "She's dead!"

"What?!" I cried. "That's right," said Emma. "They found her body near our house here, back in the woods!" She glanced in the direction of the wooded area behind our house. "She was raped, tortured, and almost decapitated when they found her."

"Oh my God!" I cried. "Didn't you know anything about this creep before you took up with him, Emma?" I was angry with her because I knew she hadn't bothered to check into Oliver Turner's background. We had always been warned by Grandmom Faya and Grandmom Miriam to get 'feedback' on people we would call 'friends.' Men and women.

"You know how it is, Ty," she told me, hanging her head. "I liked him. And I didn't care to check up on him. I wish now that I had. But I didn't!" I stared at my sister in disbelief. "What about the other girl?" I asked her. "What about her?" asked Emma.

"Didn't they do anything to him for her murder?"

"Well, Ty," Emma said, "two weeks before it happened, she told a friend of hers, who is also the person who told me about him, that she knew that he was going to kill her. *And get away with it!*" "That's unbelievable!" I said. "How can that happen?"

"Because he's rich!" she answered. "Rich people get away with a lot of things that they shouldn't! You know that!" I knew she was right.

"Who is this person who told you about Oliver, Em?" I asked her. "She works on my job," replied Emma. "She just started there a few months ago. He came up there to take me to lunch one afternoon, and she saw him. He saw her too! We had been talking. When he came over to my desk at the office, she looked at him real strangely. Then she walked away. After that, she tried to avoid me. So I cornered her in the ladies' room one day, and I asked her what was wrong. That's when she told me about her friend and about Oliver. I didn't believe her at first. Then the *real* Oliver Turner showed up!"

"What do you mean by that?" I asked. "Well," began Emma, "we were out one night at a party when a guy that I know asked me to dance with him. Oliver was outside talking. When he came back inside and saw us dancing, he freaked out. He started a big fight with the guy. The people who gave the party asked us to leave. So we did!" She hesitated before she started talking again.

"He drove me way out somewhere," she continued. "It looked like some kind of park area or something that had been abandoned. I didn't know where I was. But it was a long way from here. It was very dark and nobody was around." She paused again, then said in a voice so low I had to strain to hear her, "He put a knife to my throat, Ty!" My mouth fell open in shock.

"He told me he would kill me," she said, "if I ever talked to another guy again when his back was turned. I couldn't believe it! Since that night, he would find any excuse, no matter how small, to hit me or slap me around. He even broke my arm by twisting it behind my back once."

"I remember when your arm was broken, Emma," I said in a cold fury. "That rotten, no-good bastard. How did he get away with killing that girl? I don't understand that! Rich or not."

"Well Ty," said my sister, "they *buy* their way out of anything in the first place. You know that! Also, there was never any record anywhere that he'd beaten up on that girl before. There were no witnesses that he ever even threatened her. It's the same as in my case! She never told anybody until it was too late! I was too embarrassed to report him or file charges against him. I guess she was too. When I couldn't take it anymore, I broke it off with him. Especially after what Gina told me. She's the girl at work! She even asked me one time if he ever hit me. I lied and told her 'no'."

"You should have told someone a long time ago, Emma," I said through clenched teeth. "After all of that bragging on him that I did?" she said. "I couldn't tell anybody that this 'knight in shining armor' was beating the hell out of me every chance he got! He told me that if I tried to leave him, he *would kill* me!"

"Emma, I don't care what you say," I said, "we're not letting him get away with this! I'm going to tell the Sheriff!" "I already have a Restraining Order, Ty," she said. "It doesn't really do any good! Do you know how many women die at the hands of men, and they have Restraining Orders?" "I don't care," I insisted. "We have to do something about this maniac!"

"No, Ty," she said. "Don't you realize that my dreams of Andrew Jr. have been *warnings?*" Whenever someone dead keeps worrying you and tells you something like that, it usually happens. He told me that he would be seeing me soon. And he will!" "No way!" I cried. "I'm telling the men about this!" The thought of losing my sweet sister to some jealous clown who already murdered a woman and got away with it was unbearable to me.

"Poor Ty," said my sister softly, as if to herself. "If it will make you feel any better, you do whatever you feel you must do. But stop worrying about me! You and Gary have a whole lifetime ahead of you! You're going to be very happy, Tyla Shelley! Your life together will begin when you leave this house. Not before! Remember that I said that, okay?" She touched my hand gently. "That was another thing that Andrew Jr. told me, Ty! And guess what else?" "What?" I asked her.

"He came in my last dream, holding a big, pretty baby boy," she said. "He told me that it was your son, Ty!" she said excitedly. "But what does that mean?" I asked, confused. "Why, Tyla," she said, "I thought you knew! It's a sign that a new life is coming into the family. And an old life is ending! Our 'grandmothers' used to tell me that all of the time! It means a beginning and an ending!"

By now, I was in tears. "You act like you don't care, Emma," I sobbed. "This man is threatening your life. What's wrong with you?" "I am just accepting it, Ty," she said calmly. "If it's my time, nothing will stop it anyway! Don't you understand that? I believe that everybody knows when their time is up! I didn't always believe that. But I do now! I can feel it!" She spoke with such resignation.

For a few minutes, the two of us sat there in silence. Except for my sobbing. Then Emma put her arms around me to comfort me. "You have to promise me that you won't say anything to anybody about this, Ty," she said. "Promise me! I've gone through enough changes behind all of this! It's taken me a long time to get to this point! Please promise me that you will let me handle it, okay?"

I nodded. But deep down inside, I knew I would not let that terrible monster hurt my sister without putting up a fight. No matter what she said or what promise she made me make. I left Emma in the kitchen and went upstairs to lie down. I cried for a long time. I was glad that Gary was out of town with his father until the next day. He would surely want to know what had me so upset.

As I laid there, suddenly, I felt a warm, comforting *presence* in the room with me. I was lying on my side, so I rolled over onto my back. There, at the foot of my bed, stood Mama, who I knew was really 'Aunt Charon'. She was looking down at me, smiling. She didn't say anything to me but just kept smiling at me. I wasn't afraid.

I realized, after all those years, 'Aunt Charon' had never meant to hurt me or my siblings. It was just that she had been forced by someone wicked to give up her own life and grown resentful. Also, I knew that God had forgiven her for Andrew Jr.'s murder. Although evil and darkness surrounded our family, there was also love and light there too. I knew 'Aunt Charon' came to let me know that.

The next morning, I went to see Sheriff Bicket after Emma left home to go to work. He wasn't doing much lately because he turned most of his work over to the new Sheriff, Wilson Reilly.

Sheriff Wilson Reilly came from a big city in the East, he told me. He welcomed the change of a small town, especially after he'd just gone through a very bitter divorce. Most of the battle had been over money and property because his children were all grown up. He had been married for thirty years when his wife fell in love with a younger man who worked where she did.

Sitting down with the Sheriff, I explained everything that was going on between Emma and Oliver Turner. Also, I told him about the murder of Oliver's former girlfriend and mentioned that he was suspected of her murder.

"Tyla," said Sheriff Reilly sadly, "there's not too much that we can do to this guy unless he breaks the Restraining Order or if he presents an actual danger to you or your family." He was a very nice man. I could tell that he was very sympathetic to my problem.

"Do you mean to tell me that there's nothing that you can do until he hurts my sister or one of us?" I exclaimed in shock. "Then, what good is a Sheriff if they just hang around and pick up the bodies?!"

He knew that I was upset and sighed. "I'm really sorry, Tyla," he told me. "I know it sounds terrible, but that's the law. Emma has the Restraining Order on him, and you're telling me that he hasn't bothered her except over the telephone. There's just nothing that I can do." "Well," I told him angrily, "the law sucks."

"I know," he agreed. He really felt sorry for me and wished that there was something that he could've done to help me. "Can you at least keep an eye on this jerk?" I asked him. "I'll have one of my Deputies tail him for a while, Tyla," he said. "But that's all I can do. I hope you understand."

"I guess so," I said, calming down a little because I realized that it wasn't him who made the law. He only enforced it. "Whatever you can do, I'll appreciate it," I added. I left his office that day and went back home, knowing that Sheriff Reilly would do all that he could to help us. He was a good man. I got to know him pretty well because I worked in the office with both he and Sheriff Bicket. Since he knew me and my family very well, I knew he would stay on top of Oliver Turner for sure.

Grandmom Faya and Grandmom Miriam were both in the kitchen, and Mr. Tom was in the living room watching television when I got home. "Hey there, Maam!" Mr. Tom greeted me. "Hi, Mr. Tom," I returned his greeting. "How are you doing today?" he asked me. "I'm okay," I answered.

Mr. Tom always called me 'Maam' because he said I acted older than both he and Grandmom Faya. It was his way of joking with me, and I didn't mind. He was very dear to all of us.

Without saying anything else, I headed upstairs to my bedroom. I felt like my heart was breaking because of my sister's troubles. Mr. Tom must have been watching me as I went upstairs. I heard him go into the kitchen, where my grandmothers were, and say to them, "Something's wrong with 'Maam', Faya." Curiously, I stood at the top of the stairs, listening to them talk.

"Oh, really?" I heard Grandmom Faya say. "I don't know what it is," he told her. "But there's something pretty heavy on her mind, I think." "Do you want me to go talk to her, Faya?" I heard Grandmom Miriam ask. "No," said Grandmom Faya, "you know how Tyla is. She'll talk to us whenever she's ready."

Almost prophetically, Grandmom Miriam said, "I'll bet my last dollar in the world that it has something to do with Emma and that guy, Oliver Turner." "You're probably right," Grandmom Faya agreed. "But she won't talk to us either. I don't understand it." "Whatever it is," Mr. Tom said, "it will come to the surface. Is lunch ready, Faya?"

"Yes, hon," she told him. "It'll be ready in about five minutes." "Do you think she's hungry?" Mr. Tom asked, referring to me. "No," said Grandmom Faya, "don't bother her right now."

Dear Mr. Tom! He was always so concerned about my siblings, Linda, me, and our little ones, Angelina and Nicola. He truly considered us as his own grandchildren and great-grandchildren. Also, we thought of him as our dear grandfather in return. We loved him very much. I went on to my bedroom and lay down.

The following summer was the hottest in Maron that anybody could ever remember. It was doubly hard on me because I was five months pregnant. Gary would tease me once in a while by sticking a pillow under his shirt and walking around the house. "Oh, it's so hot!" he would say, teasing me. Then, he would give me a big hug. We would both laugh.

As hot as it was, though, I made it through the summer, even though there were many days when I didn't think I would. At the end of September, the weather was a lot cooler and much more comfortable for everyone.

I was half asleep on the morning that Emma peeked into my bedroom and said, "Ty, I have an interview this morning for a better job. I almost forgot about it. This is the one that I told you about, remember?" "Yeah," I murmured, "I remember." I was still groggy. Emma's former job finally dismissed her because she lost so much time. She had worked there for six years. A new law firm opened up in Maron and they were interviewing for a Legal Secretary."I'll see you when I get home okay?" she said. "Wish me luck!" "Alright," I said sleepily. "Good luck, Em!" Then I closed my eyes again, not ready to get out of bed. It was only eight o'clock in the morning. Gary had left for work over an hour before that.

Since the talk that Emma and I had, I wanted to know her every move. She obliged me of course! Suddenly, I sat up in the bed and hollered to her. "Emma!" She came back up the stairs and into my room. "Yes, Ty?" she said. "Call me when you get there okay?" I asked. "*And* when you're on your way home!" I added.

Emma laughed at me softly. Then she went back down the stairs and out of the front door. I didn't care though. I was still very worried about her.

That morning, she appeared to be more lively and happier than she usually was. She looked very pretty in the pale-green chiffon dress she had cut off at the knee. It was the same one that she wore at my wedding. She had the dress cut off and altered so she could wear it on special occasions. That way, it wouldn't go to waste sitting in her closet. After she left for her interview, I couldn't seem to get back to sleep. I knew that something was wrong. I just couldn't put my finger on it! I decided to get up and make myself some breakfast.

On my way down the stairs, I thought again how pretty Emma looked that morning and how cheerful she was! She was truly beautiful! That memory of my dear, sweet sister that morning would be one that would bring me much comfort in the years to come. It was a memory that I would hold onto for the rest of my life. Deep in my heart that day, I *knew* that I would never see her alive again.

CHAPTER TWENTY

When I got downstairs, Grandmom Faya and Mr. Tom were sitting at the kitchen table talking. Linda and the children were still asleep. Nicholas and Malin had gone to work. Grandmom Miriam was in the living room watching television.

"Good morning, Grandmom Miriam," I said to her. She was watching a game show that was on television. "Good morning, sweetheart!" she said, looking at me. "How are you this morning?" "Fine," I told her. "I think I'll get myself some breakfast." "Okay," she said. "Faya and Tom are back there. I think there's food already prepared."

"Great!" I said and waddled toward the kitchen. "Good morning, Maam!" Mr. Tom said. I smiled. "Good morning, Mr. Tom!" I said. "Hi, sweetheart," said Grandmom Faya. "What can I get you this morning?" "Oh, it doesn't matter, Grandmom," I told her. "Anything that you have ready is fine with me."

She fixed me a plate of pancakes and sausage. "You look pretty this morning," Mr. Tom said to me with a smile. "Thanks," I replied. I did feel a lot better that morning than I had in a long time. Mainly because it seemed like Emma was getting her life back on track. Oliver Turner hadn't been seen, parked down the road, or heard from over the telephone for a whole month. But I should have known it was the calm before the storm.

Mr. Tom, Grandmom Faya, and I were sitting at the kitchen table when suddenly the drinking glasses that were drying on the edge of the sink slid to the floor one by one and broke. The three of us watched in silence as an *unseen hand* slid each glass to the floor. "Alright," Grandmom Faya snarled angrily. "That's enough of that shit! Now, get out of here."

Mr. Tom didn't say a word. He was used to the weird, strange things that occurred in that house at times. Then all three of us shuddered from a cold, icy chill that quickly passed by us. The hairs on the backs of our necks and arms were standing on end. *There was a chilling presence in the room with us.*

Suddenly, a loud crash came from the living room. We jumped up to see what it was. Grandmom Miriam was standing up with her arms wrapped around herself, staring at something. We followed her frightened gaze. There, lying in the middle of the living room floor, was a photograph facing downward. The dust from the frame was splattered everywhere.

"I was just sitting here," said Grandmom Miriam. "And I saw that picture come off the wall and float in mid-air. Then it hit the floor like somebody threw it there." Mr. Tom put his arm around her shoulders. She was very shaken up. "My God!" Grandmom Faya exclaimed.

Slowly, I walked over, bent down, and picked up the photograph. I turned it over. It was a photograph of my sister. I looked at the clock on the wall. It was now ten thirty in the morning.

I recalled when my sister first got word of her interview. It had been scheduled for eight thirty that morning. "She should've been home by now!" I thought. "Even if they wanted her to start work right away. It's Friday! She would have to wait until Monday."

"I wonder why that happened?" Grandmom Faya said, puzzled. I put the photograph on the coffee table, hurried upstairs, got dressed, and came back downstairs. "I'm going to meet Emma and give her a ride home," I told both grandmothers and Mr. Tom. "Can I use your car, Grandmom Faya?" I asked.

"Sure, honey," she said. Quickly, I got the car keys from the hook on the dining room wall and left. I drove to the place where the new law firm was. It was eleven o'clock in the morning by the time I got there.

I walked up to the receptionist, who asked me to sign in on the log sheet. I said, "I'm here to pick up my sister." "Who is your sister?" she asked me. "Her name is Emmaline Davidson," I told her. "She had an interview here this morning at eight thirty."

The receptionist looked at the first page of the log sheet. "Well," she said, "this sheet was filled up by ten o'clock this morning. Everybody signed in. But I don't see her name here." Panic stabbed at my heart. "Do you think she might have been the one person who didn't sign in?" I asked her. "Maybe you stepped away from your desk at that time." Panic was rising in my heart.

"No," she said, shaking her head certainly. "I'm sorry. I have a relief person, so somebody is here at all times." Now, I was getting angry at the stiff-lipped, gray-haired old prune-faced woman, who was being as nice and polite to me as possible. She didn't deserve my anger, but I had to take it out on someone.

"Could you please just check with whoever was supposed to interview her today?" I asked. "It would make me feel a lot better!" I knew my voice was shaking, and she could see that I was upset.

"Alright, dear," she told me. "You wait right here in the lobby. I'll let you talk to Mr. Johnston yourself, okay?" "Alright," I replied. I sat down to wait.

Mr. Johnston, the top attorney of the firm, was middle-aged, with gray hair, tall, stout, and very handsome. "Hello," he said with a warm smile as he walked over to where I was sitting in the lobby. "I'm Edward Johnston, and you are?" "I'm Tyla Shelley," I told him. "I came down here to pick up my sister. She had an interview with you this morning. But your receptionist tells me that she was never here."

"That's right," said Mr. Johnston. "I waited for her until ten o'clock this morning. But she never came in or telephoned me. She had the job too! Her qualifications were more than what I expected. When you see her, tell her that the job is still open if she wants it. I know people have different problems. Things come up that we don't foresee."

He was still talking to me as I turned around in a daze and walked out onto the sidewalk. Slowly, I walked back to the car and got in. I started to cry. "Are you alright, Miss?" a man who was passing by asked me. He saw me crying. "Can I telephone someone for you? Do you need help?"

"No," I told him with a forced smile. "Thanks anyway. I'm fine!" But I wasn't fine. I knew that something was terribly wrong. I made it home, unaware that I had run two traffic lights and almost caused a serious car accident. When the grandmothers and Mr. Tom, who were all still in the living room, saw me, they knew immediately that I was upset about something. They questioned me about Emma and asked me what was wrong.

I couldn't answer them. Instead, I went upstairs to my bedroom, knowing they were watching me. Linda was just coming out of the upstairs bathroom after giving the children their baths. She saw me. "Ty, what's wrong?" she asked. I still couldn't say anything. But the tears were rolling down my cheeks.

"Mama," Nicola said, "is something wrong with Aunt Ty?" "No, honey," Linda lied, "she's okay. You go on and get dressed. Take your sister downstairs to Grandmom Miriam for a few moments for me, okay?"

Linda knocked on my bedroom door. I didn't answer her. It was unlocked. She knocked again, then came into the room. "Ty, are you alright?" she asked me sympathetically. "What's happened?" She sat down on the side of my bed. I was sitting down by my bedroom window, staring outside. "Ty?" Linda said again.

Finally, I looked at my sister-in-law. "Lin," I began, "Emma never got to her interview this morning." "Oh, Ty," she said as she walked over to where I was sitting. She put her hand on my shoulder. "Maybe she just changed her mind," Linda suggested. But I shook my head.

"No, Lin," I said, "something terrible has happened to her. I know it!" "Ty, you're scaring me!" said Linda. "What would make you say such a thing?" Before I could answer her, there was another knock on my bedroom door. "Can I come in?" asked Grandmom Miriam. "Is everything alright, Tyla?"

Linda told her what I said about Emma. "Oh, Tyla, honey," Grandmom Miriam said comfortingly, "don't worry. It could be any number of reasons why she never showed up for her interview. It'll be okay, sweetheart." "No!" I cried. "It won't be alright, Grandmom Miriam! It won't!" My outburst took them both by surprise. I started crying again.

"Oh, my, my," said Grandmom Miriam as she hugged me. "It's okay, honey." She rocked me in her arms. "Tell us what this is all about, Tyla, please?"

"Yes, Ty," Linda joined in. "Why are you so upset over this?" They waited for me to calm down. I wiped my eyes with the tissue that Linda gave me. Then looked into their eyes. "My sister is never coming home again!" I told them flatly. "What?" exclaimed Linda. "Oh, Tyla," Grandmom Miriam said fretfully, "please don't say things like that!"

But my sister-in-law was silent. She knew now why I was so upset. No one in our family knew how many late-night conversations she and Emma had about Oliver Turner's abuse. She'd promised my sister that she would never tell, and she didn't. A tear rolled down her cheek, but Grandmom Miriam didn't notice it. Linda was glad. We looked into each other's eyes as Grandmom Miriam was trying to comfort me.

"Mama, can you help me tie my sneakers?" Nicola asked from his bedroom. Linda left the room, glad for the distraction. I knew from what I had said that my sister talked to her about everything that was going on between her and Oliver, probably things that she hadn't even told me.

"Maybe she just decided not to go to the interview," Linda suggested to me. She hoped that she was right. Grandmom Faya eventually came upstairs to see what was wrong with me. As soon as she saw me, she knew that something was wrong. She walked over to me and took my hands in hers. "Miriam," she said, "why don't you and Linda leave us alone for a bit. Okay, honey?"

Grandmom Miriam nodded her head, as did Linda, and they left the room. Grandmom Faya closed the bedroom door behind them and walked back over to where I was sitting. She pulled up a chair in front of me and sat down. "Listen to me, Tyla, honey," she said. "I want you to tell me right now what is troubling you." "I promised her that I wouldn't say anything," I replied.

"Well," she said, "I think it's time you broke that promise, don't you? Look at you, Tyla. You're a wreck, and we can't have this. We can't have you being upset because we have to think about that sweet little baby that you're carrying. I'm quite sure Emma would understand that. She wouldn't want you to be upset like this either. So, come on. Out with it." I stared out of the bedroom window.

"Tyla, please," said Grandmom Faya. "You know that you can tell me anything, don't you? You always could, ever since you were a little girl." "I know, Grandmom Faya," I began to sob again. She waited. I looked at her sorrowfully. "Is everything alright in there with Maam Faya?" asked Mr. Tom through the bedroom door. "Yes, honey," she answered. "Everything is fine. I'll be downstairs in a few minutes."

"Okay," he said, relief sounding in his voice. "If you need anything, just give me a yell." "Okay, hon," she told him. "He's such a dear man," I said to her. "You're so lucky, Grandmom." "You are too, Tyla, girl," she said. I smiled at her.

I sighed, then took a deep breath, held onto her hands tightly, and told her everything that Emma told me about the abusive relationship with Oliver Turner. Also, I told her about the dreams that she'd had about Andrew Jr. and what he told her in the dreams.

Grandmom Faya's heart fell to her stomach, she said. "Why didn't she ever come to me about this?" she asked. "Or to Miriam? I'm going to call Sheriff Reilly." I shook my head. "I already told him about Oliver, Grandmom Faya," I told her. "He said that there was nothing he could do and that she had a Restraining Order against him! But he did say that he would keep an eye on Oliver."

"Well," she said, "it's almost two o'clock in the afternoon now. I want to report her missing!" "But don't you have to wait for so many hours before you do that?" I asked. "Tyla girl," she said patiently, "we live in a small town, not a big city! It's a little different! Now you lie down and rest! Okay?" I nodded and went over to my bed and laid down.

Grandmom Faya left my bedroom. She went downstairs to call the Sheriff. Within twenty minutes, he was at our house. He asked Grandmom Faya for a photograph of Emma that he could put into circulation in Maron and surrounding counties.

"Tyla told me about a previous murder of another girl that Oliver was going with before he met Emma," Sheriff Reilly told my grandmother. "Do you know where that was? I can look it up and see what I can find out." "I never heard that before," she told him. "So I don't know." She was right! I left that part of the story out purposely.

By the time Gary, Malin, and Nicholas came home that evening, Emma was still missing. It was almost six thirty, and we had received no word from her. The Sheriff and his Deputies began a search for her. They searched in Vaira and in Tolstoy also. Hesitantly, Sheriff Reilly and the others searched the wooded area behind our house. She was officially declared missing around midnight, which is when their search finally ended for the day. I breathed a sigh of relief when they found nothing in the woods behind our house. Three days later, my sister was still missing.

Gary stayed home from work to be with me because I was extremely distraught. Sheriff Reilly also notified us that Oliver Turner had been found in Watsonville, where he was born and raised. His parents were still there. When the Sheriff questioned them, they told him that their son had never been in Maron. It was a barefaced lie, and the Sheriff wasn't fooled.

The family of the girl that Oliver was suspected of murdering previously, Amy Hart, still lived in Watsonville too. "That bastard killed my daughter!" shouted Evelyn Hart when Sheriff Reilly went to her home to ask her some questions about Oliver. "He did it!" she screamed. "I don't care if they ever prove it or not. He killed my daughter!"

Oliver Turner was brought back to Maron for questioning about Emma's disappearance. I wanted to see him, but Gary and both my grandmothers wouldn't let me near the Sheriff's office that day. I think they thought I was going to do something to him, and they were right.

I still had the gun that Emma owned. I put it into my purse that day when they brought him back to Maron. I was on my way out of the door to go to the Sheriff's office when Gary stopped me.

"Where are you going babe?" he asked me pleasantly. "I'm just going into town to window shop," I lied. "Well, you won't mind if I go with you then huh?" he asked me. "Yes Gary, I do mind!" I said. He was getting on my nerves. "And why is that?" He knew I was up to something. I was definitely going to put a bullet into Oliver Turner that day. "I have to go," I told him impatiently as I opened the front door to leave. But he was right behind me.

"Where are you going?" I asked him. "With you, my darling!" he said. "With you!" He had a big silly grin on his face. "Why?" I asked, obviously upset even more by then. "Why do you have to go into town *today*?" he asked sarcastically. "Since when do you question where I go?" I retorted, getting angry at him. "I don't care if you get angry, Ty," he told me in a calm voice. "What's in your purse anyway?"

Angrily, I put the car keys back and stormed into the kitchen, where both Grandmom Faya and Grandmom Miriam were. I sat down at the table, pouting. The two of them looked at me, smiling. "Something wrong?" asked Grandmom Miriam.

I didn't say anything. I could tell that they had all been talking about me, and Gary accompanying me into town that day was planned. I guess in the end, I was thankful for those people who loved me so much. It would have been a terrible mistake for me to shoot Oliver Turner. He wasn't even worth a bullet. I realized that later on when I came back to myself.

"Everything will be fine, sweetheart," Gary said lovingly as he came into the kitchen and sat down next to me. Then he put his arms around me. "You have to let the law handle this, Ty. Okay?" I looked at him. Suddenly, tears filled my eyes. But they were not tears of sorrow but tears of rage. My husband knew that too. He wiped the tears from my eyes.

"He will pay, Tyla, honey," he said in a soft voice. "He will. I promise you that. One way or the other." Then I looked at him strangely. "*What does he mean by that?*" I wondered. I knew what he meant. It wasn't long after Gary and I got married that I found out that he had some rather dangerous relatives who didn't mind taking care of *other people's problems*. Permanently.

A criminal record search by Sheriff Reilly revealed a startling surprise to us. Not only had Oliver Turner been the prime suspect in the murder of Amy Hart one year before, two women had been murdered five years ago, six months apart. One in Vaira County and the other one in Watsonville. He had to leave Watsonville because of the second murder. The people there knew that he had done it, but it couldn't be proven.

Once again, his family bought him out of trouble. However, the people of Watsonville let Oliver know in no uncertain terms he was no longer wanted there. So he left. All of the murdered women had been girlfriends of his until they turned up missing.

Oliver's father, Wesley Turner, was a hot-shot criminal attorney worth millions of dollars. Oliver was his only child, born when Wesley was in his late fifties, to a woman he had an affair with for ten years. Somehow, with his money, he got custody of Oliver from the woman when he was only six months old. Wesley's wife, Anna, was the only mother that Oliver ever knew.

From the time that he was a teenager, all the boy ever did was stay in trouble. It cost Wesley and Anna a lot of money over the years to buy him out of it because he did anything that he wanted to do. He knew that his father bail him out of anything. Even murder. And he did. In a way, I felt sorry for the creep. He couldn't love anybody because he never knew what love was. All his parents ever did was throw money at him.

Two weeks passed by and there was still no word about my sister. Everybody suspected the worst by then. Although I already knew that Emma was dead. I was taking a nap one afternoon while everybody was gone from the house. The house was quiet that afternoon, and I began to dream.

I found myself in a place that I had never seen before. It was someone's house. It was a strange-looking house, and it looked like nobody had lived there for many years. It was badly in need of repairs, and it looked as if whoever owned it had just abandoned it. Curious, I went inside.

Nobody was at home. The furniture and a pot of water that was boiling on top of the stove let me know that somebody did still live there. Cautiously, I went throughout the house, looking around. But I never saw anybody. Then I went downstairs to the basement.

"Aunt Charon" was sitting down there in a rocking chair, rocking back and forth. "Hi, Tyla!" she said to me. "Are you still looking for Emma?" "Yes," I told her spirit. "Emma!!" she called. "Yes!" It was my sister's voice that responded to her call. "Tyla is here to see you!!" Aunt Charon said.

I heard the footsteps of someone coming down the basement stairs. Then Emma appeared. She was wearing the same pale green chiffon dress that she had on when I last saw her. The dress was torn, dirty, and bloodied, just as she had seen in her dream that she told me about.

I was so happy to see her that I ran over to her to hug her and kiss her. "Stop right there!!" she shouted at me in the dream. "Ty, what's wrong with you? You know you can't touch me! You know that you're not supposed to touch the dead!"

In my dream, I started to sob. "Where are you, Emma?" I asked her. "We can't find you anywhere! I miss you so much! Where is this place? I don't know this place! Please, I can't find you! Where are you?"

"Ty," said my sister's spirit kindly, "you have to stop getting yourself all upset. Think about your baby." "I don't care anymore," I said. "I need to find you!" "Poor Ty," she said, "didn't you get the address on the front door of the house before you came inside?" "No," I said. "I don't remember seeing any address."

"Come on, then," she said, "I'll show you. And don't forget it, okay?" Then she led me outside to the front of the house and showed me the address. "Don't forget that address, Ty," Emma told me. Then she was gone. "If you want to find Emma, Ty! Remember this address!" It was my brother, talking. Andrew Jr.! I saw the address and recited it to myself. It was 1364. "What is this street called?" I asked him. "It's called Townes Street, Ty," he replied.

Almost immediately, I awakened. *"1364 Townes Street!" I thought. "I wonder where that is? There's no such street in Maron! Wherever it is, that's where my sister is!"*

Jumping up, I ran downstairs. I kept thinking about my dream. I sat down on the sofa in the living room. I was waiting for everyone to return home so I could tell them about my dream. I put my head back and closed my eyes for a few seconds.

When I opened my eyes again, *there was Emma*. She was sitting on the sofa right next to me. I caught my breath, but I was so startled I couldn't speak. She smiled at me lovingly.

"Don't forget that address, Ty," she told me. "It's important if you want to find *me!*" Then her spirit began to slowly fade away as I watched. It frightened me, but I quickly calmed down. I loved Emma, and she loved me. "*How can I fear someone that I love and who loves me?*" I thought. It was then that all of the fear of the dead that I'd carried around for so long left me forever.

CHAPTER TWENTY-ONE

As soon as the rest of the family arrived home that day, I told them about the dream that I had and about Emma coming to me. Immediately, we telephoned Sheriff Reilly. He was skeptical at first, but then he recalled the *strange things* he heard about the Davidson family from the people in town. He didn't tell his Deputies about my dream or what he heard about us.

"We have a lead on Emmaline Davidson's whereabouts," he told them. "So we're going to follow up on it." Then he gave his men the *address* that was given to me in my dream. They knew there was no such address in Maron, so they broadened their search. The following day, he got back to us. "We figured there was no such address in town," he told us. "But we searched anyway."

"Try Watsonville," I suggested. "That's where Oliver is from!" Sheriff Reilly checked there too. Still, no such address could be found. Frustrated, he checked in Vaira, Tolstoy, Brewer, and a couple of other counties. He came up with nothing.

"I don't understand it," I said. "That's the address that they gave me in the dream! Emma told me not to forget it!" "It has to be somewhere, Sheriff," Gary told Sheriff Reilly. We were all confused. There had to be a *1364 Townes Street* somewhere.

"Maybe it's not a house," suggested Malin. "Yeah," said Nicholas. "But what else could it be?"

Emma had been missing for three weeks by then. My birthday was also approaching, but I didn't care. All I wanted to do was find my sister. None of us could stop thinking about the strange address that was in my dream. Not even the Sheriff. He pored over it day and night but couldn't figure out what or where it could be.

"I'll tell you what," Mr. Tom said one night at the dinner table. "We'll hire a private investigator. I know a guy who owes me a favor from years back that I never collected on. He's an ex-cop. If anybody can find this place, he can. At least now we know that *it's not a house."* "You're right, hon," said Grandmom Faya. "I just can't imagine what else it could be, though."

"Well," said Gary, "one thing about Ty's dream always bothered me." "What's that?" asked Malin. "Well," said Gary, "it's the basement, and Emma coming down the stairs." "Oh?" asked Linda. "Why is that, Gary?" "Because," he said, "it's like she was descending, or going down. You know, like what's underground."

"Of course," said Grandmom Miriam. "Why didn't we think of that, before? Charon, and Andrew, Jr. were already there, right? Emma was coming down! Of course! Gary, you're brilliant!" My husband was proud of himself for coming up with an idea that none of the rest of us ever thought of. "So," Linda joined in, "now, all we have to do is figure out what things are underground, that have numbers."

"Well," said Mr. Tom, "a lot of places have lot numbers! I'll give my friend that information. It'll help him out." And he did just that.

Beryl Matheson was thrilled to hear from his old friend, Tom Garrison. They hadn't seen each other in twenty years. But they kept in touch with one another over the years.

Mr. Tom had saved Beryl's life, when they were in the Service. Their entire company was wiped out, during a secret mission that they were on, for the government. Only Mr. Tom and Beryl Matheson survived! Beryl was shot up, pretty badly. But, Mr. Tom carried him, for three miles, to safety. They were rescued after two days. For those two days, Mr. Tom kept himself, and Beryl alive, with only water to drink.

Beryl couldn't wait to see Mr. Tom, again. And meet Grandmom Faya, and the rest of us. Mr. Tom telephoned him, on the previous night. And Beryl Matheson told him that he would be there, that next morning.

True to his words, Beryl arrived early that morning. He was a big, tall man. He was gray, only at his temples, like Mr. Tom. And he looked like he spent a lot of time outdoors. He had a sharp eye for detail, and a quick mind. For thirty-five years, he worked for a big city police department out West. Before, he retired and started doing private investigations. It sure looked like he was doing very well, too. He had been married and divorced! And he insisted that we call him, Beryl, not Mr. Beryl, or, Mr. Matheson. All of us liked him, right away.

Mr. Tom, and Grandmom Faya fixed breakfast that morning. And, as we ate, we told Beryl about Emma, and about the dream that I had. "Sounds like a mighty odd address, to me," said Beryl, gulping down a cup of coffee. "In fact, I don't believe I've ever heard of that street before."

"We don't think it's a house, on a street, anymore, Beryl," said Mr. Tom. "Oh?" he asked, puzzled. "No," said Grandmom Faya. "We think it's something underground." "More coffee, Beryl?" asked Grandmom Miriam. Linda, and Grandmom Faya noticed an instant attraction between Beryl, and Grandmom Miriam. I was too upset to notice anything like that. They couldn't keep their eyes off one another, Linda told me, later.

Beryl went to work on the case, right after breakfast. He was staying in town, at the new boarding house. Sara Cosby finally turned the gas station over to her sons. And opened her home to roomers. It was mostly for strangers passing through Maron. It shocked everybody in town. No one ever thought they'd see the day, when she trusted Jimmy and Danny to do anything on their own.

That night, Beryl came back to the house and informed us that he had a few leads that he would follow up on the next day. In the meantime, he asked Grandmom Miriam out to a movie. She happily accepted.

Linda, Malin, Nicholas, and I almost didn't recognize Grandmom Miriam after she got dressed up. She looked stunning! She hadn't been dressed up like that since my wedding day. She got compliments from all of us. Beryl's eyes sparkled when he saw her. She was beautiful.

"Well, well," said Grandmom Faya, so softly only we could hear her. "What do we have here? A budding romance, think." Then, she said to them, "Have a good time, you two!" She and Mr. Tom walked them to the front door and waved to them as they drove off in Beryl's car.

We didn't see Beryl anymore until late the next morning. He arrived at our house with Grandmom Miriam, who hadn't come home all night. No one knew but Grandmom Faya because she waited up for her.

However, I did notice that Grandmom Miriam had a glow on her face that she hadn't had since I knew her. Something happened between her and Beryl. They didn't bother to hide their feelings for one another, either.

As it turned out, Beryl Matheson was the only one who was successful in the search for the strange address in my dream. He had been following various leads for days when he got a telephone call. It was an unusually warm Autumn day, and the telephone call was one that none of us would ever forget. Also, it was the beginning of a chain of events that would change all of our lives forever.

A man on the other end of the telephone line asked for Beryl when Grandmom Faya answered it. "Hold on, please," she told him. She called Beryl to the telephone.

CHAPTER TWENTY-TWO

My sister's body was found twenty five miles away from Maron in an abandoned wooded area known as *Townes Park*. She was buried in a shallow grave! After a heavy rain the night before, part of her body had come to the surface. It was discovered by some children who were walking through the park.

Townes Park has recently been sectioned off into lots which were in the process of being numbered. It was to serve as a trailer park for people passing through the area on their way across country and needed a place to stop and rest. Amazingly, the section where Emma's body was found had been numbered *1364*. Beryl was familiar with *Townes Park*. He asked a friend of his, the same man who called on the telephone, to check the area for him. He did.

Many years ago, Beryl and his family stopped there on their way across country. First, he forgot all about it. After all, since his divorce fifteen years earlier, he had no reason to remember it. However, he carried photographs of his two adult daughters and his grandchildren to show off to people.

One night, he was showing the photographs to Grandmom Miriam. She noticed the background area in one of the photographs of his oldest daughter. She must have been around fifteen years old in the picture.

"Where is this place, Beryl?" she asked him. "Oh," he replied, "that's over in old Townes Park!" At that instant, it hit them both like a bolt of lightning! And they looked at each other.

"Okay," Beryl said quietly. "I'll get the Sheriff to go over there and check that area." Immediately, he called Sheriff Reilly, who investigated right away and found the Park. It was indeed sectioned off into lot numbers! By the time Sheriff Reilly got there, the Sheriff of that county was already on the scene. So was the Coroner! And the Police Crime Lab wagon.

Of course, my family and I were devastated. Emma had been brutally beaten, raped, tortured, and almost decapitated by her killer! It was exactly the same way that Amy Hart had been murdered! Our 'grandmothers' and I went down to the morgue with Beryl and Mr. Tom to identify the body. Nicholas and Malin couldn't take it. So, they stayed at home.

Nicolas made it quite clear that they had better hurry up and find Oliver Turner before he and Malin did! We knew my brother did not make empty threats! He had been in the Service long enough to know about firearms. And he had done his share of killing. One more wouldn't have mattered to him. At the morgue, I almost fainted!

My sister's body was hardly recognizable! It was swollen to almost twice its normal size due to the torture and beating that she suffered. Furthermore, the body had been in the ground a long time, the Coroner told us. Sheriff Reilly added that it was the work of a Psychopath.

The pale green chiffon dress that Emma was wearing was ripped to pieces. It was placed into a plastic bag along with other clothing that had been ripped to shreds. Her nylons, panties, bra, and other clothing were gathered together for evidence. One of her ear lobes was split in two from the earring being yanked out of her ear. She had no shoes on her feet when they found her. And we never did recover them. I couldn't be comforted.

I knew without a doubt Oliver Turner had murdered my sister. As well as all of those other women. I told the Sheriff that. However, Oliver disappeared as if dropping off the face of the earth. No doubt, compliments of Daddy's big bucks.

No words could describe the great loss our family suffered. None of us knew what direction to go in. For several days, after we buried Emma in the family plot, everybody walked around in a dazed silence. We felt so helpless! Most of the time, I laid in bed thinking about Emma. *"If it's the last thing that I ever do, I'll make that bastard pay for killing my sister!"* I vowed.

Every day, I telephoned Sheriff Reilly to see if he had heard anything about Oliver Turner. But there was nothing! No one could find him! Naturally, his parents took a trip to Europe the same day that Emma's body was found. I hated those people! And I didn't even know them.

Gary was worried about me. And so were the 'grandmothers'. I was filled with bitterness, hatred, and anger toward Oliver Turner and his parents. I even scared myself. Because there was nothing I wouldn't have done to hurt him for what he did! As I look back now, I realize the dangerous situation that I was in. Because there was nothing beneath me! I even picked up the telephone one day to call Damion.

Damion Shelley was Gary's first cousin. And a known hit man! He had killed nearly eighty seven people and was only twenty six years old. However, he didn't have a criminal record of any kind. Not even a parking ticket! He lived in Hawaii!

At our wedding, Damion told Gary and I that he never planned on getting married. But he would sure like to get next to Emma. And he didn't say it in a disrespectful way, either. He liked her, that's all. She talked to him all during the reception. But then she retreated to her bedroom as usual. I wished that she had talked more with Damion. Maybe something would have come out of it.

"Yeah, I'll bet Oliver would have taken his ass and gone on about his business then! And left my sister alone!" I thought. But I didn't call Damion! If I had, I knew he would have contacted Gary. And I didn't want that.

The anger and frustration inside me kept building. For the first time in my entire life, I knew what it felt like to hate someone. Most of the time, I was silent. But everybody knew what I was thinking.

"I don't like seeing Maam like this, Faya," I overheard Mr. Tom say one day to Grandmom Faya. "It isn't healthy, you know." "I know, hon," she agreed. "But we'll just have to give her some time, I guess."

Even my dear sweet husband was almost out of his mind with worry about me. "Honey," he told me, "I know how you feel. But you have to let this go! Let Sheriff Reilly handle it. Believe me, they'll get him." "Do you really, Gary?" I turned and snapped at him. "Do you really know how I feel?"

I was angry at him for being so calm and cool when I was in a turmoil inside. As soon as I said those words, I wished I could have taken them back. Of course, he knew how I felt. A drunk driver had taken the life of his brother. "I'll pretend that you didn't say that," is all he said to me. Then he walked away. I knew I had hurt him by my careless words.

My anger was so intense that I didn't care if the law found Oliver Turner or not. I wanted revenge in the worst way. Every time I recalled how my sister died, I would burst into tears.

At the funeral, my family had to pry me off my sister's casket. My dear sister was such a beautiful person! She didn't deserve what happened to her. Lying in her casket, she looked so beautiful. Her hair had been light blonde streaked, which contrasted nicely with her dark brown hair. It looked good on her. Her hair had grown down her back, and the Undertaker did it very nicely. All of the marks on her body were completely covered over with makeup.

Emma wore a pale pink negligee, which both our 'grandmothers' bought for her funeral. A corsage was on her wrist. Linda made sure that she had the beautiful ruby ring on her finger that she gave her on her last birthday. She wanted Emma to be buried with that ring. In fact, she was adamant about it.

Even Ray Jamison and his wife came to the funeral. Seeing him and remembering how much he had loved my sister made me cry all the more. *"Her future would have been so different."* I thought. Ray cried too.

I knew then that he still loved my sister after all of that time that had passed. He loved his wife. But there was a different kind of love that he still felt for Emma. Seeing him made me so sad for Emma's sake. "Why? Why, Emma, didn't you give Ray a chance?" I thought.

The words *'Beloved Sister'* were engraved on her casket, which was only half opened. The Undertaker couldn't get any shoes on her feet due to the swelling in her body. Her legs were still swollen too.

As I watched the casket being lowered into the ground, I almost passed out from the pain and sadness that I felt. Her name, *'Emmaline Davidson,'* and her birthday and her speculated date of death were atop the casket. *'Born 1970, Died 1993.'* Seeing her being buried emphasized the finality of her death for me. I would never be able to talk to her again, hear her laughter, or go shopping with her. Nothing. All because of some evil selfish maniac named Oliver Turner. She was my best friend. And then, she was gone forever.

I told Grandmom Faya and Mr. Tom that I didn't want Emma buried in the family cemetery behind our new house where the roots of all our family evil were buried. Roy, Marie, and Ole Lucy. She agreed. So, Emma was buried in the family plot at the house we moved away from years before, next to Aunt Charon and my brother Andrew Jr.

After Emma's death, the house, as well as our family, changed. Grandmom Faya was plagued almost every night by dreams of Emma. It was beginning to bother her too. I noticed that she hadn't been looking well. She began to look old. And so did Grandmom Miriam. Both of them would sit in the kitchen for hours talking about my sister. Then, one of them or both would start to sob.

Josie went about her daily duties. And Linda tried her best to keep a little cheer in the house. But it was no use. Nicola and Angie helped somewhat. They were little children and didn't understand why everyone was still so sad about Aunt Emma.

Through all of our sorrow, though, our family noticed that Linda and Nicholas seemed to be quarreling more and more. Most of the time, it was over silly things. The same things they used to laugh about when they first got married. There was a lot of tension in that house then. And things were not the same.

It was Grandmom Miriam who finally figured out that other forces were at work in that house. Probably because she spent a lot of time with Beryl at his place around then. She could sense more than we could. She was more like an outsider who could walk into a house and feel the presence of something not quite right. Since Beryl had decided to move to Maron, she was rarely ever home anymore.

"I've got to talk to Faya," Grandmom Miriam told me one day. "Something is wrong in this house. It's been here for a long time too. I think our unwanted tenants are at work. And have been for quite a while. I believe they are responsible for all of the heartache that we've been experiencing these past months. That's why we haven't *seen or heard from them*," she explained.

"Do you mean that you think they caused Emma's problems and her death?" I asked her. "And now Linda and Nicholas's problems?" "I damn sure do," she said angrily. I didn't doubt what she said for a minute. In fact, when I thought about it, it made sense. It all fit. Grandmom Miriam had it all figured out. She just didn't know it was already too late. The changes in our family were already in progress.

Then Malin announced that he was leaving home. He told me that he was going to join the Army and would probably make a career out of it. He didn't tell the others that he wasn't planning on coming back anymore. But that's what he told me. All he said was that he had to get away. Linda and I both knew why and promised him that we would keep his secret.

As if that news wasn't bad enough, Linda told us that when the New Year arrived, she and Nicholas would be leaving us for good too. What she didn't tell us that she felt Emma's presence in the house was coming between her and my brother. She thought it was best for them to leave if they wanted to save their marriage. But what she didn't know and nobody else could have guessed was that by the time the New Year rolled in, their marriage would be over anyway.

I still wondered even now if maybe that old attic that Grandmom Faya turned into an apartment for Linda and Nicholas had a hand in all of their unhappiness. The more I thought about it, the more I had to admit it probably was the cause of their breakup. So much evil had gone on up there in the past. How could any good come from a place like that? You can change everything around, paint the walls, and lay down carpet. But the evil is still there.

Gary and I thought things were becoming almost normal in that house again. I still kept track of the progress that Sheriff Reilly was making on my sister's case. But they hadn't found Oliver Turner yet.

Actually, it was only Gary and I who thought things were becoming normal again in that house. Unbeknownst to me, both 'grandmothers' were more cautious than ever before. Especially Grandmom Faya, who began to have heavy sorrowful feelings every day for a week.

"Don't worry about it Faya," Josie told her. "Look at it this way, whatever it is, I've found out from my experience there's nothing you can do about it! Whatever it may be!" But Josie didn't tell her that just before she lost her husband Georgie, whom she had loved dearly, she had similar feelings like the ones Grandmom Faya was having. The heavy feeling left her a few days before Georgie passed away. She didn't want to upset or frighten her. So she kept it to herself. Then again, she figured she could be wrong.

Since we knew him, Mr. Tom had developed a wonderful relationship with every member of our family, becoming the grandfather we never had. Nicola was very dear to him and would wait up for Mr. Tom when he took nightly walks around the town. Sometimes, he would take my nephew with him. But if he thought he might be getting back late, Nicola had to stay at home.

Nicola wouldn't go to bed until 'Grandpop' came home. He had long since stopped asking Linda to read bedtime stories to him. "Grandpop" was the only one that Nicola allowed to read stories to him. Linda was happy and glad that Nicola had a grandfather to tell him stories and spend time with him, since my brother was rarely at home anymore by then.

One night, Mr. Tom came home from his evening walk. Then he sat down in his favorite chair in the living room. He told Grandmom Faya that he felt extremely tired and fell asleep almost immediately. Nicola was disappointed that "Grandpop" couldn't read to him that night, but he was glad that he was home. He went to bed with the promise that he would see "Grandpop" in the morning.

Around ten o'clock that night, Grandmom Faya called downstairs to Mr. Tom, asking him to come to bed. She heard the television playing and figured he was still asleep. But he never answered her. After calling to him several times, she put on her robe and slippers, then went downstairs to awaken him. Mr. Tom was fast asleep in his favorite chair, his head drooped down to his chest. "Tom!" Grandmom Faya called to him. There was no answer.

"Tom," she said again, this time a little louder, "Wake up, honey! It's bedtime!" Then she nudged him, and he slid limply over to one side of the chair. Quickly, she felt his pulse. "Oh God! Oh God! Oh God, no! No!" she screamed. Everyone was awakened by her screaming and came running downstairs. Grandmom Faya sat on the floor, holding herself, rocking back and forth, and crying hysterically. "I can't take this anymore! No more!" she cried.

Linda got to her first. The rest of us followed. As soon as I saw him, I knew that Mr. Tom was dead. Immediately, I became hysterical too, throwing my arms around Mr. Tom. I cried and cried. They had to pry me away from him. I thought I would lose my mind for sure. Both Grandmom Faya and I had to be given sedatives to calm us down.

Doctor Maise, who had assisted old Doc Walker and worked at the hospital, arrived after being called. She was careful what she gave me because I was almost due to have my baby. She gave me the mildest sedative that she had. I had to have something to calm me down. Again, I was devastated.

Elisabeth Maise had gotten to know many of the longtime residents of Maron. She wasn't much older than I was and had no family. When she was eight years old, she lost her parents and grew up in an orphanage. Studying medicine, she worked her way through medical school. Mostly, she kept to herself. But she had become very close to me and my family after Doc Walker died.

Sam Evans, the Undertaker, came to the house with Sheriff Reilly after Grandmom Miriam telephoned him. He took Mr. Tom's body away after he gave it a precursory examination. "He had a heart attack as far as I can tell," he said. "His heart has probably been bad for years. But I'll have to do an autopsy on him to be sure." "He never told me that he had a bad heart," Grandmom Faya spoke up, looking at him through tear-filled eyes. Mr. Sam just smiled at her sympathetically.

The rest of that night, our family sat up, trying to comfort Grandmom Faya and me until both of us drifted off to sleep from the sedatives. As she put the children back to bed, Linda silently wondered where Nicholas was. With a sinking feeling in her heart, she believed she knew where he was.

The whole family noticed that Nicholas hardly came home at all since my sister's death. Linda heard the rumors around town that he was having an affair with a nineteen-year-old woman in Brewer. She didn't want to believe it. But she realized if she heard the rumors, so had everybody else. "They say the wife is the last one to know," she told me. She and I talked about her problems with Nicholas all the time.

Kissing the children good night for the second time, Linda began to recall the talk that she and I had a few weeks before that. "Linda, what are you going to do?" I asked her, referring to Nicholas. "I don't know, Ty," she replied sadly. "I feel like I'm helpless to do anything about it at all." Then she began to sob. I tried my best to comfort her. "Don't worry, Linda," I said reassuringly. "Maybe it's just something that he has to get out of his system."

"You're probably right, Ty," she said, wiping her eyes. "Anyway, the last thing you need is to be worried about my problems. You just think about that little bundle of joy that you and Gary have coming!"

Linda and I never told the rest of the family about Nicholas and what he was doing. And if any of them knew, they didn't act like they did. However, I would later find out that I was very wrong. It was not just something that my brother had to get out of his system. He was serious about his new love. He just didn't know how to tell Linda that he didn't love her anymore.

Sure enough, it turned out that Mr. Tom had never had any heart problems in his life. It bothered both Mr. Sam, the Undertaker, and my family. Here was a man who purportedly died of a heart attack but had never had any problems with his heart, let alone any other health problems. The autopsy revealed no reason at all for Mr. Tom to have suffered a heart attack. None.

For the funeral, Mr. Tom was laid out beautifully by Grandmom Faya. As he lay in his casket wearing a pin-striped suit, he looked so peaceful. He had been placed in the living room, and it was very crowded in the house that night. Many people from surrounding counties came to the funeral. He had a lot of friends.

Grandmom Faya held up very well during the funeral. But I fell apart. It was Emma's funeral all over again for me, and I cried most of that night and the next day. I still found it difficult to go into Emma's bedroom, and I couldn't seem to get over her death.

After viewing Mr. Tom's body, I went upstairs to my bedroom and stayed there. I didn't feel like seeing anyone. Grandmom Miriam came upstairs to see me. She held me comfortingly as I sobbed.

"Tyla, honey," she said soothingly, "there's nothing we can do about death. We just go on and remember all of the good times that we had with our loved one who leave us behind. We have to go on, though, okay?" Solemnly, I nodded my head. I knew what she said was true. But it still hurt so badly.

"I guess we'll have to be the strong ones now for a change, huh?" she asked me with a little chuckle. I smiled through my tears and asked her, "Do you think Grandmom Faya will be alright?" She smiled at me again. "We have to stand behind her right now, okay?" "Okay," I said.

After Grandmom Miriam left my bedroom, Linda came in to talk to me. "You know what, Linda?" I asked her. "What is it, Ty?" she answered. "God took Emma. But He left me another beautiful 'sister'!" I told her. We hugged each other. Linda and I loved one another very much.

As she left my bedroom to go back downstairs that night, I watched her. Somehow, I knew that I wouldn't have my dear sister-in-law much longer, either. She was seriously contemplating packing her and the children's things and leaving forever. She started thinking about it more and more, she told me.

I knew Linda was very unhappy. "The family doesn't realize it. But the evil in this house has never left us alone!" I thought. "I know those evil demons are behind all of the horrible things that are happening to us! I know it!" My thoughts made me angry.

Then as if they could hear my thoughts, I heard the faint laughter of a *man and a woman*. Quickly, I looked around my bedroom. But no one was there. At least, no one I could see. I did recognize the same eery evil laughter that I hadn't heard since the day that Linda dreamed about Gary's car. "*I was right!*" I told myself. "*They've never left!*" It seemed as if they were being silent but were still watching us and *working against us.*

The following morning, as we watched Mr. Tom's body being lowered into the ground at the family burial plot, it dawned on me that my birthday was only two days away. I would be turning *twenty one years old!*

CHAPTER TWENTY-THREE

It was Halloween and my twenty first birthday. This was the day that we had anticipated for many years. The day that was somehow our only chance to destroy the evil which tried to destroy all of us. Grandmom Faya told us that it was herself, Grandmom Miriam, myself, and another woman who would help us do it.

"The other woman who is going to help us tonight must be you, Linda" I told my sister-in-law that morning. But Linda shook her head. "Somehow, I don't think so, Ty" she told me. "It *has* to be you, Lin" I insisted. "Who else is there? We already know it's not Josie" "Do we?" Linda asked, looking at me seriously. "I don't know. But I'm sure it's not me, Ty."

For several moments, both Linda and I thought about it. "You know, Ty" Linda said finally, "I believe my being here has already helped the family somehow. Don't ask me how. But my presence here *has* served some purpose for you all. Maybe it's something that I said or did. I don't know. We may never know."

"It could be anything." I agreed. "If you feel that strongly about it, Linda." "Don't know," she said, still not sure. "But I do know that my being here had a purpose. Call me 'crazy.' But I think it's another woman in the *family* who is going to help you."

"What?" I said. "There is no one else, Linda. And I could have sworn Grandmom Faya told me and Emma that it was a woman coming who is in our family. The only one left is *you*, Linda." "Well, it's not me, Ty" she insisted. "Maybe Malin will bring a wife home today or something." She was joking with me, and we both laughed. Linda knew that idea was ridiculous. Not only because it would be unbelievable for Malin to suddenly come home on that particular day with a wife, but because he would not be marrying anyone. Malin was gay. Neither one of us had mentioned it to anybody else. But that was the reason that he left home. He was deep into a relationship with a guy he'd met in school named Charles. Charles came back to Maron with my brother. But they told nobody but me about their relationship with each other. Eventually, I told Linda. The grandmothers, Josie, Gary, Nicholas, and Mr. Tom never knew. They believed Malin when he said that he couldn't stay with us anymore after Emma's death.

"Listen to me, Ty," Linda said slowly. "Most witches and seers can only see things in partiality. Only God knows the future! It's probably only part of what Miss Faya was *seeing*. In other words, she couldn't see the actual person. It doesn't have to be *anyone* connected to the family at all!"

"Maybe you're right!" I told her. "We'll see soon enough, won't we?" She nodded her head, smiling. Grandmom Miriam and Beryl decorated the house inside and outside for Halloween. All the candy that Grandmom Faya bought before Mr. Tom passed away they put out for the children. There was nothing for anybody else to do.

Then, for my birthday, Gary and the children blew up lots of balloons. Grandmom Miriam baked me a cake. She put twenty one candles on top of it. We gave Josie the day off. Nicholas stayed out all night as usual. Linda knew he was probably with *her*.

As soon as dinner was over, Linda began to dress Angie and Nicola in their costumes. They were going out for trick-or-treat. She was very distraught over her failing marriage, which had once been so happy. She wondered what happened to both her and Nicholas. It all happened so fast, right after Emma died.

"Mommy!" said Nicola, breaking into her thoughts. "I don't like this costume. I wanted a Spider Man one!" "You look better as Superman, honey," Linda told him. And he was satisfied with that. Angie had a cold, so Linda wasn't sure if she would take her out or not, especially since they would be out late.

The grandmothers had already told her what they planned to do that night and thought it was best if both she and the children were not there. Accordingly, Linda arranged for her and the children to spend the night at Josie's house. That was great for Angie and Nicola because they loved Josie very much. Linda and the children left for Josie's house that evening.

Grandmom Miriam and Beryl had been recently talking about getting married. They loved each other, and Beryl wanted to go away for a couple of days with her. But she told him that it would have to wait until the following day. He agreed, asking her no questions. Then, on the pretense of not feeling very well, she got Beryl to leave our house around ten o'clock that night.

Luckily for us, Gary's father had taken him on a fishing trip in the mountains. They wouldn't be back until the next morning. There was nobody in that house but the three who were *supposed to be there*. Everybody else was gone.

I was lying across my bed when I heard a soft rapping on my bedroom door. "Come in," I called out. It was my grandmothers. "Okay, Tyla, girl," Grandmom Faya said as she patted my shoulder. "First of all, happy birthday to you again." Everybody had sung "Happy Birthday" to me that morning.

"Today, you are twenty one years old, honey," Grandmom Miriam said softly. "So, we've come to talk to you about what we need to do tonight, okay?" I sat up in the bed and listened to the two older women.

"Tyla," began Grandmom Faya in a serious no-nonsense voice, "what we do tonight no one can ever know about. Not even Gary. Do you understand?" "Yes," I answered, nodding my head.

"You are going to see and hear a lot of strange and scary things after we begin. But you must not be afraid, Tyla, because you should know by now what we're up against," Grandmom Miriam joined in the conversation. "Yes, I do," I agreed grimly. All of the strange occurrences and the stories of evil flashed through my mind.

"You have nothing at all to fear, honey," added Grandmom Faya reassuringly. "It is the evil that we will be destroying tonight that fears us. Remember that, okay?" "I will," I promised her. "But what about my baby?" "Nothing at all will happen to that sweet little baby, Ty," Grandmom Miriam promised me. "We will begin at eleven o'clock, which gives us exactly one half hour to get ready," Grandmom Faya said, looking at her watch. "But you said *'someone else'* would be here to help us," I told her anxiously.

"I know, sweetheart," she said. "But I don't think, in fact, I know it's not Linda. And Emma's dead. If there is another woman who will help us, we will just have to wait and see who it is." "Maybe it's *Teresa?*" I suggested, surprised at myself. Grandmom Miriam shook her head. "Teresa would have made that known a long time ago, Tyla, honey," she said. "It's *not* her either."

"This must be done by midnight," Grandmom Faya continued. "So we have to begin promptly at eleven o'clock. I'm going to have everything all set up for us. So you lie down for a few more minutes, Tyla, girl. We'll be back to get you." She patted me lightly on the cheek. Then both women left my bedroom.

With a heavy feeling in my stomach and chest, I laid back down on the bed. Even after the reassurance by the grandmothers, I was still worried. Then I felt my baby kick. I put my hand on my swollen stomach. "You don't even know that you're part of an *exorcism* tonight, do you, little one?" I said softly. Strangely, the baby kicked me again, as if to answer me. "Whoa!" I said. "Maybe you *do* now!"

As I laid there, waiting for the strange ritual to take place, I dozed off to sleep and began to dream. In my dream, Marie was chasing me and trying to grab me.

"Come here, girl!" she yelled at me. "Stop running away from me! I need you so I can become stronger!"

I was terrified. I didn't know where I was. But I kept running as fast as I could. Looking back in the dream, I saw her demonic spirit, dressed all in black, and her red eyes glowing hideously. Turning back quickly, suddenly, I found myself running right toward a *man* standing directly in my path with a horrible wicked grin on his face.

"Yes," he said with a wicked laugh, "*I need you too. You and your baby."* Then *he* opened his arms wide, as if waiting for me to run into them. I screamed in horror.

Suddenly, out of nowhere, I saw the arms of another spirit, and I instinctively knew they were the arms of a woman. The arms pushed the man to the ground, out of my way. Then a dark cloud engulfed and blinded me. Looking at the arms and hands of the spirit who was helping me in the dream, I noticed a beautiful ruby ring on one of the fingers. I had seen that ring before. But I couldn't remember where I had seen it.

The evil spirit chasing me almost caught up to me when the ghostly arms appeared again. They shoved me down to the ground. Then encircled the evil spirit that was chasing me. The strange dark cloud left me, allowing my sight to fully return. Then enveloped the two evil demons.

From where I lay on the ground in the dream, I couldn't see what was happening. But I could hear them screaming. Terrifying screams that sounded like nothing of this world. As the spirits *fought*, 'others' came from all sides to surround me. Then I saw the spirit of an old gray-haired woman standing some distance away from me! She had cold evil black eyes that glared at me hatefully! I knew instantly it was Ole Lucy.

Suddenly, Andrew Jr., 'Aunt Charon', and *another* woman whom I knew must have been 'Teresa' were there. In unison, they yelled at me to "Run! Get help! You can't be here alone, Tyla!" It was at that moment that the *arms and hands* with the ruby ring appeared again. They wrapped themselves around my shoulders as if to protect me.

With a start, I awakened! My heart was racing! I was sweating all over my body. And the feeling of terror lingered. The dream had seemed so real! Then I realized that somehow 'Marie's' evil spirit and the 'others' with her had pulled me into their spirit world. Also, I knew that if she had caught me in the dream, I would have died! *"Is that what happened to Mr. Tom?"* I wondered.

"Are you alright in there, Tyla, honey?" It was Grandmom Miriam. She came into my bedroom. I was visibly shaken from the dream. "Grandmom Miriam!" I said breathlessly, "I just had a terrible dream!" "What did you dream about, honey?" she asked me with concern. But before I could answer her, we heard Grandmom Faya say, "You'll have to tell us as we get ready, Tyla, girl*! It's time to get started!"* While we were going downstairs, I described the dream as the two women prepared for what we had to do.

"*They* are terrified of us," Grandmom Faya said when I finished telling them about the dream. "*They* are trying to frighten you, Tyla. But after this night, they will be gone forever! I promise you that!" "Who was the woman who helped you in the dream, honey?" asked Grandmom Miriam. "I don't know," I told her in frustration. "I never saw anything except her *arms and hands!* Oh, and a beautiful ruby ring that I knew I've seen before was on one of her fingers! I just can't remember where I've seen that ring! Whoever she was, those wicked spirits were afraid of *her! She was protecting me in the dream!*"

"A ruby ring?" Grandmom Miriam echoed thoughtfully. "Who do we know that wore a ruby ring, Faya?" she asked. "I seem to recall somebody having a ring like that too," said Grandmom Faya. "But who is it? I can't remember!" "With so much happening in this family lately, I can't think right now," said Grandmom Miriam. "But it will reveal itself! Whoever she is, she's the one who is going to help us tonight, obviously!"

Then Grandmom Faya must have thought back to the day we buried Emma. Because she said, "A lot of changes began in this family after Emma's death. Changes that none of us ever expected!" After a minute, she continued. "And I would bet every dollar that I have that Tom *saw something* that night that terrified him. And caused him to have a heart attack!"

Also, I began to think about poor Mr. Tom. He loved our family. But he never really got used to the eerie things that regularly occurred in that house. Then she thought about the day that Malin left us. I saw tears in her eyes. We all missed him so very much.

Malin telephoned Grandmom Faya when he got to the train station in Brewer. "Grandmom," he told her, "I didn't tell you while I was packing because I wanted to wait until I got here." "Tell me what, sweetheart?" she asked him. He hesitated. "I'm gay, Grandmom Faya," he blurted out. "And I'm in love with

Charles! I'm going away with him!" Grandmom Faya wasn't as surprised as he thought she would be. In fact, she suspected there was something going on between Malin and Charles the day they arrived at our house from college.

Charles Wayne Ross was not a young handsome man. But he was kind and he loved people just as Malin did. He came from a large family in a city on the East coast. His family disowned him when he told them that he was gay. His father even cut off his college tuition money. Charles was forced to drop out of school until he could find a job.

Although he spent the night at our house when he and Malin arrived home, the rest of the time he spent at Sara's boarding house. He and Malin were trying to keep their relationship a secret from the rest of our family. They told me and I told Linda. Other than that, nobody else knew about them.

"Are you happy, honey?" Grandmom Faya asked him. "Yes, Grandmom Faya," he answered her. "I am." "Well, that's all that matters, isn't it?" she told him. "I love you, Grandmom Faya," said Malin. "You do know that, don't you?" But Grandmom Faya didn't answer him right away. She knew there was more that he wanted to tell her. She waited. My brother hesitated again.

"Malin?" asked Grandmom Faya, waiting for him to finish talking to her. "I'm not coming back, Grandmom Faya," he told her bluntly. "You can't mean that honey," she told him. "We're your family!" "I know," he said. "But I can't ever come back there. There's too much pain! I'm leaving for good, Grandmom Faya!" Grandmom Faya felt a pain stab in her heart when he told her that. She couldn't say anything.

"Grandmom Faya, are you still there?" Malin asked anxiously. "Yes, honey," she said, "I'm here." Silent tears were rolling down her cheeks. But she didn't let him know that she was crying. Ever since Malin was a little boy, she knew if he made up his mind about doing something, he did it! She knew we would never see him again.

"It's really weird," he told Grandmom Faya, "but when I was on my way to the bus stop in town, I looked back to get a last look at the house." He paused. "Yes?" replied Grandmom Faya, waiting. "I saw Emma, Grandmom Faya," Malin told her. "She was standing on the porch, waving 'good-bye' to me. I thought I was seeing things! So I squeezed my eyes shut tight. Then opened them again. She was gone!"

"You probably did see her, sweetheart," Grandmom Faya told him. "She doesn't want you to leave us, just as we don't." "I love you all, Grandmom Faya," he said. "Good-bye!" Then the telephone disconnected.

Grandmom Faya cried openly after that. She never told the rest of the family about their conversation, only me. And when she did, I didn't think I could go on living without ever seeing my beloved brother again. I couldn't believe how all of our lives were changing. And all because of the wickedness that went on in our family *before* we were even born.

CHAPTER TWENTY-FOUR

After everything was over and done with, Grandmom Faya explained to me all of the preparations that she made for the *exorcism* that night. Earlier that evening, she went downstairs to the basement to ready the room that we would be using. The room was unusually cold while the rest of the basement was warm. But she didn't let the cold bother her.

She carried a brown leather box under her arms that she laid on the floor in the basement. She took a key from her pocket and unlocked it. After she opened the box, she took things out of it that she needed.

Grandmom Faya took a piece of black and white chalk from the box first. It looked like a marble cake with chocolate and vanilla swirling through it. She'd had it specially made over twenty years before. Just for that particular night! The woman who made it for Grandmom Faya instructed her to be sure the piece of chalk sat untouched for two decades. She followed the woman's instructions to the letter.

She drew a circle with the piece of chalk. Then she drew another circle inside that one. Then she drew a smaller circle inside that one. "Alebei Alebei Cumbahala," she chanted three times, turning around inside the smallest circle as she did.

Suddenly, the black and white circles changed into solid colors! The largest circle became solid black while the two smaller circles became all white. She smiled.

Then she got seven candles out of the leather box. Two of the candles were red, three of them were white, and one was a fiery orange color. And the last one was all black. She placed them at different points on the smaller circle. The solid black candle was at the top point. She lit them one by one, chanting as she did.

"Barubuah Alebei Spirutuah," she chanted those words seven times in succession. The flames on the burning candles turned to a beautiful blue color.

flame on the black candle turned blood-red in color. Again, Grandmom Faya smiled.

The things she used were very old and had never been used by anyone else. Grandmom Faya was glad that everything was working the way it was supposed to. It was imperative that everything be done correctly. Or it could be detrimental to herself, Grandmom Miriam, and me.

Many people didn't believe in *demonic possession*. But Grandmom Faya had seen it firsthand in 'Aunt Charon'. There was nothing she wouldn't have done to protect me from 'Marie' who was patiently awaiting my twenty-first birthday. She wanted to use her own daughter to wreak more havoc on the sisters who successfully defeated her in her lifetime.

My twenty-first birthday was the only chance Marie would ever have to possess my soul. My unborn baby would give her added power but be destroyed in the process. However, with Marie destroyed, the others with her, including Ole Lucy, would also be destroyed.

Inside the leather box was a beautiful golden amulet that had belonged to my great-grandmother, the mother of both my 'grandmothers'. It had been given to her by her father to protect her from Ole Lucy when he wasn't around.

Grandmom Faya recalled how her mother always believed the amulet, with its strange power, had protected her from Ole Lucy's wicked plot against her. Her father told her never to take it off while she was around Ole Lucy. It had great power over people. Grandmom Faya's mother gave it to her just before they took her away from them.

Earlier that day, she put the amulet around my neck and told me to keep it on. I was not to take it off. I couldn't take it off until the next day. "Why, Grandmom Faya?" I asked her. "Because it will keep Marie away from you, Tyla girl," she told me. "Today is your twenty-first birthday, remember? You're especially vulnerable to her evil power now."

I did as she told me to do. "Okay, Grandmom Faya, I won't take it off." That was when she told me the story behind the beautiful piece of jewelry. Grandmom Faya reached into the leather box again and took out a long white hooded robe that was trimmed with gold. She put it on and covered her head with the hood.

Then she got a Bible from the box and opened it to the twenty-third Psalm, the one that *Marie* hated. She laid it in front of the burning black candle and chanted, "Locallah Inyusah Alebei," seven times.

I asked both 'grandmothers' why *Marie* hated the twenty-third Psalm so much."Because," said Grandmom Miriam, "it's a prayer of protection. It mentions how, while walking through the valley of the shadow of death, you will fear no evil. And that goodness and mercy shall follow you all of the days of your life. Not wickedness and evil."

It made sense to me. But I figured Marie should have hated the whole Bible, not just one chapter. However, the 'grandmothers' explained that this Psalm was the most powerful one that we could use against her.

The last item that Grandmom Faya took from the box, while still chanting, was wrr, one was for Grandmom Miriam, and one was for me. She laid each one of them on the opened Bible.

"Seroichyah Seirocha Da," she chanted. Everything was going perfectly. She was pleased with her work. Then she removed her robe and laid it within the three circles. Then she came to get Grandmom Miriam and me.

When the three of us descended the stairs to the room in the basement, it was five minutes until eleven o'clock. Without speaking, we entered the small cold room that had been readied earlier for our task.

Grandmom Miriam put on a royal blue hooded robe trimmed with gold, pulling the hood over her head. In turn, I put on a deep dark red hooded robe that was trimmed with black and silver that Grandmom Faya gave to me. She placed the hood over my head. Then she put on her robe and covered her own head.

"Tyla," she said, "you must trust us! And do whatever we tell you to do." "Okay, Grandmom Faya," I replied, becoming frightened. But I didn't want to let them know it. However, I think they knew anyway.

"We must stand inside the three circles and hold onto one another's hands," Grandmom Faya continued. "Do NOT let go at any cost!!" She repeated emphatically. I nodded, as did Grandmom Miriam.

"Tyla," said Grandmom Faya, "you will stand in front of the black candle." I took my place where she instructed me. We proceeded with the ritual, the entire time with Grandmom Faya telling us what to do. First, we recited the twenty-third Psalm in unison seven times. The air in the room became colder than it already was. A light wind came into the small room from nowhere that we could see. It was blowing at the candles as if trying to blow them out.

"Leave this place forever!" Grandmom Faya shouted to someone unseen. "You are not wanted here! No one wants you here! Leave here now! You will leave this house and NEVER come back! You will NEVER bother any of our family members ever again! We are free of you forever!! Be gone now!! Be gone, I say!"

Then Grandmom Miriam began to speak.

"*The spirits of heaven surround us now!! You cannot touch us! You cannot touch the circles that protect us! They are blessed by the Almighty, Who Has All Power over you! Tyla is of this world! She belongs here!* YOU ARE NOT OF THIS WORLD! YOU DO NOT BELONG HERE! YOU ARE DOOMED! YOU ARE BANISHED TO THE DEPTHS OF HELL FOR ALL ETERNITY!! YOU ARE BANISHED FROM THIS WORLD FOREVER! GO NOW!"

Together, both Grandmom Faya and Grandmom Miriam began to chant "Alebei Alebei Serahlo Da!" over and over again. They squeezed my hands, signaling me to repeat those words as they were doing. I joined in.

Suddenly, the room turned to a bone-chilling cold. I had never felt cold like that in all of my life. Then we heard the eerie evil laughter all around us. Ignoring it, we kept on chanting. Closing our eyes, we saw the spirit of my brother, Andrew Jr., inside the three circles with us. He stood there with us, and even with my eyes closed shut, *I could still 'see' him!* It felt strange to be able to 'see' with my eyes tightly closed shut. It was spooky too!

"You will need help," my brother's spirit told us. "But I am not strong enough to *help you!*" Then the flames on the burning candles flickered and blew in one direction toward me! The sound of running water was heard too. But in reality, it was blood that was running down all four walls of that cold little room. It poured freely down the walls and onto the floor. But it could not enter the *three circles* where we stood. Finally, it ceased to flow! But it made a pool around us and the circles up to our waistlines. The *three circles*, however, remained as dry as a bone. It was horrifying.

The old gray-haired woman I had seen in my dream stood on the outside of the largest circle. She was right next to me. With our eyes still closed, we 'saw' everything that was happening around us. The old woman was a terrifying presence. But we kept on chanting! She glared at us. The look on her face was the most evil that I had ever 'seen.'

The *old gray-haired evil spirit tried* to reach for us as if to pull us out of the protective *circles* that kept us safe. But each time *she* tried to reach inside the circles, her hand caught fire! Several times, she tried. Each time she touched the outer *circle*, it burned her! Yet *she* kept trying to touch me. Then the spirit screamed! A blood-curdling scream that raised the hairs on the backs of our necks! But we were not moved! Then the spirit of Ole Lucy yelled at us. "*Sumatiyalo! Sumatiyalo! Birealta! Birealta!*" Instantly, *Marie* appeared next to me. And Roy appeared next to Grandmom Miriam. They were *both* laughing. An evil laughter that was not of this world!

I felt myself becoming more and more frightened. Terror was enveloping me. But I remembered what both 'grandmothers' told me. I stood my ground! I knew they were depending on me to do my part in the ritual as much as I was depending on them to help me. My hands clutched theirs tightly.

I could 'see' Marie banging on my arms with her fists, yet I couldn't feel it. *She* was trying desperately to scare me into letting go of my 'grandmothers' hands! The room began to move from side to side as if the 'spirits' were trying to make us fall out of the circles! At one point, it turned so far, it looked like we were *standing on the ceiling* instead of the floor. All of a sudden, a deep red-colored mist covered the three of us! We could 'see' the evil spirits inside the mist with us. *They weren't really inside the circles*, but *they wanted us to think they were!* They were hoping we would be too scared to continue with the ritual!

The entire time, the evil ones were screaming! "*Satanomah! Grevahto! Nat'el!*" at us over and over again. We 'saw' the realm of the dead and hell itself inside the red mist that covered us. At that instant, all of the demons of hell began to reach out for us! We were surrounded by terrible evil! Andrew Jr. was gone by then. My 'grandmothers' and I felt our hands slipping from each other's. Then we could hear each other's thoughts.

"Oh no!" I heard Grandmom Miriam thinking, "we are going to be defeated!" I knew that my baby and I were in grave danger. Without warning, the deep red mist turned pitch black. Horrified, we chanted louder. The *screams* of those who were in hell drowned out our chanting. And I felt my 'grandmothers' and I were lost.

Above the screams of the damned, we heard a familiar voice. "No!" It shouted at the evil ones who had once again become visible to us. The spirit of my sister joined my 'grandmothers' and I inside the three *circles*. She smiled at us. And a wave of relief flooded through me.

With outstretched arms and a great force of power, Emma threw each one of the demons away from the circles, one by one. It was their turn to scream in terror. And their cries rang in our ears. As suddenly as they had appeared, they were gone. Emma's spirit stretched its *arms* out to the three of us as if to envelope all three of us at once. As it did, we 'saw' the beautiful ruby ring on *her finger*. It was the very same ring she was buried with! The one Linda gave her.

"*Lay your hands on my hand with the ring on it!*" We heard her say to us. We did as she told us. As soon as we touched her hand with the ring, we saw the fires of hell blazing all around us! Burning in those fiery flames were the *spirits of Marie, Roy, and Ole Lucy*.

There are no words that I can ever find to describe the horror and anguish of their screams as they were being destroyed forever! As I think back now, just the memory of it makes me shudder.

"*They will never bother you again*," we heard Emma say to us. "The family is free now! Only those spirits who are good and kind will remain here. F*ear no more, Grandmom Faya and Grandmom Miriam! You are free now. Open your eyes and see.*"

As we opened our eyes, the little room was as normal-looking as it had been *before* Grandmom Faya had set everything up for the exorcism! The *spirit* of my beloved sister was gone. Then we heard the church bells ringing outside. They rang twelve times, signaling to us that it was midnight. The evil that had plagued our family for years was gone forever. We were free at last.

Neither Grandmom Faya nor Grandmom Miriam ever thought it would be Emma who would be the *unknown woman* to help us in the ritual that we performed! "All of these years," said Grandmom Miriam, "and I would have never guessed it was *her!* Even after Tyla had the dream about the ring! I still didn't make the connection!"

We were exhausted when we stepped outside of those circles. The little room became warm and cozy. "*They* really are gone now! Forever!" said Grandmom Faya, "I can feel it!" "Me too," Grandmom Miriam said, chuckling softly. "Thank God!"

Then Grandmom Faya sat down on the basement stairs. She had been so preoccupied with the many things that had been happening in our family lately. She never remembered the ruby ring that Linda gave to Emma on her last birthday. She too couldn't believe it was my sister all along who was to help us! "I never would have thought of Emma," she admitted, shaking her head in disbelief. I thought about the conversation that Linda and I had earlier that evening. My dear, sweet sister-in-law was right. Her coming into our lives had served a great purpose. No matter how indirectly. It was she who gave Emma that ring and insisted that it be buried with her. Neither Grandmom Faya nor Grandmom Miriam ever mentioned anything about that. They didn't have to.

I knew then that Linda gave Emma that ring for a reason! Later on, I began to search many books on the supernatural. They always mentioned a ring that was anointed with supernatural powers. The ring could be placed onto the finger of a deceased person, and that person's spirit would return when its loved ones were in danger.

Finally, it all came together for me. Who better to fight in the spirit world than another spirit? And one who had been endowed with supernatural power?

I doubt if Emma could have reached out from the grave to help us without that ring that my beloved sister-in-law gave to her. I didn't know for sure. But I had a suspicion that the ring had belonged to Linda's mother. Many years later, after finding a letter that Linda gave to Emma when she gave her the ring, my suspicions proved to be true! *The ring had belonged to Linda's mother.*

Grandmom Faya stood up from the basement stairs, and we began to clean up the room. She placed all of the tools we used back inside the leather box. She told us it had to be buried at dawn. Never to be used again. No one would know where but herself.

Once we finished cleaning up, we went upstairs to the kitchen and sat down at the table. Grandmom Miriam made us each a hot cup of tea. Briefly, we discussed what had happened and what we had done. But after that night, we never talked about the incident again to anyone. I never even told my husband.

As we sipped our tea and talked, someone came into the house. We hadn't realized so many hours had passed by that time. The footsteps slowly approached the kitchen where we were. "Hey there, girls!" It was Gary. "You ladies are up early!" He couldn't have known that we had never been to bed that night.

He was home a little earlier than I expected. "What are you doing back so early?" I asked him. "The fish just weren't biting, sweetheart," he replied. "So here I am!" I offered him a cup of coffee and some breakfast. He, my 'grandmothers,' and I sat there talking for a while. "*If only you knew, Gary!*" I thought. "*If only you knew!*" But he would never know what we had done to obtain peace in that house forever.

CHAPTER TWENTY-FIVE

Later on, that same morning, Grandmom Faya buried the leather box. It would never be seen again. Nor would the contents of it ever be used again. There was no more need for them. She buried the robes that we wore with the box. After that, she went into the kitchen and sat down with relief and peace for the first time in a long, long time.

Beryl called for Grandmom Miriam that morning, and she told him she would be ready around noon. They were going away for a few days. I was glad that she had somebody who loved her.

Then, Grandmom Faya wondered where Linda and the children were. "They should be coming home soon," Grandmom Miriam told her. But when they hadn't come home by noon, Grandmom Faya telephoned Josie, who was still over her friend's house.

"I'm sorry, Faya," said Josie. "But Linda came by last night around nine o'clock then left. All she said to me was that she was going home."

Grandmom Faya became worried. She couldn't have known that when Linda left Josie's house, she and the children went directly to the airport in Tolstoy. They were going to board a flight to Paris. Linda *was* going home, but not our home. She was going back to Paris! When their flight was announced, she and the children walked to the departure gate. "Mommy, where are we going?" Nicola asked her. "We're going on a long trip, honey," replied Linda. "We're going home!"

"But home isn't a long trip, Mommy!" he said. She ignored him. She wouldn't let either one of the children see the tears in her eyes. Then, Nicola became excited when he saw the big airplane. He had never seen a real one before, only a toy one.

Linda was very sad. She was leaving the only family that she had and a husband whom she still adored very much. But it was over, and she *had* to leave. So much had changed in their lives in such a short period of time. She knew she was never coming back to us. Her tears rolled down her cheeks as she looked out of the window of the airplane. She began to sob.

Quickly, she got up from her seat and ran to the ladies' room. She stayed there and cried for a long time. She thought about how her marriage was over and she didn't even know what had happened. She dried her eyes after a while and returned to her seat on the plane. The only thing to be seen out of the window by then were the clouds in the sky.

"I should telephone Sheriff Reilly," Grandmom Faya told Gary and I. "Linda and the children should have been home a long time ago." It was two o'clock in the afternoon by then. "No, Grandmom Faya," I said softly. "Don't do that!" Gary looked at me strangely. So did she. "Why, Ty?" my husband asked me.

I looked down at the kitchen table without answering. Then I sighed. "She's gone, Grandmom Faya," I finally said. "And she's not coming back! Their marriage has been over for a long time now. Everybody in the family has known that."

Grandmom Faya couldn't say a word. She knew I was right! "Oh my Lord," she said, putting her head in her hands. Gary put his arms around me. "Are you alright, baby?" he asked me. He knew how much Linda and I loved each other.

"Yeah," I said. But truthfully, I wasn't alright. And I wouldn't be for a long time. Over the years, Linda and I had grown very close. Then she was gone. I would miss her terribly.

When we went to look in Linda and Nicholas's apartment upstairs in the attic, all of Linda's and the children's things were still there. They had left with only the clothes on their backs. "I had no idea she was that unhappy," said Grandmom Faya in a low sorrowful voice.

"She was, Grandmom Faya," I said. "She was!" I never told anybody that Linda telephoned me when she got to Paris. She gave me her new address and telephone number. But I knew I would never see her or my niece and nephew ever again. We talked on the telephone a long time. Linda told me how she felt and how she couldn't handle the heartache anymore.

Although I didn't want her to walk out of my life, I knew I had to let her go! She deserved to find happiness in her life. I wished her all of the luck in the world.

Two days after she left, Nicholas finally decided to come home. When we told him what had happened, he wasn't concerned at all about Linda. Only about the children. This made Grandmom Faya angry. But she still didn't interfere.

It wasn't long after that when Nicholas himself stopped coming home altogether. Several months later, he came home to collect the rest of his belongings. He packed them all into three suitcases, kissed the 'grandmothers' and I goodbye, shook hands with Gary, and walked out of our lives. He never bothered to tell us where he was going or with whom. But he didn't have to tell us with whom. We already knew her name was Carmen.

Darius Andrew Shelley was six months old. He was a great joy to Gary and I. And spoiled by my 'grandmothers'. Gary's parents and sisters did their share of spoiling our baby too. They cuddled him and held him all of the time. He was a beautiful baby boy with big deep dark brown eyes and sandy red hair. He always had a ready smile for anybody who came into contact with him.

"I've got big plans for you baby boy," Gary said to him one day holding him high in the air. Then I thought about my sweet little nephew Nicola. I thought about how he told us that was the name his 'Aunt Charon' used to call him. I missed my nephew my niece and Linda.

"We'll probably have another boy Ty," Gary announced. But I didn't say a word. I recalled the dream of my father Andrew. In the dream he had brought two children with him telling me they were mine. In the dream the boy was clearly the older of the two. I knew that our second child would be a girl.

When Darius was eighteen months old we were eagerly awaiting the birth of our second child. Gary and I decided it was time for us to buy our own home. I wanted to be sure that everything was alright with my 'grandmothers' before I left them.

Grandmom Miriam and Beryl Matheson finally got married. They stayed in the house with Grandmom Faya. Who was also seeing another elderly gentleman from town by then. Even Josie Marshall had a boyfriend after all of those years.

Then Gary tragically lost both of his parents in a car wreck. They were coming home from a party at a friend's house one night when they were hit head-on by another car coming in the opposite direction from their car. It was raining and the driver was speeding! He lost control of his car and plowed into Ernest and MaryAnne's car.

All three people involved in the accident were killed instantly! It was a horrible time for Gary and I and his sisters. They already lost their brother in a deadly accident many years before. Now they lost their parents! After the funeral Amelia and Dana decided to move out West. However, they still kept in touch with Gary and I.

Since that Halloween night which seems so long ago things were normal in that old house. In fact even the dreams stopped for both my 'grandmothers' and I. Everyone was at peace. There were no more unwelcome or unwanted visitors. None. Everything was peaceful and everybody was happy.

Often we still thought about Linda and wondered how she and the children were doing. We never heard from Nicholas. But somebody told Grandmom Faya that he and the young woman he ran off with had moved to the East coast.

Gary and I had a little daughter just as I knew we would. I named her *Emmaline Faya Shelley* after my beloved sister and 'grandmother'. Right after she was born we moved into our own house in Manchester. A lovely quiet county located outside of Watsonville. I talked with my 'grandmothers' every day though.

CHAPTER TWENTY SIX

As my mind came back to the present I realized I was looking out of my living room window. I just got back from Nicholas's funeral and decided to unpack my suitcases later. I was very tired.

I wrapped my arms around myself as if to keep warm. It was a cool Autumn day. I looked at the thousands of different colored leaves lying on my lawn. "*I'll have to get Darius to rake them up for me,*" I thought.

Looking out of the window I watched my five-year-old grandson Michel as he came running toward the house. He and his father, my son Darius, moved in with me after his wife Janet died last year. They were married for seven years and only had the one child, Michel.

My daughter Emma was coming home from college for the semester break soon. She wrote to me telling me that she was bringing a young man home with her. I smiled. Our children made Gary and I very happy and very proud.

Without warning my mind slipped into *a day-dream*, something I still did from my childhood. The day I received the letter from Carmen, the woman that Nicholas left Maron with, I knew that it was bad news before I opened it. He never did write to me or telephone us after he left. I think he realized how badly he'd hurt our family. But he was too ashamed to apologize. The handwriting on the front of the envelope was unfamiliar to me. I tore open the envelope and read the letter. It became apparent to me that Nicholas kept track of us even though he never contacted us.

Carmen informed me in the letter that Nicholas had been murdered. He was standing on the corner waiting for the bus to go home. Nearby where he stood some young hoodlums were gambling. Evidently they had some very vicious enemies. They drove past them in a car and started shooting. He was shot in the head and died instantly. An innocent victim who never knew what hit him. "*The way he treated Linda,*" I thought, "*I don't know how he could've ever thought that he wouldn't be paid back for that!" I didn't like my thoughts. But I always believed, 'What goes around comes around!'*

I tried my best to find Linda and the children. But no one knew where they were. As far as I knew, Linda and Nicholas were never divorced! All the authorities in Paris, France, could tell me was that they had left the city a long time ago.

I wondered why she stopped calling me. Somehow I thought they might be back in our country. Still, I didn't know where to look for them.

At the funeral, I saw that Nicholas had aged just as I had. Yet he was still very handsome. Carmen was very nice to me. And she reminded me a lot of Linda. They were both sweet and kind-hearted women. I regretted she and I had never met before the tragedy. She informed me that my brother talked about our family a lot. Even his wife and children. The funeral service was nice. But I was glad to be home again.

At Nicholas's funeral, I couldn't help but think about Malin. I thought about my brother a lot. We never saw or heard from him anymore, either. I always believed he would write to me or call me. But he didn't. My 'grandmothers' worried about both of my brothers until the day they died.

Grandmom Faya and Grandmom Miriam passed away exactly one year apart. I always thought that was very strange! Stranger still, the Coroner's report listed both of their deaths as heart attacks.

Grandmom Faya was sitting in Mr. Tom's favorite old chair and simply fell asleep. She never woke up. Just like he did. The next morning, Grandmom Miriam found her body.

Then, sadly, six months later, Beryl had a stroke and never recovered from it. He slipped into a coma for twelve days before he passed on. As with Grandmom Faya, Grandmom Miriam went to bed one night and never woke up. It was one year to the day after Grandmom Faya passed on. The Coroner said that she had been dead for two days. I tried to telephone her. But I figured she was out somewhere when she didn't answer the telephone. After the second day, I got worried about her and went to check on her. That's when I found her dead in her bed.

The funerals of both of my 'grandmothers' were well attended. I remembered how peaceful and beautiful they looked. However, I was also sad because I lost two of the best friends and loved ones that I had ever had.

The house was left to my brothers and me. But I never wanted to live there again. "It wouldn't be the same," I thought. Instead, I had all of the furniture covered and the house itself boarded up. I had thought that if my family kept growing, I might return there to live someday. That was four years ago.

After the deaths of my 'grandmothers', only little Michel gave me the energy to go on. Even Gary couldn't comfort me. I felt as though everything I loved was slowly being taken away from me.

It was then that Janet, our daughter-in-law, fell sick with cancer. I knew I had to be strong for Darius and Michel. Michel was a dear little boy who made me think of my nephew, Nicola, every day.

Nicola was a grown man now. He probably had a wife and children of his own. We never saw him, Angie or Linda ever again. I hoped with all of my heart that she had found happiness. So many years had passed by. But it was after Emma was murdered that everything truly changed for all of us.

"Emma!" I thought sadly. A single tear rolled down my cheek. But I smiled. After all of those years, I still missed my beloved sister. It was almost thirty years since that horrible day when we got that terrible telephone call. I would never forget that day as long as I lived. To make matters worse, Oliver Turner had never been found. I hoped with all of my heart that somehow God made him pay for what he did to my sister and to our family.

Three years ago, Gary passed on tragically, leaving me behind to cherish his memory. I was so lonely at times. He was inside a grocery store in Vaira County when it got robbed. He had gone there that day to visit an old friend of his. He offered to go to the store to get some more beer for them. My dear husband didn't even drink. The robbers, trying to make a woman in the store stop screaming, got nervous. They were going to shoot her. But Gary jumped in front of her, pushing her to the floor. But in the process, he was mortally wounded. The robbers were never caught and only got away with $35.00.

Whenever I would think about it, I would get angry at Gary for being so gallant but foolish! I stayed angry with him for a long time for his thoughtless action. Darius and Michel helped to ease my pain and loneliness. I still pined for my beloved husband, though. I couldn't imagine ever being with another man. We loved each other so much. And we'd been married for many, many years. Gary's passing left a huge void inside me that I knew would never be filled.

"Hi, Grandmom!" cried Michel, snapping me out of my daydream. "Well, hi there, sugar plum!" I said with a smile as I picked him up in my arms and kissed him on the cheek. He saw the lonely teardrop on my cheek.

"Are you crying, Grandmom?" he asked me. "No," I lied. "I just have something in my eye." "Are you sure, Grandmom," he asked suspiciously. "You look sad to me!" He was such a smart little boy. "Well," I said, "maybe just a little bit sad." "Why are you sad, Grandmom?" he asked me. I thought about it for a moment.

"Why am I sad?! I've lived a wonderful life, surrounded by a dear, loving family!" I thought. Although I missed my loved ones and had wondered every day where my brothers were or if they were still alive, I truly had no reason at all to be sad. I never gave up hope of seeing them again before it was my time to leave this world.

Michel was all the world to me. I loved my Grandmom more than anything in the world. Both of them! I felt fortunate to have lived so long. Long enough to see both of my children grown up and happy, as well as becoming a grandmother myself. I was glad that Nicholas always thought of us. I knew that after receiving the letter from Carmen. But there was still Malin! I wanted to hear from him desperately.

"I guess I just miss your grandfather, is all," I told my precious little grandchild. "Let's go see what we can find in the kitchen for a snack, okay" "Okay, Grandmom," he answered happily. When I became a grandmother, I realized first hand how it felt for my two dear 'grandmothers' to love my siblings and I more than anything else in the world. I understood their love perfectly.

All of the hurt and heartache of the past would disappear in time. I knew the light of love and peace had struggled for a long time to cut through all of the darkness that had a hold on our family. I looked at Michel and thought, "*How could any sadness, evil, or darkness survive all of the love that I've known in my life! Past, present, and yet to come?* " The 'light' was still shining and had been for a long time.

Michel and I settled down in the kitchen with some slices of cake that I brought home from the funeral. I didn't know who made that cake. But it was incredibly delicious. I *had* to bring some home with me. "Who is that, Grandmom?" Michel asked me, pointing outside the kitchen window.

I turned to see what he was pointing at. A taxi cab pulled up in front of my house. A man who looked very familiar to me got out of the cab. At first, I couldn't believe my eyes! Jumping up, I went to the living room window to get a better look at him. As he approached my house, I recognized his face. He had hardly changed at all after nearly thirty years. His hair was now mixed gray, like mine. I couldn't believe it!

"Grandmom, are you alright?" asked Michel. "Do you know that man?!" I knew the big smile on my face could have lit up the whole world. I ran to open the front door as Malin approached it. Tears of joy rolled down my cheeks. I was so happy to see my long-lost brother.

"Yes, honey," I answered happily. "I *know* that man!" I was overjoyed! I could hardly contain myself. Neither one of my brothers had attended the funerals of our 'grandmothers'. I didn't know where they were. Then it dawned on me that

"Nicholas knew all along! He knew about our grandmothers. But was still too ashamed to face us. That's why he didn't come to the funerals."

As my brother came up the walkway toward me, he was smiling too! "Hey, Ty!" he said. "I told Grandmom Faya that I was never coming back! But I couldn't stay away any longer! Can you ever forgive me?"

I threw my arms around his neck, and he put his arms around me. We hugged and kissed each other for what seemed like forever. "There's nothing to forgive," I whispered into his ear. "Welcome home, Malin!"

Then I grabbed his hand and led him into the house. "Who is he, Grandmom?" asked Michel, unsure who the strange man was. "Grandmom?!" exclaimed Malin. "You've grown old, *Tyla, girl!*" We both laughed. Then a sad look came across Malin's face. Calling me *"Tyla, girl"* reminded him of Grandmom Faya. She always called me "*Tyla, girl!"*

"I'm so sorry that I missed both of their funerals and Nicholas's, Ty," said Malin sadly. After I told him about our 'grandmothers' and about Nicholas, I reached for his hand. "They understood, Malin," I told him with a smile. He smiled back.

Then I asked him about Charles. He informed me sadly that Charles had leukemia for years. He had passed away the previous year. I was sorry to hear that. I always liked Charles. Malin smiled at Michel.

"Hey, there, big guy," he said, "what's your name?" "My name is Michel Gary Shelley," said my grandson, "and I'm five years old! Who are you?"

"Well," began Malin, "I'm your Grandmom's brother and your great uncle, Malin. I'm pleased to meet you!" He put out his hand to shake Michel's. I saw tears in his eyes when I told him about Linda and the children leaving us and we never heard from them again. Also, I told him about Gary's passing on. In turn, I had a lot of questions for him, too. I was curious as to what he had been doing, for all of these years and where he had been. However, there was no rush. After all, Malin and I had all the time in the world.

THE END

www.ingramcontent.com/pod-product-compliance
Lightning Source LLC
LaVergne TN
LVHW012014060526
838201LV00061B/4295